Cary J. Lenehan is a former trades assistant, soldier, public servant, cab driver, truck driver, game designer, fishmonger, trainee horticulturalist and university tutor (among other things). His hobbies include collecting and reading books (the non-fiction are Dewey decimalised), Tasmanian native plants (particularly the edible ones), the SCA and gaming. He has taught people how to use everything from shortswords to rocket launchers. He met his wife at an SF Convention while cosplaying and they have not looked back.

He was born in Sydney before marrying and moving to the Snowy Mountains where they started their family. They moved to Tasmania for the warmer winters and are not likely to ever leave it.

Looking out of the window beside his computer is a sweeping view of Mount Wellington and its range.

Warriors of Vhast Series
published by
IFWG Publishing Australia

Intimations of Evil (Book 1)
Engaging Evil (Book 2)
Clearing the Web (Book 3)
Scouring the Land (Book 4)

Warriors of Vhast Book 3

Clearing the Web

by
Cary J Lenehan

Clearing the Web

Book 3, Warriors of Vhast

All Rights Reserved

ISBN-13: 978-1-925956-49-8

IFWG Publishing International
Melbourne

www.ifwgpublishing.com

Acknowledgement

It has been a while coming, but the third book of the series is in your hands now. I would like to thank all of you who have been reading either the books or the short stories (currently only available through my Patreon page).

I hope that I continue to entertain you and that you keep reading, sharing my world with your friends, and posting reviews.

This may be the third book, but it is just the start of the adventure. There are five more books (mostly written) to come. After that I hope to see come out, collected together, the short stories, the maps, the recipes, the plants and animals, and even the Tarot deck.

I do appreciate feedback from my readers and I look forward to meeting or talking to you all at one stage or another.

Cary J. Lenehan
Hobart

A cast list and glossary of terms used in this novel can be found at page 383.

As well as my wife (potter extraordinaire) Marjorie and my mother, Eden, I would like to dedicate this book to my friend and beta reader Pip Woodfield. She knows my characters better than I do in some respects. I would have difficulty keeping track without her.

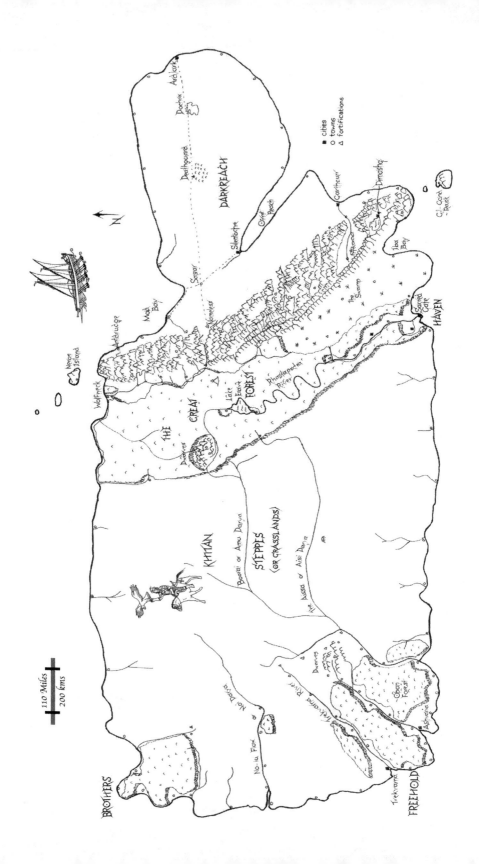

Delving deep the Dwarves dug long
Giant galleries are greatly growing
Dare to disturb the dangerous denizens
Dreaming darkly of devastating doom

Calamitous conflict claims cavernous chambers
Covetous curs cause cacophonous clash
Base brutes bring blighted beasts
Bloody battering and bruising blows

Ancient ancestors and awful ambition
Afflict agony and angry anguish
Depraved desires deal out dark destruction
Dwarven deserters draw discordant dispute

Soul-stealing spirits sew Strife-strewn stairs
Sanguine strife sees Serpentine sleeper
Hallowed histories help haunted homeland
Hag-haunted halls now hope-filled

Sublime sound of singing staunch steel
Stalwart seekers stalk soul-stealing spirits
Fierce foes fall to furious frenzy of
Formidable friends and famous Crown-finder

*Djill Tale-bearer, Dwarven skald
(extract from Double-damned Dharmal and Dread-filled
Dwarvenholme)*

Map of the Lands
East of Lake Erave

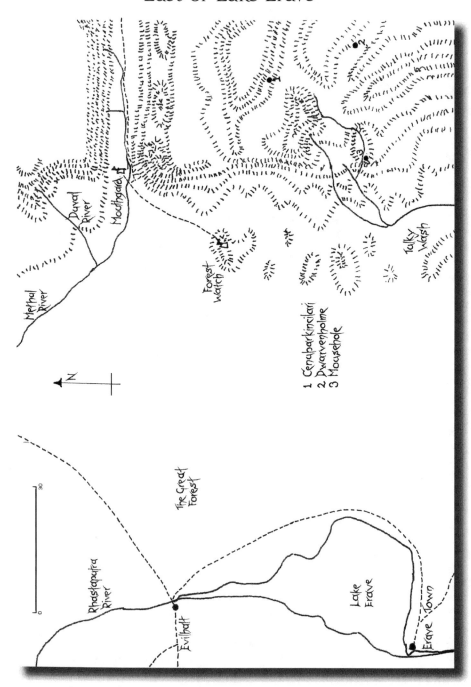

Chapter 1

Rani
3rd November, the Year of the Water Dog

I guess that it is up to me, as the Battle Mage, to think of these things…but did I have to think of it on the way to bed? "My dear, something for you to think about tomorrow. If we are to succeed, we will need to have at least one device that will directly target at least some of these Masters so that they do not overwhelm us."

O dear Ratri, as expected, my wife has started thinking about it straight away. I knew this would happen. Once again, I end up alone and bored while she plays with a slate instead of me. She sighed. *Even if I choose to pleasure myself, she will probably not notice.*

Rani
9th November

*I*t has taken her a full week to determine that the best they could do would be *to enchant some of the weapons that they would be taking with them.* Looking at what people were using already, or had decided to train with, the most common weapon was the mace, of some sort or other. So that they had more than just knives to fight with, Bianca, Kāhina and Verily were all being trained in them by Hulagu and Ayesha, rather than by Stefan, who was busy teaching sword to the villagers who would stay. Naturally, the two teachers favoured their own weapon when teaching.

Theo-dear had reasoned, as Thord used a hammer, he could, with ease, change to a mace as well. However, I am not used to working with Dwarves. I had heard that they were stubborn and fixed in their ways. I just had not realised how much this was true. "My hammer is already enchanted," said Thord. "perhaps not as strong as the ones Princess 'll provide, but ha' an extra enhancement agin undead on it anyway. Besides, I be used to it." *It seems that is the end of it.*

Oh well. We only have five to make. If we can get facility with the spell, we might try changing it for some of the other weapons that we will use. That will be harder, but we still have several weeks before we can set out. Theodora argued that she was the stronger of the two mages and so she should be the one to create the weapons as she could forge a stronger spell. Rani found herself arguing that undead lay in the realm of water and she was a fire mage, so anything she made should be more effective.

Theo-dear won the argument by reminding me of some basic theory which I have been trying to ignore. "Once the spell is cast, it is not focussed. If it were, you would be the more effective. It will be controlled and constrained, and unless we are creating something that specifically uses the elements, the item will work the same regardless of who makes it. You can better spend your time making more arrows with Robin, or something to give us light as we stumble about under the ground."

Sticking her tongue out at me ruins the logical argument, but it does help us move to another subject far less germane to the task at hand, but far more fun.

Theodora explained it to the students. "Each weapon will take me three days to enhance. The first day creates the matrix. The second lays in the enchantment against undead that should encompass a wraith or something else of that ilk. It is a charm that will only work on very good blows, for I cannot afford to create anything that works all of the time."

"If the Masters are more powerful, say if they are liches…that being the usual name given to mages who have refused to die and who have raised their own bodies from the grave, or rather kept them from it, by force of will and so have kept all their power…then we will all die. The third day allows us to add a casting to make it easier to hit targets."

Better not leave it at that. "However," Rani added quickly, "if they are liches, then between them they probably would have been able to remove the shield that we put in place over the valley, and we think that it is still intact against them because the Hobs were not warned of our wards on the path. We may be lucky, and these wards will be powerful enough for them. If they are not, then we have included enchantments to enhance damage and the ability to hit them. These will also make good blows more likely.

"Remember that magic has its limitations. The first is that, no matter how powerful you get, you are never powerful enough to perform everything that you want to do. The second is that, because of the first, you are always trading off one thing for another. Thus, with these weapons…to make them work better against a more powerful undead, we have to decrease how often they will work when we do hit. I would like to make them work all of the time when they hit. I cannot do that."

"Hulagu," interjected Theodora. "It is time for us to start. Give me your mace." Hulagu reluctantly handed over his mace as the first to be worked on. *It is obvious that he is not too sure if he wants the experiment done on his weapon, but we are not giving him a choice.*

Theodora made her casts. When they were finished, she nodded in satisfaction.

"Now," said Rani, "until we have finished working on Hulagu's mace and locked it, no-one can cast any spells unless they go to practice in the mine. Why is that?"

Bilqīs raised her hand. "Because if we do, it is possible that Hulagu's mace may not negate undead, but it will make a nice cup of tea," she said with a smile. *At least they are picking up the ideas.*

W e need to keep up the investigation of the hidden talents of Mousehole. *Most people have something that sets them apart from their fellows. I already know about Verily and her ability to smell magic. That is a rare skill indeed and I have been working on training her to be more precise in her evaluations… Try and get her to tell an item made under the auspices of the moon of the tiger, say, from one that was made under the moon of the dragon…although both are fire spells. There has been some success, but it is not consistent. Do we keep this up?*

But we really do need to know who has any skill at all first. Before we find that we have a need for a skill and have not explored it. I suppose that of the skills we have discovered so far, some were almost predictable. Harald couldn't smell magic, but the smell of butter, or of the sea, meant gold or silver to him if there was enough of it, or if it were close enough. It was a valuable talent for a miner. Was it why he took up the trade? Even the new priest has Harald and Thord excited by admitting that he knew if gems were within a metre of him. He doesn't know how, he just knows.

Parminder was often to be found sitting in the stables, listening to horses or a cat. *I have proved that she could not 'hear' any of the sheep or chickens or goats or cows, but she should always try to hear any new animal that comes in sight. It will be better if we can get her to increase the range at which she could hear…or if we can get the animals to hear her.*

She is able to tell that the horses liked Ayesha nearly as much as they liked Bianca, and that the cats loved it when Stefan, Ayesha or Bianca came to the stables and paid attention to them. She did not know why. The girl had decided that the only thing that was different between Ayesha and Bianca was that Bianca responded more to her animals than any of the others did.

Our other discovery is a real surprise. Danelis had said "I have always tried to ignore this. I grew up thinking that it made me a witch and I didn't want to be that. It was only when I came here that I found that it was sometimes useful, but it is only a tiny thing and I did not know how to make it stronger. I will show you. It is easier to show than to explain." She sat down and looked at Rani's dagger at her side.

I feel something shifting. My dagger is slowly coming out its sheath. It is moving slowly through the air and has stopped on the table. "I have to concentrate hard, and it has to be close…no more than three paces…and I can only move it slowly and it is very tiring, but…well that is it." *Danelis has sweat standing out on her brow from the effort of what she has done.*

After that, Rani had her trying to lift heavier and heavier weights, further and faster and with more force. *If it were not for the fact that the only mining that she and Harald were doing now was for some pieces of stone for building, I would have her absolutely exhausted when she went to bed each night. This could be useful.* "It is far easier lifting stone," Danelis said.

Christopher
11th November

Theodule stood in front of Christopher and seemed to be embarrassed. *He has surprised me. He has mentioned nothing in his confessions. I am curious.*

"You know that I was sent here to fill in while you are away as your vicar," he said. Christopher nodded, "and part of the reason that I was sent is that I was a widower," again Christopher nodded. "It seems that your village has struck again. Today Ruth has asked me to marry her. I pointed out my age as opposed to hers, for I am almost exactly twice her age. She pointed out that this was not important. Many men were older than their wives as many did not settle down until they had enough wealth to keep a family.

"I pointed out that I might be sent elsewhere as a priest when you came back, and she pointed out that she could travel as well as I could. I pointed out that I didn't love her, and she pointed out that most marriages didn't start with love. They were arranged, and that love was something you learnt together over time. I admit that my many happy years of marriage have made me disposed to agree with her plan. I have been happy once before, so I am sure that my Kale would not mind if I were to become happy again."

Christopher just grinned through his shock. "When do you want the wedding?"

Chapter II

Theodora
11th November

"Iha' worked out how to read t' diary." Thord said.

"Diary?" said Theodora, "What diary."

He looks impatient. "On t' day we arrived here you gave me a book and told me t' it might be Dharmal's diary. Did you just give it to me to waste my time?"

"No, no, I had just forgotten. So much has happened…did you find out what is in it?"

"Yes. He records his quest for t' door to Dwarvenholme 'n' details his route. I can now walk you t' exact path he took. He was very precise with detailing everything t'at he did. I t'ink t'at he t'ought he was starting to write history for his children." Thord chuckled. *It isn't a pretty chuckle.* "He records his meeting with t' Masters. He saw four hands of them but, 'n' he gives no grounds for t'is, he t'inks t'at t'ere were only half t'at many. He is convinced, but he was just working on a hunch."

"Even hunches are sometimes right but you are also correct, we cannot rely on it."

"T'ey took over his body 'n' he could not move."

"I had forgotten that. They seem to like control spells…I wonder…" *I have forgotten Thord. He just coughed.* "Sorry, I just had a thought. I think that we will be trying to make everyone a new ring. It may not work, and it may not be needed, but then again, it may. Is there anything else?"

"He records seeing t'em walk, rather t'an float. He is definite on t'at point 'n' when, he saw t'eir hands he mentions that t'ey are just bone."

"Perhaps we may be lucky. Undead are almost always created by someone. It is very rare for them to just arise on their own. When people make them, they are usually made as a form of skeleton. It is easier. What Rani and I have been afraid of is if they are all liches. Liches are undead, but they are very nearly alive…they have real bodies with wants and needs and lusts."

"A skeleton mage can be made powerful, not just like the ones that wander around near Evilhalt, they can easily be as powerful as most mages who are alive, but they lack the full power of a liche. Just think for a moment about the power of someone who has thwarted death by just refusing to accept it."

"What lacks the power of a liche?" asked Rani, entering the room.

"Thord has deciphered Dharmal's diary and is telling me what he wrote in it." They filled her in on what had been said so far.

"That would make sense," said Rani. "We had worked out that they lacked imagination and creativity. That would accord with them being skeleton mages rather than liches. Skeleton mages lack much free thought, among many other things. We can only hope."

Christopher
13th November

I think Theodule is a little disappointed that the men of Mousehole respected his office and gave him a very quiet pre-wedding party. The wedding itself was very straightforward, with Stefan as groomsman and Bianca as the maid of honour. Rani gave the bride away.

What is nice is that the last marriage I will do in Mousehole, at least until more men arrive was so…normal in all of its aspects. Its most notable attribute is that we were able to hold it on the feast day of Saint Homobonus and Saint John Chrysostum. While Saint Homobonus has little relevance to the village yet, being patron of cloth workers, Saint John Chrysostum is at least the patron saint of priests.

Christopher
14th November

It turns out that Mousehole has one more surprise in store for me at least. Ayesha came up to him when he was talking to his wife in the courtyard enjoying the morning sun. "We need to gather Rani and Theodora and go down to the guard house. You told me to get someone to help me with the Hob, and

I asked Verily, because she is the least human of anyone here—and I include Thord in that."

She would not be drawn on any more detail. "It is not my story to tell." *The door to the cell is open and Verily is sitting inside the cell with the Hobgoblin prisoner Saygaanzaamrat and holding his hand. Interesting...why have I ignored him? No-one has mentioned him, but still...we have all ignored the Hob.*

Christopher looked at him, really for the first time. *He is a big man, taller and heavier than any of the rest of us and totally bald. He has prominent and strong incisors on both his top and bottom jaws that overlap up and down and he has grey skin that is, in appearance, more like that of a lizard than most people except Basil. I can also see that, for the first time since I first saw her, Verily lacks composure.*

"Well," said Rani from behind, "we are all here now. Why is the door open and why are we here?" *Her words are meeting silence.* "Is anyone going to tell me?"

It was Saygaanzaamrat who replied. *In Hindi, not very good Hindi, but it is Hindi.* "Me want to join Mousehole, village yours," he said, with a heavy accent, "and me want to marry Verily like all you marry. She not pretty, all hair and she does not even have the teeth that Cat girl has, and she not very strong, but me like her to talk to and she make me feel nice...soft and warm...inside. Me want protect her and hold her. She tell me she want me to do this."

I hear the sound of crickets...someone needs to say something. "Verily, what do you say?"

It is her usual velvet voice, but very quiet. "I am sick of Human men. They only want me because of my body. They do not want me. Men see me as beautiful, and what has it gotten me? Ten years of being raped by men, and by women, all of whom I hated and who only wanted to possess my beauty. You heard Saygaanzaamrat. He thinks I am ugly. He is bright and strong, and he wants me for who I am inside and he wants to protect me. Do you realise what a relief that all is?"

"Strangely," Bianca spoke next, "I do, in a way. My beloved husband thinks that I am beautiful. I pray that he stays as deluded, but he is the only one who does. I was judged all my years for being plain and an orphan and poor. Here, and with Christopher, I am accepted for what I am. I imagine you feel the same sort of way." Verily nodded. "If this goes to a vote," she turned to the Princesses, "they have my support."

"But," said Rani, almost speechless "is it right to mate with another race?" *Theodora is blushing as she leans close and whispers in her ear. I remember something from the Confessional...something I can never mention, about her encounter with an Insak-div. I wonder if that is what she is talking about. It certainly has an effect on Rani. She is giving her wife a very odd look.* "You don't even know if you are built the same."

"We fit," said Verily, blushing, "very well indeed."

"You might not be able to have children." *Rani is clutching at straws and all of the others, including her wife, are smiling at that poor attempt…well it might have been a smile that Saygaanzaamrat has on his face. It took only a moment of looking at the faces around her before Rani realised that the same, and more, can be said about her marriage.* She added "Oh," after that pause. She looked around at the others. "You all think that she…that they…. He is a prisoner." *I keep making excuses, but she does come from a culture with no mixing. She is working on it.*

"So was she," Christopher found himself saying mildly.

Saygaanzaamrat is turning to me: "Verily has talked about her beliefs, but I not understand what she saying very well. Spirits failed tribe. We could have been all die. Spirits supposed to make prosper, not get all killed. I not happy with spirits. I happy to talk to you about your spirits."

"In that case, I will talk to you as often as you wish. I hope that I make sense to you."

"I give in," said Rani. "I suppose that you want to move him from here to your room?" she asked Verily…*almost sarcastically.*

"That would be good," *I don't think that she even noticed the tone.* "This bed is both very small and very hard and he needs teaching in more than I can give him. Trust me; you will learn to like him. I have. He wants to stay with me."

The five left, leaving Verily to help Saygaanzaamrat gather his few things and follow them. *As the pair come out of the guard house hand in hand, the first thing they see is Ayesha talking to Basil and Astrid outside the barracks. Verily is nervously approaching the two. This could be awkward. I can see Verily looking around the courtyard. I can see others looking cautiously at her. She is getting nervous. She stands nearly five hands shorter than the Hob and she has grabbed his hand for support.*

Basil and Astrid are just standing there. Astrid, as she almost always does, has her spear in hand. Verily is walking slowing but keeping her course. My most unpredictable parishioner is whispering with her husband…they are both nodding to each other.

Astrid

*A*s we agreed, Basil speaks first and uses Darkspeech: "Welcome to the world of Humans, fellow monster," *and his grin is genuine.* "My male ancestor was Kichic-Kharl and changed his name to Kutsulbalik when he married my female ancestor. From all of the Kichik-Kharl I have met, he must have looked far less Human than you do and he managed to have a long and happy marriage with lots of children. I hope that you two do the same."

My turn. "I hope that you don't hate me for killing your tribesmen and stabbing you there." *I point at his groin.*

"It was battle," he shrugged. "In battle, you do what you do. I am now well there." *He glanced at Verily as he said that. Verily noticed that. Is that a faint blush appearing on her face?* "I am Saygaanzaamrat, but," and he now addressed Basil, "if you say I have new name to show I am new me...that sounds right to me. We choose new names when adult anyway. You will choose new name for me. Choose well." *And I thought that I had a toothy grin.*

A lot of people are watching us. "We monsters have to stick together," *I need to make a point.* More loudly and this time in Hindi: "Welcome to Mousehole." *I need to do more for the rest of the village to see.* She put her spear down and went to Saygaanzaamrat and gave him a hug, then while Basil was reaching up and doing the same, went and hugged Verily.

"I hope you are as happy with your monster as I am with mine." *Make it more cheerful.* "And it will be nice to not be the only one who gets sideways looks occasionally. You will get used to it and they do get less over time." She kissed Verily and hugged her again, getting the little girl lost in her embrace. "Do I get to be the maid of honour?"

Oh shit. The calm and collected Verily, the one who never shows emotion, has almost collapsed in my arms. She is weeping like a young girl against her mother's breasts. I think that I heard a muffled 'thank you' but her body is just shaking with emotion. Saygaanzaamrat and Basil are looking at us with that dumb look husbands get...useless the pair of them.

"Basil, you two are not needed here. Go and show Saygaanzaamrat where Verily's room is, and put his stuff there and then show him the village. Verily needs a woman to be mother now and we may be a while." The men hurried off from this display and she led the weeping girl over to the veranda and took a seat.

Verily lay there, curled up, shaking and sobbing in Astrid's larger lap being held tight, as if the last ten years of Verily's life had finally caught up with her. Astrid stoked her hair and rocked her and softly sang an almost wordless song to her. *I hope this song helps…it is almost all that I remember from my own dead mother.*

Theodora

"The Cat seems to have found a kitten to care for," said Rani. "I would not believe that Verily would fall to pieces like that. Mind you, how could she fall for such a creature?"

"She has been…you barbarian westerners are so…" *I have not been angry with my husband before. I am now. I don't know what to say.* "I fell in love with you, and that was something that I was not expecting to do. People fall in love with who they will. At home, all of our races marry each other. Admittedly those women that marry Insak-div men usually do it just because they…well they like the sex. They cannot have children, but everyone else does.

"Basil's great-grandfather was a Kharl. He was short, had no hair, had green skin and very big teeth and tusks and yet Basil's great-grandmother fell in love with him. My ancestor, whom I will point out, is not human either, and Basil's general, who is, both trusted him with my life. If I took Basil home, they would make him an officer and heap rewards on him and praise on Astrid."

She turned on her heel and stormed off into their house. *I am livid. I can see Rani doesn't know what to say back. That is her problem. She can go and ask Christopher or one of the men. She needs to work it out before I can even speak to her again.*

Theodora locked herself in her study by putting a chair behind the door. *I can hear that Rani is trying the door. I am ignoring her. I am still mad.* She didn't calm down until night time. *Outside I can hear housework being done, but much more quietly than Valeria usually does it.*

Theodora worked off her anger at Rani by thinking on the theory of the rings to protect the hunters from the Masters. *It is hard. Controlling humanoids is a water spell, so I am best doing it, but the best way that I can work out to cast a suitable spell requires far more mana than I can safely handle without being overdrawn and, with this many rings to make, that could be dangerous. It is something that I will only suggest if it is an emergency.*

How many will we need? I wonder if there are other ways around the problem…and if that is a way out. I am taking in new spells fast since I left home. We all have a fixed number of spells that we can learn that grows as we do. Yet I wonder if I am going to run out of the ability to learn more at this rate. This spell will take a lot of mana, but if I make the spell specific only to the people of Mousehole, instead of having it being able to be used by anyone, then…

By the time she emerged she was ready to see Eleanor. *I am still ignoring my husband…even if she has been waiting here the whole time. She has to be made to realise that if you rule a place that has different races in it you should treat none of them differently to the others.*

I just realised that this is the secret to how Granther has kept his Empire together for all this time without too many problems. It isn't just through people like Basil or through the power of his magic. Father Christopher seems to realise this straight away, why doesn't Rani?

As Theodora walked past her husband, she told Valeria to tell Rani, who stood beside her, that if she asked, she would be back in a while and left the house and went to see the jeweller.

Rani

R ani slumped and stood dejected for a while. *Love is supposed to be perfect and happily ever after, and it has been that way until now. I had better see one of the men, one with common sense who might understand my wife better than I do. Basil knows her best, but he is probably still with the Hob…I suppose that it has to be the priest then.*

W hen Theodora came home, Rani apologised and said what a fool she had been and told her about going to see Father Christopher and what he had explained to her. Rani had also been out into the fields and had found some of the first spring flowers and had gathered them into a bunch and had them hidden behind her back. She brought them out now and handed them awkwardly to Theodora.

I feel such a fool doing this. It is just a handful of plants. Her wife smiled happily and, took the flowers. She laid them on the table beside them, then reached up and drew Rani's mouth down to hers for a long and deep kiss. *It worked. I am forgiven.*

"See, if you are going to be a princess, you have to think like one. The world is much bigger than Haven and the way you were brought up is much smaller than the way it is elsewhere. Now, help me find something to put these flowers in and we can go to bed and make up properly before Fear comes home from school."

While they were walking back to the kitchen she added. "Now that I have the maces made, I also have a solution to the Master's control spells. I have been to see Eleanor and we start on them tomorrow. We need to work out how many we need."

Chapter III

Rani
5th November

T o sort out what is next we need to talk with everyone. I think that we will need to have a meeting after the evening meal tomorrow. So many have started living entirely in their own houses now, even if they still draw food from the common kitchen, that we cannot just pass the word around at a meal. I have to send Valeria around to tell everyone about it.

W e are last...everyone is already there. Those who are definitely going hunting are more-or-less sitting together. Shilpa, Elizabeth, Danelis, Tabitha, Dulcie and Umm are in a clump, and there are several groups of married couples while Fãtima, Bilqīs, Goditha and Parminder, of the young mages, sit well apart. Away from everyone else, but Astrid and Basil that is, is the last clump of the priests, their wives, and Verily and the Hob. Even I can see that all of the children in the room are looking at the Hob from the far side of mothers or sisters and several are peering at him out of folds of skirts.

Rani sighed. *It looks like my reaction is already being shared by others here. My Theo-dear is looking at me in a meaningful way. It is going to be my job to sort this out, isn't it?* "By now you will have heard that Saygaanzaamrat is no longer a prisoner and that he has asked to join the village as Verily's husband." *Well, that got them all leaning together and muttering.*

The Hob unexpectedly stood up. He made everyone else, even Hulagu and Astrid seem small. He spoke up in his broken Hindi: "Me no longer Saygaanzaamrat. To celebrate that me new person Basil has given me new name. Me now Azizsevgili. You can call me Aziz. Me not tell what it means, because me embarrassed."

Rani looked around, *Basil and Astrid have innocent looks on their faces and from the smiles on Ayesha and Theo-dear, even though they are hearing the name for the first time, they know what it means. Right, I will find that out later.* "Me am put old life behind. Me am study to learn this language and want to be good husband. Me am hunter and want to look after my little ugly one. Me hope you learn to like me. Basil and priest say you will and me trust them. Astrid tell me have to tell you that if you are tell monster stories to children, me can act in them for you."

That broke some of the tension and caused a titter of shocked amusement to go around. He turned and looked at Astrid meaningfully. *She has a huge grin on her face.* "Me thought she making joke of me." He sat down.

I will try again. "That aside…what we now need to know is who is going to come on the next stage of the journey to attack the Masters, and who is going to stay in the village and look after the children, and keep both the children and the village safe for our return." She paused.

"It will not be safe to come, and it may not be safe to stay. The Masters have already sent people here to invade us and they may send more. Whoever stays must be vigilant, must keep up the watch at the lookout and must keep watch on the hills around the valley. Although it is hard to come that way, it is not impossible. We will finish blocking the way we came in before we go, but there will be other ways we don't yet know of. We also have to decide when to go and how to go."

Hulagu stood. "I have been thinking about the second of those. I offered to take my köle back to the tents, so I was thinking of leaving a few weeks after the snow clears, but they said that they want to stay with me until I am finished. This meant we could go sooner, but then I thought; if we sit here as if we are all staying, the Masters may think we are not coming. If we then sneak out, we may surprise them." He sat down.

Yes, that could work. If the Masters had an early attack on the valley planned, then we will still be in place to deal with it. It looks like we don't have very far to go and a week or so of quick and stealthy travel would see us there, so we have all of spring and summer to get to our target.

The only drawback I can see is that several women are pregnant and so this would both slow us down and make the women clumsier as time grows on. Still, it is actually better than what I had planned…They are all looking at me and waiting for me. She eventually spoke up. "I agree, now who wants to go…please raise your hands."

I am not going to push them. It is up to them. There are whispered conversations everywhere. Eleanor keeps trying to put her hand up, but Robin is objecting. Norbert has two women telling him he is staying and Goditha has Parminder pointing at her belly. On her small frame her pregnancy is showing more than on many of the others.

Aziz and Verily have obviously agreed between them what they will be doing and they both have their hands up without consulting. She nodded at them and they put them down. *We will have beauty and the beast with us. Bryony must have worked it out with Stefan as well. Her hand is also raised. Nod to her. Valeria has hers raised as well. Otherwise it is only the original party who are interested in going.*

"Thank you all. Eleanor and Norbert; do not be disappointed, but you will not be going. You are needed here. If the valley is attacked, the bulk of the fighting will be on you two. Valeria, you are staying as well. We cannot take Fear with us and we need you to care for her here."

"The rest of you are free to stay and listen to what we discuss, but you can leave now if you wish. I just want to talk a bit about weapons and what we now have with those who are going." Most stayed, but they quickly realised that nothing really interesting was being said and went home. The rest were not kept long either.

A s they walked home Theodora spoke up. "Now we have more time to cast the spells, I am going to extend my mace spell and make some spears, and perhaps even swords. With the rings, that should give us a better chance of coming back to Fear."

Now that we have extra time, we can do more training. We can all get fitter and stronger. I can have our trainee mages practice in the mine…away from charging items and we can set up a plan to fool anyone watching from outside the valley as well.

T hord, Goditha and Harald have made sure the entrance above the village is properly plugged. Gradually we change the watch at the lookout. Astrid has Darkspeech words my wife doesn't. She calls it a maskirovka. The people that came from outside Mousehole appear less and less often. The ones who are seen outside on watch and hunting, with someone watching over them from the lookout, are all the ones who will be staying behind.

Between them, Theodora and Norbert have made new spears for Astrid, Bryony and Stefan. They are broad-bladed hunting spears with a cross-piece like Astrid and Bryony are used to, ones that will have a better effect on anything that is just a skeleton, than the type that Stefan normally uses, with a narrow blade, which are meant for use mainly against cavalry, or by it.

Theo-dear is getting used to this making of magical weapons, and Norbert is even starting to show her how to work the metal. They will have time to make a sabre for Anahita, a scimitar for Aziz, who is very pleased, as well as the two new shortswords for Basil.

Basil looked at them and immediately went and got two new scabbards. "I will take these, but they are shortswords, they are small. I am taking my old ones as well." *The old ones were strapped to his legs while the new ones took their old position for his high cross draw. My wife and I don't need new ones. We have good blades and should not be in the front row of a fight anyway.*

My Princess' last few days will be best spent making wands. I have been doing that, and a few other things, all along and we now have several bundles of wands, each bundle in their own pouch. I plan on using them freely...I remember the skeletons that attacked us on the way north to Evilhalt in a time that seems so long ago...this time it could be even worse.

Astrid
27th November, the Feast Day of Saint Fergus

Aziz was baptised three days before his wedding. *Our priest is delighted that he can do it today. After all, Saint Fergus is the patron saint of the 'greenskins', the general and sometimes derogatory name of the Kharl races and so probably of grey-skins as well.*

After the religious solemnity of the baptism, the men's party for the marriage is to be held on the same night. Aziz has told Verily of Hobgoblin wedding customs and she has insisted on it being then. The men, and of course Goditha, discovered why when they arrived. Aine had been hard at work and none of them were capable of doing much work the next day, to the annoyance of us wives. Even Christopher and Theodule are more than a trifle indisposed.

I don't blame Verily for shunning her birthplace and insisting on wearing what Hobgoblins do when getting married. It is just a surprise what that meant for me. "Are you sure?" *The couple both nodded, so I have agreed to make it, and to wear it. Now that I am committed, I will make the wedding clothes all by myself and secretly to maintain the surprise. I have to admit that the fun bit was telling Theodora.*

Christopher
30th November, the Feast Day of Saint Andrew

S urely this day marks our last marriage for a while. I wish it were more auspicious a day to have one, given its nature, but even I can draw nothing from the feast day of the patron of fishermen, however hard I try.

The groom is arriving to the sound of drums. Kāhina even hurried to make a special one to play on this occasion after Aziz had described it. I wish that she had not. It is very large, and it sits on a stand high above the floor beside me and the end, at the same height as her head, is being hit with two padded sticks. It is very loud beside me. It sounds like one would think the heart-beat of a dragon would sound like close up.

Basil is the groomsman. The two are wearing just a short leather kilt and sandals. Aziz was looking even larger dressed almost in just his greyish skin and, for the first time really, most people can see that Basil's skin does have similar patches, green not grey, that show his ancestry. Both have marks painted on their bodies with ash and clay.

Now the door opens, and it seems the bride is coming. There is no change in the music. Astrid, as the maid of honour, is at the door. I am glad they warned me. She is dressed the same as the men, but wearing her rubies and, from her broad smile, her ancestry can also be seen.

The bride is the only fully human member of the wedding group. She also has just the kilt and sandals. Her jewellery is an ancient and ornate necklace of jet, a lace of stones a hand wide, one which matches her black hair and shows well against her pale skin. It seems that Theodora really wants to make her point with...her husband. She is giving the bride away dressed the same way as the rest of the party, but she has the jewelled collar of her favourite dress around her neck.

Outwardly she may appear calm but, as her confessor I know that she has never before appeared in public wearing so little. All three also bear painted marks that, I am told, said to any who could read them that they came in peace as wedding party. All three, as a point of pride, are staying dressed the same for all of the night as well.

Theodora has told me that, when they return, all of the children and, if they wanted to, the adults will also be taught at least Darkspeech of the Darkreach languages. If they were going to end up with traders coming past, people will be better off talking to them in their own tongue and, after all, her daughter should be able to speak to her great-great-great grandfather if they took her to see him. She had been sure that Basil, at least, will agree with her and Astrid

21

has been loudly complaining for some time on the subject.

Rani
35th November

I t did not take long for him to be accepted. The children love him. Aziz is walking around the village, followed by all five of the children. Suddenly he turns and raises his hands and roars and they all run off with shrieks and giggles, to return and follow him again. I just wish this game hadn't led to a new fashion among them…leather kilts.

Fear came up to Rani and demanded her own. "But dear, it wouldn't be right for a little girl."

"But Presbytera Bianca wears one and so do Anahita and Kāhina and Astrid, and even Teacher Ruth wears one when she is running and throwing things and mummy Theodora wore one to the wedding, and so I should be able to as well," *She says this with all of the conviction a child with logic that they know is unassailable can muster.*

A sharp look towards Theodora. *She has the effrontery to be amused at me even while she stays silent…she is laughing at me inside. I can see it in her twinkling eyes. Damn her twinkling golden eyes. They change shade with her mood and I can read them easier than I can most faces now.* Rani gave in to the request. Soon, if it was warm enough, all of the little girls ran around in them. *Children seem to be very hard on clothing. At least this way it saves on material. We can always easily get more leather. Cloth we are short on.*

Rani
31st December

F inally, all was ready, and they could not delay their departure any longer. The horses were to be left behind and they would walk, despite the objections of the Khitan. Riding would only gain them an extra day of travel, and they would either have to leave someone outside to look after the horses, or let them wander outside, prey to any of the many possible unknown dangers of mountain predators.

We need to leave Sajāh in charge of the Mice, but Eleanor in charge of defending them. Everyone who is being left behind has to agree to obey these two and, if we do not return, to accept their decisions as to whether to stay in the village or to go. The herd cannot be taken up to the top meadow until we return, so as to keep the much smaller number of people together.

They decided to go in the early evening, just after the watcher had come in from the lookout. Bilqīs, who was the best observer of those staying behind, was given this special outside watch. "There is no sign of movement on the roads or in the forest below, no smoke…nothing at all. It is all just as it almost always is."

Parminder spoke up. "I tried very hard and listened to the mind of an eagle soaring above us and what I could see from her eyes showed the hills around us and there were no people and no sign of fires except from the Bear Folk of the south. Again, there was nothing unusual."

Sajāh

Sajāh faced Theodora and Basil. She looked at them. *What do they want me for?* "If we do not come back in two months you must take these," *the Princess is the one that speaks as she hands me something…letters?* "And get them to Darkreach. You will be rewarded and it will not bring you ill. Mine is about Fear."

Sajāh looked down. *They are all sealed with strange devices imprinted in wax and have writing on them. I have a little Darkspeech and one says 'Hrothnog.' It is written in a different and more elegant hand to the other two and has a simple seal. Of the other two, the first has 'His Imperial Majesty, Hrothnog' written on it, and the other says 'Strategos Panterius—Intelligence'. The first is from Theodora, the others from Basil.*

Basil then spoke, "You must hand these to any Darkreach merchant, or even better to an officer at Mouthguard. Mine must be delivered by your hand or by Eleanor. She should be able to get there safely. I can tell you what mine are about. The Strategos, and that means he is a general, is my superior. I must tell him if I am dead, so that he can tell my family. The other—well, if we fail, then the Emperor will succeed, and he needs to do that to keep you safe."

Sajāh looked at their serious faces. *I know how capable these people are and how well equipped and prepared they are, and yet they think that failure is a real possibility.* She shuddered at that. "I will do this. Good luck. We will pray for you and may Allah, the Merciful, the Just, bless your task."

Chapter IV

Astrid
31st December

W e are leaving into the cool of a quiet and overcast spring night...a nice night for hunting. The only sounds audible are the little ones, the insects and the night birds, the soft 'ttcch' made by hoppers when they are talking to each other, and the near-as-soft thumping noise of them landing when they move about.

I can feel no touch on my charm that would tell me that someone is looking for magic, so given the darkness, we might be leaving unseen. The smells around me are simply the damp small smells of the forest night.

This time I am not the only one in the lead. I have charge of Bryony and Aziz and we run ahead...as often off the path as on, running through the fairly clear understorey and stopping to stoop in a little clump to look at possible signs that other people might be around. I have missed this. While we stay around a hundred paces ahead of the rest, I need to remember to keep one of us just in sight of the main group as we have fun exploring ahead.

The others stay on the roadway in a tight bunch and keep slowly moving down this path. Theodora has said that she hoped that her charm showing the empty trail might provide protection for the main group. If we are seen at all, we could well be a hunting party out for some night sport. Bryony and I have only bows and spears, and Aziz has a bow, so we look like we are hunters and, we are trying to look for tracks when we stop, so we are acting a lot like hunters.

This is a path that we have traversed once before on our way to Mousehole, and many times while out hunting, but it is springtime now, not autumn or winter. We move along the path as it follows the contours and meanders on the flanks of the mountains. To the right is the occasional small cliff.

The valleys are full of an upper storey of tall red cedars, myrtle-beech, and celery-top pines, with their long straight trunks and a rounded clump of their odd leaves at the top. Under them are the Blackwoods, then shorter wattles and other plants. I can smell some even at night. There are rivulets running down from the flanks of the hills behind, the area around the water crowded with the tall trunks of ferns and lush carpets of moss.

Sometimes I hear or see a waterfall. Higher up on the slopes are the giant gums, over a hundred paces tall, which provide a top canopy over the Blackwoods and smaller gums, and the occasional broad-leaved conifer and slightly smaller myrtle beeches. On the ridges grow the groves of the smaller beeches, just starting to re-grow their leaves after winter. Although there is none between the trees, in the larger clearings in the valleys, the grasses are lush and prolific.

Around us are the wildlife of the night: the small deer and rock hoppers in little groups, and a number of other small hopping creatures in ones or twos. Sometimes a bandicoot or other little creature scuttled away from them, quickly trying to lose itself in the night. There is no sign that anything else sentient stirred. It would be fun to be actually hunting tonight...although I suppose that, in a way, we are.

A gentle breeze is coming up from the south-west; there is just a hint of warmth in it. According to Dharmal's diary, we have two days of travel to the north before we can find the path into the mountains that he used.

Towards the end of that night they came upon an old campsite that they had used on their way south. *It is showing signs of further use...the bandits and the Darkreach traders at least.* Astrid went back to the main group.

"Do you want to use the campsite or stay away from it?" she asked Rani.

"We had best stay away. The first thing someone scouting the area will look at are the campsites. Can you find us an area off the trail near water with a cliff behind it?"

"Only every half hour," replied Astrid. *I know that I have said it to Basil, and I may have even said it out in public, but some people spend far too much time in towns and not enough in the wild. How can Rani not have noticed this?* "We will stop at the next." She went back to the lead group to give them instructions.

Bryony stayed near the track and the other two veered off to the right to find a campsite along their path. True to her word it wasn't long, in fact just in the next valley that she gave Bryony the signal and she, in turn, began signalling to the main group and pointing to the right. *The daylight is growing.*

Astrid was stopped in a small flat area that was covered in an aromatic grass. *The rivulet is around forty paces away and, after the flat patch, the grass runs down a small slope to meet it. Behind the flat area is a small cliff of around two hands of paces high that runs, with lower patches, for some way in each direction. Good campsite.*

"Aziz is checking the top of this cliff, but we have seen no sign of people in this area. You can just see the track from here so, as we keep watch, we should see if we have followers. I will head back now and cover the tracks that you herd of giant lizards will have left behind you." She turned to Basil: "Darling, I would love some breakfast when I get back," and was off.

Astrid
32nd December

During the day, the vigilance of the watches was rewarded with the sight of parrots and colourful rosellas and many other small birds flying among the trees. The parrots and rosellas made the day vibrant with their plumage and their cries. More quietly, small yellow-winged honey-eaters sought out the newly appearing flowers of spring. Raucous wattle-birds mixed seeking flowers with mating flights, dancing around in the air as display and challenge.

Above them all, in the clear sky, were the rare sightings of a huge wedge-tailed eagle or a smaller hawk. Some small lizards moved on the cliff behind them as the day warmed up. The only larger creatures were a small, and very surprised, group of goats who came down around the cliff, obviously to a favoured watering hole, to discover a group of travellers. Their lack of immediate reaction showed that even hunters were rare in the area.

Bryony strolled over to Astrid as they shared the first watch. "Have you looked at what we are sleeping on?"

"Not really, I know little of these southern plants."

"We need to come back here when this is over." She bent down and pointed. "This grass is Lying Miriam. You can make a nice little poison to smear on blades from its roots. It is more painful than fatal, but still. And this," she pointed at another tall grass with sharp looking leaves, "is Sweet Ali. Dry and shred fine its roots, and you can make a lovely tisane. It not only is nice to drink, but it makes a curative potion if it is gathered at the right time of year. That is the herbal scent that we can smell.

"You could harvest a good bit of these from just this little meadow and make a fair bit of money in a town. Those goats probably come here not just for the water, but also for the Sweet Ali. The roots of that probably help keep them all healthy. I wonder what other things have flourished around our valley undiscovered in the last hundred years. We need to look." *She is looking around...calculating.* "Our Princesses are women of the cities. I wonder if they have even thought how far the rule of our village should run."

"In Wolfneck, we claimed a day's walk beyond our furthest hamlets as ours and keep an interest for a week beyond that. Our Rangers patrol out to there and check what happens. I have spent time with them. In summer, we use our canoes or run and in winter we use our skis."

"If the mages pay no attention to the outside, then I will suggest to them that they allow us to do the same. A week, down, will put us near your Swamp, and the Bear-people, if what I have been told is right." Bryony nodded. "A week up should put us near the Darkreach gap, I think, and below some of their hill forts. Behind us is the old land of the Dwarves, and south of there lies the Caliphate. I think that, as we start to climb, we might see Lake Erave in the distance to the west. I think that sets our limits."

"I will want to settle down and have a place to raise a family. Basil and I may visit his family, but I don't want to see mine. Although there is someone that we do want to see in Wolfneck, we don't want to see him for long, we just want a couple of things from him," *I guess that I should not grin like that.* "And we want to start our own family soon."

"Mousehole will be our home and I want to see it, and my family, safe and wealthy. We will need money, and earlier on we didn't settle exactly how we would all share in the mine and the other wealth that is already there. This land outside might be what we need. I was waiting until we got back to pin it all down as I thought it to be of no use trying to think of these things when we don't even know if we will still be alive."

They went on further that night. The travel was a repeat of the previous night, except for the scouts finding a bear off to the right and carefully steering the main group around it and stopping Theodora from wanting to see its cubs. Toward the end of the night Astrid came back.

"Somewhere around here should be our turnoff into the mountains. We are fairly certain that we have not passed it yet. From the ridge, ahead we can see a major rivulet. It should be the headwaters of the Tulky Wash. This means that our path lies along this slope...somewhere. I want to lie up until it is daylight and then we will look for it. This time we will take Verily with us."

Verily looks surprised. "I know more about finding loose money rolling around on the floor than I do about finding tracks."

"Yes...and the three of us will find the track. We need you as we have no chance of finding a spell that would tell the Masters that we are on the way. If we can think of putting an alarm on the road from the falls, they can do the same to something that leads to their front door. You should at least have a chance of sniffing it before we put our foot on it."

Rani nodded. "Good idea. Off you go."

"By the way, watch the sky." She pointed far to the east where the bulk of a huge mountain could be seen outlined against the growing daylight. "Aziz tells me that there is a dragon living in that mountain you can see at the start of the Tulky. We didn't tell him much of what we planned, or he would have mentioned it."

"His people live directly beyond it in a valley. Like all that are of that race, the dragon is not often seen, but if the Masters can rouse the Hobs, they might be able to rouse it as well. Theodora might be powerful, but I doubt that she can take that on, and unless she has better magic arrows than those that you have given us so far, I know that I cannot."

"A dragon?" asked Rani and looked at her partner.

"Umm, yes" said Theodora. "I seem to remember something about that. It is one of the reasons the hill forts are so solid and largely made of solid rock. Still, sometimes Darkreach loses one and it has to be rebuilt, but generally the soldiers can shelter inside if it passes."

"What type is it?" asked Rani.

"Red" said Theodora and Astrid at the same time, naming the largest and most violent of the fell beasts. *Luckily, they are also supposed to be the rarest of them all, not that most people ever get to see one of any type.*

"Keep good watch," said Rani. "That might be one of the reasons that there are no grazers left in the top meadow at Mousehole. How did we get the good fortune to have an eater of armies right next door?" *I notice that no-one has an answer to that.*

Astrid
33rd December

Once it was day, the path into the mountains was easily found. Dharmal had written of a marker on the main path, a rock with old carvings on it in a Dwarven script that he could not read. Aziz found it and called Astrid over. She looked at the flat stone. *It is covered in leaves left over from last year.* She gently cleared these off and looked at the stone.

It is a pace across and three paces long. One third of it is blank. Another third is covered in writing in Dwarven script. She looked at it: "Damn. It sort of isn't from the Dwarves at all." She called Thord and Basil over. "Can either of you read this?" Both shook their heads. "How do you write then?" she asked Basil, and without waiting for an answer she continued. "Anyone else read this?" They gathered around to a shaking of heads.

"This is how we write at home. It is in Darkspeech, not in Dwarven."

"No, it isn't." said Theodora.

"Yes, it is. At any rate, it is proper Darkspeech...how we write it at home. It says: 'If you pass by this spot you enter the land of the Dwarves. Abide by our rules or accept that we will punish you. Do not touch the rocks or leave this path without...' part of that word is gone, but I think it says 'permission.' 'We watch anything you do from here on, and you will answer for your deeds. If you come in peace, we welcome you. If you do not, then beware of our justice.' I think this used to stand in the ground so that all could read it."

Thord cleared the rock better and looked at it: "I t'ink t'at you 're right. Look at t' base. It has been broken. T'is used to stand in t' air." He looked to the side. "See t' rock here is an old road. Not just a path. T'ese 're t' remains of cobbles, hundreds of years old perhaps 'n' buried 'n' disturbed by roots.

"All we ha' to do is follow t'is 'n' we'll find Dwarvenholme. It'll take us straight t'ere. T'is looks far older t'at what we have previous t'ought. T'at would be why no-one has reported finding it. Most of it must be buried or destroyed." He started striding along the ancient road. "Here is t'e first Dwarf to rightful pass t'is way in cycles of cycles."

"Stop!" called Verily. "Oh too late. I didn't smell it until it triggered. Either I wasn't concentrating or else I guess I cannot smell traps. I think that the Masters now know that we are on our way."

"In that case," said Rani, "we will press on hard until we have a defensible position with some overhead cover before we stop for a long break."

Astrid nodded and waved to the other two with some hand gestures and they ran forward. *I am glad that I have been teaching them how to talk without noise between them. It may be important.*

"Sorry," said Thord, contritely "I was excited."

"It doesn't matter. You heard Verily. You had no way of knowing and she didn't sense it, for that matter, neither did we...now lead us out. You keep watch at your feet for traps that are more physical. Hulagu, you go next and keep an eye on the three up front.

W *ith us running ahead, the rest can follow slowly behind. We need to keep rotating so that we have fresh eyes at front and we keep to the left, the higher ground, to look for a place to lie up.* The morning kept the same chorus and screech of birds. There were occasional glimpses of little hoppers, and once, some goats.

It is near to lunch and this is a good place to lie up. We *have connected piles of stones with a tree growing up in the centre of them. Plenty of shelter.* She sent Aziz off to bring the rest of the group. Astrid waited in the centre under the tree, where it pushed through one of the piles with Bryony just outside the stones. As they approached, Astrid made a circling motion and pointed at her eyes and then out. Aziz and Bryony nodded and ran off.

"What is that you are doing?" asked Verily, waving her hands around in the air in some vague imitation of what she had just seen.

"In Wolfneck, our few military for the village are our Rangers. We scout more than we fight, so we have to be quiet. I am teaching these two how we talk to each other in the field. Being quiet can mean your life." She grinned. "It also helps when you are out hunting or when you want to chat in a crowded room."

"Look around...this used to be a building. This tree," she hit the trunk, "is old. We see these sometimes in the south of the area we patrol. It is a type of pine. We like to use them to build our ships when we can find them. They are rare. One this size is probably well over two thousand years old. It must have started growing here soon after the Second Age ended at Evilhalt."

"That tells us how old these ruins are, and possibly even how long it is since this road was last used." She turned to Thord. "No wonder your people have never found Dwarvenholme. They were looking for something lost only a short while ago." She turned and went out of the ruins.

The hunters started to prepare for a break and eventually the scouts return- ed. "We think that we cannot be seen from above but, not being birds, we are not sure. It is all clear for a few hundred paces around," said Astrid. "There is no recent sign of people that we could pick up.

"Now, seeing that you lot have been lazing around and we have been doing all of the work – you can keep watch during this stop and we will put our feet up." Rani opened and closed her mouth. *She may be used to military discipline on an expedition, but I'm not. I do it my way.* Astrid made some more quick gestures and Aziz and Bryony grinned before going to Verily and Stefan and to get some food.

"You love having a joke, don't you?" said Basil. "Did you teach them how to tell jokes first? What was that about?"

"Oh," Astrid grinned and gave him a quick kiss, "I just said 'too crowded to have sex here'. I hadn't taught them how to say all that, but they guessed what I meant. I figure that one," and she demonstrated, less quickly, "is pretty much the same everywhere." She nodded towards Aziz and Verily. "Have you noticed that since she has discovered Aziz, Verily is actually behaving like a human being? She just smiled."

Basil nodded. "Now she even talks sometimes without having to answer a question. It took one of us monsters to bring out the human." He grinned and fed Astrid some food."

"How can you tell the age of the tree?" asked Basil.

Astrid answered with a grin. "I cannot tell you that. You just have to learn how to ask a tree a question" she said and refused to be drawn further.

R ani had decided to wait there where they had some protection until the next morning. Now that they were known or suspected to be on the way, they may as well use daylight and travel both a little faster and a little safer.

At about dusk, when they would have been setting out, the forest around them suddenly went very quiet. Ayesha, who had been up on the ruins keeping watch came scrambling back down. "Everyone keep quiet and get close to the tree," she said urgently. They all scrambled close and Rani went to ask a question. Ayesha put a finger to her lips. In a minute, the sky above grew darker as a vast figure went overhead. The wind of its passage rustled the leaves above.

Once it was passed, everyone huddled still for a bit. They were starting to move when Astrid shook her head and made motions at Aziz. He climbed up to where Ayesha had been looking out; his grey skin harder to see against the rock than the others would have been. He looked around and then made some more gestures and froze.

"Still and quiet," hissed Astrid. Again, the huge shadow swept over them and down the track. This time there was a massive gust of wind from above and they could feel the wind push down on the earth as the dragon took a slow beat with its titanic wings. *Aziz is holding his hand up to stop.* Again, they huddled, silent. This time the dragon could be heard. It was beating its way back uphill. The last time it must have circled around, but this time it was coming directly up the road.

One more time it came back down the long slope and once more, now in full darkness, it flew up. Eventually Aziz gave a sign and Astrid announced that they could now move. *Basil and I were hugging each other tight. I hadn't noticed that before.* She grinned and kissed him long and hard. "When you may die," she said, "you hang on to that which is most precious to you."

"Well, it looks as if the Masters may have some control over the dragon," said Rani. One or two passes could have meant that it was looking for food. That many transits surely meant that it was looking for us."

"When it beat its wings," said Aziz, "they only just cleared the highest trees. Its head was moving around to look for movement or colour. It was looking for us."

Sound slowly began to return to the forest and they set up for the night.

That is interesting. When we are stopped Aziz and Verily spend a lot of time with Christopher and Bianca and, while Verily talked to Bianca, Aziz and Christopher were head to head in an earnest discussion. My dear priest is in full teaching mode. Anyone can see that. Oh well...better the Hob than me.

Astrid
34th December

The next morning, they again hid under the tree and delayed their start and their patience was rewarded. *Four times the dragon passes over us before heading off again.* "Perhaps, if we can hide well, they will think that the warning was an accident or that we have gone another way. We shall keep off the old road as we move." Her scouts nodded back and moved off.

If we have to cross it, we jump and, when we land, check that we have made as few marks as possible. Four days they travelled with the huge bulk of the mountain looming larger above their left. They stopped early and left late. Each night the scouts found a place that gave overhead cover.

For the first three days, they saw the dragon at dawn and dusk. It was on its last flight that Astrid saw where it came from...*a huge cavern half way up the height beside them. It is titanic, bigger even than I had imagined in my worst nightmares. I have heard of the three greens to the east of Wolfneck in the mountains, but not seen them.*

This monster...its wingspan is surely wider than the valley where the flocks graze just outside the wall of Mousehole below the mine. They must reach over a hand of hundreds of paces wide. Its head alone is at least forty or more paces long. If it finds us, we have no chance of defeating it. We will surely die, and we have to walk under its home. It gives urgency to our attempts to stay under trees and hidden. Now we truly are just like mice scurrying along and hoping to avoid the gaze of this vast creature.

Chapter V

Astrid
2nd Undecim

F *ive days in and we find it.* Astrid came back to the rest of the hunters. "I think that we have found the main road from the north. It is at least as old as this one, but as we cross it, we are going to have to walk on it. We are going to keep to its right for a while. They had the last trap around a hundred paces along this road, so do not walk on it until I wave at you.

"By the way, Aziz's old tribe live past the mountain up the valley ahead. We are going between the ridges to our right. I am guessing, but if I am correct, the little creek we camped beside last night may be the start of our river at Mousehole. We could probably get back to the valley by following it." She grinned. "Of course, there may be a few cliffs in the way. I know that Aziz's tribe did not follow it when they came down to raid us, although he does not know why."

She went on, and eventually waved at them and then pointed across the road. There was a cliff a hundred paces away. Bryony was waving at them from under an overhang. "Verily, do you smell anything?" Verily shook her head. "To be sure, when you cross, run across there. We will wait for a bit before going on." *At least they do as they are told.* Astrid stayed behind, anxiously glancing at the mountain. *Now I get to cover their tracks.*

When they were ready to head off again she said: "I think that we still have several days to go. The dragon might explain why some searchers did not come back, Aziz's tribe explains others, and the Masters themselves will explain still more. Now that we know how old the track we are looking for is, and roughly how far it is that we have to go, we should have an advantage." She headed off south.

That evening, when they stopped, Rani pulled out the map from 'My

Travels Over the Land and Beyond' and pointed as she showed things. "We have found the road he talked about. The dragon must have been asleep when he passed. But he shows the mountain…and the valley that goes to your old village Aziz. Now that we know this we can see that those dots must mean that is where he thinks our river goes, so Astrid is correct. This mean that she was also accurate, if I am judging our travel times right, with how long it will take."

"I wish that I had taken some classes in geography," Astrid said. "I never thought that I would need them. It looks like I will be at school with Ruth when we get back as well. However, it also looks like this old Simon's book is right in all that it says. We need to carefully read more of it when we get home to see what else it tells us."

Astrid
5th Undecim

D *ay follows day and now there are eight. We have the huge mountain range looming large on our left. We walk at least a thousand paces below its first row of lower peaks and hug the base of mountains and sometimes walk along the foot of cliffs. At any time, something could happen…we could be attacked. It is exciting.*

To their right, a valley grew that was five hundred paces below them at its base. It came to an end where the road passed, but continued on, far smaller now, above the road. "I think," said Ayesha, "that when I left the Caliphate, I flew over this valley. If we followed it up into the mountains, we would get to my old home."

Around us is a forest clinging to the slopes and reaching above us…so different to those of home. The old, and almost invisible, road we follow lies a few hundred paces below us where trees give way to bushes and then to low shrubs rear us. Astrid stopped and looked around. *The flowers of spring are well out now. The hillsides are covered in whites and muted mountain hues with the bright splash of poppies and other things.*

She looked at a large flock of mountain rosellas making the sky noisy. *We are seeing lots of birds. Small ones fly low and the large ones ride the thermals, seeking prey. Yesterday I even saw one of the flying furry-winged lizards doing the same, and following it with my eyes, saw it land and some others take off. There was an eyrie of them above us.*

We must be close to our destination. I think that I will stop us early tonight and camp here. There is a safe spot against the cliff to hide. If we go on and find the gate, we could not be sure of a good spot to stop. We scouts will go on in the morning and search.

Rani agreed, and they set up a place to camp. *Perhaps this will be our last night outside or, for some of us, the last night. If so, it is a lovely night. The breeze is blowing warmer from the south-west and there is little cloud. Both moons are nearly full, and the night is bathed in light. I have chosen well in finding a spot for us to stop. We are above the road and can see for a bowshot in all directions. The trees have been cleared for some distance by a massive fall of rock which extends in a talus slope down over where the road runs.*

Christopher

Towards the middle of that night they were attacked. *Is it just luck that I am on watch already? Now, to start my praying…this is a fight that I was born to.* Those who were asleep were woken by Bianca and Verily. "Undead," he could hear being said behind him. *Coming awake they would see where I am facing.* He kept up his chanting.

There are vast numbers of skeletons, but they are not together. They are spread out. Whoever sent them must not have known where we were. They must have spread out from their source. They might even have been doing this every night since the alarm was sounded. They might even have been doing it for years. "In nomine Patris et Filii et Spiritus Sancti, et anathemati te…"

Rani

The next batch crumbled to dust before the priest. *Once the word, if that is the term, had spread among them, they must have started to converge. Luckily, they did not wait back and concentrate, but came on to attack as soon as they arrived.* She surveyed what they had.

Father Christopher is standing forth as a priest ought in such a case. In one hand, he holds Bianca's Bible, and in the other he holds a crucifix. He is intoning prayers in Latin and telling the unquiet dead to leave and disperse.

It is evident that he is far stronger in his faith than his friend Father George had been, from the number he is dealing with. Some came close and heard his exhortations and fled, and when they came in small groups, some just disappear in clouds of dust.

More and more are arriving, and they are starting to arrive faster than our priest can impose his will on them. Aziz and Ayesha, who had been standing beside and behind him begin to advance, making sure that the undead could still see and hear the priest.

Rani yelled for Bianca and Verily to move to back the other two up, she directed them to guard the back of the more experienced fighters and to stop them being surrounded, while the others who were still armouring, made ready to join in. Soon all were engaged. *Some of the animated skeletons 'die' instantly when they are hit, but some are stronger and take several blows to dispatch.*

Christopher

I *will keep up my exhortations, although I have been forced to take my old staff in hand to defend myself. I thank the Lord that I insisted on bringing this and I thank Astrid for her lessons. This staff, enchanted as it is against evil, does far more damage against these lesser undead than I could have done with a mace. I am still even getting some to turn away before I can hit them.*

We have formed a semi-circle anchored against the cliff. I stand in the centre, as I should. Basil and Thord hold the ends. One mage is on each side and Rani has given some of her wands to Theodora. Gouts of flame from them make the night sky even brighter. Those with spears just sweep them back and forward in front of them. They do not have to aim. A target is always there.

Silently, the attack keeps on and on. The only noise is the splintering of old bone, the grunts and sometimes cries of the Mice and my chanting. My voice is growing hoarse. Some of the animated dead attack with just their bare bones and empty hands; some use rusted and ancient weapons and some even have the remnants of shields on their arms.

At one stage, they were almost pressed back against the cliff and were in some danger of tripping over their own packs.

Eventually the attack slackened, and then it dwindled, and then there were only a few coming at them and finally there were none. *It is evident that we have won, it is time to leave the last few attackers for the others and enter into my main role as their healer.*

Picking up the Bible and crucifix again, he went to his pack and removed his bandages and healing salves and berries and went to work. *None, apart from me, are free of all damage. Anahita is our worst at hand to hand combat. She bears terrible injuries, is nearly spent and has to be helped to me. It is time for me to get to work; clear an area, mark out a sacred diagram, and pray so that she is healed.*

"Now that I have this done, Verily, you are next and then Stefan and then, you, my dear. Lastly, I will see Basil. The rest of you I will bind and use berries and potions on, but these will need more."

"I think we can assume that the Masters know that we have arrived by now," said Rani.

Ayesha spoke up. "Did anyone notice anything about our attackers?" she asked.

"Yes," said Thord. "T'ey were t' skeletons of my people. T'ose Masters have not only stolen our halls, but t'ey have taken t'e bodies of our ancestors 'n' are using t'em agin us. Even if t' rest of you turn back at any time, I have to go on. I canna allow t'is insult to t'e honour of our race to continue. I must either kill t'em or die. I would be shamed forever for allowin' it to continue. Dharmal was damned for his other actions. For allowing t'is to continue, he'll be doubly damned. Our priests must be told so t'at t'ey can take right action agin his soul."

They settled down for as much rest as they could get for the rest of the night. Several had trouble getting back to sleep. *As a reminder of what lies ahead of us, in front of where we are trying to find rest a mound of bones over a pace high forms a macabre rampart. I am exhausted. With my head on Bianca's lap, I will be asleep quickly.*

Christopher
6th Undecim

M orning prayers may be very important today. More so than usual...we could face anything. After they had eaten, the scouts set out, keeping up near the cliff rather than down on the road, which was now a hundred paces below them.

While they are gone, we need to ready ourselves for the day that lies ahead. We are all showing signs of the fighting last night with bloodied bandages and tears in our clothes. Astrid can fuss over them, but she did not have time to repair all of the damage to them.

The scouts have hardly left, and yet Bryony is back and waving at us from the edge of the clearing. Shouldering their packs and picking their way across the fallen rocks, the rest of the hunters soon reached her. "We camped nearly next to the gates," she said. "Simon told of the rock-fall we camped at the top of. It must be the one that covers the bottom of the path."

They travelled only another hundred paces through a thick grove before breaking through the trees onto a level platform made of massive blocks of stone. Christopher looked around him.

The trees form a border around the platform. The cliff above it towers in a massive overhang that darkens the area around the doors. The view of the road is blocked by the trees and, against the cliff I can see two colossal doors of iron with Aziz and Astrid looking at them. The doors stand at least five paces high and each is a good three paces wide.

"You can see the final reason why this place has not been found before. The road from below has been deliberately obliterated," said Astrid, waving her hand around, "And, while you can see that these doors used to be surrounded by relief carvings, they have gone as well.

"Even from the air it is likely that the shadow of the overhang would stop people seeing the entrance, unless they knew what to look for." She looked at the mages. "We have found your gates for you. It is up to you now to find a way in for us."

Chapter VI

Thord
6th Undecim

*H*ere we are standing in a rough row in front of the massive closed gates, with most of us facing out and looking up. If the dragon is called now, and comes, we need at least some warning; otherwise we will be trapped here and will certainly die. That would be annoying when we have just found the way home.

I will first try what Dharmal said had worked for his people. He stood in front of the doors. "I am a Dwarf coming home," *Now wait…nothing happening…oh well. It was worth a try.*

"Never mind," said Rani. "They probably removed that spell when they discovered that it worked. That it worked for Dwarves would also rancour with anyone who called themselves Masters and thought of this as their home."

Thord nodded. *What else could open them? I can see that the doors shift, but I cannot detect any sign that there was a hidden trigger that would cause them to open. By the Ancestors, this is frustrating. It should be me opening them.*

The mages are saying a variety of the words of opening, phrases that are conventionally used to open a public gate. They are trying in Dwarven, and in deference to the age of the artefacts that are confronting them, they try High Speech. After what Astrid had pointed out with the writing on the road marker, Theodora even tried in the Darkspeech tongues.

They were so long at it that Astrid, in impatience, came back from where she was watching to the north from the trees. "Have you tried pushing the doors?" she asked. Thord looked at the mages. The mages looked back. They all looked at Astrid. She returned their gazes with an upraised eyebrow.

"Such gates are always held by a charm of some sort," said Rani.

"That is nice to hear," she said. Astrid went over to the gates and shoved hard on the right hand one. "Thord," she called, "push on this one as well." Together they heaved. "Can you feel some movement?" she asked.

"Yes...I wonder..." he went to the other gate. "Now push, not as hard as you can, but try 'n' match my push, start weaker 'n' gradual push harder."

He began to push again, and Astrid pushed her side. *With the enhanced bracers on, she is far stronger than I am, so she has to try hard to pull back and to match my push.* Eventually she must have gotten it right, because all at once and very smoothly considering their age, the gates parted and swung wide.

"It is an old Dwarven trick. I shouldn't say t'is because some towns still use it. If t'ey do not have t'eir bars in place, all you have to do to open t'em is to push firm, with t' same force, on each side. If t' bars are down, you'll not open t'em 'n'," he looked inside and pointed at some large stone hooks carved out of the rock inside, "t' bars are missing." He turned to the mages. "Princesses, it is up to you to lead us inside, but I will take t' lead in. It is only proper for Dwarf to be first."

"It is," said Rani, "but first I want you all to gather around." They did so as she opened a large pouch causing a torrent of light to spill out. "I thought long about us seeing inside. Dwarven towns use light spells, thousands of them, frequently cast on crystals, to make the light seem brighter and more beautiful. I am guessing that the Masters have destroyed these crystals and have their own methods of finding the way."

She began to empty the pouch. "I want each of those with shields to hammer one of these to the face of your shield." She began to hand out small nails. *When you shade them, it is obvious that each one glows like daylight.* "I also want those near the front to throw them forward so that we can see what lies there. As we reach where we have thrown them, we shall look for places to leave them in the walls."

"Bianca, get as many small pieces of timber as you can that you can put a nail in and sling ahead of us if we need to. That way we will have light before us all of the time and it will be harder to attack us. Each time we reach a corridor that goes to the side we must halt until it is lit for some way, so that something cannot lurk in the dark for us."

"This pouch is full and, if I fall, so is a second one here on my belt. There are more in a small green bag in the left pocket of my pack." She indicated where and soon sounds of quick hammer blows rose as the fronts of shields became lanterns.

"Stefan, you are carrying your shield on your back and holding your spear. You must take the rearmost position as we move in case something causes darkness behind us. As we move, you will somehow have to keep looking back behind us while facing forward."

"Hopeful Dwarvenholme is built along t' lines t' at most towns still follow," said Thord. "If it is I should ha' some idea what we face. It's a pity t' at Harald is not with us. My town was built different. He grew up in more normal Dwarf town."

"He had to stay. Both his wife and Mousehole needed him there. On the other hand, we needed to have some of you here, and you will notice that everyone here who had a partner has them with them. In such a case as this I would not split a couple up, even if one would have been better off staying. You each have a right to be with those whom you love or...or whatever arrangement Hulagu has with Anahita and Kāhina." The last two named grinned at each other.

W e are as prepared as we ever will be. Ahead of me the old tunnel pierces the mountainside like an arrow plunging in. The whole thing excites me and scares me at the same time. Every Dwarf in existence today would want to be me, and yet it is terrifying...now I need to pay attention to what I see. For instance, already I can see rooms opening off the main shaft and there are lichens growing on the walls...lichen.

"T'ese doors must oft lie open," said Thord. "See, t' lichens here near t' entrance ha' lots of colour in t'em. T'ose t'at are deeper will be much paler 'n' 'll have to live off t' light t'ey are able to garner from spells 'n' anything t'at may find its way inside. Many of our settlements ha' giant crystals 'n' mirrors to bring sunlight inside, but I imagine t'at here t'ey'll most be broken. T'ey ha' closed t' doors just because we're coming." *Head in slowly. Look carefully at all four surfaces around me. Remember that we are a cautious race.*

Rani

I hope that I have considered this properly. I have Basil, Aziz and Ayesha in a line across the corridor behind the Dwarf. Basil is in the centre and has his shortswords drawn. Ayesha has her shield on her right arm, for she can use either hand equally well. This way she can be on the right and have her shield facing an attack from that side.

Aziz takes the left. Behind them are Astrid and Bryony. Both have their bows on their backs and spears in hand. They stand ready to thrust over the heads, or between those in front of them. Hulagu stands between them. His mace is sheathed and is ready to cast his darts, or to throw nails forward as is needed.

We are next. Theo-dear has her shield and I have my main-gauche in our off-hands. We both have wands instead of swords. Behind us are the Khitan girls, Kāhina & Anahita. They have bows in hand. I don't think we will need bows, but we are sure to see some caverns where they may be needed and, if need be, everyone could move to the sides and allow the girls to fire along the corridors. The short Khitan bows are ideal for this task, as they fire with a flatter arc than most of the other bows except Astrid's.

Verily, Bianca and Christopher are next to last. The women have their maces sheathed, and have ready the weapons with which they are happiest... throwing knives, and lots of them and most of them enhanced. Although these may be hard to use against an animated skeleton, I think, or perhaps hope, that there cannot be too many of them left inside, given the hundreds that we faced last night. I hope that any opponents are more substantial than the animated sets of bones. Our priest has his mace in its holder and he leans on his staff.

She looked back. *Stefan is where he should be, bringing up the rear. He keeps checking behind him and the three in front of him kept checking on, and past him.*

As they advanced Rani showed her military training by softly barking out orders to keep them in place. *I have no experience with this sort of thing, but I talked with Basil before we left about how his police search an area, and I hope that I am right in using that to guide me. Mother Prthivi, I pray that I am right.*

We have reached the first opening. It leads off to the right. "Hulagu, Astrid, Bryony...go past it and watch ahead." Thord entered, followed by Basil, Aziz and Ayesha. Hulagu cast a nail ahead of him (although the light from outside was still strong here) and then another into the opening. *There is a room in there. I will send those four with Theo-dear in. We will wait outside.*

"Remember... Call out what you see and make sure you can hear our replies."

"It looks to be guardroom," called Thord. "T'ere 're piles of fungi. I suppose t'at t'ey 're where t' furniture used to be long ago... I am looking around before going on to t' rooms t'at lead off t' first...I cannot see any rocks t'at could move 'n t' doorways are all open. It looks like t'ere used to be doors here as t' rock is carved for hinges."

"I am going into t' first room. It is bare...again t'ere 're fungi. It is big 'n' rectangular. It may once have been t' barracks as t'ere 're niches carved in t' walls of t' right size to be for sleeping. ... Basil has put a nail into crack, so it is now lit up. … We're going to t' next room… … it is smaller."

"Basil has put in another nail. T'is room has several other exits in a row off it…each of t'ese is small…t'ey may ha' been cells — or small storage rooms — no, cells, I can see t'at t'is one has some remnants of bars jutting out of t' walls of its entrance. T' iron is good on t'em ,so t'ey may ha' been removed rather t'an rusted 'n' t' air is dry. We ha' left it alight"

He is getting muffled "T' next is t' same…'n' t' next…'n' t' next. We are back in the main room. We 're going to t' last doorway, which is on t' left. It is also large…t'ere 're hooks 'n' other t'ings driven into t' walls. We have lit it. I still canna see anything t'at would move or open. I would say t'at t'is was an armoury or storeroom. We 're coming out now." *I can see the shadows and lights moving towards us.*

"Do we have to go t'rough t'at each time we find gap?" asked Thord when he re-emerged.

"Yes, for the present. At least until we are in the main complex I want to ensure that we know the way it is all put together, and make sure that we leave nothing behind us in a room that we didn't search that can then attack us from behind. We have plenty of food with us, and if we do run out, we can return to the entrance. Astrid and Bryony will, I am sure, be happy to do some hunting for us."

She turned as she said it. *They are nodding at each other and making hand talk already. Perhaps they don't like the silence ahead of them. I don't. Even to me, this is a different silence to that of the forests. Here in the underground there isn't even the faintest murmur of a breeze, no sound of water, no whirr of wings.*

My ears are straining to hear something…anything at all. The smells around are all of dust and mould. It is hard not to sneeze. We may not yet have come very far, but we have already left behind us the feel and smell of fresh breezes and the scent of spring and growing things.

Ahead there is a large widening of the corridor. Why? It then closes in again to the same size and keeps going further. Perhaps it is a place for wide things to pass. Pusan, guide our steps.

They followed the same pattern of searching at the next three openings, but already, as Bryony and Astrid waited, they could see that there was a much larger space ahead of them as the main entrance corridor opened up into a vast blackness that the light behind them, and even that on their shields, seemed unable to penetrate.

There is now little light left coming from outside and what there is left is only a dim sliver going into the dark ahead. It can only be seen clearly if we cover the nails. The next two openings are very much the same inside as each other, one bigger than the other, but of the same pattern.

Thord is right...stables make sense. "T' larger room is for visitor horses 'n' t' smaller is for sheep like Hillstrider. So far t'is is following t' pattern of most Dwarven towns. If I am right t' next should ha' several large rooms leading off central one 'n' smaller one, well away from t' others, with running water 'n' drain." *He was right.*

"So, what is that?"

"T'at is where herd animals from outside 're brought to be penned if need be, 'n' t' small room is for slaughtering t'em for food," he replied. "T'ere would be spells 'n' magics to stop sound or noise panicking ones not taken. If'n all follows right we'll next ha' t' main gallery. It'll be round 'n' ha' at least two levels."

"T'is is where t' shops 'n' t' artisans who make small goods'll work, not t' metal smelters or t' blacksmiths, or anyone else who is too loud or too... smelling...but everyone else. It is all so much bigger t'an home or Deafcor, which is north of Kharlsbane 'n' t'e only other town I've been to, but it has followed t' same pattern."

"We Dwarves 're usual very traditional 'n' Kharlsbane is unique in t' way it is constructed. Even t'ere, with most of t' construction above ground, t' buildings 're laid out in a similar pattern if'n you know how to look."

W e're at the end of the corridor, and the light from our shields only goes a tiny way inside, but it is disturbing something. As we approach and from above the entrance, I can hear a chittering sound, and there is the rustling sound of many flying creatures...bats? There is a foul stench coming from the cavern ahead and the floor is white with droppings covered in fungi. Yes, bats.

Even I can see some trails in the fungi, as if animals come from outside after grazing. They disappear quickly into the gloom. We need more light.

"Bianca, cast some of your pieces of wood into the room...cast some high so that we can see what is above, but from the curve of the room that I can see, you will also need to cast them long. Those at the front keep watching below. Don't all of you watch where the light goes."

The first piece of wood, with its nail, went soaring into the air. As the partial globe of light, flickering as it flew as the wood turned and tumbled, went sailing up in a long arc, they could faintly see the room. *It is a huge dome. The light is disturbing the occupants. A horde of small and large bats are showing their agitation by taking flight and letting out a chorus of squeaks and other cries.*

Some tried to come their way to the tunnel to the outside, but returned on finding it still brighter in the corridor. For a while bats flew all around them making their noises as they fluttered around. Eventually they fled further back into the darkness.

Bianca cast more sticks into the dark, and pockets of light began to spring up in the centre and around the walls, disturbing more bats. One bounced off a flying bat and then caught on a projection and lit up a broad stone shelf with square openings behind it. *The shelf has been carved out with the native rock left behind as pillars to help support it and to also leave a balustrade. I can see a set of stone stairs leading up and down from near where the stick landed.*

"See...t' concourse," said Thord. "T'at one is caught two levels up and it looks like there 're another three levels above it. This is huge. You could put every dwarf alive now into these shops and still ha' lots of room left over. We once must ha' had the largest city in the Land. Deafcor has two levels and even Copperlevy, our largest town, has no more, even if it is supposed to be much larger around. But it still is nowhere near as big around as this."

Bianca cast to the left and right. *Two openings are leading off the main concourse. They are each as large as this one. Another long cast reveals another one also lies straight ahead. The two at the sides are opposite each other, and the four corridors form a regular arrangement. Bianca's cast ahead has not reached the wall, but lies near a hundred paces closer to us. Only a fraction of that wall is lit up, and that dimly. The cavern is around four hundred paces across and possibly over two hundred high.*

"One of 'em, probable t' one going to t' left, but not always, 'll be t' way to t' stairs up 'n' down to other levels 'n' t' shafts where goods 're moved between 'em. One'll probable lead to another concourse with metal smiths or else to farms for fungi 'n' other delicacies 'n' t' last should lead to where most of t' Dwarves lived."

"Other levels 'll hold t' Royal rooms 'n' meeting areas 'n' caverns to practice combat in...'n' temples. One'll ha' t' main water store 'n'... Oh, I don't know what else...treasure perhaps. T' Masters 'll be somewhere."

Thord is finding it hard to contain himself. He is nearly jumping up and down with excitement. At the moment, it is obvious that he doesn't care where the Masters are. He is seeing Dwarvenholme. I am sure that no-one has ever seen a Dwarf, normally so reserved and inscrutable, both so animated and happy before. "I'm not sure what you'll want to check next, but we'll ha' to leave t'is entrance behind us to see any more."

It seems like most of the place is covered in bat excrement. A bat cave is a very unclean place. Ganesh guide my thoughts. Rani felt the pungency hitting her nose and shuddered in disgust. "Let us stay under this balcony for a start. It is cleaner here. We will move to the right and try and explore this level a bit before we go elsewhere."

They set off. *As we move, we have unconsciously drawn our formation tighter. It will be in response to the vast blackness that lies beside us with pools of light scattered around it. It sets up an eerie spectacle.* As they continued, something fled from ahead of them. *I only caught a glimpse of it. Even Thord isn't sure.* He moved ahead a few paces, stopped and pointed down.

"Cave deer." *He is pointing at something that may have been faint hoof prints.* "T'ey 're like other deer, tiny 'n' very shy, but t'ey have huge eyes. T'at means t'ere must be some light here. I'll bet t'at, if we dowsed all of t'ese lights, we'd see t'at t'ere is enough light from fungi to see dim by. We might e'en find hunting here without going outside. If'n t'ere is deer here, t'ere might also be cave pigs—t'ey 're not real pigs—t'ey 're large fat rodents like big rabbits, but t'ey run not hop. T'ey eat fungi 'n' 're good eating." He rubbed his stomach.

"We'll ha' to watch out t'ough. Not only are t' Masters here, but if'n t'ere 're t' plant eaters, t'ere 'll probable also be t' things t'at eat 'em…otherwise t'ey would breed until t'ere was nothing left for 'em to eat. It'll most likely be t' animals t'at are leaving t' tracks t'at we can see."

He looked around into the cavern for a while. Rani followed his gaze. *The bats are hiding away from the light, but seem only to be agitated by our presence. They are not aggressive.*

Thord continued: "T'ere are two flying t'ings to real worry about, 'n' a few nuisances. One is a bat t'at, while you're sleeping, will land on you 'n' drink your blood. They're only small 'n' you'll only have major problem if'n t'ere are lot of 'em. We ha' to watch for 'em when we sleep as they're very quiet 'n' 'll even creep up on you on t' ground."

"T' other is far larger 'n' t'ey 'll attack at any time. T'ey 're like bat, but t'ey have hard beak 'n' t'ey fly very fast 'n' bury themselves into a body 'n' 'll drain blood until t'ey 're full like tick 'n' t'en t'ey 'll drop out 'n' crawl away or fly slow. T' main problem is t'at, when t'ey bury themselves, it could be in something vital 'n' you'll die. T'ey not bright. Oh, 'n' if'n you see what looks like black parrot, kill it. T'ey 're mainly nuisance, but t'ey bite —hard— 'n' t'ey eat flesh."

"T'ere 're many flesh-eaters on t' ground. T' best rule is; if'n it moves towards you, try 'n' kill it fast. Some're very nasty. Usual, you only find 'em in big cave systems with exit outside, but…" he waved his hand towards the cavern beside them and started off again to the right.

Next tunnel we need a break for food and to regain focus. "Hulagu go to the limit of light and plant a nail somewhere." *Now we will all have some food.*

Astrid

I *don't feel much like eating. I have never ever gotten seasick. I have dealt with the stomach contents of a whale. Why does the smell of this bat shit make me feel queasy?* She forced some food down, but she lacked her usual hunger.

Time to stand up, and I nearly throw up. We just get to the first side corridor of the main avenue and I can feel my stomach rebelling. Damn it. Astrid dropped her spear as her gorge rose, and she knelt down and vomited. She stood up again as Father Christopher came rushing up.

She raised her hand. "I feel better now. I know it sounds silly, but I do." The priest handed her a cloth to wipe herself with, "Thank you," she muttered as she cleaned her mouth. *Next, he is handing me a small green ball. What is this?*

"Suck on this," he said.

"No, I feel better."

He grinned: "It is not for the illness, we don't know what that is yet, although I might have an idea...but it is for your breath. Lakshmi made me some from mint before we left. You wouldn't want to kiss Basil like that now, would you?" *Good point.* She took it and began to suck. When he came back, she had to explain to a very worried Basil that she felt fine.

Rani

They went to the next passage leading off and searched. *It looks to have a single large round room at its end, but I don't want to go into it, so other things may lead off the far side.* "Possible practice area, or meeting room," said Thord. *So far nothing dangerous has appeared. Either the rooms we are seeing are empty, or else they just contain fungi, lichens and dust...lots of dust. I am a little worried. In the empty rooms, the dust lies thick and causes people to sneeze. I know of diseases that start that way.*

As they prepared to go into the next hallway things changed. A small cloud of flying creatures came boiling out. *They are flying straight at the four of us nearest the entrance. Basil is the first to be attacked, but he is facing the door and uses his shortswords to cut two out of the air.*

Thord has managed to get his shield in the way and one ended up impaled in the timber, while another is deflected up. He has swatted it with his hammer as it spun in the air. Aziz deflected one with his shield, but grunted as another one has speared itself into his stomach. Damn. Ayesha is concentrating on dodging three of them rather than trying to hit any.

Rani raised her voice. *This I can deal with.* "Archers, watch each way. Spears face out." *Damn, all I am doing is hopping around, trying to get a clear shot with a wand.*

More coming out of the door...but not making it to their victims. Bianca and Verily have started throwing knives and these put up a wall of steel, impaling squealing creatures. Most of them haven't died, but the blades stuck into them stop them flying. They can only flop around on the floor making high pitched squeaks until Christopher is able to dispatch them with his staff without getting too close.

I am still unable to do anything. Basil has looked at the two women drawing blades and throwing them as fast as they can, and turns his back to the entrance, dispatches first one and then a second of Ayesha's attackers. She has used her shield to drive the third against the wall. Basil has turned around again in time to cut another out of the air. It is the last. Thord squashed the one stuck in his shield against a wall.

"Sorry," said Bianca, "we ran out of blades before we ran out of them." *Verily and Christopher are already moving towards Aziz. He mutters in Hobgoblin as he grasps the thing with his hand to pull it out.*

"Don't do t'at," yelled Thord. "Let me. If'n you do it wrong, it'll leave bits of itself 'n' lots of poison inside you." Thord knelt, and grabbed the beast around its beak, and twisted it and gently pulled. *It comes clear with a wet sucking sound...twisting and struggling and squealing like an upset pig. Its wings are furiously trying to get it free as blood now flowed out of the wound.*

Christopher dived towards the wound with a pad. He held it there for a while and then grabbed a crying Verily's, hand and replaced his hand with hers so that he could wrap a bandage around the Hob, lifting his leather jerkin to do so and reaching around his body. *Thord has been left with the blood-sucking beast flapping like an enraged rooster in his hand trying to get itself free. Its squealing is continuous.*

He put his hand down and squashed it with his boot carefully near the wall. Blood still squirted around—its own and Aziz's—as the furred flying creature gave a bleat like a baby goat and expired with a popping noise.

"I suppose that you warned us about them," Rani said to Thord.

"Yes. They 're t' cokhane, but I've never seen, or even heard anyone tell, of so many. T'ere were...what...over twenty?" Usual you only see one or two, t' most I've heard of is six. T'is lot...may've been sent."

When he had finished with the bandage, Christopher reached down and took a flask off his belt and pressed it to Aziz's lips. The Hob took a small swallow, and then Christopher looked at him for a while and felt his pulse before making him take another. Aziz coughed and sat up, colour already returning to his cheeks. "Spicy...thanks."

"Another thing I had Lakshmi make up. One thing our valley produces on its flanks is Healbush. The potion you can make from it does not produce a major curative effect, but I have a lot of it." He pointed at several flasks on his belt. "Bianca has another flask if it is needed and there is more in my pack."

He turned to Aziz. "I will leave the bandage. The damage inside you should repair over a little while and you will feel better already, but the wound will stay soft for a little while yet and may tear again. You will be tired from your body healing itself so quickly. Even the best herbs take a while to work and I think that you have a mild poison in your system from your pulse. It is running very fast. I want to see you each time that we stop."

Bianca came up to Verily and handed her the knives she had thrown. Absentmindedly she put them away, her attention on Aziz. "There, there, I am fine, don't cry. Makes face all wet," he said and kissed her. She gave him a hug, and a loving look, and stood again, looking on the floor for her knives. "You have them," said Aziz and pointed at her side. She patted her sides and, realising that they were there already, blushed.

Anahita let go an arrow back towards the main room as Stefan yelled. "We have visitors. God's blood...what are they?" The arrow exploded.

Rani looked back towards the main concourse. *Bounding towards us are two large, cat-like creatures that seem to be made of a golden metal. Their eyes are glowing like Theo-dear's do, and they have a series of spikes along their backs.* Another arrow exploded against one of them.

"Spears," called Rani. Astrid and Bryony reached Stefan just as the two metallic beasts roared and leapt into the air. All three grounded their spears, without dirt to dig them in, putting a foot against the butt spike and crouching down as they felt the others take position behind them.

One arrow hit each of the beasts and exploded just before they reached the points of the spears. Flame wrapped around Rani, as she let go a bolt from her wand. *Got a bolt in this time. There is a whooshing noise and the other cat rocked a little. So did my Princess...and their attempt to leap the spears failed as well. Stefan and Bryony have pierced one, Astrid the other.*

"They are still alive! Keep them pinned with your blade as you would with a boar," yelled Astrid as she tried to wrestle it onto its back, her hunting spear buried to its cross-hilt in the beast's chest. She is sliding backwards. *A normal spear would have been useless in this fight.*

Hulagu and Thord pushed past and attacked the beasts with mace and hammer, as the spears kept them off balance and did more damage. They were dispatched. Thord immediately drew a dagger and started prying out their eyes.

"What are you doing?" asked Theodora, with a hint of disgust in her voice. Thord didn't reply, but he held up the eye he had gouged out. When it had been pulled out, they could all see that it was a gem, resembling a star ruby, but brighter. He removed the other three and straightened.

"I ha' not heard of t'ese for a while. If'n you 're alone when you meet one, you die. Don't ask me how a beast of metal can exist, or rather how a beast can grow a metal shell 'n' ha' gems for eyes. We call t'em war tigers." He pointed at them.

Now that they are lying stretched out, I can see that their flanks bear black stripes on the bronze of their skin. "Legends say t'at they used to be taken into battle by a far-past ruler." He held up the gems for all to see. "See...t' first treasure reclaimed from Dwarvenholme."

"I would wager that these two were supposed to attack us at the same time as the others were." *How strong were they? Let us see, they took four of my arrows, two bolts and a lot of other damage. Even an armoured elephant would not have taken half that much to die.* "We are lucky that they didn't."

W hen Thord came out of the corridor he said: "T'ere 're several rooms in t'ere, from t' fittings I'd say t'ey were workshops or factories. I found shaft leading down. It's too difficult for us to use, but something could fly up it, if'n it were made to. I'd say t'at t' Masters sent t' blood suckers up from below us. I dropped coin 'n' heard it clinking for long way as it hit t' sides."

"One more," said Rani, "and then we need to think about where to spend some rest time."

"Rest," said Astrid. "I wouldn't bet on that. They will just keep sending things against us until we fail. Let us attack them instead."

Rani thought for a while, waving the others to silence. *Do we rest or push on? What is best? I need to decide one way or the other quickly.* "You are right." She turned "Thord, if the way down was on this side, should we have found it by now?"

He nodded. "It's usual just off t' main chamber. It'll probable be t' corridor opposite t'is."

Rani nodded and turned to Father Christopher. "Do you have anything in your pharmacopoeia that would take away our tiredness?"

"Of course. Lakshmi said that the bandits had brought some leaves back to her from the forests below. I have never seen this before, and she told me to take it with care...even one sip has been known to lead to addiction. It is called Sleepwell, and that one sip will make it as if we had just risen from a good night's sleep." He started rummaging in his pack. Rani looked in. *It is a big pack and it seems to be almost completely full of bags, bottles and packets.*

"Find it and keep it close. We will take it when we reach the next level. Hopefully there is only one." *I doubt there will be, but I can hope.*

She turned them around and they headed towards the other corridor, again keeping them close to the wall.

They made it into the far corridor before they were attacked again. Bianca cast a piece of wood ahead. *That looks like a huge swarm of large moths flying towards us.*

"Flame 'em!" yelled Thord. "Quick ... burn 'em afore t'ey get here. Don't leave any alive." He started backing up and ran into Rani moving forward. *He is in panic. I hope he knows what he is talking about.* She pushed past and fanned her hands out, her thumbs joined and with her little firepot hanging from them, as she started chanting.

The first of the moths was nearly upon them when she finished and a sheet of flame burst from her hands. It washed down the corridor, filling it with fire, as she moved her hands up and down leaving behind floating ash and a burnt smell. When the fire had gone, none of the moths remained.

"Would you like to tell me now why I just used my entire stock of mana for the day on wiping out a cloud of moths?" she asked Thord.

"T'ey were Night Moths. I didn't mention 'em afore. I didn't expect to find 'em. You don't want 'em to touch you. Flame 's t' best t'ing to use."

"I know of them," said Ayesha, "they exist sometimes in the mountains. They poison you by touch and, even if you survive their attack, you can oft later die of a wasting disease that eats you from inside. It wasn't a waste of anything to kill them. Once you are dead, they will then settle over and around your corpse and eat your body once it has rotted. No scavengers will come near if they are there. After that they mate and lay their eggs in the soil around. They can lie there for many years until they are born."

Thord nodded. "Hold your breath until we're past t'eir ashes 'n' try to avoid getting any on you. Even t'eir ashes can kill you from t'at wasting disease." He thought for a bit and then added. "If'n t'ose are here, t'en we should be very watchful for something else with like effect. T'ey're called Deathshrews. T'ey look like normal shrew, but t'ey swarm in large swarms. One can only nibble you, but t'ey have poisonous breath 'n', if t'ey touch you, t'en you'll like catch Flashfever."

"I cannot cure that," said Christopher. *He sounds surprised.* "I am not strong enough yet and may never be."

"Anything else you want to tell us about?" asked Rani sarcastically.

"T'ere is so much," Thord replied seriously. "T'ere are jellies t'at move, t'ey general don't like flame either, t'ere are rats t'at, like war tigers, 're made of metal 'n' we ha'n't seen any undead since we entered 'n'...'n'..."

Astrid came up and clapped him on the shoulder. "That is what I like about you, Thord. You are such an optimist. In a few weeks, we will be sitting in the hall, drunken as Freehold lords, making up tales for those that stayed behind and laughing about all this." Despite himself Thord smiled. *Even if it is a trifle sickly.* "Let us go," said Rani and waved them on. *I wish that I felt as confident as I am trying to look.*

Chapter VII

Rani
6th Undecim

H*e did say it would be just off the main chamber. It is huge…round and over fifty paces across. Around its edge is a huge staircase that winds around above and below us. The staircase alone is five paces wide, and has a carved and pierced railing carved out of the same stone, and over a pace high and two hands wide.*

Once, when it was all lit up, it must have been magnificent. Now it exhibits the signs of age and is covered in lichens, and shows signs of dampness from water seeping through the walls. There are even some stone snail trails like in our mine. Filling the rest of the room is a huge hole.

"T'is usually extends from t' top to t' bottom of a town. It should ha' a wooden platform in it with rails. It goes up 'n' down on command 'n' is used to move heavy loads between levels. I am not sure if any Dwarf mage could even make one nowadays. T'ey 're hard pressed just to maintain t' spells on t' ones t'ey ha'."

"I don't know about Dwarven mages," said Theodora, "but I am sure that I would not be able to do it alone. Lifting a slab of timber that large and still have it carry things…the weight would be just so… It is incredible. You say that each town has one of these?" Thord nodded.

"My dear," *she is talking to me now.* "We have some State visits to do after this is over. I want to see if they will trade me for the spell. I can trade the one I used at Mousehole for it. I cannot even think how to construct this one."

It seems that a new spell will always distract her. "Later dear, now…up or down." She looked at Thord.

"T' t'rone room 'll be up. We've been attacked from below, but t'ey 'll ha' been driven creatures 'n' t'ey could've been compelled from anywhere.

However, I suppose t'at, if'n t' Masters t'ink of 'emselves as t' rulers of t' Land, t'en t'ey 'll be in t' t'rone room."

Rani nodded. *I suppose that was obvious.* "Up it is then," and she waved them on towards the stairs.

They were moving up the stairs when Theodora, who happened to be on the outside and ahead of her, glanced behind her. She screamed "watch out," and fired a bolt from her wand. Rani turned. *The air bolt grazed Anahita from the way she was flung aside. Princess is firing out into the shaft and up to the next coil, about twenty paces above. What is she firing at?*

"Light, give me light." The others turned their shields towards the shaft, mystified but obedient. *By the Destroyer. What are they?* Rani gasped at sensing a flock of almost invisible floating beings, folds of dark in the dark, drifting towards her people and she started firing at them as well. Everyone backed up against the wall.

Stefan had to drag Anahita back. She is just standing there, not moving. Princess threw the wand she was using away...drew another one...fired once... She is looking around anxiously. She is moving forward cautiously. "Bring me light," she said. Hulagu came forward and she pointed up. He tipped his shield so that the light shone up the shaft. "I think we got them all."

"All of what?" asked Hulagu.

"Look at Anahita."

Christopher is already tending her. "She is not responding. She is just standing here." *He is waving his hand up and down in front of her. Her eyes are not following his hand at all.* He felt her pulse. "Her pulse is normal and, apart from this tear, I can see nothing wrong with her. What just happened?" He started dressing where the skin was torn from the air blast.

"Our people have to deal with them sometimes at Deathguard Tower," Theodora began to explain. "They are called Moonshadows. They are easy to kill, but if you cannot sense the invisible, as mages learn to do, then they will usually be able to kill you. They don't often come when you are awake. It is usually during the night that they drift up. They attack when you are asleep, and once they have chosen a victim, they will follow until they have drained them completely."

"Anahita is un-minded. She cannot think for herself. That is why I blasted it off her. It affects each person differently at first, but if one attacks and stays attached to a person, she loses her mind, her ability to speak, her hearing or being able to move at all, one or the other. Eventually when all else is done, she dies."

"We will have to lead Anahita around now and feed her and clean her. If we can get her home, then we will have to try and find a cure. I have heard of it being done, but I do not know how." *Kāhina has gone up to Anahita and hugged her, but there is acknowledgement from Anahita, and Kāhina is starting to weep. Dhatr be with her.*

"I have never heard of more than one coming at once. I think that there were a dozen here at least. We were lucky that I glanced around and noticed them. If I had not noticed them, and they had struck us from behind, then we would all now be dying."

"I will lead her as we move," said Christopher, detaching Kāhina from her friend. "You can care for her when we stop. I am sure that, inside, she knows that you care for her. Perhaps she can still hear you."

"Can you do nothing?" asked Hulagu.

"Not until we get back to Mousehole, unless..." He turned to Rani. "Can we go back down the stairs for, say half an hour? I want to do a quick Mass, which might be a good idea anyway, and ask the Lord to help her. She is a good girl, and I am sure that He will not mind that she is not a worshiper. She is still one of His children and a part of my responsibility."

I have been brought up to respect the priests and their rituals. I may not be strong in my faith, but I will still pay respect. This man may not be Brahmin, but he is certainly a good man who works hard to heal and care for people. "Half an hour."

I *should pay attention to this so that I understand my people better.* With his congregation facing out and on guard, Father Christopher drew a complex pattern with chalk and placed Anahita inside it. He then began a shortened Mass in Latin, going to his worshippers to hand out the wafers, which he had in a separate pouch, rather than the other way around.

All of that he has done before. He sought the intercession of Saints Winifred, Cosmas and Damien. *He has talked of them before. They are some sort of avatars of healing.* He concluded with a heartfelt prayer, reminding the Lord that he had not asked for Divine Intercession before and pointing out the work that he was doing in His name. Aziz was mentioned and pointed out. Lakshmi and Parminder were referred to as well.

All of that is new and interesting. It is almost like an impromptu spell without form. It is just an expression of desire and faith. He thanked God for the blessings that he had received and uttered the Benediction.

There was a brief pause as Christopher stood there looking at the Khitan girl and then Anahita shook herself. "What am I doing here? Ouch. Why am I hurt?" she asked and wondered why she was smothered in kisses from Hulagu, Kāhina and Bianca before saying "oh" as memory flooded back.

Unbelievably it seems that she had been conscious through it all. Christopher beamed and then received a huge kiss, first from his wife on his lips, and then another from Kāhina on both sides of his face.

"Thank you," said Bianca, tenderly.

"Thank the Lord, not me. I just asked. We will do another Mass of thanks as soon as we can."

Aziz came up to him with wonder in his voice. "Can you teach me to do that?"

I would not have believed that Christopher's smile could grow broader. "Gladly...gladly."

If I wanted proof of the priest's holiness, I have just seen it demonstrated in the most tangible way. He cannot hold even a fraction of the mana needed to restore Anahita's spirit with a normal Miracle. Bringing a lost spirit back to the body is far beyond a mere cure. It is far beyond what Princess and I could hope to achieve together.

What I have just witnessed is a direct intervention of Christopher's Deity in answer to a Holy Prayer. I have heard of such, and indeed the priests even tell you that this is always available as an option if you are strong enough in your faith and...well...lucky. I have heard and read of such before, but it is all in the past. I have never known of anyone doing so successfully.

They were about to set foot on the stairs again when Rani looked at the faces around her. "We are all tired. Father, share out some of that potion of restfulness, or whatever it is. If we cannot have a night's sleep, it is as well to feel that we have just arisen."

Christopher nodded. He began by using up all of his mana by laying his hands on first Aziz's stomach and then on Anahita's abrasion. Then he gave everyone a sip asking them to tell him if they felt strange in any way afterwards. They set out again.

The stair is rising above us and, with the light we have, I cannot see its top. Looking up I can see the coil above us, and I can see the stairs carved into the other side of the room, but more than that is just a suggestion.

Astrid is looking queasy again. "Father, are you sure that I am..." she ran for the balustrade and vomited over the side. *It seemed that she had little left in her stomach, but still huddled there, clutching the rail. Basil has run up and is holding her hair out of the way. She smiles weakly at him before again lurching for the rail. As suddenly as the attack had come, she has recovered and is standing erect.*

"Here you are," said Christopher and handed her another of the mint balls. She shook herself. "You are not worried?"

He has felt her pulse and her temperature. "No. I'm sure that everything is as it should be. I am also sure that the feeling will pass soon. Let us go on. The sooner that we get all of this over, the better it will be." *He may not be worried, but I am.*

$\mathbb{W}$e have reached the last of the nails that we set into the walls on our previous climb.

"You had better refill my bag of these," Hulagu is saying. "It is as well that we decided to come this way. I think we would not have had enough of them to do the rest first."

"I did not expect the place to be so large. We could fit a goodly part of Pavitra Phāṭaka in those pieces that we have seen so far. The Dwarves were never numerous, or so I had thought before now. We should be quieter. We should soon be up to them. Ayesha, as we climb, do you have the ring of stealth and that which protects from magic ready?" She nodded.

"Then do not wait for me to say anything. If you see the Masters, and have a chance to do something to them, put the rings on and...do what you do. Remember to be careful getting clear of us. I would hate for you to be hit by mistake. If you fall, we may not be able to find you. Astrid, you may need to do the same."

We continue up the stairs. We rise in only a shallow curve, going up only one pace for every five that we take forward. It is a long hard trudge. Looking down at where the light showed we have been; there are ten coils of the stair behind us. We are probably even now only at about the level of the top of the main concourse. She looked up. *There is still no sign of the top above us. How far does it go?*

Christopher

$\mathbb{W}$e keep climbing...twelve...no thirteen coils of the stairs...oh Dear Lord. "Lacrima Christi, let me past. Look to the right." Everyone did so. *They are still too far away, but rushing down the stairs towards us, like a giant wave, are the last of the old residents of Dwarvenholme, a horde of their animated skeletons are defending their old home for its usurpers. From what*

I can see there might be more here now than there had been outside...many more.

"Father," said Rani, "try and do what you do from behind the line. Get those opposite. Your job will be to heal us as we fall out." Christopher stopped his rush and nodded. *That makes sense.* "Those with shields, form a wall. Spears get behind them. Archers, fire at them as they come down until you run out of exploding heads. If you can, then get new ones from those in front."

She and Theodora started firing their wands as fast as they could at the oncoming horde, tearing gaps in their ranks. The others hurried to take their places and get set. They were just in time and Aziz, Ayesha, Hulagu and Thord had just been joined by Stefan, coming from the rear, when they were hit by an almost solid wall of moving bones.

I am not sure if my prayers are having any effect...there are too many at once. The archers and the mages could scarce miss their targets. They were packed tightly and in seeming limitless numbers.

The five at the front were hard pressed. The sheer weight of numbers of their foe pressed them slowly back down the stairs. Cries and the sound of blows echoed through the vast shaft. Christopher moved from a prayer into a chant.

It is easier to use such a familiar thing rather than extemporise. It provides an odd, almost musical, backdrop to the combat and is having some effect, but there were so many of the godless undead that really all I am doing is slowing their advance, as some tried to turn and became tangled with others. I suppose even that is some use.

Suddenly Stefan and Hulagu are both being forced back out of the fight towards me. Hulagu is bleeding from multiple cuts through his leather armour. Stefan has taken a thrust from an attacker armed with a broken rusty spear. It had appeared from between two others who shielded it from view and the point had been planted in his ribs. It is still there.

"Father..." gasped Stefan. Astrid sprang forward into the gap as Christopher ceased his chant and leapt up the stairs, heedless of the combat above him. *Get them and drag them clear...change to another prayer...pull out that blade.* He finished and looked at them both. *No, they still need more... Betterberries.* He began forcing berries from a pouch onto them. They chewed and swallowed and went back forward, but too late.

Silly girl. Even I know that a spear without a shield in front of it has no place in the shield wall, no matter how fast the person wielding it is. Astrid had been duelling with several be-weaponed opponents and suddenly she gave a scream and fell, back down into the two coming back. Bianca and Verily tried to take over the gap with Bryony behind them.

Astrid fell and rolled down the stairs, her spear clattering after her. Basil jumped to stop her fall, "Puss!" he cried. *There is blood pouring from her shoulder and her eyes are open and staring. That is a bad blow.* Christopher put a bandage in Basil's hand.

"Stem the blood." He shoved Basil's hand against the hole in her mail and the gaping wound beneath. *I start praying again even as my hands tend the smaller wounds with salves.* Eventually, her eyes blinked weakly.

"Good, now drink this…again…and again." He was pulling her mail over her shoulders now. "Basil, use force directly on the wound. We must get her jacket off." He started stripping her top off where it was revealed under the mail and then tightly binding the pad to her shoulder.

"Will she live?" asked Basil.

Christopher was feeling Astrid's pulse and then placed his hand on her stomach. *Yes, I was right.* "They are both fine," *What a relief.*

"Both?" asked Astrid weakly as she returned to consciousness.

What a way to tell them. "You, silly girl, somehow you missed out on realising that you are pregnant…now rest for a while. Only stand up if it is an emergency. You are healed, but it will have to take effect before you are much use." He looked around for her spear and found it. He moved it to beside her. "Basil, be useful, go and see what has to be done to make sure your baby gets home safe." Basil kissed Astrid and stood up.

The battle is nearly back to us already. The Princesses are already behind us. Kāhina came over and took those of Astrid's arrows that remained in her quiver. *She is grinning at Astrid. She obviously heard what I said to her.* Anahita was gleaning some arrows from the stairs where they had been spilled by someone. "You need to move back" Christopher said to Astrid. Reluctantly, she obeyed him.

Next, it was Aziz's turn to fall out of the line. *His thicker skin gives him some protection, but otherwise he has only a shield and his light leather jerkin. Back to work again: bandaging…prayer…and another draft. Just as well it is not addictive. Back on his feet, and now Stefan is back again.*

The sound of explosions has ceased. The Khitan girls must be out of arrows. I have barely healed and dressed Stefan when it is Ayesha coming to me holding her side. Christopher looked at her wound. "I am sorry, but you will need to take your jerkin off. I cannot bandage that wound with it on."

She may be holding herself with blood coming around her hand and in obvious pain, but she is hesitant. Stubborn girl. I am not interested in lusting after your breasts. "Ayesha, I need to save your life. I am a married man. I love my wife. I see the girls at Mousehole half-naked all of the time and no-one else will see you. I am sure that your god would prefer to see you alive and fighting rather than clothed and dead."

She nodded and between them they removed her top. *At last I can see it properly. At least the wound is long, rather than deep. It runs directly across below her breasts, but it runs deep enough that her ribs were exposed on each side.* "I would like to have time to sew this. I am afraid that I might leave you with a scar." Her hand fluttered dismissively.

Christopher bound the wound and started to put her top back on her. *Ayesha is looking up. Hulagu has moved back and is now sitting beside her, holding his head with blood coming from between the fingers and swaying, but with his eyes locked and entranced by what he sees before him. Ayesha is blushing, her lack of upper clothing making this more apparent.*

Christopher looked from one to the other. *At least Bianca and I were not as bad as this. Still, I wish that one of these two would talk to me so I can say what the Metropolitan said to me. I suppose that they will when they are ready...if we live.*

He hurriedly helped her regain her top and shoved a bandage at her. "Quick. Hold his head. He is about to collapse." So, with her top on, but unlaced, Ayesha cradled Hulagu's head against her breasts while she tried to stem the blood from a large flap of skin hanging loose on his temple.

Christopher rummaged in his pack for more supplies. He turned and took over, tightly binding the wound. Hulagu's blood was all over Ayesha. "Lace yourself up and go back. I have him now."

He felt inside his head. *Saint Winifred, patron of healers, be with me. I should have used all of my mana for the day, why do I feel as if perhaps I have a little more to give. Am I growing? Maybe I have one more small prayer in me without overdrawing my prayer account.* He tried. *I was right.* He finished tending Hulagu and moved him to where Astrid sat slumped.

"Did Ayesha...did I just see...did she hold me?" he muttered in Khitan, barely sensible.

"You did, and she did. I am sure that you will remember the sight fondly in your dreams tonight. Now drink this...and then chew on these and rest."

He stood up and looked around. *The torrents of the undead have stemmed, and no more are coming down to them. The remainder are so close that Rani and Theodora would have been unable to fire at them, although all I see from here are empty pouches. Theodora has taken her place in the line.*

Rani has joined Basil behind it, waiting to see if any break through. She has her sword and main-gauche out and so they both lack a shield. The hunters now stood shoulder to shoulder with shields locked and with a hammer, maces and swords, lacking all subtlety, just rising and falling, rising and falling, smashing skulls as they did.

Suddenly, it was over. *We have won. Looking at the lights above we have retreated nearly half a turn of the stairs.* Bodies soon slumped to the ground... exhausted. All of them bore signs of battle, armour was torn, and wounds bled. *It is time for me to get busy binding the minor cuts. Ayesha is still sitting down, but she is also tending wounds. She must be feeling better.*

Christopher

W hen all was done, he looked up. *Rani is moving around, checking how everyone is and taking exploding arrows from those who still have them, and giving them to Kāhina and Anahita regardless of how strong a bow they were meant for, and whether they were three or four fletched.*

Anxiously he took stock of his flock. *Everyone, except the mages and me, bear visible bandages and the clothing on several is stiff with drying blood. The vigour of only two hours ago is gone, and again, we are exhausted. Astrid and Hulagu may be healed, but the strain on their bodies shows in hollow cheeks and grey under the eyes. Astrid is being made to drink some water and nibble on some food by Basil, while his köle fuss over Hulagu.*

"Don't you dare die on us," said Anahita. "You have sworn to find us good husbands and you would be leaving your duty behind." He grinned weakly.

Saint Luke, patron of physicians, grant me wisdom on this. I am sure that we will not survive another battle. I have to give this counsel. Christopher went up to Rani. "I don't want to do this," he said. "But either we need to retreat, or we need another draught of Sleepwell. The Masters cannot be far away. I am not sure why they are not attacking us themselves now, for I am sure that we couldn't fight off a moderately determined rabbit at present."

Rani looked around and looked at the bones heaped ahead of them. What more lay ahead? "Do it. We cannot retreat."

Theodora came to him. "Father, before we go on, will you hear my confession?"

She was the first. Before we can move on, I have granted absolution to all of those who are directly of my flock and performed a short Mass of thanksgiving on the slope of the stairs. I wish that I had a confessor here.

Ayesha has prayed by herself. At least, if they were not to survive the next, and hopefully last, encounter, they would at least go with a clean conscience.

I have difficulty separating myself from my office when it is Bianca's turn. I will always have that conflict. She admits to the sin of envy, as she has done before, but this time it is envy of Astrid for being with child. After granting her absolution, he kissed her. "I am sure that, if we try hard enough, we can fix that little problem after this is over, if you still wish it."

Before setting out again, he shared out another sip of Sleepwell to them all, and they had some more to eat and to drink. The effects of the draught were obvious and immediate. Hulagu sat up and came alive. *He is stealing* sideways glances towards Ayesha. *She has noticed and is trying not to meet his eyes.*

After a short while, Astrid threw up again. Basil was fussing over her and holding her hair out of the way. *At least she can now eat. I have not mentioned this, but I pray to Our Lady, patron of mothers, that this potion has no effect on the unborn, as some do.*

He looked at the Khitan girls. *From being close to them, if I am right, they might be finding husbands somewhere else, but they will also be leaving babies in the valley. I need to ask Bianca what effect that will have. She will either know already or else she will be able to find out.*

Chapter VIII

Basil
6th Undecim

*I am to be a father. Who would have thought that when all of this started?
We have started out around what must be the last few turns of this seeming
endless stairs. We have to crunch our way through the bones of the Dwarves.
Ahead, Thord keeps alternately muttering apologies in Dwarven and promising
retribution for what we have been forced to do.*

*Another three turns and we are at the top. There is a huge platform here
at the head of the stairs. Only one vast corridor leads away, but I can dimly
see two others coming off it at the limit of the light. Pay attention. We must be
near the end of this…one way or another. All I want is to be somewhere safe
with Puss.*

"Where now?" asked Rani.

"Straight ahead unless we're attacked. T' side corridors 'll just be rooms
for guards or for visitors to wait in."

*On we go, still putting nails into walls as we do. Ahead, it is possible to see
that the corridor opens out into a large room.*

"T'is area ahead of us may not be where t'ey are," said Thord. "It could
be an antechamber. If'n it is, I suppose t'at we should still expect something
to be waiting t'ere."

*We are trying, but it is hard to go cautiously when you have a series of
bright lights shining ahead of you and moving around as the shields they
are mounted or shifted.* The chamber opened up ahead of them. *There is a
dragging noise from ahead.*

"Bianca," ordered Rani, "a light stick—straight ahead."

Bianca had been ready for this, and the globe of light sailed up and out
through the dark. It lit the roof as it went. *This chamber is smaller than the*

concourse below. It landed. *What in hell is that? That gasp was from Theodora beside me.*

"Blasphemy," said Rani. *There is revulsion in her voice.* "Abomination."

What is emerging from the opposite tunnel looks like a giant snake; so large that some of it is still inside the tunnel. In place of a head there is the naked torso of a giant woman with six arms. Her eyes are black and flat, and she is smiling a hungry smile. In each of her arms there is a massive weapon: a whip, a sword, an axe, a mace, a flail and a sickle. She…it…is moving towards us.

"It must die!" Rani said softly.

"Lamia," said Theodora. "Do not get close to it, or it will take control of you. Ayesha, it can see you when you are invisible, do not even think of it… and it can bring in other creatures of the spirit world and demons. Even if it just hits you with any of those weapons, you will die in both your body and your soul." *Great. Now I have two women I have to try and stand between to protect and it can destroy with a touch.* He pushed forward a bit.

Anahita and Kāhina had started firing over the heads of the others. Bianca had her sling out and quickly started despatching bullets.

Rani is chanting. It closes and still Rani chants. Shit. This is a big spell. Half way across the chamber, and it has been hit by several bullets and more exploding arrows. They seem to have made little effect on it. We are backing to the entrance of the corridor now. It is only thirty paces away.

Theodora has pulled out a wand and is pointing it. I can feel the rush of air, but see nothing. Wait…there are dents in its skin…that is all. Suddenly, Rani has stopped chanting…she is throwing her whole firepot at the creature. The firepot has become the centre of a huge ball of flame that is growing as it flies through the air.

Rani has collapsed in a heap…the fireball has struck…there is a mighty roar. A wash of heat born in a scalding hot wind. Basil felt himself knocked off his feet onto the smooth stone floor. *At least I am not the only one. Beside me, Bianca is also climbing to her feet.* He blinked. *I can hardly see.*

He looked around at the others. *They are doing similar things. We were all blinded by the light.* As his vision cleared, he could see that the Lamia had lost her human top and the amputated snake's body that was left was thrashing around the room spraying gouts of blood. He checked on his charges.

Astrid is just standing there. Theodora is turning to Rani. She is lying on the ground. Screaming in anguish, tears already starting, the Princess threw herself on her husband, to be pushed aside by Father Christopher. *If I ever doubted that her love has become real, there is the proof.*

The priest began checking her, first holding his hand flat above her heart. "She is alive," he said. He checked her pulse, "her heart is weak, but she does not seem to be in danger…what happened to her? I need to know." He stood up.

Theodora threw herself back down on Rani and cradled her in her arms weeping and rocking her. "She has used all of her mana…and more…too much…perhaps several days more. I thought that she was dead. She is at least unconscious, but she may never fully come back to us. Please…what can you do?" She raised a tear-soaked face to the priest.

Christopher shook his head: "Nothing…until I know what is happening with her. She could just wake up. If she sickens I will know, but at present I can do nothing. It is not much, but her life is not in danger at the moment. That is all I can tell you." He looked around. Basil followed his gaze.

Everyone is just standing, arms hanging down, watching the mages and waiting for direction. Christopher gently addressed Theodora again. "Princess, the rest of us need you now. We need to know what to do." Theodora paid no attention. *One of us has to take charge.*

"We wait." *That was Verily. Her voice has returned to the flat tones that we first heard.* "Father, get the mages into the corridor. Stefan, go back to looking behind us—something could still be in one of those corridors. The rest of you start looking to the front. We cannot do anything until that…thing finally dies. It could still crush us like little bugs if we try to cross before it stops moving. So, we wait."

That makes sense. Aziz is looking strangely at her, but she makes sense. We are all obeying her. Basil turned and joined Ayesha in ushering Theodora back into the corridor while Astrid carried Rani. Gently, she laid her down with her head in Theodora's lap and, opening her backpack, took out a cloak and put it over her.

They settled down. "Bianca," said Verily, "How many sticks do you still have?"

Bianca felt in her pouch. "Three."

"The last one that you cast hit the Lamia and bounced off to the left of the entrance. See if you can cast another one to the right, so that here is no shadow there for something to come through."

Bianca did as she was told.

Time passed. *The writhing of the snake is slowing to a twitching.* Rani groaned.

"My love, my dearest." Theodora smothered her with kisses.

"So, I am alive then?" Rani asked weakly. "Sorry to worry you. I had to do it…give me a proper kiss and tell me you love me. I need it." *She may smother her with that number of kisses.*

After a few more minutes, Verily handed control back to Rani and meekly asked: "Can you tell us what to do?"

A feeble shake of the head. "I am useless now. I am out of mana for at least another day. Even if I took that potion, I would have none. I am completely exhausted. You will have to leave me and go on." She closed her eyes. *That we are not doing. Theodora will want to stay with her and we need her.*

"That is too dangerous," said Verily. "Even if the Masters didn't send something, you could not defend yourself from anything that might happen along attracted by the smell of blood."

"I am staying with her," *It is almost like a spoilt child being told its toy was being taken.*

"No, Princess," *Verily, back into her flat voice.* "We need you, and we need Rani to direct us." She turned to Christopher. "Give her more of the potion. She will not be a mage, but she can direct us."

"But three doses?" replied Christopher. "In one day? She could be addicted so easily"

"Better to be addicted than to be dead. I know what it is like to do things to avoid dying. Addiction is nothing. Give it to her."

"No...no...no" started Theodora. *Damn it, Verily is right.* Basil knelt down and gently held her to stop her from interfering, while Christopher poured some Sleepwell between Rani's lips. She shuddered and opened her eyes. *At least they have life in them.*

"You did the right thing," she said to Verily. To Theodora she said, "Darling, I am fine, really, I am. Now dry your pretty golden eyes," and she kissed her. She stood up. "Somehow, I feel that this should be our last obstacle. Get your weapons ready." *She is looking at each of us, in turn.*

"I think that we only have one more fight in us, and hopefully we only have the Masters left to overcome. Ayesha, I think that you should put your rings on now and just stay clear of us...no, Anahita, carry your bow without a shaft and hold Ayesha's hand. Now we will know where you are. Anahita, say nothing, but take an arrow out and knock it when Ayesha lets go. Is everyone ready?" *All of us are nodding.*

"Then let us go. Remember that they will probably be casting spells at you as we run. Unless they use a more expensive area spell, even the best mage still has to hit their target to hurt them. Move and dodge as best you can. Put your shield in the way if you have to. That will take some of the sting of a small bolt. If you are closing, do not take straight lines. Try not to die. We still have a destiny to fulfil." *Try not to die...I might just listen to that one.*

They went to the left. *The snake skin of the Lamia is still faintly twitching as we skirt it. We are all avoiding the huge pool of drying blood that its death has left spreading across the floor. A sharp metallic smell like hot iron is overwhelming any other aromas. I have smelt blood before...but not like this.*

We are moving across to the far corridor. Ahead I can see the corridor, and dimly, not too far away, it opens up again.

Chapter IX

Theodora
6th Undecim

I *must concentrate. My love is alive and will recover, but now I am really the only mage we have. I am needed…unlike my life in Ardlark, here I am making a difference.*

She emerged from the corridor. *The chamber ahead is filled with light. There is a tingling feeling and a sharp smell in the nose like the scent of a thunderstorm. Air magic…they use air magic. Ahead of us, over two hundred paces away, I can see a semi-circle of perhaps four hands of figures, robed in deep purple robes. Cowls cover their heads.* Anahita knocked an arrow. Theodora dropped her pack. *Except for the priest, all of the others are doing the same.*

He is doing a blessing on us all: "I ask for the blessings of Saint Anne, protector against evil, patron of those who fight the undead, on all of us." *Around me I can hear people saying "Amen." One of those voices was mine.*

"Behold the so-called Masters… It starts now," said Rani. *At least my husband sounds confident.* "Archers fire first. Keep firing, as long as you have shafts, any shafts. The rest of you…we need to get closer…stay clear of the path of arrows." *I just felt a peck on my cheek and she has drawn her sword and main-gauche and headed off. I will just follow her at a jog. We are soon leaving Anahita and Kāhina behind.*

The first arrows hit. *Both of their targets staggered but did not go down. Behind me, I can hear Kāhina giggle tensely. I can detect a touch of hysteria.* "Damn. That was for a stronger bow. I hit the one behind him." *Basil, his shortswords still sheathed, quickly drew level with Rani and even more quickly passed her…now Astrid…Stefan. They are already running as hard as they can. We are being left.*

The second shots went past them and exploded among the Masters. *One is down. Other shafts are following as fast as the girls could fire now that they have the range.*

Basil is half way across the chamber. And the Masters finally act. Bolts of lightning come from them. Basil must have seen them raising their hands and was expecting this. He is already moving in a different direction. One bolt grazed him, but the rest missed. He returned to his course, aiming for the right, daring them to fire again.

Astrid headed to the left. Stefan follows her. Arrows are landing among the Masters now and not exploding. The Khitan women had been left with only two good enhanced shafts each. It is hard to see if the normal shafts are having any effect, but at least they must be providing a distraction.

I forgot the ring we gave Stefan from the bandits. Lightning bolts are flying back at the Masters. Stupidly, they just stand there and do not attempt to dodge. They must have been expecting that these were spells, which they could easily resist, rather than magic from an object. Two are staggering from hits. Stefan dodges and fires.

The Masters raise their hands and cast again. Most aim at Basil. He is the closest. This time, he threw himself on the ground and rolled to the side. I can see why he has not drawn his weapons yet. He knows that he is drawing fire, and is using his full agility to avoid being hit. He continued his roll and, regaining his feet, kept running. The bolts passed over his head and to the side.

Three aimed at Astrid. She also threw herself on the ground, but was slower getting back up. This almost proved fatal, as she was scarce moving again when three more bolts landed where she had been. Basil is nearly at the line and has stopped dodging. His blades are coming out. The Masters are drawing weapons from beneath their robes. A bolt from the other end of the line went close behind him as he closes. That Master had misaimed.

Basil is engaged. He has taken one of the Masters immediately, his short blades chopping at head and body at the same time. There is a sound in the air…a thin high scream erupts in my ears…with a rattling noise, as if he had hit a sack of bones and torn it wide open, the now empty cloak fell to the ground. Even from here a rank smell of old decay spreads and fights with the lightning smell.

The Master's concentration on the charge of Basil and Astrid and Stefan has allowed us to close on them without interference. If I am to cast it must be now. I will use your own air against you. Start the chant and…I risk a miscast by not concentrating fully as I run, but I have little choice, it is a long incantation.

Just short of the Masters I stop…fan my hands as my lover did against the night moths...last words and a sheet of lightning blazes out. I strike the centre of the Masters formation...faint thin screams. Five or a hand of the enemy collapse in heaps. They may have had some resistance to a spell, but I blew it away...feel my strength and die!

Both Hulagu and Verily are chanting as well. As they run, they put their maces in their shield hands. Their chants are shorter, the spells weaker and close cast. But both are successful. Verily stops after casting. The Master she is targeting had, instead of casting a spell itself, readied with an axe. Before closing, she follows up her casting with four quickly thrown blades. They hit inside the cowl of the robe—smart girl—the Master is at least distracted by them, clawing at its face as she closes and starts striking.

Theodora looked around. *I have done all I can as a mage. The others are too close to risk casting another spell, or even the use of a wand. Draw my sword and start running again then. One of the Masters at the rear is falling. That must be Ayesha. Now concentrate. I am in a fight for my life. I sense others around me ducking and weaving, but only to stay clear. Human yells... strange high noises...the roar of an enraged Dwarf...I notice that he is the last of the main pack to join the fray. The air is full of noise.*

She despatched her opponent. *He is swinging a hammer, but lacks a shield and it is this lack that finally does him in. I saw an arm of bone. He is, in reflex, raising the arm in defence as if it were used to a shield's presence. He doesn't use his hammer to parry. I use this with a full head shot, I am still weak but if I swing as hard as I can... It is enough. The arm is raised, and I splintered it and the blow continued to the head. The Master ceased to be with a scream.* Her nose contracted, and she sneezed at the smell.

Theodora turned. Astrid stood a way off. *She has not thought to go invisible. Her spear is moving far faster than the Master's sword...she needs no help. Beside her, Stefan is hard pressed. He has two of them against him and is solely concentrating on defence.* She struck at one from behind, but too late. Stefan blocked an axe only to have a hammer strike him in the chest. *He has gone down.*

Theodora took on the axe-user and then, standing over Stefan, engaged the other. *I must protect my people. Christopher?* "Move forward off him," said the priest. *He must be ignoring his safety and tending the wounded in the middle of the fight.* Stefan had at least damaged this Master and she despatched him before looking around.

They are easier to kill than the wrights were. Christopher is tending Stefan, but Bianca already stands protectively over him. She has her mace clasped in the same hand as her shield grip and a throwing blade in her right hand. She spots a target and throws. It took a Master in the...eye? The eye socket at least.

It seems to have no effect on his vigour. He is fighting undiminished, but at least it looks as if he has lost his vision on that side. He turns to favour it. Hulagu notices this and is first to move…quickly dispatches it by moving to that side and continuing his attack as he moved around in a circle.

Theodora looked around. *Kāhina and Anahita have joined the fight and the inexperienced Anahita is already down, as is Verily. Aziz must have seen this as he gives the roar of a dragon and leaps several paces. He crashes into the Master standing above her, and it flies off its feet to be sliced in mid-air by his scimitar as it recoiled from him. Aziz now drops down beside Verily. It is all very confusing. Now run to attack the one Kāhina is defending against. Between us, it is despatched.* She turned around again.

They are all down. Yes, the others of the hunters are all looking around, dropping to tend the wounded and to bring them to where Christopher is working. My delicious brown-skinned lover is running to me. Why does she look concerned? Suddenly she felt a pain in her side. She raised her hand and first felt the lames hanging loose on her armour.

There is a gap I can put my hand in. The lames are hanging loose. She felt further. *The padding is cut through as well and it is damp. That is blood… my blood…lots of it. I am wounded. I hadn't noticed…that hurts…a lot.* She recognised that as she was going down on to her knees. *I have dropped my sword. I am going into a swoon.*

Christopher

T*hank the Lord this didn't happen as soon as I left the monastery. I wouldn't know what to do.* He looked around trying to see who needed him most. *Yes, Stefan first, and then Verily, Anahita and lastly Theodora.* After stopping Stefan's bleeding, and shooing away Bryony he drew a pentagram around him with chalk and began to pray.

Stefan regained his feet, weak, but able to move readily. *He is cured enough to move. That will do for now.* Bryony hugged him and moved him away. He gestured at Aziz and he carried Verily over and put her in Stefan's place. *Soon she is on her way and it is Anahita's turn.*

Lastly, Father Christopher beckoned to Rani and she brought Theodora closer. She *is worse than I thought. That was not just a theatrical collapse then…it was so elegantly done that I mistook it. How much do I have left?* Soon, she was moving away as well. *It is starting to look as if we are all going to survive this experience unless there is yet another surprise waiting for us in the surrounding rooms.*

Chapter X

Ayesha
6th Undecim

She looked around her. *The last of these so-called Masters are down. It was a hard fight, but they were limited in how well they can fight. They were better at influencing things from afar than actually fighting. I can take the ring off now. We have won. May Allah, the Victorious, be praised and thanked.*

The victory cry of a Dwarf filled the chamber. *It may have been the first time this has happened in over two thousand years. As our Christian priest has finished with his healing, they are all gathering and starting to hug and kiss each other.*

Ayesha began to walk about to see if any needed help, as the priest began his work. Tears are pouring down Bryony's face. "Conan...father...you are both avenged...can I let you sleep now?" she said quietly as she held Stefan, still weak after his healing. She went silent briefly and then said softly as she looked down.

"Come on Stefan...smile at me...think of the glorious sex we will have when we get back. I have you almost trained as I like it, and am used to you now, and want to keep you healthy and with me." *I am not sure that was meant for anyone but him. At least he seems to have heard.* He smiled weakly back and coughed in pain. *He was throwing himself at opponents without much regard for his own safety and, as a result, is now very low on life force...he is very brave, just not very smart.*

Basil and Astrid are sitting down together facing each other. They are pointing at places and things, and obviously are going over what happened, and who had done what and when. Basil placed his ear to her stomach, and spoke to it, and she playfully swatted at him.

Aziz and Verily have hugged and kissed each other, then checked each other for any wounds that might need attention. Now they have separated. Verily is off to start fetching packs, while Aziz is looking around at the piles of bones. These are all that remained of the beings who had terrorised his people for many years. He is kicking a pile.

"You do not look so fearsome now." *He is speaking loudly in his own tongue. Obviously satisfied, he went over to his new priest and began watching what he did as he was working.*

From what I know of Aziz's people, a priest who ignores his own safety and begins healing in the middle of a battle will be regarded as being even braver than a mighty warrior. In a way, they would be right, and it will make the Christian priest a leader to follow for the Hob. He will want to become a priest next. I had been hoping to have a chance with converting him, but I guess that is not to be.

Hulagu and Kāhina are fussing over Anahita, making her drink and eat as she recovers. Ayesha looked on. I am jealous of the attention being given to Anahita…and the intimacy that the other couples share. I fought. I even killed several of the Masters on my own. Am I still invisible? Had Hulagu even thought to check on me? Why do I even care?

Verily brought her third load of packs back and began going around sniffing at the Master's weapons. "They are enchanted. They are all enchanted." *Her voice has regained the happy tone that we have become more used to since she found Aziz.* "They once must all have been mages…before."

"Not mages. Did you see 'em? Look at t'eir weapons. T'ey used to be t' druids…our priests. If'n t' druids became t' Masters, it may e'en have been t'em who brought down Dwarvenholme…from within. I don't know why or how, but t'at is what I t'ink may ha' happened. T'ere doesn't seem to be anyone else here. However, I don't know. If'n t'ey were t' druids, why were t'ey using lightning 'n' not earth magic? It doesn't make sense."

Theodora

It *makes sense to me; my brain may be only just ticking over. I have never hurt like this before…but this does make sense to me. I will keep quiet on this and talk it over with my kaf-skinned husband later, when we are under the shield in the valley and snuggled in bed.* She realised that she was a little chilly and very light-headed.

I am sitting on the stone floor, half naked with my armour and top off, and with Christopher working on my wound and Rani fussing around me…I like that bit. She surprised herself by speaking. "We know they collected at least one book from Dharmal. There may be a library here. If there is, it may hold more clues. We need to find it."

Thord pointed to beyond where the combat had taken place. *There is a series of corridors, rather than just one, leading off the chamber.* "T'ose would be t' private chambers. T'at is probably where t' Masters…lived. It'll be where we find anything t'at t'ey ha' left."

Rani

I *don't want to be impatient, but I know that I am. If there is anything else around, I need to know about it. If there isn't…I need to know anyway.*

It has taken a couple of hours, but eventually our priest seems to be as happy as he can be with our condition. He is letting me start us moving again. We can keep the same formation. People are used to it. It will give them confidence. We will need it, if anything happens.

We have no more explosive arrows left and only a few normal ones— none of which are matched to Anahita or Kahina's bows, so they will be less accurate. Neither my Princess nor I have anything beyond a couple of wands with light fists of air left, and they are only capable of firing at short range.

More seriously, Christopher is almost out of healing potions and is completely out of Betterberries. I don't even think he has a spare bandage. We have been expending magic at a prodigious rate. Months of brewing, making, and enchanting have been used in a couple of days. I hope that there are no remnants or servants of the Masters left hidden.

We are in no condition for a serious fight or even a casual one. We badly need rest and we need a re-supply. It is almost certain that neither will happen soon. There is certainly no chance of supplies for us closer than Mousehole.

The first set of corridors led to a series of small individual rooms. *Each has a…for want of a better term…bed in it. The beds do not look like they belong in the rooms. They must have been brought in at some time in the past. They are each made of stone and lack either cushions or covers, and each looks like the top of a sarcophagus; perhaps that is what they once were.*

In each room there is a rack, obviously for the weapons that the Masters were carrying and a hook for a robe. There are few possessions and, according to Verily, no magic.

They had left the complex when something occurred to Rani. She went back inside and counted. *There were four full hands of Masters, according to the empty robes on the floor where they had died, but there were five hands of rooms that seemed to be tenanted.*

Does that mean that there is a hand of Masters somewhere else? She groaned to herself. *I won't mention this at present...not until we are at home.* When they were moving to the next corridor, she made sure that she had picked up some of the bones of the Masters and put them in her pouch.

The next complex of rooms held treasure. *The Masters did not keep the spoils of their conquest of the Dwarves in their rooms. It is all here. It is almost as if they did not value the wealth that they had stolen. Then, why did they steal it? What is it all about?*

All of the timber is decaying, the iron is corroding, and much of the silver is more than tarnished, but the gold and gems are still there...and the coin, and the items made of the precious stuff. They all lie jumbled in a heap along with the remains of ancient weapons and unidentified objects. Some of the weapons and other items, those that were at the fringes, are still intact, so this pile of neglected treasure must be what they did with the loot the bandits brought to their Masters.

It has been brought here, and then they just dumped it in a heap, paying as much attention to it as a city dweller does to a pile of rubbish. Looking at the expressions of wonder on the faces around me, I can see that the same thought is on several minds. If the Masters didn't value the treasure that was collected for them, what were they after?

Bianca

This *old backpack has all sorts of things in it...religious things. Unlike the rest of what is here, they have all been gathered together and kept in one place...and a new backpack at that...as if to shield them from sight.*

She first replaced her own wooden crucifix (kissing the old one and putting it in the bag) before putting a new gold one around her neck and then went around to all of the Orthodox and handed out silver and gold crucifixes and rosaries. Going up to her husband she handed him a beautiful golden pectoral cross with an icon in the centre and jewels on its limbs and gave him a kiss. "You didn't receive a present at our wedding. Let this be your present."

"The Archangel Michael, General of the Heavenly Hosts. This is a good image to wear to battle. Thank you my dear." Bianca was still rummaging in the bag and its pockets. "Anything else?" he asked curiously. She opened the side pockets on the pack and pulled out of each a flat wooden box that, when opened, revealed an icon. Each was in a frame of gold leaf and had small jewels in the corners.

Christopher is looking at the first. It shows two men dressed in robes that have more than a hint of the Caliphate about them. Around them are medical tools. "Saints Cosmas and Damien, they are the patrons of healing. This is very useful. It would have been beneficial to have had it available earlier, but we will have it from now on."

He looked at the next. *It shows a bearded man holding an oar in one hand and a book in the other. Behind him is a boat.* Christopher grinned. "Saint Jude...the patron of hopeless causes. I have prayed to him often on this trip. This will never leave my side when we are away from the valley."

Thord

I t is done. *Not only have we found Dwarvenholme, but we have defeated those who held it and, quite likely, those who caused it to fall. It is time to recover some of the wealth now.*

Thord found, buried in a small pile of fungi, *which probably meant that there had, long ago, been a wooden box,* a small pile of mithril coins with Dwarven markings. *Mithril; we are rich.* He looked around. *No...we're richer.* He scooped up the coins and added them to the growing bulges of his pouches. *I am not even touching the gold...apart from mithril, I am merely taking the gems.*

Digging in one heap he found a magnificent gemmed crown. As he raised it, he looked at it and the runes written on it. *I turn it around and around and my eyes must be like orbs. I know what this is. Every Dwarf alive knows what this is! Now, I am really famous.* When he spoke to the others he realised that his voice had suddenly became solemn, almost reverential in tone.

"I t'ink t'at t' next King of all t' Dwarves 'll ha' t' Crown of t' last. T'is I'll take with us in trust." *They may urge me to try it on, but I won't. I am not the King. I am more than content to be the Crownfinder...to be the one who gets to choose the next King.*

Rani

I can see that people are gathering what they wanted from the almost limitless supply of the Dwarves and the produce of centuries of theft. Packs are filling up again. I must make sure that they are not overladen.

"Do not burden yourselves too much," said Rani. "We still have to find the books and get home. We will return with horses later."

The third set of rooms revealed the library. *It doesn't look like any library that any of us has ever seen. Only one room has books. They are all on one stone shelf that runs right around the room. At least everything is not in a heap like the treasure. You can actually use this place to look at the books if you stand.*

Some of the books are too old. They are decayed and falling to pieces. However, many are much newer. There is even another copy of 'My Travels Over the Land and Beyond'. Someone has, many years ago by the look of it, underscored the section on Mousehole in a now-faded ink on the fragile vellum.

"They found the valley through the book," said Theodora.

Bianca thinks that she has found the book that started her on this road. At any rate, the binding on it is very similar to that of her Bible, so it may come from the same place. It is in High Speech, but an old form, and it talked of places and had maps. "Again, we will read it when we get it home."

Christopher has claimed for the village an illuminated set of what he calls Gospels. It is very old and quite heavy. "The one I took to Evilhalt was no heavier. I will get this home." He looked at the next book and then exclaimed: "Ayesha…come here!" She hurried over. "Here; your people need this. It is your own Qur'an, and a beautiful one as well." *Ayesha reverently stored it in her pack, throwing out mere clothes to do so.*

Theo-dear has taken charge here. While people are looking at books for themselves, she has gone around and selected all of the important looking books and given them out, at least two each, to carry back to Mousehole. We have thirty or so books that are in the best condition, and a couple that are not.

The other rooms in this section each have a pentagram on the floor. They are all very similar. There is writing I don't recognise. She began towards one when Verily called out. "There is magic here, Air magic."

Rani looked at the diagram ahead of them. "Thank you. This must be charged." Taking care to stay clear, she looked as closely as she could at it. To

Theodora she confided: "I would venture that, as well as for normal casting, each of these that is similar will control a different pentagram somewhere. One of these was for Dharmal. One was for Conrad, and so on." Together they counted the rooms. *There is one large one, and twelve smaller ones.*

Rani looked at her wife. "This is something that we will have to come back for. We need to think if there is a way of finding out where they connect to, and if we can close them down. What would it be like if some of these patterns can physically bring a person or a Master here? We will have to be cautious about what we will find here when we return."

Chapter XI

Bianca
late on the 6th Undecim

After the previous two, the last set of rooms is a disappointment. They are smaller than the others and revealed nothing at all except fungi, and the dirty and unidentifiable remains of what had been there. From the stone fittings, I would be willing to say it was once some form of accommodation, but even that is unclear.

There are privies though, and that means people. Seeing that there is running water from a stone spigot in one room that goes into a pool and flows out the other end, Rani has decided that this is as good a place as any for us to get some rest. Real rest is something that we have not had for a long time.

There are a number of stone rectangles beside the water and along the walls. Thord thinks that the room was once a garden. Rani has said that we can keep our watch outside the entrance to the rooms, with one of us wandering through our small complex in case anything happens. What a relief to have something as normal as a watch ahead of us.

In the second watch, Bianca had just re-joined the group outside when her husband came to her. Christopher's hands were shaking as he handed her a flask. "This has the last doses of the Sleepwell," *His voice is full of pain. Why?* "Do you remember that I told Rani that it may be addictive?" Bianca nodded.

"It is. I had to take more in the last combat to gain the mana to heal everyone. Now I am addicted. I want to have more. I do not want to sleep. I just want to take some more, and then more and more. The craving is burning through my blood and my body like a fire in my veins. I have resisted it so far, but I do not know how long I can last."

"Take the bottle and give it to someone, and do not tell me who. Get them to hide it from me, but before you give it to them, make them hold their hands out like this." He held his two hands out flat, palms down. *Both of them are quivering violently.* "If they shake like I do, don't let them have it."

"I will face away from everyone. Choose someone, either awake or asleep, and do this. Come and get me before the end of the watch. I will be praying and trying to ignore what is happening to me. If I get violent, get them to restrain me and; whatever I do or say, or even if it kills me, remember that I love you very much and anything else is just the drug talking through me. It is not me."

He kissed her and went outside where the guards were and, without another word, lay on his face with his arms outstretched and his legs together in the shape of a cross. Bianca looked at her husband and tears began to trickle down her face.

I love him so much. I cannot lose him…first…his bidding…who is the most stubborn of the hunters? I remember the stoicism of Verily when she was found, and I remember what she endured and survived. She looked around.

Verily is on watch with us, looking curiously back at me. Bianca went over, holding her finger to her lips. Verily raised an eyebrow, and Bianca gestured for her to follow and went inside the set of rooms. Choosing a vacant room, she explained what Christopher had said.

Verily is looking back at me. She sees my anguish and my tears and gives me a hug and kiss. "Your husband is a good man. God will not ignore him, and I am sure that He will help him overcome this. He will struggle, but he will live and be back with you. Now, go back outside and I will work out what to do with this." Bianca nodded and silently went back outside.

She spent the rest of the watch sitting, crying, near her husband lying on the ground. *I can see his body shaking and can hear him reciting litanies and prayers, over and over again, trying to keep his mind off his agony. He has settled on one. Over and over he says the words* "Kýrie Ii_soú Christé, Yié tou Theoú, eléi_són me ton amarto_lón"…'*Lord Jesus Christ, Son of God, have mercy on me, a sinner,*' *as he tries to draw on the inner strength that he is granted.*

Eventually, as the watch was due to change, she roused him and took him to a vacant room to try and sleep. *We end up spending the rest of the rest time with me holding him as he sweats and shakes. His eyes hardly seem to recognise me as he tries to keep up his litany.*

When everyone is waking, Rani comes to us. "Can he walk?"

"I think so," said Bianca and she stood Christopher up.

"I can," said Christopher in a tense voice. "It hurts, but then everything hurts. I feel like I am on fire. I am afraid that I will not be of much use if anything happens. I will do a Mass if anyone needs it, but otherwise, just let

Bianca lead me. It hurts to have light in my eyes, so I am keeping them closed when I can do so."

Rani has agreed and now she leaves to gather the others and we will leave the place of our victory. If I lose him it will be a hollow victory indeed.

Bianca led her husband out of the room and saw that all of the others were there ready to go. One by one, they came up and hugged her husband and herself, some murmured words of comfort to either Christopher, who hardly seemed to hear, or to Bianca. *I am sure they mean well, but the words they say are just...passing.*

Rani
very early on 7th Undecim

T *his will make it difficult. We now lack our priest. Bianca is now useless as well. We need to get home as quickly as we can.*

Rani sent them down the stairs. *I must make sure that we keep as much vigilance going out as we did coming in. It is easier this time...we are not being attacked as we go down the turns of the stairs, crunching through bones to the light of the nails.*

"Do we leave these here?" Astrid asked, as she waved at one of them stuck into the wall beside her.

"Yes. We will be back, or others will be back, and these may help keep at bay some of the things that are surely still in this complex."

Christopher has nearly fallen several times as he walks down through the bones. He has lost his concentration and his co-ordination, and has to be helped through them. He is now walking leaning on Astrid, as Bianca lacks the strength that is needed to help him.

We have reached the level where we entered on the stairs and now get to head back to the entrance. I wonder how deep it is? "Hulagu, do you still have some nails left?"

He checked his pouch. "A hand's worth."

"Then throw one down the shaft, and we will see if we can see how far down it goes."

Hulagu did as he was told. *The ball of light, which fills the shaft at this level, becomes smaller and smaller and eventually a tiny speck, only as big as a copper dirham coin. It is staying that size...that must be at the bottom of the shaft.*

Rani looked up to see how big the circle of light was at the top where they had come from. *It is at least four times that size. It is a long way down to the base…if that is indeed the base and not just the bottom of these stairs. How many other levels are there? What lies below? Is that where the missing Masters are?*

These are things we will have to find out later…probably much later. For now, we have to get the priest back home, and only then can we see what we have found and what it means to us. I don't even know yet if this is the finish of the quest, or just the beginning of a longer one that lies ahead.

They went down the corridor and out into the concourse. *The bats are all still there, packed together and trying to stay outside the lit areas.* Under the lowest of the huge circular balconies they passed around the huge circle to reach the tunnel to the entrance.

Ahead of us is a square of light that is brighter even than the radiance of the nails along the corridor. It looks like it is morning outside. I have completely lost track of time while we have been inside. For us it could be any time of day.

I t is good to direct my people down this broad entrance corridor. I may have cast the spells that light behind us, but even I love that the light from outside is starting to gradually overwhelm that from my nails. It is a bright, shining and hopeful day outside. Yes, I think it is morning.

Eventually, they emerged from the gates into a new day and the sun shone brightly on them as, now laden down with books and with treasure, they set out back on the road to Mousehole.

Chapter XII

Rani
7th Undecim

W*e may have broken the power of the Masters, at least for now, and found Dwarvenholme, but our joy is being overwhelmed by what is happening inside our Christian priest. We have not even gone half a day from the gate and Astrid has cut two saplings and made a stretcher. She and Aziz are having to carry the man.*

He is strapped to the stretcher, his hands tied down to stop him gouging his eyes out as he tried to do earlier. Still, his hands are oozing blood from where his nails had dug into his palms before this was noticed, and padding to stop him doing it was tied in place. A pad is placed in his mouth and bound there to stop him biting his tongue. His wife has to keep wiping the sweat off him as it poured from his body. His eyes are staring wildly and blindly at the sky, and his whole body shakes in a continuous and painful ague.

I hear her as she whispers low: "I love you and you cannot die…you promised me children, and you are not a man to break a promise. When I sleep I keep dreaming of us surrounded by a large family, and you told me that you wanted to make my dreams come true."

"I may not be as good a healer as your priest," Ayesha said to Bianca at one of their stops as she checked him. "I cannot do what he does and sense the life force within, but I can read his pulse and it is strong but very erratic. His body seems to be fighting itself…that is why he is burning up. We must make sure he does not lose all his water. Keep his gag wet and try and trickle some, only little bits so that he does not choke, around it." Bianca started to do this, and Ayesha kept checking Christopher every time that they stopped. There was no sign of any change in his condition.

As we move, we now only have Bryony to check ahead of us, and she stays near the path. Perhaps, if we move fast, we will only have to contend with normal beasts until any absent Masters return. Of course, there is still the dragon, so we must keep a watch on its mountain, which now lies ahead of us.

If we are lucky it will have fed itself well while we were inside and, without the Masters to prompt it to stir again, it might stay quiet for another year at least. Asvayujau, please make it so. Despite moving with less caution, we are moving a little slower than we did on the way up. Although we are carrying less food and medicines and arrows, we now have to carry Christopher and the books and the other treasure.

Rani
7th Undecim

L*ast night our camp was subdued. Christopher made the most noise. I heard his muffled groans throughout the night. From what I am told, Bianca tended him the whole time, wiping away the sweat and dribbling water, until she fell asleep over him just before dawn. We had to wake her so that she could eat and drink. She is almost moving like an automaton. Who would have thought it?*

They left that site and continued on for several more days in the same pattern. *Bianca is showing no response to the still chill air or the noises…to nothing but her husband. She had even failed to react when a large hopper burst out of the vegetation beside the track and bounded down slope away from them. It took Aziz saying to Bianca as he ate that he missed the Father's prayers to wake her a little from her total focus on Christopher…that actually made her shake herself and look around a bit wildly.*

"How long has it been?" she asked.

"Five days," replied Ayesha. "You have not replied to us at all, whatever we have said. We have been able to get you to do things, but you have not really known that we were here, even when we were handing you things."

"That is not what my husband would have done, I am sorry. I am not a priest, but I am the priest's wife, and I am the best qualified here. I have forgotten my duty to you." She looked around at everyone preparing to eat. "Now, let us pray." *It seems that she remembers most of the prayers and rituals that her husband performs on the road, and now she has begun to lead all her believers through them.*

"If the Church thinks that I deserve a title, it is going to get some service out of me. I know that Deacons can lead a service, and perform everything except one of the Sacraments. And a Presbytera has to be at least worth the same as a Deacon."

Bianca
12th Undecim

O ne by one, they tell me that they have been on edge...deflated despite their victory, and now they feel a little more peaceful. Even Ayesha has told me that she was becoming familiar with the priest and his services, and as for not having them as a part of the background to her daily life, even she had begun to miss them.

Saying the prayers is a balm for my soul as well. I can feel my faith building again. My hands clutch this icon of Saint Jude, and I know in my heart that my husband will regain his mind and all will be well. I may still be concerned, but by showing a better face to the world, it is rubbing off on the others.

Bianca
13th Undecim

A t least there is no sign of the dragon, and we have reached the junction of the old road down from the Dwarven road, where it headed down to the path along the base of the mountains, without incident.

They had been on that road for a day when something happened. That night, after they had stopped, Bianca was leading them in prayer. There is another voice, a thin and weak voice that has joined in. Christopher...my husband. Bianca stopped immediately and threw herself on him with tears of joy.

"Don't let me stop you, my dear," Christopher said weakly. "Finish what you are doing and then we will talk...go on...finish." Bianca kissed him and returned to the prayers, adding a few more in fervent thanks for him starting to recover. It was only a partial recovery. He was weak from his ordeal and he said that he still felt a craving for the drug within him. At least he was able to sit up and sip the soup that I held for him. Now I can just hold him while Hulagu carefully uses a spell to heat him some more.

Bianca
14th Undecim

The next day Christopher was still too weak to walk, but he started to take a little solid food, and when they stopped that night was able to slowly rise and take himself away from where they had set up to relieve himself. He walked away from them like an old man, supporting himself on his staff, and was still very shaky as he staggered from tree to tree. He came back and rummaged in his pack and brought out some stems from a package.

"Please cut these up and boil them and put them in some soup for me. No-one else eat of the result," he said. He paused and then added, "Unless you have had some difficulty with a tightness of your bowels, in which case, pray join me." He gave a weak smile. "For myself I will give a prayer of thanks that Lakshmi made me bring these just in case."

That night he held a service for them all and the next day he felt strong enough to start walking, despite still shaking a little. *I notice that Aziz and Astrid just looked at each other and packed their stretcher along just in case. And just as well, it was needed again well before we took a mid-day break.*

Although they had time to go further, they camped that night again under the strange pine tree inside its ruins and set out early the next morning. By the time that they had reached the base of the trail he was walking strongly and had started trying to carry his own pack. *And he can forget about that. He is far too weak, and it will make him worse again. But thank the Lord that he is getting stronger. He can now walk for much of the day.*

They turned left onto the path for home and, with Mousehole only another night away, even Father Christopher had a spring in his step as they picked up their pace. *Tonight, we will spend under the cliff off the road, and then we will be home.*

Rani

Soon after they re-joined the path Astrid appeared waving at them and hurrying back. "It is a new beginning," she said. "You will never believe who we are about to come up on from behind. It is an omen of our future."

I wish that she would just say things instead of making us guess. "What are you on about? Haven't we had enough of omens?"

"Oh…" replied Astrid dismissively. "Personally, I am not even sure if we are finished with that first lot yet. No, we have our Darkreach trader ahead of us. It is Carausius and his guards: Karas and Festus, the ones you didn't like me following. I just thought that I would tell you that I am about to go up and say hello. If you hurry up and keep low, you will see the fun." She grinned and turned around to head back.

Even though she now has problems every morning, she seems to enjoy them for what they signify, and her irrepressible nature keeps re-emerging. I wish it wouldn't. "But why do we want to stop them?"

Astrid stopped and turned around again, returning. "Firstly," she said, "it will be fun, and we could all do with some fun. Second, and even more important, Mousehole will only survive if it is prosperous." She patted her stomach. "I want my little Kharling to be really wealthy, not just prosperous. We will only get that way in Mousehole if we have traders beating a path to our door. These are traders.

"We need cloth, we need men, and we need so many things for a village that you can't even imagine. I mean, Sājah makes candles for us, but they are not very good. Even you must notice how much they smoke when alight and you do not have the time to make us enough magical lights. We are lucky because the girls have taught themselves to make do with so little, but there are things we can do really well, and we need to sell these to get the things that we cannot make.

"Wolfneck survives with whales and fish, fur and some plants. We sold these to everyone else. Most other things we bought even most of our cloth. We have so much more for us in Mousehole. Instead of being at the end of a road pressed against a cold sea, we own this whole track and everything around it.

"Just from the gifts that we know of, well…Bryony and I think that we can sell plants. Between them, Aine, Sājah and Lādi, and all of our entertainers can make the Hall of Mice famous, and people will want to come here to hear them and eat our food. We have our mines. We have lots of mages, we have the grazing lands, but for any of this to work we need people to come to us.

"We cannot send out our own caravans to trade. There are not enough of us. These traders ahead of us will spread the word if we want them to." She stood there with her arms crossed and with a determined look on her face.

My wife is nudging me. "She is right, dearest," said Theodora. "We may have defeated the Masters for the moment, and we can and will bring all their treasure down to Mousehole, but treasure doesn't make you wealthy. What good is wealth if our people are not happy and well-fed? You cannot eat it or get Fear to wear it. We have to do something with it."

Theo-dear has turned to Astrid. "Go on and see your Caracticus, or whatever his name is. Welcome him to our land and tell him that his first trip through will be free, and that he can call in to see what he can sell to us in the village or what he can buy from us."

Astrid

I am going to cheat and use the ring. I run up the path and then dodge through the forest. I know this area and can be almost silent. I'm now ahead of them and stop behind a tree and...take the ring off.

Peering around, it she saw some of her people's heads appear behind the trader, peering over the ridge. When the three were about twenty paces away, she stepped out from behind the tree with her left hand open and raised palm first in greeting, her spear held upright in her right hand and her bow cased in its woollen cloth roll on her back.

"Carausius, Karas and Festus," she said in Darkspeech, "how nice to see you all again."

Karas started to raise his bow, but he has quickly realised that, if this was an ambush, it is a very odd one and actually raising his bow might provoke someone putting an arrow through him. He is not dumb then, even if he and Festus are looking wildly around. "Who are you? I have never seen you before" spluttered Carausius. "Why are you stopping us? How do you know our names?"

Astrid grinned. "I have my ways," she said. "You haven't seen me, but I have seen you, and listened to you when you were heading down to the Swamp to trade last autumn and when you returned so happy to Darkreach."

"But..."

"But nothing. Oh sorry, I did not introduce myself. I am Astrid the Cat, from the mighty village of Mousehole. When last I saw you, we were not open for business, but now we are and I want to invite you to come in to see us, and to stay at our inn, the Hall of Mice, and perhaps you might have something to sell us or perhaps you might like to buy from us. I think that we have some things that you will want to see, and we will have more in times to come."

"There is no village here...we went through last year." Astrid was nodding with a smile on her face as he said this, and her mocking expression made Carausius just peter out in what he was saying without completing the sentence.

I will wait until he stops. "Yes, there is. We are just hard to see if we don't want you to find us. I will introduce you to our Princesses when they catch up, and we will then be going on towards our home. We might not see you at the campsite tonight, but we will let you know when you come up to our village.

Remember the old bridge a day south of here?"

Carausius nodded. "Well, we live near there. Now, don't panic when everyone catches up, for there are quite a few of us, but we mean you no harm." She gave a little bow, waved back towards the others and started to walk down the road towards home. Bryony and Aziz had come jogging quietly up from behind them while Astrid spoke. They came level to the three who were now stopped and looking around.

"Hello," said Aziz in Darkspeech. *All three jumped and spun around. Aziz has pointed at Bryony.* "She would say hello too, but she not speak this tongue. We will see you later at home," *and now they are coming to join me. We will wait now and watch and listen to the rest.*

"Boss…" Karas, who was at the rear, had turned and noticed the others approaching the three men. He turned again and spoke to Carausius, "there are more of them." *The three traders are just standing dumbfounded as they go past one by one.*

Everyone is saying hello, many in Darkspeech, but I notice that Theodora is keeping her eyes shaded. Probably a good idea…that can wait and, at the moment, might be too much of a shock for the poor men who, by the time we have all passed are already looking a bit stunned. Now it is time for us to head on. She motioned with hands and the three ran ahead again.

Theodora

"**N**ow we are past them, do we push on tonight, or use the hidden campsite. You have all forgotten my eyes. If anyone from Darkreach sees me, they will know exactly who I am, or at least who my family is. I don't want that known until we are safely home."

Rani thought for a moment. "We will have to pass the traders again if we used the hidden site, but that doesn't matter. That way they will know we mean no harm to them, and a little mystery as to where we were camped will not hurt them and will add to our legend in their eyes. It never hurts to be thought to have more powers than you actually have. Anyway, after Astrid's show earlier they will already think we are more than a little odd."

Astrid is right. We were careful, and we could see them clearly from here *as they went past. Now, in the clear morning's light, as we prepare to set out, we can see the smoke from their fire. Our valley will be alert to people coming in along the road.*

Astrid
15th Undecim

W*e have set out nice and early and we are upon them before they have set out.* "Hello, we are here again" *They have stopped what they were doing as once more we come up, this time all of us at once. I might tease them a bit more.* "Tonight, you can sleep in the Hall of Mice as our first guests. Is there anything we can tell the cook to get ready for you?"

"Ummm…anything from Darkreach." *From his face Carausius is feeling lost.*

"I will see what Kutsulbalik can arrange," she replied. "We will see you then."

Again, the party filed past the traders and, this time, each of the Mice bid them good morning in one tongue or another, before hurrying on their way back home. *I note that once again Theodora has kept her eyes hidden with her head bent under the cowl of her cloak.*

Chapter XIII

Astrid
15th Undecim

Just short of where they had ambushed the bandits, and when they were temporarily out of sight of the watch point, Rani called Astrid back. "We don't know what has happened in the valley while we have been away. Remember what we have done to over-confident people as they have approached what they thought of as a safe haven. I want you and Ayesha to put on your rings and go ahead of us. Go up to the cave and check that no one is there, and then go on up to the watch point. We will come along very slowly. You are to let us know if anything is amiss."

Astrid nodded, slung her bow and put out her hand to Ayesha. "We had better stay in touch, or else we won't know where the other is. Let us go then." Holding hands, they put their rings on and disappeared.

Astrid looked back before they went out of sight. *Rani has held the main group stationary for a while. This time she is making them move slowly and, remembering what they had done to the confident bandits, with more than a little caution…good. We need to hurry, though.*

Lakshmi was up on the watch area, dressed in leather, and carrying a horse bow as well as her knives. She was relaying news excitedly on the return of the wayfaring group through a Talker, when first Ayesha and then Astrid took their rings off behind her.

"Boo," said Astrid quietly, and was rewarded with a strangled sound and a startled look as the very young-looking girl (who was actually older than

Astrid) spun around pulling out a hastily drawn short-sword with her free hand.

While Lakshmi hugged and greeted Ayesha, Astrid stood up and waved to the returning Mice. Just coming into view in the distance over the ridge behind them were the traders. Astrid then grabbed the Talker.

"Hello, anyone who is listening. This is the Cat. Can someone find either Sãjah or Lãdi?" *We need Mousehole's head domestic and cook now.* "And let me talk to them please. Who is here anyway?" *It turns out to be the young mage, Fãtima, who is on the roof watch and she is already calling down below. Apparently, the village is already a hive of activity.*

Astrid let the village know about the merchants, but wouldn't be drawn about what had happened. "Let the storytellers tell everyone when we are all together. I am not going to ruin the tale with my rough version. The main thing for now is that we are all back safely and it is a lovely day."

Rani

The travellers returned to a welcome from almost the whole village. *They cannot wait. They are all at the gate already.* Fear flew at Rani and Theodora, trying hard to hug them both at once. *It is not just us though.*

I worried about him fitting in, but Aziz is being mobbed by the other children, all dressed in their kilts, who want their monster back to play with. He is roaring at them and they shriek and run away to come back when he kneels to let them swarm all over him. Who would have thought that a Hob was so good with children?

His wife carries his shield and he gathers them up and carries them all back to the village in his arms or on his shoulders. Our recovered priest is grabbed by Theodule and Thord by Harald. It is a scene of general rejoicing.

"What is this about traders?" Sãjah asked Rani.

"Remember the ones who passed last autumn? Astrid has invited them in to stay at the Hall. She thinks that we should encourage them."

"Indeed, we should," said Sãjah. "We are getting the rooms ready now. Hagar and Shilpa are already hard at work. Do we charge them? Are we now an inn? What do they have to trade?"

"I guess that we are an inn of sorts. But I don't know whether to charge them, and I don't think that we have time to work it out. I think it best if we tell them that, because they are our first visitors, they are to be our guests for this visit. I think Astrid was having too much fun playing with them, and pulling their legs to ask anything practical about what they might have to trade to us. This time they have five pack animals and they seem to be very well laden, but what it all is, I don't know. What can we sell them?"

Sãjah thought briefly and started trying to call instructions over the general din. "Lakshmi…oh, she is outside. Giles, Eleanor, Aine," she had named the four who had the most likely saleable produce at hand: herbs, cheese, jewellery and spirits. "Come here, please. Goditha, be a dear and get your weapons, and ask Lakshmi to come in and do the rest of the watch, please. Tell her to think about…oh no…I keep forgetting the Talker. I will do that."

Rani called Astrid over. "Seeing that these seem to be your traders and you can speak to them, you wait at the gate and show them in."

"That is fine. Basil will be busy upsetting Lãdi in the kitchen anyway. It is about time she learnt some more of his way of cooking things, if we are going to get more people in from Darkreach. They will be more relaxed when we trade with them if we have them full of the food they are used to…and beer."

"Better get Shilpa or Ruth ready to do the dealing with them. They both used to be traders, but neither speaks Darkspeech well enough, so if you can get your wife to translate…" She stopped and grinned, "Well, one sight of her eyes and we should get very good prices on everything." She handed her pack to Tabitha and asked that she take Basil's as well, so that he could go straight to work in the kitchen.

The Mice returned excitedly to the village. Everyone was again told that explanations would wait until tonight, but that it would be worth the wait.

They were nearly back to the village gates when Sajãh came over to Rani. "I forgot when we saw you first, but you may need to know," she said. "We have prisoners, and perhaps three new residents…that is, if you do not mind having them."

"Prisoners? New people?"

Sãjah nodded. "Five days after you left, two men appeared coming south on the path with two women and a little girl. Robin was on duty, and after checking with Eleanor, he let them in as if he were a bandit. They are slavers, and they had been told that new girls were wanted here, and they were bringing the first of them in.

"The little girl and one woman are both from the Brotherhood, and the other woman is from near Greensin, we think that she may want to go home, but we are not sure. The bandits are in cells in the back of the guardroom. That is why Eleanor is not here to see you. She is making sure they are secure and locked up tight, so that we can ignore them when the traders are here. I didn't think that taking prisoners and questioning them was something we wanted to talk about in front of any visitors we want to make a good impression on.

"We thought that you should try them and let the Presbytera find out what she can before we do anything with them. Several of the girls were brought here by them, and we all know that they have been here before, so they are guilty.

"They have not been gentle when they dealt with anyone, and we have to make sure that they are secure, as a few of the girls have wanted to kill them already, but we thought it best if we waited for you before we did. The Presbytera may get them to talk before they die. I have been telling them that, but I am not sure that they believe me"

Christopher

W*hile all the turmoil is going on, and before tonight, we should have a quick service of thanks. I will see who we can gather. It is, after all, the feast day of Saint Jude and our hopeless cause has actually succeeded, and what is more, we are bringing home an icon of the Saint all at the same time. It would be wrong not to take the opportunity to thank God and the Saint at the very first chance. We would not want to be seen to be ungrateful.* He turned to Theodule and explained why they needed to gather some people... even a few.

Astrid

I*t is nice to just wander out to the watch point and sit talking to Goditha on the stone bench. Instead of tramping with a full pack and expecting a dragon, I can just talk and watch the sky and the birds wheeling in it until the traders draw close.* Eventually, they approached the bridge and she went down to greet them.

They are obviously surprised that there is something here in what had seemed to them just a useless side valley, one of many that they had passed, but they looked to have recovered from the shock that I gave them earlier. Wait until they see Theodora.

She waved up to Goditha and went towards the village with the three men and their horses. The shod hooves of the horses clattered on the stone of the path as the water roared past them. The men were at least polite, and only quietly smiled when she told them the name of the village.

They went through the gate to the valley. *Their eyes are growing wider and wider.* She explained the gate to them. *Rani had not mentioned that, but it is a good idea for the rumour to get out into the world that Mousehole is impregnable. I will have a child living here soon, and I want her to be safe from the world and all in it.*

She pointed out their fields and their flocks, and explained that the valley was ringed with tall mountains and cliffs. She could see that the traders saw the watcher on the roof of the Hall of Mice. "That is one of our mages. We have ten now in Mousehole," she said proudly.

I may not have seen a real town yet, just my home and Evilhalt, but I have been told that some of them didn't have ten mages. Wolfneck has only seven, and Bjarni isn't any better than the junior Mice mages, and neither Magnus nor Leif, the two senior mages, come anywhere near to matching either Rani or Theodora.

Verily was waiting at the village gate for them. "Rani said to bring them straight to the hall. Lãdi and Basil have some things ready for them to eat and drink while they are trading, and Theodora is waiting there with Shilpa and Ruth. Rani thought it best to get the trading over with while we are all sober, and then we can all relax and hear the story of what has happened while you were away."

Verily was staring at the traders with wide eyes. *Apart from the male Mice, she has never seen men who did not want to abuse her, and while she is married to a Hobgoblin, these were some of the Kharl of legend…and much more visibly so than either Basil or I.*

"Stop looking at them like that, Verily." Astrid used Hindi. "These are Karas and Festus. They are part-Kharl, the same as Basil and I am, and they are just as much people as we are, or Aziz is…and I am sure that they can speak at least a little Hindi." She turned to the traders.

"I am sorry, but the people here are not used to strangers who are not going to hurt them…I am sure that you will hear the story later, and apart from my husband and I, they have never met an Insakharl before." As the traders went up the courtyard they could see people moving around and working, while little girls wearing just short leather kilts peered from around skirts. *It all gives our one short but wide street a general bustle of activity.*

Waiting outside the hall were Bianca and the Khitan. "We are here to help you unload your goods so that you can show us what you have," said Bianca in Hindi. "Do you want to show us what you want taken off, then we can unload the beasts and take them to the stables." Carausius was surprised. *He obviously isn't used to this amount of help from customers, and is, at least a trifle nervous. The guards are looking around and eyeing the number of armed people all around them as if weighing up their chances. Not very high…so relax.*

"Stop worrying. If we had meant you harm, it would have happened already. We outnumber you and we could even have taken you captive when you slept. The fact that we haven't done so, should show you that we want much more from you than just one lot of plunder. We want to trade with you. What do you have for us?" Quickly she was given a summary of the goods that they had with them.

Carausius had the pack horses unloaded and taken away. *He is looking ready to go inside. It is time to make him a bit more nervous.* "That will all be brought in. You need to follow me," she paused. "If I might give you some advice…it might be an idea to bow once you enter. One of our Princesses is used to that," and without any more explanation she strode through the door and bowed herself.

I am right. Theodora is glaring at me for that. She is sitting on one of our biggest chairs up front with Aziz and Thord on each side of her and the two traders on one side…so she deserves it.

"Your Highness, I bring you the trader Carausius from Ardlark and his guards, Karas and Festus from Mouthguard in your old land of Darkreach. They bring…" She spoilt the impression a bit by forgetting exactly what they had, "I cannot remember the names, but they bring cloth to trade…should I get Fortunata as well?" Theodora nodded, and Astrid spun around to get the dressmaker forgetting the sight she wished to see.

Theodora

H a…*she has missed their reaction. This Carausius is addressing me as he would any other barbarian village headman, his men noticed though. So much for me being anonymous. I should have put my disguise back on…they are flat on their faces at my feet. Now he notices them and he looks again at me…at his guards and then again at me. Ahh, now he notices my eyes, stops speaking in the middle of a sentence and joins the others on the floor. I should have expected it.* "Stand up all of you…get up. Do you want to trade or not?"

Astrid set it all up, didn't she? "We are not in Darkreach now, and I am not my Granther. Someone please bring them some chairs and food." *Oh, curses, I meant that to calm them. I think that I just made it worse. I just confirmed to them what they just thought likely before…that I really am a Princess of Darkreach. All three men are hugging the floor even tighter. It looks like it will take several more minutes for others to calm the traders down and get them off the floor.*

Astrid returned as this was taking place. "Damn," she said. "I should have waited a bit. Was it fun?" she asked innocently.

It turns out that, not only do they have cloth, but most of it is unusual. It includes khmel, cloth made of camel hair; gotar, cloth made from the fleece of goats and of several types; walla, the cloth made from the llama and alpaca; and sh-hone, cloth made of a seaweed. Some of that we need for our mages.

The rest of the load they stated was just made up of several types of hemp cloth, mainly as serge, as they had not been able to get enough of the others. *Fortunata and Astrid are interested in any cloth but they are trying to avoid showing it. I know that the hemp will enable them to make durable everyday clothes, and that is what we have the least of.*

On a small table nearby were some samples of gems and herbs, and a couple of pieces of cheese and two bottles. The trader was plied with food by Bilqîs while Umm had sat the guards down and was looking after them, and was asking them about their journey and where they were from.

I should be listening to what they say as well as the trading. I note that both of them have some Hindi, but that they both have a little more Arabic, as they had both been guards for trips to the Caliphate. Poor trader, he is not sure whether to look at those he is bargaining with, or me as the interpreter... and he is scared to look at me. I will be glad to get a deal struck.

Finally, we have a deal. "Would I also be able to ask you to take a message to Ardlark for my family please?"

"Certainly, my lady." *Oh dear, he has realised who I meant it for and now he is all flustered again. He definitely does not move in Court circles, does he? Now I have to calm him down...again.*

It looks like Basil is going to tell us that we have food. Good. Why is he coming over to this Carausius? "Could you deliver a message for me, please, when you go home?"

"Yes, I could." *He is looking at Basil with relief as just a normal person. Basil already has it written and hands it over and he looks at the addressee. Oh dear...I can see that it says Strategos Panterius and Basil is making it worse as he hands over a small diamond, one that we had brought down from Dwarvenholme...tiny really...as payment.*

The letter has one of those Antikataskopeía sigil things on it in a green wax. Carausius has read the address and looked at the size of the diamond and his mind is working hard as he wonders again what he has stumbled into. The panic on his face is evident. Will we ever get him calm?

Rani

W ith the traders here, and presumably returning straight home, the secret of Dwarvenholme will not remain a secret for long. We really only should stay home for a day and then, this time with horses, we should return to empty the treasure room and the library. We could explore the rest of the old Dwarven complex...no...in two thousand years, and given the size of the piles in the treasure rooms, most of the items of value are likely to have been brought into that one place. She leant over to speak to Theodora.

Theodora

I t is nice to have some of the food of home. I have not had Garthcurr Hopper on rice for a long time. I didn't know that we had the spices for that sort of thing. Now that we have eaten, what should I put in my letter to Granther... and what has Basil already put in his?

Although we want to get more of the treasure that is there, we cannot keep Dwarvenholme for ourselves, there are not enough of us to hold it, and anyway it belongs to the Dwarves as a whole. Besides, we already have a very good home of our own.

The secret of Dwarvenholme will soon be out and people will be racing there. This could spark conflict in the mountains near to Mousehole. It would be best for us to forestall this, and to gain some goodwill by telling the Dwarves about it ourselves, instead of them getting it second-hand. I wonder if Thord could travel north with the traders to see them on their way, and then go on to Kharlsbane and lead a group to Dwarvenholme before coming back to Mousehole...that is if he wants to return to us. I have to discuss this with Rani.

"We need to do something with Dwarvenholme," they both said at the same time. Astrid, who was coming up and had been about to ask them when everyone was going to be allowed to hear what happened, nearly exploded with laughter. She turned to the hall. "Not only do they complete sentences for each other," she said. "Now they have started saying the same thing as each other at the same time."

She started laughing at the discomfiture she was causing. *Why did she have to hear that? I can feel myself blushing. At least Carausius, seated next to us, looks scandalised at Astrid. He is right. Such obvious disrespect is not the way that the Imperial family should be treated in public. How do I stop her?*

When Astrid had recovered from her mirth, she asked her question. I am looking at my husband and she is looking at me. I am sure mine is the most important question. Rani took Theodora's hand and started to move her away from everyone, so that they could have a quiet conversation without being overhead. "Wait a minute," she said over her shoulder to Astrid as they left. "Talk to your trader, we need to discuss what we each thought of."

Astrid

W*ell, I am going to sit down and not stand to talk to a seated person.* She sat in Theodora's chair. *Carausius is looking shocked again. He does that a lot.* "You cannot sit there like that" he said.

Astrid bounced up and down a bit. "You are right," she said and stood up. *Carausius looks relieved.* "I don't know how Theodora puts up with that chair. It is so hard. She must be much better padded than I am." She grabbed a cushion and put it on the chair and sat back down again. "That is much better... now tell me...are you pleased with your deal here?" *Carausius' expression is back to that of shock. It may as well stay that way.*

I can see Carausius is not sure how to answer that. "I have made a good profit, perhaps not as good as I could have gotten in the Swamp, but I have cut near a month off my round trip and so might get three trips in for a season for the same costs." *He answers slowly. You can see his mind turning over. If I am right, he is thinking, 'What right has this girl with the strange accent, who claimed to be Insakharl, but looks and sounds like none he had ever seen, have to ask him? Why does she treat the Princess with such disrespect, and how does she get away with it?'* Basil came up and gave Astrid a kiss.

"Carausius, I want you to meet my husband, Basil. He is with Hrothnog's intelligence service...looking after the Princess at the direct order of the Emperor who sent him to her." *I guessed that most people do not openly talk about that service, and I have the poor man spluttering into his drink...again.* Astrid grinned and Basil turned to his wife.

"Puss, we need him to come back here with more trade. Stop trying to do your best to scare him off." He turned to the trader. "I apologise for my wife. You know what our Insakharl sense of humour is like? Well, she has inherited more than her fair share. She enjoys, more than anything else, making practical jokes and watching how people react to them. She is always teasing the

Princess. If the Princess would only stop blushing, she would not get teased half as much." He turned to Astrid again, "Would she?" *I may try and look innocent at that, but Basil's raised eyebrow shows that it is not working at all.*

"I forgot to mention," he continued to Carausius, "if you do intend to come back here, let the officer you give my letter to know when you are thinking of coming. You may have a reply to bring back to me. You will be paid for that as well. I need not tell you that, despite what my wife thinks, it is best not to mention to anyone else who you are carrying messages for. It will probably be far safer for you that way." He kissed Astrid again. "Now stand up and stop being nekulturny." He indicated behind her. "The Princesses want their seats again."

"Thank you, Basil," said Rani. "Can you quieten them down please and see if everyone is here. If they are, then Ayesha is going to tell them all what we have been doing. Make sure that they all have drinks and are comfortable. It will be a long story." She turned to the trader, "Are you all going to follow if the story is in Hindi?" He nodded. "Good, I am not a storyteller, but my wife tells me that doing it in two languages is harder."

Basil

A strid stood, and Basil did as he was told and, for a good part of the rest of the evening the audience sat entranced as the tale unfolded. *I think that the story has even more of an effect on the traders than finding Theodora had. They are a little more used to seeing the progeny of Hrothnog than to the places out of legend coming to life before them. I wonder, seeing that the story will soon be out, what the next move for us will be.*

Astrid

T hat night, after the tale was told, Theodora went around and talked to Thord, and those who would go to back to Dwarvenholme. Thord was eager to carry the news, and agreed to take his time with the task to enable the treasure to be gathered and brought back down. After all, as he said: "I've t' Crown. Everyt'ing else is replaceable 'n' every Dwarf would eventual understand t'at t' Finders need reward." He grinned. "What is even more important about t' Finders being rewarded, well, I'm one of t' Finders."

After a while, as small groups had earnest conversations together and people ducked out of the room and came back, it became obvious that something was afoot. Especially once people started to make sure that they were ready to leave at first light, before they re-joined the party. Carausius asked nervously what was happening.

Rani has insisted that I sit here and look after the traders. I could lie…but, if we are to keep seeing the traders, we should be mostly honest with them. "A group of us will be leaving again early in the morning to fetch some things that are needed." *That will do. Now to change the subject.*

"Tell me more about Darkreach. My husband has told me some, but I am sure you have seen more." *Basil has told me a lot, but I reckon that he must be biased. I know that he wants to take me to his old home for a visit. I want to find out more about where he will be taking me before I agree to it.*

Rani

We need to have a smaller group going into the mountains this time, and it will not be able to fight as well as those on the first trip. We are taking a risk that no Masters have moved back in, but Princess and I will still make as many wands as we can during the trip. This time we will travel with horses and the cart. Basil will be coming, but not Astrid, although she is sending him with all of her magic.*

Christopher and Bianca will come with us, with Bianca having charge of all the horses. Hulagu and the Khitan girls will take over the scouting duties. Neither Stefan nor Bryony can fight from horseback, but both will be coming as they can at least ride acceptably. Ayesha would, of course, be going, and we are adding the former Havenite trader, Shilpa. She is experienced with pack-horses and can help Bianca.

Our main problem is the cart. Naeve is the best at handling it, but she is far too pregnant. The only other person who can use it well enough is Goditha, and Parminder is not happy with that idea. For once, Astrid has been useful in pointing out that she is allowing her man to go without her, and offering to allow Parminder to stay with her while their husbands are away. We will equip them with swords and other things. Goditha has some tools that would be useful if the cart broke, and at the advice of Bianca, some axes and other tools for the road itself.

Verily

While she was in the gaol, where the weapons were stored and getting the others equipped, Verily had a long and hard look at the prisoners. *I know that one well. He has taken me twice before…and not gently. The other I know by sight, but he has never taken me on his visits.* "I look forward to watching you both die."

That night Aziz and Verily had their first argument. *Aziz insists that he has to go. I know that he is the strongest and they could need him to help with the cart if it breaks, and to bring down the treasure quickly. He has already managed to convince Rani that his walking will be as quick as the cart. Convincing me he has not yet done. I do not want him to go. I really do not want to be apart from him for that long.*

Theodora sat her down. "From what I have heard in Darkreach about pregnancy between different races, the babies are often more…fragile. Seeing that you had Christopher bless your union, you are very likely to be pregnant, and so you will be best staying home." *I guess that she is right.*

Now I have Astrid here offering me a place in her bed with Parminder. It will make me less lonely…but does he have to go?

Rani

Bianca and Shilpa had slipped out on the night's feast and have looked at the available beasts and equipment, and returned to say that as well as the cart they had equipment for ten pack horses, including my horse, Juggernaut, who has his own tack. It seems that they have already loaded feed for the trip up. They have figured that we will be able to cart, with the saddlebags on the horses, nearly four tonnes and surely there cannot be much more than that of value in the room. If there is, we can just take more and move slower.*

Lakshmi has been hard at work while we were away and the one thing we will be well supplied with is healing potions. Christopher had been concerned at going back without a supply of them. Astrid overheard that conversation on healing herbs and interrupted…again, and now it seems that we have to take her and Lakshmi to that first camp site as we leave.

As they were finishing with these arrangements, Rani turned to Theodora: "You get to tell Fear that we leave in the morning."

Chapter XIV

16th Undecim

They left before dawn. Astrid, Naeve, Lakshmi and Ruth would be with them for the start, although they were likely to be left behind during the day as they were walking, even if they were walking as fast as they could. They would be headed for the camping meadow below the cliff to gather plants.

They would take only a single horse with them, the second plough horse from the valley. It was going to have sacks slung over it with the jars that had been used to help with the hiding spell in them. Lãdi had said that no-one wanted to use them for anything else now, so Naeve and Lakshmi could have them for planting in. There were also some flat boxes, but due to there being no more pack frames they were going to have to improvise how to carry everything when they headed back.

Fear had not been happy when she was told what was happening. She had her mummies back for only one night, and now they were going away again and they could not say for how long. She had insisted on sleeping with them that night. Rani and Theodora just looked at each other. "I am too tired anyway," said Theodora.

Carausius

They feed us well here, but where is everyone? I asked, and was told that many had left already. Where to? No-one is stopping us poking around.

The whole place seems like a normal village, but with not enough people in it. I knew that some were going, but I thought that Astrid was one of those staying. Now she is missing as well.

Thord is one of the few that I have talked with and he is already waiting alongside our animals near the Hall. I have never even seen inside their stables. I don't have any idea how many horses they have. Well played, those women. I surreptitiously counted people last night, and I think that I have the right number, but I cannot be sure.

People kept coming and going...and that was made worse by at least two of the women, the storyteller and Astrid, disappearing and even handing things around to some of the others to try. It is time to be off and on the road. We will find out what we find out, and with at least one Antikataskopeía here, it is perhaps best not to be too openly curious.

They set out through the gate. *There is a pregnant woman, clad in armour and with a kite shield and spear, up in the watch position. I thought that might be where Astrid was. I have never seen such a shortage of people to do the work needed. The pregnant woman, Eleanor, that is her name, is still standing guard in armour at a stage where most people would not be getting ready to fight if needed.*

Thord will not be pressed too far on anything, but he does admit that a lot of their women are pregnant, but they needed to keep working as there is no other choice for them yet. Her Highness did say that they needed more people last night, as well.

Carausius
16th Undecim

It was not until the next morning that Carausius found out where Astrid was. They had just left the campsite, with Thord taking the lead on Hillstrider, when she was seen approaching him with three other women, at least one of them very pregnant as well. *They are all fully armed and they have a horse with them. It is dragging two poles behind it over the stones of the road.*

Obviously, they didn't have time to make a cart, just to knock this frame together. The poles have a platform connecting them, and there is a large heap on the platform, but whatever the pile is made of is completely covered in bags. I very much wish that I knew what is there. I feel that I will be trading for it in the future.

Astrid ran up to Thord and gave him a kiss, "Have fun being the Hero Who Returns," she said. "You may as well go. Christopher won't let me get drunk with you until the baby is born." She patted her stomach. "Just make sure that you are back for then. We are going to get stinking drunk in celebration and tease the Princesses." *She is pregnant as well.*

The two groups took their leave and parted. They had only gone a hand of hands apart when Astrid turned and called loudly behind her in an afterthought to those who were headed north: "I look forward to seeing you all in a few months," she said. The others acknowledged her with waves and, from Thord, a broad grin.

Astrid

I *will probably get sick of it soon, but it is nice to have some peace and quiet, and a normal life. Naeve and Lakshmi have started digging a new bed on some of the last flat ground near the river, near where the path began to ascend, for the new crop. They have encouraged as many of us as can spare the time to come and help them. I am pretty useless at it.*

While they plant the herbs, I can at least wander around with others and pick up rocks from the meadow and start outlining where the stone walls will go for this new herb field when Goditha returns.

We have already got some new clothes sewn for the littlest girls, and I will be doing that for a while. The children can run around in their kilts most of the time, but Ruth has put her foot down, however, and insisted on dresses or tunics and trews being worn in class.

We may have more cloth than has been in the store since we arrived, but the hemp cloth, a good grade, is quickly being used up. Some cloth we are not touching. There is a lot reserved for the new mages. According to Rani, when she was giving instructions before she left, having them wear the right cloth helps them to cast. Who knew?

Apparently khmel, hemp, gotar, sh-hone and walla are all cloths of special significance to some mages—one of the reasons the traders had selected them to bring so far. With the rough woollen cloth that Fātima and Umm are already starting to produce, we have half of the astral signs covered.

Chapter XV

Thord
22nd Undecim

"I noticed, t'at you seem to ha' very little on your pack horses, but you seem to be happy. I take it you got a good price t'en."

"I probably should have gotten a better one, but your Princess is...off-putting when she is the translator and your two merchant women know their business. You may have a strange village in Mousehole...I take that back, you *do* have a strange village in Mousehole, but I can see us making quite a few trips there."

"I had exactly one thousand, two hundred and seventy-five ells of cloth on these five horses. They were well laden. I am going back with nothing in the way of bulk goods, just a few draughts of potions, along with a few small bags of rubies, sapphires and other lesser gems and even some tasty food and drink for the way." *His voice shows his satisfaction.* "This is going to work out very well." *Unconsciously he is rubbing his hands together at the thought.*

"They even gave me orders for the next trip. Your man Basil...the one with the letter. Karas, he used to be in the army...he tells me that the man that it is sent to is the head of the Antikataskopeía." *He is looking for a reaction. I will try not to give one.* "I suppose that fits with your Princess. He wants me to bring in a bolt of spilk for his wife, and I will have to get that from Southpoint. I will either have to order that specially, or get it somewhere else at a higher price."

"I also have to bring silk and velvet and all sorts of things. They even want candles and iron. I was going to sell in the Swamp, and buy some of their potions and a few other things that I would have sold at Nameless Keep. Then I would have made up another load and returned."

"This is a much better trip. I will go on to Ardlark to sell these, and so make up my load there. I will only get two trips in instead of three, but I should make so much more on each run. I think that I will get at least one more horse and a handler for the next trip. My wife will be very pleased when I get home. I told her that trading outside among the barbarians…not that your little village would really count as being barbarian when it has a Darkreach Princess…" he hurriedly added, "was worth the gamble."

Thord had been keeping his eye out, and four days after saying farewell to Astrid and the other girls, he noticed something to the right. He dismounted and looped Hillstrider's reins to a bush, knelt down and looked. *I was right.* He stood up and walked a little way into the scrub, jumping up and down and kicking away some dirt to reveal stone beneath.

The only reason that everyone has missed this road to Dwarvenholme is that they were looking for something much younger. Now that I know its true age it is fairly easy to spot, and it looks like our Mousehole road is actually turning off the main road and we are now re-joining that. I suppose that I should explain…

"I wouldn't bother going t'ere. No-one will live t'ere for a long time yet and t' entrance is hard to find anyway. If you want I might take you up t'ere next season, if t'ere is anyone living t'ere yet."

Thord
29th Undecim

It was another seven days before they came down into the Darkreach Gap, and passed behind one of the border forts standing out on a small isolated mountain in the forests to the west of the mountains. "Unfortunately, we have to go away from home to get home," said Carausius. "Everyone leaving or entering Darkreach has to enter through Mouthguard, and get their permits stamped. Otherwise we are treated as smugglers. So, we have to go down river to there, get our permits stamped, and then come back up river to Nameless Keep."

"T'en how'd you find t'is road?"

Carausius looked a mixture of embarrassed and proud. "More or less by accident," he said. "I thought that there had to be a way to get down to the Swamp without going through every town along the way and paying tolls. I was just expecting to travel along the hillsides, and we started out looking for a good place to head south off the main road and do this, and then one stop, when he was out getting firewood, Festus found this road. It seemed to be going the right way, so after we had registered as going out, we came back and followed it."

"I think that was when your Astrid saw us. So, we have a secret way to get to you. I don't think that you are large enough to attract too many traders, so I might be your only way into Darkreach for trade for a while yet. I think we will all be very happy," *He sounds smug at that.*

They turned left and joined the road going down to Mouthguard.

A t Mouthguard they got to stay in an inn, The Roving Isci-Kharl. There was a painting of some sort of Kharl on the sign. *I am not impressed. I am spoilt by Lãdi's cooking...even Karas says the same thing.* "When you get travellers, not us of course, you will be able to charge them a lot for that cooking" he said fondly.

Explaining why I came down the road, but have not been into Darkreach, took some doing. Fancy having to get hold of the letter from Basil to his general off the trader, and wave it at the officer who was stamping passes, and who controlled access across the bridge, before I had any chance of being heard. Carausius' dream of being the only traveller on the road is just that—a dream.

I had better warn the officer of what lies ahead for him. This is the only road that I know of to get the Dwarves to Dwarvenholme. Without mentioning my destination, I need to tell this pompous officer, an Insakharl called Mellitus, that I will be back in a few weeks, probably with a large number of Dwarves, and that we will be crossing the river, but not going on to Darkreach. All I am telling him is that we will be "goin' into t' mountains."

Next morning, Thord and the traders parted. Without the three on foot to slow him down, Thord was soon heading off to Kharlsbane, and could now travel much quicker, with Hillstrider happy to oblige, while the other three were headed back up the valley and into Darkreach.

Chapter XVI

Rani
32nd Undecim

A t least the old road along the base of the mountains was easy to travel *on with the cart. Under the top layer of soil that had drifted across it over the years there is still a hard and solid stone surface. There are few trees forcing their way through it, but those are easy to clear. It has lasted for a long time and had been well maintained until fairly recently—probably until the Burning.*

I think it is smoother than that I rode on in that cursed chariot to Garthang. The road up to the mountains is a very different proposition. I have to have Aziz off the cart as often as he is on it, helping the cart over obstacles and even clearing branches. The riders in front even have to drag away some smaller trees that have fallen over the track. We had to take the cart right around one particularly large tree that lay fallen directly over the path. Will we get around it on the way back?

Rani made sure that someone was always watching, first the sky, and then the mountain itself, for any sign of the dragon. They didn't stand a chance of defending the animals if it appeared. They would just have to scatter and run.

It seems that everyone is going along well so far. Goditha has admitted that she misses Parminder, but apart from that is enjoying herself. She hasn't been outside the valley since she was brought there. It is hard work with the cart, but also fun.

I notice that she has thanked Aziz often, both privately and publicly, for forcing his way onto the trip. As for the Hob, he spends a lot of his free time with Christopher. Part of the time he is learning to read, the rest of the time he is learning his new religion. The Khitan are all happy. They are riding in a land they regard as theirs.

The only one with problems is Bianca. Her horses are jealous of the attention she has to give to the pack animals and the two war horses are a trifle bored. They do the things horses do when they have been without exercise and penned up for a long time. As well, Sluggard doesn't like being tied down to a fixed position.

Bianca has tied the other pack horses to him and that means that he can no longer just go where he wants. She seems to have solved it a bit by getting Ayesha to ride her horse, Sirocco, for her. The war-horse seems to tolerate her, "At least he gets a bit of a gallop this way," she said.

T he road to Dwarvenholme is very different. For most of the way it was an easy path to follow, but unlike the Mousehole road, as I am already thinking of the path past our valley, and which runs parallel along the foothills, this one has suffered a lot more over time with disuse. In some places, it is covered in scree from landslides, in others the path has been forced apart by the roots of giant trees.

There are many places where trees have fallen across it and it is hard to see the former road as more than random rocks. In some cases, the damage is so old that fallen trees (their width far greater than any of us riders are tall, even on our horses) could be easily cut open to allow a path through them.

For others, we have had to cut a path around them. I didn't think about these things on our last trip. I wish that I had. We might have been better just bringing packhorses and even making two trips. It is too late to reverse that decision now.

Chapter XVII

Thord
3rd Duodecimus

I *t has taken me ten days, but I am at Kharlsbane. Now, how do I go about this? I have never talked to the Duke much. He doesn't have time for mere shepherds, but I am not a shepherd now. I am an Ambassador. I know; I will act just as Astrid would.*

Bjarni the Talker was, as usual, stationed at the gate. "So T'ord, had enough of t'world, ha'you? Been left behind by your Darkreach friends, ha'you?" he asked, with more than a touch of sarcasm. "Ready enow to come back among us 'n' become respectable Dwarf?"

"Not in any way is t'at goin' to happen," said Thord. "I'll be living somewhere else 'n' hopeful I'll total 'n' complete fail at being respectable for all time. However, I need to see t'Smasher. I bring message for him from my Princess."

"Your Princess, say you?" Bjarni said in a mocking tone. "What...ha' you gone 'n' found Dwarvenholme 'n' given it King now, ha' you?" This jest caused hilarity for the other two on guard but Thord just ignored them.

"You just tell me where t'Duke is," replied Thord wearily, giving nothing away. "If he thinks t'at you need to know, I am sure he'll tell you eventual."

"Watch your lip, young T'ord. I don't care where you've been. I am t'Guard commander here 'n' you'll treat me with respect."

"Oh yes sir," said Thord lightly and without much respect and touched his forehead "Lots of respect I ha'for you." *I am doing well at this. I have been around Astrid for far too long already.* "Now, I'll ask again, where is he?"

Bjarni looked at him, surprised. *His face already says that this was not the same Thord the Shepherd who had left here only a few months ago.* "I suppose t'at he be up at t'hall," he reluctantly admitted.

Thord thanked him, more or less politely, and left. He found the Duke without much difficulty, but the Duke saw no reason to see him alone. "What can you ha'to say t'at everyone cannot hear? You are a shepherd who left his flock behind," he said dismissively.

Thord sighed and shrugged. "All right, just remember t'at it is your choice." He raised his voice so that everyone around could hear him. "I bring you greetin's from my Princesses, t'rulers of Mousehole," *I really am hanging around Astrid too much...but the blank looks are fun.*

He dug in his saddlebag that he had brought in with him, and pulled out a bag and drew a letter from his pouch. Still speaking to all around him he continued loudly: "Some of you may have the wits to remember t'Darkreach bard t'at I left here with." *Even the Duke nodded.*

"She was a travellin' in disguise. She is actual t'great-granddaughter of Hrothnog." Again, he paused and looked around for the looks he was getting. *Looks like a stunned cavy.* "We joined up with some others 'n' have wiped out nest of bandits in t'mountains. You may ha'heard about t'trade disruptions..." *at least they are nodding to that...* "Well, t' bandits were responsible for t'em. We have taken over t'eir base, which is called Mousehole. T'is letter," again he waved it without handing it over, "sends t'eir greetings 'n' invites trade."

"Trade with tiny fleapit of part-Kharls? Why would we want t'at?" The Duke looked around at the Dwarves gathered around as if he were making a joke. *They seem to agree with him.*

"Rubies 'n' other gems, antimony 'n' potions, for start. I'm now quite rich. Additional, we have ten mages in our tiny fleapit 'n' most of t'people t'ere are humans anyway. I am t' only Dwarf, but I want to change t'at as well. Oh...also... I almost forgot to mention,,," he paused and looked around while he picked up the bag and started to withdraw what was in it. "We a found Dwarvenholme."

He pulled a velvet bag from his pack and removed from it the Crown, which he had polished, and held it up where all could see it easily as beams of light caught it and bounced off its gems and around the room to dazzle the onlookers.

It is something every dwarf can describe in their sleep and they are having no problem with quickly realising that my story must be true, and I hold the proof in my hands. His last words were almost drowned out in the ensuing pandemonium. "Our Princesses want to know if'n t'Dwarves want to take it back, or if t'ey should keep it?"

Smasher is staring at the Crown. It is made of mithril and encrusted with gems and its description has been passed down in Dwarven legend. We may have forgotten where Dwarvenholme is, but every Dwarf present could have described the Crown in minute detail, from the memory of the stories they were told over and over as children.

Belatedly, he is moving and grabbing the letter lying on the table. He has given a quick glance at the wax seal, mouse rampant, standing upright on its hind legs with one front paw raised in the air above the other, torn it open and started reading the Dwarven script.

"Who is t'is Theodora? Who is t'is Rani? Where did t'ey come from? Why do t'ey make you t'eir Ambassador? How is it t'at you and these humans found what Dwarves ha' sought for over hundred years since t'Burning start?"

"Actual," said Thord, "t'at's a part of why it was never found. Bring me chair 'n' something to drink, as a befits honoured Ambassador, 'n' I will tell you a story…'n' if you wouldn't mind … I t'ink t'at my parents'ld like to hear what I've to say as well." *Act with confidence. Astrid does. No doubts allowed.*

The Duke spluttered a few times, but then nodded and waved, and Dwarves scurried off to comply. Thord would say no more until he had greeted his parents and asked of their health, and then seen them settled and everything was just as he wanted. By then, many more Dwarves had intruded and the room was getting crowded, but the Duke was so distracted he didn't order his Hall cleared. When he was finally ready, Thord launched into his story without asking permission.

"So, you see t'at, due to t'time t'at had passed since t'Fall most of t'treasure has either rotted or corroded." Thord started to wind up his story before his rapt audience. *I don't have to quieten them. If anyone tried to interrupt me the others would silence them quickly. My subject matter more than makes up for my inadequacy as a storyteller. Even the Duke is hushed.*

"Even t'silver is gone into corrosion. Of course, t'ere could be more in t'areas we did not go into 'n' I'm sure t'mines're still there. My Princesses invite t'Dwarves to reclaim t'eir ancestral home, but lay out t'limits of our territory for you to respect. You'll need to let t'other towns know of t'is 'n' 'll need to prepare."

"In particular, 'n' I speak from our experience t'ere you understand, you'll need as much in t'way of light spells as you can make before you go. T'arrangement we had is still in place, but it only covers a very tiny fraction of t'amazing place t'at is t'real home of t'Dwarves. We don't know all of it. We don't know what lives t'ere. T'ere is so much we ha'still to learn about it." He finished his story, sat back and took a large drink. *Now the questions will start.*

It was late that night before Thord was able to get himself free and go and talk more to his proud parents. *Nice to see the pride on their faces in a child who had been a part of the greatest thing that has fallen on the Dwarves for centuries. From now, I will forever be called the Finder in the legends of the Dwarves.* After greeting them, he let them know what he wanted, as quietly as he could. *I will stay as a part of Mousehole and am now very wealthy.*

With my new fame and my wealth, I will be a target for every Dwarven mother and ambitious unmarried female Dwarf, and even perhaps for some that are married. The best way to forestall problems is to get my mother to find me the right bride, and to make it known that this is what she is doing so that possible brides, and their parents, go to her and not to me.

This is, of course, something every Dwarven mother is always eager to do, and although my human companions seemed to rely on chance to find the right someone, I am old-fashioned enough in some respects to happily follow tradition on something as important to my future as this. Having given his parents instructions as to what he wanted, he now had set this in train.

Next day, the Duke sent messages out to the rest of the north-east; to Deafcor, Diamondroot and Northhole. Those messengers went by foot. Groups of Dwarves on fast sheep were sent to Copperlevy, in the Hills in the Northern Plains, and to the Dwarves of the South-West Mountains.

From his face, the Duke is very pleased to write out and send the one to Copperlevy. He signs it with a big flourish and stamps the largest seal he has down on it. It is Duke Thorfinn Deepdelver, who rules there and he has more Dwarves living under his rule there than all who are living in all of the rest of the Dwarven areas put together. Even I know that he has pretensions to rule over all of the Dwarves. Now, the rule of the Dwarves, whoever I decide holds it, would return to the real Mountains where it belonged.

Smasher is looking pleased…wait…in his eyes…he is just realising that I am the Finder. I have not claimed the Crown nor given a hint as to whom it will go to. I still hold the Crown, and there can be no King without the Finder recognising and crowning him. That will be my final role in the story and none can take it from me. That much is very clear from the legends and Dwarves follow their traditions whenever they can and, sometimes, they do it even when they shouldn't.

Mind you, I am trying to avoid that question. I have no intention of claiming the title. I can see full well the work that comes to Rani and Theodora in our own tiny village. Rule the Dwarves? You would have to be kidding. Put two hands of Dwarves in a room with a question, and you will get three hands or more of different opinions. That is part of why I got the Princesses to write the letter naming me as their Ambassador to the Dwarves. Rani had just looked blank and not understood the reason behind my request, but Theodora just smiled at it and very quickly agreed. I presume that she explained it to her husband later.

During a pause, he looked around him at what was going on, a goblet of wine in his hand and a tray of meats, pickles and cheeses beside him. He sighed contentedly. *I am already very wealthy, and I am going to be even more so. I still haven't revealed my pouch full of mithril. Some of it will to go to my parents, the rest…well, I am sure that I could afford to buy Kharlsbane if I really want to, and I have some gems with me as small change and I have an income from the mine.*

I am forever going to have a major part to play in Dwarven politics and life, as much as I want to play, if I choose to. I have entered the legends of the Dwarves. In them, the part of the others will gradually be forgotten until only the Dwarven remained. What is more, I am even going to get a wife of high rank. Life is good, very good, and there may yet be even more adventures to come.

Chapter XVIII

Astrid
5th Duodecimus

I *have grown used to Parminder waking in the night with bad dreams and having to hold the young and tiny pregnant girl tight until she falls asleep. I have even gotten used to Verily's sharp elbows, although I am starting to regret choosing to take the middle position in a bed full of pregnant women. However, this is different.*

Parminder had woken startled and was crying. On top of her dreams she was concerned that, now she was pregnant she would lose her looks and Goditha would no longer love her. *Nothing seems to reassure her.*

Careful of waking Verily, Astrid stroked Parminder's hair and reassured her that she was still beautiful and would stay beautiful to Goditha. Parminder had responded by kissing her. *It now seems that she wants to be reassured of her beauty more physically. Oh well, it looks like I am about to find out how the sailor's wives console each other in Wolfneck.* She tried to be quiet.

In the morning Verily said. "I thought that the others were joking, but you really do purr," and smiled. "Don't worry, I won't tell anyone. She certainly needed it, and I think you did as well from what you have been saying in your sleep. I will let you know if I need consolation as well, but you could not be Aziz."

I am not sure how to respond to that. "And neither of you could be Basil, but you are right. I think I needed something. My dreams may not be as bad as Parminder's are, but they have not been good ones. I am anxious about my Basil."

Chapter XIX

Rani
34th Undecim

W e have arrived at Dwarvenholme. The Khitan have already started trying to clear a new track to the path up to the flat area outside the gate while the cart is brought around the rock fall that covers the bottom of the old path. It is hard work and I am counting days in my head and hoping that the Dwarves take their time to gather.

According to Father Christopher it is Saint Vitalis's Day, and we are already a week behind schedule. I am starting to regret sending Thord off so quickly. Perhaps it would have been better to have done that only after we returned from this trip. It is not as if there were any rush in revealing what has remained hidden for centuries.

There is plenty of room inside. We can take the cart and the horses to the stairs and use the horses to bring things down to the cart before finally filling their packs to return. Most of the bats are still here, clustered high in the roof of the concourse, squeaking and adding to the noisome mess below them, but it seems that there were fewer of the flying beasts now. Perhaps the light is upsetting them, and they are moving their roosts from here further in to the vastness that is the old home of the Dwarves. Where they will go when those Dwarves return to it, I do not know.

They moved as cautiously as they could, all of them on foot with the extra riding horses tied into a string. Their caution was rewarded as they moved into the stairwell. A patch of darkness moving from the stairwell. She blasted it with a bolt from a wand, as it wafted towards the horses. "It looks like we did not remove all of the Moonshadows. Everyone has to keep checking the person near them. I hope Thord remembers to warn the Dwarves about them."

Leaving Anahita, Goditha and Stefan with the cart, the rest started to ascend the stairs. Some wands were left to deal with any more Moonshadows that appeared. Hopefully Goditha's work towards becoming a full-fledged mage would let her spot any that came towards them.

The skeletons of the Dwarves still remained, almost filling the level where they had fought. *I am glad that I brought a broom along. It is more respectful, particularly since the living Dwarves would be arriving soon, to clear a path through them rather than just crush them underfoot.*

They kept going and reached the level of the throne room. The stairs actually kept going after this point but were much narrower. *It might be a good idea to see what lies, at least a little way, up them. I will send Christopher, Theodora and Hulagu, all with nails still in their shields to light the way, to find out. The rest can go on towards the throne area.* "Only go a few turns past where the light from here fades and keep an eye on each other, and call loudly if you need help," she said.

Hulagu

They went up a further three turns around of the stairs. *There is a small misshapen lump of stone on the balustrade ahead of them. It is very out of place with the precision of Dwarven carving. I think it moved.* "What is that?" he asked. The others stopped and looked as well.

"A baby," cried Christopher and sprang forward, moving slower as he approached it. He began to sing, or at any rate chant, in Latin. *He sings that during his worship.* Reaching forward he picked up the small lump and held it on his hand...*like a very heavy hawk. It stirs sleepily, but allows itself to be handled.* Proudly, Christopher returned to them, holding his burden close to him.

"It is a young gargoyle." He showed them as he stroked it. They all reached out. *It is an odd feeling stroking a skin that feels like warm smooth-hewn stone.* "If you are lucky, and find them when they have just been thrown out of the nest they will sometimes accept you and stay with you. If we are lucky we can bring it back to Mousehole with us."

"Why would you want something that small and ugly to come home with us? It makes Aziz look like Verily."

"Gargoyles will eat most meat," said Christopher, in the tone of a teacher, "but what they love to eat are demons and many other evil creatures. When they are found, many in the Church try and tame them and keep them near their church. Happy and protected is the village that has a church with its own flock of gargoyles living on it to help protect it from the Adversary and his creatures."

"Let us go back down now. You can see from here that the stair keeps going for a long way still, and we are getting well away from the others. Besides I want to look after…" he lifted his hand to peer at the gargoyle more closely, "Her. I will wager that her parents left her here on the stairs to feed off the Moonshadows and quietly grow. She wouldn't get much to eat off them, but she is only small, and she could fill up on bats." Christopher returned to chanting as they went back down, and he stroked the gargoyle as he walked.

Rani

N othing has moved into the old throne room, and the path back to the treasure and the books is clear. The hard work of loading began. After a while Kāhina, who was outside on guard, called and they all looked up and grabbed their weapons, running back out to where she stood.

Christopher is approaching us, and he has set up a continuous chant. Are we being threatened? I cannot see a threat. The other three are approaching us at a walk across the wide room and Christopher seems to be holding something.

"It is all right," called Theodora. "The Father has found a pet he is trying to keep with us." They all gathered around, and as he stroked the small ugly beast Christopher explained what it was. On his hand, the tiny creature opened and closed its eyes…*almost as golden as Theo-dear's, but slit vertically like a cat's.* Christopher transferred it to his saddle horn, and it opened and closed its wings and yawned before seeming to go to sleep.

"I think that she has accepted me," he said. "Now," he continued cheerfully, "on that good omen, let us all get to work."

The business of transferring the treasure began. The remaining books were taken first. Although probably of least value, they also had the potential to be of the most use, even though many were almost completely rotted. The first load was taken down to the cart.

In light of the presence of another Moonshadow, either Theo-dear or I should be with the horses as they move, and seeing that Christopher assures me that the gargoyle will be proof against the unseen menace here, the other should stay with the cart.

The cart rapidly filled up. They had brought some boxes for treasure, but only gems and coins were put in them. The bulky objects, things like ceremonial light sticks (their spells expired after so long without maintenance), the weapons of the Masters, and other objects such as goblets and plates, were to just ride on top of the load, or were just casually stuck down the sides wherever they would fit.

It has taken us three trips to fill the cart. When the saddlebags are all full as well, there is still some treasure left. Rani looked at it. "We have more than enough. We have all the gems, all the jewellery, and all that is left is only gold. Fill your pouches with as much of it as you wish. We will leave the rest of it for the Dwarves."

It had been a hard day, and when they had re-joined the cart, she looked around at everyone and then said: "We are all tired, but I do not want to sleep inside here—or anywhere inside really. There could still be a lot to harm us here. I think that we will go and camp outside near the doors, and start out for home early in the morning."

Chapter XX

Astrid
7th Duodecimus

T here are two problems that Rani forgot about. One doesn't matter, the slavers are not going anywhere, and the women of the village do enjoy going to feed and taunt them. The bigger problem is presented by the three females that the slavers brought with them. How are they to fit in?

It is obvious that, regardless of what else is decided on, the child will stay. She is only five years old and quite sweet. I had thought that Fear was stuck with a bad name, but Repent of This Thy Wickedness is an even worse thing to have as a name, and surely a cruel irony for a child destined to come to this place.

Still, Repent is a biddable and well-behaved girl, and Eleanor and Robin have already taken her into their flock. She was shocked by the way the children run around in kilts, but after a couple of weeks, she has a kilt of her own and only blushes if she sees a man when she is in it.

Luckily, we have few enough men, and during the day they are busy...even more so as the pregnancies continue to show. It seems that either Christopher is very good with that bless spell, or the men of Mousehole really do want to breed like their namesakes. It has become apparent that only the unattached women remain without child.

Make Me To Know My Transgressions, the grown girl from the Brotherhood, is another matter. For a start, she insists on being called by her full name and does not answer to the short form. What is more, she does not believe what she has been told about her planned fate as a slave of the bandits.

To keep her behaving the slavers had treated her well, and her master, when he had sold her, told her she was being taken to be a slave to a Prince in the mountains, and that once she was there, she would care for his children.

She even helped keep an eye on the other two to stop them running away.

The girl is obviously not right in the head. She not only still believes in the religion that she has been brought up in, but she has decided that we are deliberately keeping her away from the family she is supposed to care for. Twice now, we have caught her trying to free the slavers.

Verily has tried to convince her of her error, but Make does not believe her. In an attempt to show her how wrong she is, Verily even got Fear, while Valeria held on to her, to tell her story. Fear ended up in tears and crying for her mummies, and it took a week before Valeria would even talk to Verily. Make didn't budge in her opinion.

She has her belief and what she believes is more important than anything she might be shown. She is scandalised by the way the children dress, and often has to be stopped from upbraiding Repent. She has refused to go to school with Ruth. "It is not right for slave women to learn more than things they will need about the house. Your master, or the preachers, will tell you all you need to know," she said haughtily.

I would have laughed at that, if it had not been said so seriously. Verily did laugh, but that only made my cause harder and Make more obstinate.

I give up on the girl. I had heard the expression beautiful but dumb before, but have never seen it so well expressed. The stupid girl insists on keeping the clothes that she arrived in and refuses to wear any others. She still wears a triangular linen head cloth the whole time.

Astrid finally agreed with Sajāh that there was nothing to be done until the Princesses returned. The only thing they insisted on was that she had to attend Father Theodule's services and listen, even if she neither sang nor took communion.

She sits there with either a grim or a sulky expression the whole time, usually sitting between Verily and me. Occasionally, I hear her muttering about idolatry or corruption. Mostly we just leave her out of sight working in the kitchens; at least she works hard. She seems happy to stay away from the 'wickedness and sinfulness,' as she calls it, that lies outside the door.

We do, however, have to make sure that the keys to the cells stay with whoever is on watch, instead of just hanging up where they usually are, and she is not allowed to go near the prisoners.

The third newcomer is a girl from Greensin called Maria. She is fifteen years old and unsure whether she wants to go or to stay in the valley. She wants to know if her family, who had just set up a new assart, are still alive. The slavers refuse to talk about the subject. That refusal alone makes me think that they are dead. If they are still alive, then she will go back to them.

Finding out if they live will also have to wait until the return of the Princesses...well actually for the return of Bianca. I have tried to prepare the slavers by telling them about Bianca, and her previous successes, and what she uses to get information. Until she can find out her fate, Maria is happy to work with Naeve doing the milking. She is used to that task.

Naeve is very glad for the help. While she can still work on the cows, it is getting harder for her to reach down to milk the sheep and the goats. She wants a bench and a crush to be made so that she can lead them up and get them to stand on it to be milked, but we need all of our cured timber for houses first.

Chapter XXI

Thord
16th Duodecimus

Dwarves from the other towns of the North-East were the first to start arriving: Baron Ironfist of Deafcor, Mayor Stronghand of Diamondroot and Baron Cnut Stonecleaver of North Hole were soon there. Each had brought a hand of hands of Dwarves with them.

Smasher has started to grumble about the cost of feeding and caring for them all, as if he didn't have the taxes from their towns coming in to his purse. He has never given them much in return for their taxes before. Maybe he should start to. That was a particularly loud complaint, and I don't want them to leave yet, so I think that it is time to publicly show the power of Mousehole.

He looked around...*yes there were more than enough people in the hall for the word of what he was about to do to spread around well*...and reached into his purse, and did some silent counting in it. He stood up and waited until the Dwarves in the room were all looking at him. *A nice solemn tone then.*

"If it be t'much for some t'spend, let t'Princesses of Mousehole not only find Dwarvenholme for t'Dwarves, but let 'em also pay for t'eir return in triumph." He went up and, one by one, with a clicking sound as each was put down, laid out ten large, but light, round mithril pieces on the table in front of the Duke.

Rather let Dwarvenholme pay with these ten ancient tólf-pundr from the treasure that we found. None of the Dwarven towns made tólf-pundr today, and, despite the hardness of the metal, only a few worn coins were left from the old days and those mostly sat in the town treasuries or were traded between them at need.

My reward is seeing the expression on your face, and hearing behind me the younger Dwarves being told excitedly that each one of them is worth twelve platinum pundr, or one hundred and forty-four tólf-skillingr of gold. The last is a coin that people are more familiar with hearing about, even if very few would have held one of their own.

What I have laid out on the table is more than enough coin to feed a whole large village well for a year or more. Thord looked around at everyone's faces. *I have to remember to tell Astrid about this moment. It is almost as good as when he had brought out the Crown. Seeing Smasher's face alone has been worth the money. He has accepted the coin, but his authority will never be quite the same again. Even in his own town, my suggestions will be listened to.* Thord grinned widely.

It was another two weeks before a delegation came in from the Dwarves of the North-West. They had travelled hard and fast, but the delegation only had five hands of Dwarves in it, even if it was led by Count Snorri Trueheart, the ruler of Copperlevy itself. "The Duke is worried about talk of war outside the mountains to the west," said the Count to Thord and Smasher. "Without seeing the Crown, he does not quite believe the courier."

The Count took one look at the Crown, and sent one of his men back immediately, without even a night's sleep. I must be getting better at this story. After hearing the story from me he sent another after the first.

With each new set of arrivals, Thord repeated his story again. *I am getting practiced and better. I thought that those who first heard it would be tired of it by now, but the story of the finding of Dwarvenholme seems to be a tale which no Dwarf will ever weary of.*

He actually found himself cornered by two bards at one stage. Both wanted to hear the story over and over, again and again. One was trying to write a cycle of songs about it, while the other was memorising the tale in every detail to be made into an epic poem. *They seem to have reached some sort of agreement over who would have each of the tasks.*

The Dwarves began debating whether to go without a delegation from the South-West and it looked like the Duke was going to exert the last of his authority to force the move when, remembering what Rani had asked him to do, Thord stood and said, "T'is is t'return of t'Dwarves to our traditional city of Dwarvenholme. All of t'Dwarves should be represented. I'll not go without 'em. We'll wait."

I have amazed myself at my boldness. Before my adventures, I would scarce have spoken like that before my parents. Now, I am telling my old Duke, a Count, two Barons and a Mayor what to do. And they listened to me—quietly and without demure—and several nod in agreement with what I said.

Astrid will be proud of me. I just wish that, instead of having to get drunk with another person's wife and boast of my deeds, I could do so with my own, but my mother has said that it will be a year or even far more than that before she found the right one for me. The word will not even have reached all the Dwarves yet, and she is just starting to get letters of interest from local parents, and is still a long way from interviewing any of the potential brides that the letters talk about.

Chapter XXII

Rani
1st Duodecimus

The start back home ran into trouble the moment that they had to leave the platform and start down to the road. The horse had to be unhitched from the cart and everyone had to handle the vehicle down to the roadway.

It has taken us three days to cover a distance of less than a bowshot as we inch down the rocky slope. It is lucky that the dragon did not appear and that nothing has attacked us. It does not bode well for the rest of the return trip. I had not expected such difficulties.

Goditha is not happy. She is continually concerned with the state of the cart and had to reinforce one of the sides on the second night after the load shifted. "Why didn't you just make three or four trips back to Mousehole with the horses?" she asked crossly.

I am starting to ask myself the same question, but I cannot really admit that. I should have realised how bad the trip would be from what we had dodged around on the last trip. Bianca was the only one of us really familiar with using a cart, and on the way back she had been…distracted and none of the others knew enough to have advised me. I will make sure I don't make that mistake again.

Goditha
2nd Duodecimus

E ventually we are on the road and heading back. Despite us having a clearer path this time; and riders going ahead to clear more obstacles, the increased weight in the cart on the old and decayed road makes it a far slower trip. I am pleased that I brought so many tools with me.

She was even more pleased when, as they tried to get around a huge fallen forest giant, one that they had decided was too big and too new to chop through, a wheel broke.

I have never tried to make and replace a single spoke on a wheel before and I suddenly have three of them to do. I am glad that I spent time before the forge with Norbert, as I first had to remove the iron rim and, now the spokes are replaced, put it back on. It looks like making the spokes is the easy part. Fixing the wheel and getting around that particular tree took five days.

Rani
31st Duodecimus

I t looks like the nine days that it took on their first trip to Dwarvenholme for this leg, instead of being slower due to caution and hiding from the dragon that had been trying to find them, is going to be far quicker than we can travel now. This trip is going to take us at least four weeks.

I wonder where the Dwarves are, and if Thord has been able to delay them enough. The Year of the Water Dog turned into the Year of the Water Lizard somewhere along the way. The change went almost unremarked by them in its passage.

Chapter XXIII

Thord
27th Primus, the Year of the Water Lizard

*E*ventually, the Dwarves of the south-west did arrive, tired and dusty from *their summer travel. They had force-marched the whole way. Unlike the Dwarves from the North-West, these Dwarves were happy to believe the tales. We have both of the Barons from there, Bjorn Strikefast and Hrolfr Strongarm. They had left their villages, and each had brought many Dwarves with them, in all three hands of hands.*

With over two hundred Dwarves, this was more than the other rulers combined and caused Smasher to call in more Dwarves from his lands to go along. *He hadn't been worried about the numbers, and had been preparing to leave immediately, until I casually mused to him about why there were so many who had come here from the South-West. I admit that I had to hide my smile at the reaction.*

After some time, they were ready to leave. It had been many years since this many Dwarves had set out together in a host, with Shepherds riding ahead, and pack sheep and horses with supplies travelling along with them. As they approached Mouthguard, Thord rode there ahead of the rest to prepare the way.

Mellitus must have somehow received word of our approach. He is very nervous about this many Dwarves together, and damn him, insists on sending a patrol ahead of us to ensure that we turn off the road as we promised to do. Even then, he will only allow twenty Dwarves at a time to pass through his little fort. I am not pleased with that.

"If'n our expedition is success," Thord told him, "you'd better get used to t'is sight. When we recover Dwarvenholme t'ere'll be many coming t'is way or t'other. If'n Darkreach places obstacles in t'way of Dwarves goin' from one of t'eir areas to another, it'll not be good.

"We ha'right to go where we want in mountains. We may decide to build our own bridge 'n' village further downstream 'n' you would t'en lose our custom here. If'n I were you, I would quick seek instruction on t'is matter."

Before the Dwarves were even turned off onto the road along the mountains, a fast rider had passed them. *I guess that is the courier with a letter asking for instructions.*

The Dwarves set out following the road that Thord and the traders had come down.

Chapter XXIV

Astrid
8th Primus

"I am not much used to the world outside," Sajāh said to Astrid one day as she stood on top of the Hall of Mice looking up at the mountains, "But aren't they taking a long time? I thought that they would be back before now. Rani told me that they would be quicker with a cart and horses."

"In forests it is usually quicker with two feet," Astrid replied. "That is why we don't use horses in Wolfneck. I don't know much about carts, but I don't think that Rani thought about the amount of time that has passed since those roads were last used. She is used to her own land, which I am told has many real roads in it."

"I am just hoping that they get back before the Dwarves realise that we have all the treasure of their ancestors here. If they don't realise just how much we have, then they will not be so upset. If they see a cart and ten sets of full horse packs, then they may decide to just quietly take it from us. All we can do is keep a good lookout and hold Mousehole for them."

"Remember that I have my man up there. Verily is the same. She is just hoping that Aziz comes back. Parminder is just the same. You should try getting a good rest in our bed. It has three pregnant women, each missing their partners and it is complete with three sets of bladders with babies pressing on them. It is a miracle, firstly, that we are able to get up the mornings and get to make kaf, and secondly, that we haven't killed each other...yet."

Chapter XXV

Basil
9th Primus

*I*t seems that we are taking forever to return home. I am glad that Astrid is not here. She would have been pushing and shoving as hard as Aziz is, as I am doing in her place, and I don't want her doing that at this time. It has been five weeks, not the four that Goditha hoped for, that we have been on this road.

It is with great relief that we are turning onto the road that leads down to the Mousehole road below, without seeing either the dragon or the Dwarves. Behind us, Hulagu and the girls are trying to cover as much of the cart tracks as they can. It will soon be obvious to the Dwarves that a cart had used the road, but exactly when might be unclear. I am sure that we all hope that the Dwarves will press on, rather than come looking for us.

Chapter XXVI

Astrid

W *e are now spending a lot of time fretting and worrying. Will our husbands be back? What has happened to delay them? I may be confident in public and Verily is her usual self, but in private we are starting to do more than fret. Who else can we turn to but each other? Mostly we just hold each other as one or the other of us cries and expresses our fears, but sometimes we seek more physical relief.*

Eventually, and one by one, they made confession to Father Theodule. *At least he proves himself to be understanding and gives only light penances, reminding us that our vows will only allow us to love and truly cleave to our chosen partners. We are all happy with that, it is our worry for them, and the sudden changes in our moods, and the feelings that are washing through us that we have been concerned with. Our long-term affections are unchanged.*

N *ew Year's Eve has come and gone and there is still no sign of the treasure party. It has been nearly two months since they had left for Mousehole and I am really starting to worry. This is worse than waiting for a boat to come back from whaling. Am I a widow now? I really do understand those women now.*

Chapter XXVII

Thord
36th Secundus

Regardless of the weather, as we move along the road we are already hard at work on it. Trees are cleared, fallen rocks are moved aside and in one case, a short section of road is quickly replaced where a landslide had carried it away. Once we have passed a spot, it is cleared of centuries of overlain dirt.

Twice three hands of hands is a large number of Dwarves, and we are restoring the way to our ancestral home. We would have gotten there in far less than half the time if we had just walked, but all it took from me was a mild suggestion that we should show the world that the Dwarves are returning to their home and others had taken the idea up.

The road is not being fully repaired, that will have to wait until later, but it is now obviously a road again and could be seen to be heading to someplace that is important. Even I have pitched in.

The newly remade road wound around past the dragon's mountain and for a while the Dwarves did not watch the road as much and paid more attention to the sky above, and then behind, them. *It seems that the dragon must have fed or at least to have gone back to sleep. He is not to be seen. I think that he will be a major problem at a later time.*

I have to admit that I am relieved to see that the lead Dwarves are throwing themselves so much into the operation that there is scant attention being paid to any tracks that might exist. We nearly passed the turnoff down to the valleys, and I failed to see any tracks there and no-one seemed to notice the side road until I pointed it out.

I guess that I had to. They might need to know of it eventually and we can clear the start of it as well. I am glad that we have taken so long upon the road, but from the tracks I have seen, I need not have worried. We must have missed each other by over a month…at least.

It is now Mid-summer, and there is a continuous trail of pack animals going back behind us for food and supplies. At least after the turn-off the going is now a little easier. If anyone among the Dwarves have noticed that some of the clearing has been done already, they have not said so where I can hear.

Where the road to Mousehole split off the original road was over twenty thousand paces directly behind the Darkreach watchtower. *I can see its signal fire twinkling at night. People are starting to debate whether it is inside land that the Dwarves should claim. At least my having emphasised rebuilding the roads makes sense to everyone now. It weakens the claim of others if the Dwarves are maintaining the roads that had been long ignored.*

Chapter XXVIII

Rani
10th Primus

At last...we are on our own road. I hope that we don't have another broken wheel. Both are now repaired, but not as well as they could be. As long as everything held together, and that is not certain, we could be no more than three days from home.

I could send someone back with the news. Aziz, Basil and even Goditha would all volunteer, but I cannot forget the over-confidence of the bandits on almost getting home. We need to stay cautious. We need to increase the attention we pay to our surroundings, even though the scouts report that there are no tracks visible on the road.

After all Astrid, when she moves, hardly touches a road and always moves alongside it when she could for that exact reason. We need to send the scouts further out and keep them active and alert.

Chapter XXIX

Thord
23rd Tertius

W *e have finally reached Dwarvenholme. This time it is not me, it is the two rulers from the South-West who are slowing things down upon seeing the rocks covering the road.* "We have cleared and repaired the road up to here," said Bjorn Strikefast. "It is only right that we should repair it all the way to the gate. No-one should enter Dwarvenholme until that is done. We cannot leave it like this." *I guess that he is right in that.*

It took them, even with so many Dwarves hard at work, a full week to clear away the landslide and stabilise the slope. After that they had to remove the trees that had grown up in the way and lastly replace the road where it was needed—and that was most of its final length. When they had breaks, many Dwarves could be seen going up to the platform. There they stood and just stared at the gate or peered inside the lit path. None ventured inside.

Thord
30th Tertius

E ventually, all was ready. *The massed representatives of the Dwarves of the entire Land stand in a semi-circle outside the doors of Dwarvenholme, and not one seems to want to be the first inside. I guess that going in first might seem to be a claim to be King, so it is up to me then.* Having gone just inside, he turned around and addressed the Dwarves.

"We, the Mice, have already been in here when we killed the Masters. Now, enter and see the greatest work of our Dwarven ancestors. Remember that we did not clear all of the halls. There may still be Masters here, and there are definitely many other fell beasts."

"Remember what I told you we faced. Beware, and keep watch on those around you. Travel always in groups." He spun on his heel and strode down the corridor uncovering the nail on his shield as he did so. After a brief pause, the Dwarven horde began to follow him.

Chapter XXX

Astrid
llth Primus

The three women had just gotten out of bed late and were helping each other dress when Tabitha knocked on the door. "Harald has just taken watch outside. He thinks that they will come back tonight. He sees smoke to the north from a fire and he thinks that it was left burning late enough that it could be no accident—and they put green stuff on at the end to make sure it was seen." *It is about time.*

That afternoon the party hove into view. The Khitan were the first to be seen galloping forward to look ahead and then back to the main group. It was obvious that they wanted to get back home although probably not as much as some of those waiting wanted them back. They waved to Dulcie, who had the last watch and went up the valley.

Luckily for them, while they were away Harald had been improving the entrance to the valley by chipping away the rock that had made the track seem just like a natural shelf, and although the work was not finished, and the road was still very rough, it was now much more like a proper path, and so it was easier for the cart. Losing a wheel and having the cart fall into the river at this stage would have been a disaster. Why the original inhabitants had left it as rough and almost un-hewn stone none of them could guess.

When they had passed through the gate a feeling of release swept through the group. Seeing Mousehole ahead with their partners, dressed in their good clothes, and their friends waving and yelling, brought to them the relief of being home at last. And, hopefully, safe for a while. As they came up to the village, the Mice ran out to greet them and that night they had a proper welcome home celebration.

Father Christopher's little pet, which somewhat to his surprise had stayed with him through the entire trip, was shown to the children, and had its significance explained carefully before it was fed and placed above the door of the Hall of Mice on the roofline.

Chapter XXXI

Sajāh
13th Primus

*A*fter the emotions of returning home and the tearful re-unions that followed, few of the returnees, apart from Christopher and Bianca, are up for
morning Mass. It is very quiet this morning.

*I am happy with the way I ran the village. It had been hard with so many
people away.* She looked with relief out over the courtyard, as the people
started to go about their business after the service. *Although it seems to be but
little different to the way it had been the week before, the prosaic scene seems
somehow to be happier.*

*Everyone is going about their tasks with a more cheerful air. People are
sounding in good spirits, talking to each other with more joy. Small jokes
cause people to laugh and the children are running around before school
and playing.* Ruth came out and called the children together. *See, they come
running and laughing, instead of the silent walking that has been common
over the last few weeks.*

Rani

*A*part from not being able to make love to Theo-dear, if I feel like it, the
worst part of having Fear in our bed is that she cannot learn to sleep in
and, when she wakes, she cannot get out of bed stealthily. Now I am awake,
and my wife has rolled over and gone back to sleep.* She got up, dressed and
went to sit in the morning sun to think.

Today we need to work out what to do about the prisoners...no...that can wait another day. Let us have a day without that pain first. We need to put the treasure somewhere and find out how much we have. I suspect that, leaving aside the magic that Haven has accumulated over centuries, and we will never equal that, my little village may now have itself a treasury to equal that of the entire southern Kingdom.

I wonder how Thord is, and what he is up to with the Dwarves. Have they accepted the boundaries that we set out in the letter? Will Thord even come back? He is now the only one of the Mice out in the dangerous world. While we can still be attacked in the village, it is a place of some safety for us. She smiled.

Forget the land of my birth, here is now the real Haven...outside these cliffs lies who knows what. Some of the Masters may still be out there somewhere, and in all likelihood their agents are scattered all over the Land. We cannot necessarily trust any stranger that comes through our gate.

Perhaps we would be able to trust our first traders who came to us totally unsuspecting of what they would find, but how many others will come with instructions to pry and spy as much as to trade?

It seems that Bianca and Christopher will have to greet all our newcomers: Bianca to use her sense, whatever it is, and Christopher to try and feel good or evil in a person, as priests seem to be able to do somehow—in a similar unexplainable fashion to the way that mages sense magic.

We also have to work out what to do with the slaves that had been brought here. Astrid has told me briefly about Make. We cannot just send her back to the Brotherhood and her owner. She would just end up being sold again to pay another debt. Equally, we cannot keep her here if she is always going to be a threat to the village.

Astrid doesn't even think that she can be sent out into the world on her own as a free person. Surely the girl cannot be as stupid as Astrid has said she is. I will need to find out. I didn't see the girl last night. I don't think that I have seen her since our return.

Much as I dislike looking at the cards to discern my own future, I am going to have to do so again for the welfare of the village. Further back in the house, she could hear Theodora, now up as well, and Valeria trying to get Fear fed and out of the door because school would start soon. *I have to worry about them as well. I have taken on these responsibilities, which now spread to,* she did a quick count, *over eight hands of people and they rely on my choices and decisions.*

It is now far too late to back out of all of this and go back to being just a Battle Mage and teacher of Haven. I have broken caste, perhaps irretrievably, and thrown in my lot with these people. And those eight hands, judging from what I can see, would soon increase by at least two hands soon; and possibly even more. Hulagu's women are not letting anything show, but I suspect that they have also joined the ranks of the breeders.

Anything we do now, before next summer at least, cannot be done with the full strength of the village. Perhaps more importantly, from now on we will always have behind us the knowledge that we have children to protect, whatever else happens.

During a day filled with re-acquaintance and rest, with repair and renewal, Rani sent Valeria around to everyone to get them to gather after the evening meal. *The message was that they needed to work out what was the next thing that the village had to do. I need to have a word with Father Christopher myself.*

That night, when all were gathered and either seated comfortably or standing for a better view, Rani stood to address them from the front of the hall. *My chair and a small table are behind me. My cards are sitting openly behind me, lying on the table.* She looked around. *Except for the watch on the roof of the Hall of Mice, and I have Theo-dear taking that, everyone is gathered around.*

"Thank you for interrupting your evening and gathering together. I am happy to say that we appear to have completed at least some of the destiny that was placed in front of us nearly a year ago. For those who have forgotten, when we set out to come here we were guided, not only by the personal prophesies we mentioned that some had received, but also by a reading that I did of my cards and by a verse from the Christian Holy Book that Father Christopher found."

"I have gathered you all here now so that we may do the same sort of thing to find out what next lies ahead of us. Father Christopher will be doing his reading after he has said Mass tomorrow, but I will do mine now." She moved to behind the table and sat down. *I have thought hard about whom to call on next.*

"Lakshmi…" The woman that she had named jumped a little with surprise. "In so many ways you have been one whose life has changed the most by what has happened to you since you were taken and brought here. I would ask you to represent the village and to come here now and to shuffle these cards until you are happy with them."

Lakshmi has stood but she seems hesitant to come forward. Harald pats her on the bottom and nods at her. She is moving forward very nervously. I could be wrong, but from the way she looks at me, she knows of my family and seems scared by what she knows. I will ignore that.

"As you shuffle think about what lies ahead, not just for you, but for the whole of Mousehole. Those who have been here for some time, and those who have arrived more recently."

Lakshmi picked up the parchment cards and began to shuffle them. *Despite her normal deftness she nearly dropped them twice.* Eventually, she put them down in front of Rani and quickly moved back beside Harald, who gave her a quick kiss and a hug with his arm, which he left around her for comfort as Rani prepared to look at the cards.

"Normally, when a reading is done, you use more cards than I will use tonight and you take a lot more time. In the last two readings that I have done however, because of the restrictions that have been placed on true sight I have only used four, and possibly because they were so important, their meaning was obvious."

"We will see what happens this time. It may well be that we have only completed a part of our destiny. I do know that some have said this very loudly." *I mean you when I say 'very'.* She looked meaningfully at Astrid. *Damn, she just smiles at me.*

Rani laid out the four cards without doing anything to them and paused for some time before turning them over in order. The first card turned showed nine goblets standing on each other with water cascading down from the top one to the bottom three. There was some writing on the card. On one side of the card was a person kneeling and seemingly petitioning a ruler—a man in a throne with a crown on his head. "The nine of cups."

She turned the next card. On each side of the card was a man arrayed for war, one of whom held a woman, who stood between them, by the arm. Also between them, but below them, as if a part of the contest, was a sheath of three swords. "The three of swords."

She turned the third card. Again, it bore some writing and two figures, but this time the figures were a man and a woman. The woman had a club in her hand, while the man bore a drop spindle. Between them was a sheaf of four rods and around them were words in the same script as the last card. "It is the four of staves."

She turned the last card. It was upside down and showed the two moons with only part of each one lit up in a crescent. Beneath the moons were two women. One played a sitar while the other danced. Behind the women was a rural scene with a woman archer shooting at a stag. "The moons—reversed."

She closed her eyes and held her hands, face down over the cards. *Now to divine what the cards mean in the context we find ourselves in.* She emptied her mind of her own thoughts, holding the cards in the sight of her third eye.

As she spoke, as it had in Evilhalt, her voice became slightly more detached. "The first card stands in the position of the enquirer, the person who is asking the question. In this case it is we the Mice, the people of Mousehole. The card is the nine of cups and the writing is in Old Speech and says success."

"In this position it signifies a place or people of a new beginning, and with difficulties overcome as well as, possibly, a favourable agreement. This card describes all of the persons in this room, in one way or the other; some have one meaning attached to them, others two and indeed some have all three."

"The second card stands for the history and influences, those things that hang over the question, often without the knowledge of the person who asks. Here we see the three of swords. It is a card of conflict and, in most readings means that there is strife between two mighty forces for possession of something or of someone. On the card two warriors lie in dispute over a woman."

"We know that some of us have been given destinies. We know that evil was in this village and the source of it lay in Dwarvenholme. We thought that those destinies were done, and we were possibly finished with them. I believe that what this card tells us is that the battle is far greater than what we have known before. Perhaps it is just one battle that is a part of a larger and more extensive war and, indeed, is merely a tiny part of the whole."

She paused. "The third card is what should be done. In some ways it is a contradiction. It is the four of staves. This is a card of peace. The words say 'love' and 'pleasure' and 'respite'. It is a card that says to do little but attend to our own affairs, to take some time away from the battle. Perhaps it is best said that we should not seek trouble, but that we should tend to our own interests as best we can for a while. It will only be temporary, but we should look after ourselves and care only for those around us for a while."

"The last card is upside down, which is called reversed. The card itself is the major card of The Moons and in itself is a card of significance for all women. Reversed, this card will usually mean that there will be the light of dawn with clarity becoming apparent. It means a new hope for the querants and particularly for the women among them."

Rani lowered her hands, and opened her eyes and looked around at the onlookers. "I am surprised," she said. "Unlike my last reading, which counselled urgent action to bring people to justice, these cards tell us something very different." She pointed at each card as she spoke.

"We have here a new beginning in our valley. For all of us, in one way or another, the past is put behind us and we are new people. Around us rages a vast conflict of which we have seen only a tiny glimpse. I would venture to say, from what I feel, that we are caught in the eternal battle of good and evil and, for some reason that I cannot discern, have been thrust into an important role."

"We should, however, now take some time out from our battle for ourselves and our partners and our children. There will be birth and growth to be experienced and enjoyed. We should enjoy calm before our next move, perhaps, a greater battle, the nature of which shall become apparent as we do what we feel we have to do."

"It is an odd reading, but very clear in its meaning. I can only say that I very much look forward to what the good Father has to add to this tomorrow."

She looked around the room. "Again, I thank you all for coming. We will hear from Father Christopher in the morning…and then we have some unpleasant business to transact as well. Sleep well and think on what you have seen." She gathered her cards and wrapped them in their cloth before placing them in her belt and leaving to tell Theodora what had transpired.

Rani
14th Primus

M*ass is very well attended this morning. Our chief priest has made special mention of the fact that today was the feast day of Saint Hilary, the patron of lawyers, and that we have matters to consider later today concerning judgement. He sought the intercession of his Saint to assist us in making a wise decision. I admit to a rare prayer to Ganesh on the same subject.*

When Father Christopher had finished the service, he moved to behind the tall table with a box on it that he was using as a lectern and looked around. "It is now time for me to see if I can add anything to what the Princess said last night. I will again use only the older books, partly because that is what I used before, and partly in deference to those who do not use the Gospels." He looked around the room. "However, first I will ask all of you who can in conscience do so, to kneel in prayer and I will ask for guidance to be given us."

After the prayer was finished, he closed his eyes and reached in front of himself for Bianca's Old Testament. His hands found it and allowed it to fall open on the table, after which he placed his finger somewhere in it at random. When he had it placed, he opened his eyes and looked down.

"I am reading," he said, as he looked up again, "from Isaiah, the thirtieth Chapter and the eighteenth verse." *His eyes return to where his finger lies on the page:* "'And therefore will the Lord wait that he may be gracious unto you, and therefore will he be exalted, that he may have mercy upon you: for the Lord is a God of judgement, therefore blessed are they that wait for him.' Amen."

He is looking up from his reading and directly at where I sit beside him. "I believe that once again, as we did in Evilhalt and earlier here, we have a concurrence of opinion between our two sets of guidance. God has clearly guided us and we are instructed to wait and that judgement will come in time." *He is turning to the others now.*

"Like the Princess, I am puzzled by this and what can come from it, but what I have just read seems to be quite clear and in agreement with what we heard last night." He bowed his head silently for a moment before he gave a short prayer of thanks, followed by the benediction and urging everyone to move off to have breakfast. *I need to think and pray as well. There is no doubt on what we must do, but why? What are we preparing for?*

Chapter XXXII

Rani
14th Primus

*H*ow do we question and try the prisoners? They are going to die. From what the girls have told me, I know that. However, before they die, it is essential that we find out what the prisoners know. This 'time of waiting' we are having is also a time of renewal and rest and regrouping. Surely a part of that is gaining information to help us stay safe and for seeing what comes to us.

It is a time to reflect on what lies ahead and to think. We already have the rough location of one of the Masters' pentagrams, somewhere on the docks in Pavitra Phāṭaka, and Conrad, who used it, is now dead, but the device is still there and could have others using it. If we can locate the users, then we can get other names as well.

These men probably know who one of the Masters' people was...Astrid's former betrothed in Wolfneck. What we need to know is how far the whole network spreads. There has to be at least one contact in the Brotherhood, possibly one in Darkreach and there could be several in Freehold.

Bianca has said that the bandits had placed men with her caravan by getting a friend to poison some of the guards. That should mean that there is at least one agent in Toppuddle, at least temporarily, and somehow, they knew of the old book that was on the caravan. That would mean that they had at least one person in a position to find that out.

There may even be more there, seeing what Theodora told me about what the Metropolitan said about Freehold preparing for war. Is there someone also working in the Caliphate? Ahmed and his carpet had apparently visited there regularly, but it is possible that may have been for his own reasons. We have no idea. What is more there is almost certainly at least one in the Swamp.

Conrad had not known where, but it seems inevitable.

Each of these areas presents its own problems. Can I even go back to Haven now? The Brotherhood will kill most of our people on sight as devil worshippers. Ayesha may have difficulty in the Caliphate, as will most of our women.

Freehold will be as harsh on Father Christopher as the Brotherhood will be, and I am reluctant to go anywhere without our healer. He has kept us alive, at great cost and risk to himself. In Wolfneck, the man we seek probably has the backing of the community and Astrid will not necessarily have that.

Apart from visits to the Metropolitan at Greensin, ironically possibly the only safe place for us to actually start will be Darkreach. Who would have thought that everything that I have been taught about that place is now overturned, and it will be possibly the one place we can venture with some degree of security, that is if we can find any shelter at all outside our valley.

I can put it off no longer. I discussed what to do with Bianca and Astrid and their partners last night. Bianca had told me what she thought about why the questioning had become easier as time went by and the time has come, with Ruth having the children in their classes now, to put everything into place.

She sighed and dressed and got Theodora to do the same and sent Valeria to get the rest of the players ready for their little play. *I hope that those who will unwittingly be both the audience and also the key players will take the lines that they are supposed to use and react to the planted cues properly. Is this what rulers really do? Is it all really a play and a bluff?*

The prisoners had been shackled and gagged and were brought by the farmer Giles and Hulagu, two of the largest of the men, to the hall. *They are staring wildly about them. Basil, by far the smallest of the three, led them and he makes it obvious that he is in charge of them all.*

The three village men are all dressed in black leather and look as close to being in uniform as we can make them. We sit on the largest chairs up at the front wearing our Court garb. Beside my Princess is Aziz, dressed in his leather kilt and with his huge heavy scimitar unsheathed and laid across his crossed arms.

Beside me is Bianca, dressed like the men in black leather, but with most of her knives strapped on the outside of her clothes for a change and looking very menacing. She has Verily behind her dressed all in brown leather, as we cannot put her in black, but she also has her knives strapped on visibly. She looks like an assistant. Father Christopher stands beside Bianca in his vestments.

Most of the rest of the village stood around in a ring with a gap in the centre. They had been told to dress in as warlike a fashion as they could. *It is an utter failure for little pregnant Parminder and tiny Bilqīs is not much better. She looks more like an angry Gnome than anything else. At least she has chosen to dress and look like a mage and the slavers will not know that the wands she has strapped to her are just empty sticks at present.*

Rani looked to the side. *Bryony and Goditha hold Make fast between them so that she can see what happens. Both look alert to the likelihood of her doing something stupid.*

The men were forced to their knees in front of the Princesses. "I am the Princess Rani Rai and this is my partner, Princess Theodora. If you look at her, you will see that she is from Darkreach, indeed, that she is from the Imperial line. I believe that you have already talked with Astrid. Between you stands Astrid's husband. He is an officer in Hrothnog's pay."

"Before we start, I should in conscience tell you that your lives are already forfeit...not for being slavers as such, but for being slavers who sold children for sex. We have followed Darkreach in this area by making such a sale a capital crime, wherever and whenever it was done."

"Your lives are also forfeit for what you have done to some of the women here when you have been selling people to the bandits that ruled here before us, their rape and maltreatment. The only thing that is in question for us now, is for us to decide exactly how you are going to die. I think we will largely leave that question in your own hands and let you, to a degree, decide your own fate."

She paused and looked around at the women and drew a breath. "I believe that Astrid has told you how others have died at our hands. This," and she pointed, "is the Presbytera Bianca. She is the one who Astrid told you about." Bianca smiled sweetly at the men and started, as if unconsciously, slipping one of her knives in and out of its sheath just a little way. *Their eyes widened a bit at that. She looks so innocent.*

"We have decided that the first one of you who talks, the one who tells us who gave you orders, who gave you messages, who gave you shelter and anything else you know...the one who satisfies the person who is asking you questions first, that one will die quickly. The other will be handed to the ladies, some of whom you know intimately, to do with as they will."

"Previously, we have been rushed for time and we have made them finish an execution with the fall of the dark. Now we have far more time available to us, and we may let them take more time, perhaps even a week or more."

The men are straining at their gags, twisting and staring wildly at the women behind them. The women are beginning to look both wild and happy at the same time. Some of the women have the faces of feral beasts instead of their own...quite scary.

"If neither of you is willing to talk when you are first asked, then the Presbytera will have to talk seriously to you, before you get to leave this plane. As well, then I will not say who will go quickly and who will go slowly. You will pass away from this world only as the ladies behind you allow you to. Nod if you understand me."

The men are both nodding. Sweat is standing out on one man's brow and his gaze is fixed on Verily. Rani turned her head. *She has a knife in her hand and blowing the man kisses and then making cutting gestures with her hands as she points to his groin...not nice.*

Rani looked at the men's attendants. "Take them out now and keep them separate. Record exactly what they say, and the first man to have his recorder back here with a full confession will win a speedy death." She nodded, and the men were hauled to their feet and carted off.

I can see from his groin that one of them has already wet himself in his fear. Bianca silently followed one, and Verily the other to remind them of the next step if they did not talk.

Rani waited until they were gone. "Thank you all for coming like this. I think that we will see them back soon, so you can either wait or you can go and get some rest, or you can even go and watch them confess. You will not miss anything here as we will make sure to call for you when they come back." She stopped talking. *Let them work out whether to go or stay...now the next part.* "We would like to see Make and Maria next."

Several of the women were hurrying out of the room, *possibly to cheer on the questioning.* While that was happening, Make was brought forward, while Maria came up by herself. Rani turned to Theodora. "Well, that seemed to work well."

Theodora nodded. "I was taught that a brave man dies only once, but a coward dies a thousand deaths. These men are surely evil men, and I think that evil people have some flaw inside them that will make them weak and, at heart, cowards...that is if you can find the right thing to break them. I think that we have found that thing."

Make is now standing nervously in front of us. She is wondering on her fate. Rani looked at her. *She is trembling and looks ready to collapse, she keeps stealing glances at Theodora and at Aziz.* "Someone bring the silly girl something to sit on." Valeria quickly brought a stool and the girl collapsed on to it.

She looks terrified. "Make, you have done nothing wrong and will not be punished. You are here because I have been told that you think that these men were helping you, and that you were going to a happy place. Talk again to any of the women here after this is over. They have told me that you refuse to listen to them and quote from some strange book that is used in your old land in place of the Bible that Christopher uses."

"This time when they talk, listen to what they say. Particularly, you should listen to all that Verily tells you. She was brought here by men just like this when she was only a little girl and she was used badly. The man that sold her believed exactly what your master believed when he sold you and lied to you about it. Verily's old master was evil and the man who sold you is evil. These men we are condemning here today are evil. Soon you will hear them speak of their wickedness and what they have done." *She still looks terrified and, yet she shakes her head.*

Now I need to say something to the other girl. "I am sorry, Maria, there is no easy way to say this, but we think that they killed your family, or had a part in killing them." She looked from one to the other. "It does not matter what they told you, or what you were told by your old master," she looked at Make, "they were bringing you both here to be used for sex by other evil people. You both need to realise this. Now we will all wait to hear what they say."

Make is still shaking her head. She really is as stubborn and fixed in her belief as Astrid said and she looks set to continue to refuse to believe any proof we give her.

*I*t has been about half an hour and people are sitting around and talking. No-one wants to leave. We have refreshments, but the atmosphere in the room is very subdued. Make, on her stool, has been moved to sit beside me with her attendants standing beside her. From where she is now she will be able to see the faces of the slavers.*

Maria was on the other side of the Princesses sitting on another stool but with Danelis, who also came from the north, seated beside her, holding her hand for comfort. *She will burst into tears any moment. Outside a voice can be heard telling people to gather again, but it seems like near everyone is here already.* Suddenly there was a commotion at the door and raised and desperate voices could be heard.

"I was first," said one.

"No, no, it was me," said the other.

There were two slapping sounds. "Silence, both of you." *That is Basil.* "I want nothing at all from you until I tell you to speak."

The two were brought in and forced, again, to their knees, glaring at each other. "It seems that these two prime examples of humanity are brothers, in both senses of the word," said Basil. "They both have the same father and they come from the Brotherhood and still attend its services."

"Which was first?"

Both men started to claim it was them, until Basil again slapped them both hard on the side of the head, hard enough to rock their heads. "I have told you to be quiet," he said. *He seems to have already lost patience with them. One now has a trickle of blood coming from where one of Basil's rings seems to have cut him.*

Addressing me he continues: "To be honest, I think that they both put their foot on the step at the same time. So, they are both first, and they are also both last. You will have to decide which dies easily and which does not."

The men started to clamour again, and again Basil slapped them hard enough to make their heads rock. They went quiet.

"I will do that after we have heard them. Do we have their words written down?" asked Rani.

"We do. We have names, we have places, we know where they are from and who gave them instructions and it is good information. They both gave as their main contact a man who works under, what they call the First Disciples or the Heads of their so-called Council of Elders, who are apparently Brother Enoch and Sister Will-of-the-Lord Malachi."

Rani looked sideways at Make. *She is shaking her head again.* Basil continues: "It seems that all the women, and some of the men have these stupid long names. This person is in charge of their taxes, what they call tithes. He tells the slavers who is having trouble paying their tithes and then they visit him and, if he has a pretty girl in his household, they convince him to sell them that girl to get his taxes forgiven."

"While Make was born a slave of a slave woman, the man who sold her was her father. But apparently Repent was the man's own full daughter from his real wife. I will let them talk now. Which one do you want first?"

Rani disdainfully pointed at the man whose trousers were stained with the proof of his cowardice. The man swallowed once and then started. *He keeps looking fearfully about, particularly at Verily, who stands beside him with a very fixed expression on her face, as cold as ice and as still as a stone statue, a picture of detachment and cold vengeance. Kali would love her.*

"I am Amos," he said. "I have been doing this now for six years. Micah, he is the man that the policeman mentioned, asked me to do some work for him to pay my debts. None of my females were pretty and so he asked me to bring a slave here. It is dangerous to bring pretty girls through the lands of the Khitan unbelievers. They are sinners and thieves and may try and steal a slave away from you. Now we bring one or two here each year, they are almost all children and they are usually not here when we come back next. We brought one that the policeman tells me you still have here alive. Make and Maria are the first full grown females that we have brought here for quite some time."

"Did you know what you were bringing them here for?" *The man swallows and nods.*

Christopher stepped forward and interrupted then. "How does this sit with your beliefs? Surely you know that you are a self-condemned sinner?" he said. He turned to Rani: "Sorry, I could not help myself with that question and, while I am talking, I have to mention that he absolutely reeks of evil. Any priest, from any religion, should know this. If he is going to his Church and none have noticed, it is because they all smell the same."

"Interesting." Turning back to Amos, she said: "Answer the good Father. Why do your priests not condemn you?"

The look Amos gave our priest was pure hatred. "All women need firm direction from their betters…from men. Females have less of a soul than men do anyway, and female slaves have no soul at all. We are told that what is done to them does not count as a sin. Selling them is like selling a chair.

"We fornicated as we wanted while we were here, the same as you do with your slaves, but here you don't have to worry about breaking them and losing money. But we know it was not as if it were with real women with souls, so our slate is clean and our marriage vows remain unblemished."

"So, you admit having sex with the girls here?" *I hope that Verily, whose face has just gotten even harder, if that is possible, does not lash out with that knife. The man nods and looks sideways at Verily. He seems to be hoping the same.* Rani turned to Make. "Do you hear what he is saying?"

"You are making him lie," she said. "You have told him what to say."

"Then would you like to ask him a question that I could not have given him an answer to?" asked Rani.

Make's face looks puzzled. Finally, she spoke: "What was the name of the family that you were bringing me to so that I could care for their children?" *She looks smug as she sits back. I don't believe it. She seems confident that she will soon have an answer.*

"Don't you get it, you dumb bitch?" said Amos, and was rewarded with a hard slap from Basil that nearly knocked him over. He recovered, the side of his head already growing red. *He nearly said something to Basil, but stopped himself. He turns again to Make.*

"There was no family. The God-forsaken bastard that is your father was desperate. He had owed his tithes for several years, and we had threatened him with the Flails-of-God, to enquire as to his faith and to take everything from him. He gave you to us this trip, and we were to come back next year for his own ten-year old daughter by his wife."

"You know that she was sick when we left, otherwise we would have her now as well, but we were to go and get her when she was well. He just told you that story so that you would come quietly. It worked, and, what is more, the story was even his own idea as well." *Finally Make looks a bit shocked, but there is still a stubborn look on her face.*

Amos shook his head and spoke to Rani. "I hope you take this into account when you make your decision." He turned to face Make: "I was even promised that I would have you first. All that modesty and hiding away while we were travelling was getting me excited."

"We could have had you any time on the trip, but decided not to as the better you were treated the more biddable you were. You…" *He stopped what he was going to say and glanced at Basil* "…should listen to what they are saying. I am not an evil man, no, that is wrong, I am a goodly Church-going and God-fearing man, but what I do to you does not count against my soul. I can fornicate with you all I want, and God will not judge me. I can lie to you, I can punish you, and I can know you in any way I want. You do not count against my sins as you are not really a person. You have been to church, even though you are not saved and never can be. If you have listened to what was said there, then you should know this."

He turned to Rani. "Do I have to say any more to her? She is so dumb that…well…no wonder her master wanted to get rid of her. It is a wonder she can dress herself." *Now there is a look of shock on Make's face.*

"Very well. Now let us hear from the brother." She turned to face the other man.

"I am Matthias, and I am also a God-fearing man. I have done what I have said I have done, but I will die with a clean conscience because what I did is sanctioned by the Church. Brother Micah told me so himself. The Church uses this as a way to raise money from the pagans outside the lands of the Blessed."

"These girls are only property. They have no souls, and so we commit no sin. Even though they can talk and act as if they are real people, they are not, so they may as well help the Church by giving it money for its Crusade against the Devil worshipers that surround it."

"We sell them here, and we sell them in Freehold, and with the money we raise we better equip the armies of the Lord to eventually vanquish you all and rule you sternly in the name of the Lord. We are simply good stewards in using the gifts that God has given us to have dominion over." *He sounds proud and defiant.*

"So, you believe that you are doing the work of the Church?" *I look at my own priests and both of their faces are red, and they look almost ready to explode.*

"Yes, and I know that you will make me a martyr because you are servants of Satan and seek to bring down God's church. I know that you hate us because you cannot bear hearing the Truth that is held inerrant in our Holy Books. I would just prefer to die quickly rather than risk becoming apostate through pain."

"Do you hear this, Make?" Rani turned. *The girl cannot answer. She has her face buried in Bryony's bosom and is weeping silently. Bryony's face, looking at the man, almost mirrors that of Verily.* Rani turned back to face the men. "What has happened to Maria's family?"

"They are dead," said Matthias. Maria began weeping as Danelis tried to comfort her. *She starts to stand and sits down again.* "We did not kill them." Matthias continued quickly and dismissively. "Some Unbelievers did it for money. We decided to add to our stock on the way and we asked them if there were any pretty virgins in the area and they told us there was one. We gave them instructions on what to do, and they did what we told them to. It does not matter what happens to her and her family anyway. They are predestined to be condemned to hell as Unbelievers. We just had them sent there sooner."

Rani shook her head. *I don't quite believe what I am hearing. I feel sick in my stomach.* "I don't think we need to hear any more from you. You both condemn yourselves out of your own mouths. I look forward to stepping on you in your next lives." She looked up at the crowd. "Does anyone have anything to say on how they should die and if either deserves any mercy?" *This starts a clamour from the women, but Christopher stands forward.*

"These men are evil," he said. "I had not understood quite how evil they were until I heard them condemn themselves and felt what I feel from them… but, having said that, there has been enough suffering in this valley. We are risking our own souls here. Although the Bible says, 'an eye for an eye', it also asks 'who can have compassion on the ignorant?' and 'let not mercy and truth forsake thee'."

"I pray that they both be given a quick death so that we can show ourselves to not be the same as the people that used to live here." He turned to face the crowd. "By our mercy, and only through our mercy and love, can we show that we are better than the bandits."

"We need to show ourselves that these people," *he waves a hand towards Amos and Matthias,* "are truly the forsaken of God, sunk deep in the pit of evil, and we, by showing our faith through our works and deeds, are fully justified in our faith and not just making a noise with our mouths. Let the most grieved kill them certainly, but let it be a quick and merciful death." *He stands back and reaches for his wife's hand.*

Now what do we do? I promised these women the lives of these men, and yet Christopher is right. Rani turned to Christopher: "Does your holy book not say that blasphemers should be stoned?" *Christopher nods.* "Does what they have said count as blasphemy?" *Christopher nods again. He is not sure where I am going here.*

"Well, I think that there are many here who are grieved by them, but I agree that their deaths should not be drawn out." She addressed the crowd. "Bind them and take them down to near the river where there are many rocks of different sizes. You may all throw rocks at them until they die. Personally, I believe that Father Christopher is right in what he says, and I hope that you use large rocks and that their death is quick, but the choice is on your own consciences and I will not judge anyone on the choice that they make."

"When you have all returned," *Maria is already rising to follow the others.* "we will determine what is to be done with Maria and Make." *Make is about to faint.* "Not that they are about to be punished or harmed."

Protesting and pleading for a quick death, the two men are dragged away. Their hands are already being grabbed and bound behind their backs. Father Christopher went with them urging them to repent and confess their sins so that they may die with their souls cleansed and was rewarded with being spat upon by Matthias. He just wiped away the spittle and kept up his work.

Once they have left, I turn to Make. "Do you now see that what we have told you is true?" *Make is crying and she turns back to me.*

"I don't know what to believe. I really don't. I cannot believe that my Church is evil, but if what they say is true, it must be. I am confused. I know that I am not like a chair. I…I promise you this…that I will talk to the other women and this time I will listen." *She pauses and then in a despairing voice adds:* "I don't know what to think." *She returns to crying on Bryony, who is patting her hair awkwardly.*

The return is swift, given the distance. "What was done with the bodies?"

"We threw them in the river," said Verily "As would have been done with the children who they brought here, and would have happened with any of us when we were killed. We killed them quickly, as the Father suggested. I was tempted to do otherwise, but on the way down I realised that the Father was right. I am better than them. I will not lower myself to their level. I will show mercy. We threw big rocks at their heads and they died almost straight away."

Her resolute firmness suddenly dissolves and she runs to Aziz and buries herself in his arms. The Hob wraps his arms around her as she sobs against his chest.

Maria indicated that, knowing what she now did, it was likely that she would probably stay here, but that she remained unsure. *She is too upset at present to make up her mind and the matter is put aside until later.*

Chapter XXXIII

Rani
14th Primus

The next issue that had to be dealt with was the treasure that had come from Dwarvenholme. Rani had it all brought into the hall and looked at what was put before her. The books had all been taken away and, with those that they had brought out on the first trip, had been put in the library to be looked at and studied later. Christopher and Theodule and Ruth were, however, already having some excited conversations about some of the volumes that they had glanced at.

Now we have a pile of objects. There are weapons, light stands, plates and goblets. There is also jewellery of all kinds. I see necklaces, rings, bracelets, brooches, arm bands, torques and cloak-pins. We have seeming mountains of gems; and golden and platinum and even some mithril coins. It is all too much. What is more, we are not even really using money. It seemed that each is just doing what they need to do, sometimes helping another who had helped them, and sometimes just keeping on doing what they had done under the bandits.

If what is here was added to what was already in Mousehole and we then shared it out and we all went and lived in a city, then not one of us would ever have to work again. Our children's children would still be living well. Having said that, no-one seems interested in leaving, so that is irrelevant.

Perhaps the best thing to do is to just share out those things which could have a use and put the rest in store. Someday it might come in useful for us. How it will be useful, I don't know, but there is enough wealth here to buy an army, even to buy an army that was arrayed against us. Perhaps that may, one day, be the use that Mousehole will gain from it.

Rani had Valeria fetch Eleanor, who had returned to her home. "Take anything that you need to help you with your making of jewellery. Take only what you need now, you can always get more of it later."

Eleanor looked at the pile and started picking through the jewellery. "I will take all that needs repair," she said. "One of the best ways to learn and get better is to repair things. That way you see how they were made, and you have to force yourself to look at the work of different craftspeople and to follow the way that they made them."

She hurried away and came back with a bucket and began to pick over the pile, and placed broken pieces, or those missing a gem, into the bucket. After she had finished that task she went and got a smaller bucket, and began to pick over the gems, taking gems of different values and different sizes that might fill some of the gaps that she had noticed.

The two buckets normally used to hold water, between them hold enough wealth to buy whole large towns as well as the land around them. Red and blue and green and yellow light reflects off the contents and they make a noise like gravel in the bucket of a builder when they are hefted. It is…awesome.

While Eleanor was working, Rani was looking over the pile of objects. *I should be able to rekindle the magic in the light stands. Having been used once for this purpose it should be easier to do it again, I think. I have never tried. This way, each house will have at least one permanent light source, and then candles will only occasionally need to be used. That is a good idea. It will mean that everyone will be able to have some of the treasure for themselves as proof of their wealth.*

Rani looked at the plates and goblets. *Some are too grand for everyday use…well, maybe not for Princess. But for everyone else they are.* She started to sort out the ones that could be shared out like the light stands. She realised that what she was collecting was a fabulous set of plate. *Like our best clothes, which we save for important occasions, these can be saved for important dinners or when we have visitors that we want to impress.*

She had Valeria bring Sajāh to her, and she shared these thoughts. Sajāh agreed with her and, summoning help, began to remove the chosen pieces and select more. "There is a storage room in the Hall of Mice that I can get Dulcie and Tabitha to work on with shelves and a better door, and we can make it a strong-room for the plate," she said smugly. "This will polish up beautifully and we will have it there ready for when we need it," she said proprietarily as she looked over the collection.

Rani then went over the jewellery that Eleanor had left. There were still many pieces there. Some were nearly as lavish as Astrid's ruby necklace, some were only small rings. *Some of these should be shared out, but we need to keep some for the wedding gifts, and even more so, some should be kept as gifts for outside the village.*

She went and got Theodora, and asked her to choose some pieces that would be suitable for rulers. *My wife is more in touch with both jewellery and the tastes of the nobility than I am. Darkreach, Haven, Freehold and the Caliphate should all be provided for.*

Next, she got her to pick lesser pieces, ones that would be suitable for the rulers of individual towns and villages if they decided to hand them out. When this was done, they took these items to the hidden cupboard in the Hall of Mice.

Next, they picked over the pile looking for wedding gifts, trying to choose pieces that would suit each of the unmarried women of the village. To help them in this they gathered in Astrid, Verily and Bianca, who had been talking outside when they returned to the hall. They all had fun making suggestions as to what would suit each person.

When this was done, they still had a small heap of jewellery left over, something that perhaps would fit into two more large buckets with a bit left over. *Outside of our valley this would be a major treasure. Here it is the leftovers. Tonight, I will invite everyone to take a couple of items that they want for themselves.*

The rest of the gems we will put in store against need. Once we work out the exact orientations of the mages, some will be needed to make them items to add to their ability to cast. Just as I, as a fire mage from the moon of the dragon, work better with a single ruby set in mithril on me when I cast, so shall all of our apprentices have their aids…when we can work out their exact moons…and that is one thing I intend doing over the next few months.

This leaves the coin. Deciding to keep it is one thing. Where to keep it is another. Eventually she realised where. *There is already one place large enough and with a lock. We have the Masters' contact room in the mine. It is ideal. We can keep the spare gems there as well. The few weapons that we found and brought back we can take to the armoury until Father Christopher has determined what they are, and whether it is safe to use them. I already have the helpers handy. It is time to get the wealth stored away.*

That night Rani announced her plans for the wealth of the valley, and asked if anyone had better ideas. It seemed that no-one did and they all had a fun night picking and choosing items from the pile. There were a few minor disagreements over who saw something first, but there was really so much there that they were soon smoothed over.

Rani
15th Primus

T his wealth that we have really has become a joke. Naeve is going out to milk the cows, with Maria to help her. She is wearing her most comfortable dress for her pregnancy, her leather kilt. She has refused to have a new dress made that will only fit her when she is this size. So, she is proudly wearing just a kilt and sandals, along with two arm rings that would not have looked out of place on a lady in the Maharajah's court in Haven.

Rani could scarce stop herself laughing at the sight, but then stopped. Coming from where I did, such wealth is natural. What Naeve, a woman who has come from a long line of milkmaids, has on her arms is far more wealth than has ever been seen by all of her family in all the years that she has been alive, and she is celebrating this by wearing the bands just because she can. What little precious objects her ancestors have owned they probably kept on them or near to them. She is just doing the same.

Chapter XXXIV

Theodora
4th Secundus

A s the cards had said, the summer was turning into one of peace. *The days have become filled with work and training, and the nights are often spent communally. Even when people choose to eat in their homes, they often drift down to the hall afterwards where there are music and entertainment and people sit around quietly talking and amusing themselves.*

The Khitan decided that some of the flocks should be taken up to the meadow and this was done. This added to the chores with the cart making frequent trips up and down. Dulcie, Goditha and Tabitha even began to make a second cart.

As time progressed, Father Christopher confirmed that every one of the married women (except for the mages and Goditha) was pregnant. He even admitted that Hulagu's köle were going to be mothers as well. When he said this, those listening all looked at Bianca, but she just smiled. *How the pregnancies will affect the relationships among the three she might know, but she is not telling.*

Theodora
7th Secundus

T he conversation among several of the unmarried women has turned to *their prospects and not necessarily in a good way.*

"What man of the Caliphate will have me?" asked Lãdi bitterly. "I have not been a virgin, in any part of my body, for the eight years since those animals brought me here. I have seen thirty years and was the oldest slave here. It is only my skill with a spoon, with flattery and in bed that was keeping me alive with the bandits. Even with those, I know that I would not have lived much longer.

"I am not sure if I would want any man who would want me, as I could end up as the fourth wife of an old man who just wanted me to cook for him, or where I would have to use what I have learnt here to coax him into getting up when he was tired, and the other wives didn't want him. They all want young and silly virgins who will give them back their youth, not make them feel old."

She turned to where the Princesses sat on cushions. "If you are going somewhere else, see if you can find me a man, like Aziz loves Verily, who will want me for myself and what I can still give. I may not have long to do it in, but I want children and something more than lust. I have been with a woman before, we all have here, but I don't want a wife or a woman as my husband. I want a good man. Is that too much to ask?" Several others among the women murmured their support for her.

Theodora sat up from where she had been lying with her head in Rani's lap. "I need to visit my home soon, after Astrid has delivered and is in a condition to travel. We cannot go before, as I don't think that Basil will leave without his wife and he won't let me leave without him. When we go, I may take you with us and we will see what we see. I think that the Muslim men of Darkreach may be more practical than the ones you are used to. Perhaps we can find one there who suits you."

Christopher then spoke up. "I also need to go back to see the Metropolitan. I will ask him if there are men he can send as suitors. I cannot promise you anything, unless you are willing to trust me to be your matchmaker to make a contract on your behalf, but we might have some success. We need more people in the village anyway."

The women begin to think about this and start talking about what they might seek in a man. At least they are not all asking me. Some prefer to trust Bianca to find someone and some ask Astrid rather than a Princess or the Presbytera.

Many are still scarred from their time as slaves, and simply want a man who will be gentle. It is a relief to all that they do not have to think about the wealth of the man they would marry. I would not know how to approach that subject. They can choose a person just because they like him.

At least coming from Mousehole has the advantage that the wealth of a suitor is never going to be an issue. Having survived their past, and not really needing money, they can concentrate on other matters.

Bianca loudly made one general announcement on this issue. "Despite requests from several of you on the matter, I am not asking to inspect any man physically. The women I find men for will have to take that as they find it."

Ayesha

T*he others are all busy, but none of the Muslim women have come to ask my aid, but then, Lādi is right. There are not likely to be any worthwhile men in the Caliphate who will take them as a first wife.*

This left her wondering about herself. *I am the only virgin in the village, except for the two new arrivals and probably Rani, and Rani has made it clear that she has no intention of knowing a man now, and Maria, at least, has already talked with Astrid.*

Am I, Ayesha, going to stay a virgin forever? Should I seek a husband myself? Will a man from the Caliphate expect me to stay in his home and to leave Mousehole? Could I, a ghazi of the Caliph, accept a man from Darkreach?

How do my dreams about Hulagu, which I am still having, even with him away in the meadows, fit in with all of this? Can I take him as a husband? Will he accept me, a woman who is not a tribeswoman, and who has no intention of ever being one? Will he even stay in the valley once his köle are delivered and he goes back to the tribes to find husbands for them to allow them to be free? In the end, it will all turn out as Allah, the Compassionate, wills.

Astrid

W*hy is Fātima taking me aside? She looks embarrassed.* "The others are asking for their ideal man, and I want mine. Will you agree to not tell this to anyone who does not need to know?"

"Yes…of course"

"Then, well, I actually miss some elements of my old life under the bandits." *She is blushing, and her voice has gone very quiet.* "I want a man who will give me…when I want it…some pain. I have found the only time I can really…find release…is when I am being punished and treated fully as a slave and I want this…sometimes. I like men, but I actually enjoyed some of the attention I received from the bandit women. I don't want someone who will be too rough and actually damage me, as sometimes happened with the men."

"I do not know how I am going to raise this subject with a man, but I will try and help you," Astrid answered her. *You may be grateful now, but wait until*

I succeed before you celebrate. I have no idea how to find a man who can be what Fãtima wants. I may have been sworn to secrecy on this, what I say with my husband does not count. Maybe he can help me in this.

Theodora
9th Secundus

E veryone was excited when Theodora decided to teach as many as it was possible how to use the carpet. "Although Air mages are better with them, any mage can use one and often many people who are not mages, but who could possibly have some magic."

In the end, we have the mage trainees as well as Hagar, Eleanor and Lãdi who are able to control it to my satisfaction. Once this was done, on fine days, the carpet was often to be seen floating around the valley and going for longer and longer trips, up the valley and finally into the upper valley.

Although the watch at the entrance to the valley was not abandoned, with a carpet and a Talker they could even keep a good watch on the whole area around Mousehole. *My husband, thinking about how easily we approached the valley, has deemed it prudent to make this an extra precaution, rather than replace what we are fairly sure will work. I think that, as usual, she is right.*

T he books that they had brought back mainly had mentions of Dwarvenholme or of Mousehole, although several were works that more broadly talked about the world. *I am spending a lot of my time in the library. Astrid, in trying to learn the languages that others use more competently than she does, has surprised herself by also coming to love being among the books and, as her pregnancy progresses, is spending more time there.*

Ruth was also often to be seen there, in her little amount of free time, and sometimes Rani or Bryony, who actually knew something about the subject of geography before she had come to the village.

I am surprised to discover that there is indeed a 'Beyond.' I need to apologise to Astrid over my earlier doubt. There seems to be a lot of Beyond. It is much bigger than just the ice land to the north that Astrid had described. There are other places like the Land. We have several books that talk of another land to the west, giving it different names but all agreeing that it is wild and untamed. Two talk of a land to the east that runs from near the ice to the north nearly down to the ice in the south.

"Astrid, is there ice in the south?"

"Not that I know," she replied. "I thought that it got hotter and hotter. Ask your husband. She is from the south."

That land has many different people in it and, according to the books there is even a race of lizards that talk and made tools. Some of the drawings of one of the places there look sort of like Darkreach, but with only humans in the kingdom. The only Kharl mentioned live in their own kingdoms. They are not a part of a larger Empire.

"But it is said that Granther made the Kharl, and he has never mentioned other lands having them as well. Why would they be there if he doesn't pay any attention there; that I know of at least…and I am sure that we would all have heard if he were away from Darkreach for long, to the areas outside The Land?" Astrid did not answer. She just shrugged.

There is one land that is talked about where everyone who lives there is black, where magic does not work the same as in other places, and sometimes does not work at all; a place where no-one can speak to the inhabitants. The people who live there wear no clothes and do not use metal unless they are given it.

They exist in a blasted hell of heat and sand that is raised high all around above the sea. The few travellers who reach their land, according to the one book that mentions the place, leave as soon as they can. It said that there is no water there and that it never rains except along the edges. No other place is as hot or as dry.

Along with many islands, some large and some small, one other land was mentioned in a few books. It was called the Great Southern Land. Theodora and Astrid both noticed that, although several books mentioned it, even if the authors had been very good at describing everywhere else that they had been, they were very vague, and indeed often contradictory, about what was to be found there. "It sounds like some very good air mages live there and turn peoples' thoughts away from it."

Astrid
10th Secundus

N ow that is very interesting. The northernmost isle off the coast of the Land had borne another name once. We people of Wolfneck and Skrice simply called it the Shunned Isle. Once, it had been a lively city called Arnflorst. Now it is a deserted ruin and a prohibited place.

The sailors from the two villages in the north will not land there…ever.

They will not even fish in its waters, and they definitely will never take shelter in its lee during a storm. It is regarded as an evil place.

Apparently, once it had been a bright and shining city, its people travelled all around the world and, if I have it right, the runes on the stone marking the path to Dwarvenholme are neither Dwarven nor Darkspeech, or rather they may have once been both of them. They are the writing and the speech of the city.

This is even more exciting. I have heard tales of the Sea Nomads. I have never met them of course, but I have heard tales, even if I do not believe them, of towns that float and of their boats, as tall as the tallest trees. One book talks a lot about them. "I wonder if these people still live or if they died during the Burning. Wild fire on a ship would be devastating."

Rani

N ot all of the books are about geography. Some are books about magic: why it works and how it works and speculations about it. When she stops looking at those others with Astrid, I need to get Princess to look at these. They may help her with new spells.

I idly delved into this section of the library at the University and now I find that we have a copy of one of the books that was often mentioned there: Dar Lagrange's 'Speculations on the Nature of the Physical and Non-Physical Worlds.' We have a book that was thought to have been lost forever.

Several days later, she had to admit that even she found it hard reading. *It talks not only about magic, but also of physics and the connections between the two. It is a very thick book and very dry and makes me question everything I know.*

It talks about the tiny particles that the world was made of, and how these particles are mainly made of nothing. It talks not of the four, well-known, elements, but of many, many, more. It is very confusing. I will need to have a lot of time to sit down and seriously read it, with no interruptions and plenty of time to think.

One book is a series of speculations on what might lie beyond the world itself. It called the world that we live on Vhast and describes the use of telescopes upon the moons and talked of using them to look at the planets in the sky.

It contains many numbers and it talks about why Vhast and the other planets go around Kron, the sun, and even why that is similar to the flight of an arrow. It leads to us spending time on the roof pointing our small telescope around the sky on dark nights. We need a better one, if we can get it, to see all that is talked about in the book.

"I think, my love, that if these books talk of other lands, and the Masters collected them, then they might not have wanted others to know about them. Of course, it could also mean that they were interested in them themselves and that might explain where the other Masters are. There are, after all, more of their diagrams in Dwarvenholme than there are likely places for them to connect to in the Land, unless there is more than one in each area."

Lakshmi

Lakshmi had taken over an empty residence and workshop beside Harald's house for her own workshop. *I may be married to Harald, but there is not enough space for me to work in his house. With his charcoal and slag and dust, he makes my work untidy.*

We have plenty of spare buildings and I want a downstairs area where I can prepare and store my potions and another, upstairs and more private, where I can look after the women that are coming more and more to see me.

Since I have come here, I have more experience with stopping pregnancies than in assisting with them, but I still know more than our other healers on the subject. The men who know physiking know little on the subject of childbirth and Ayesha has a lot more learning in caring for people after a battle than in helping women in labour.

I will want help to deliver my own child…so Ayesha needs to learn more. From the expression on her face, I may have put her off childbirth forever. "I do not mind killing people, but I am not sure that I want much to do with the problems that you are describing. Please be trouble free." Lakshmi smiled.

Lakshmi even made sure that there was one large room set aside in the upstairs of her workshop for the priests. *From my time in the slums of Pavitra Phāṭaka, even when everything goes well with a birth, there are far too many women who have problems. I know that some women tear badly and bleed and then die, or catch a fever after the birth and die, or die for one of many other reasons like poison of the blood. I do not want to be one of them.*

We have priests here, and Christopher and Theodule can make sure that they have a sanctified area set aside for if they are needed. The largest room upstairs was cleaned and painted, a pattern added to the floor and then consecrated, and Father Christopher proudly set up the icon of the Saints Cosmas and Damien on its wall. *Now we not only have a healing chapel set aside, but it even has its own appropriate icon. I am sure that few villages can boast of that.*

As summer went by, she took others with her as she wandered around the hills looking for herbs to add to her store. *I have even had Bilqīs practicing her glassblowing. I may have a selection of slightly wobbly and often odd-coloured jars and bottles, but it does let me store the things that I have found and made. No longer am I confined to the few bottles that we have left over from the previous owners of Mousehole.*

They usually used the carpet to seek out the plants on the slopes of the valley and in the upper valley. On the first expedition into the upper valley to find out the resources there, she came back excited, waving some small branches. The plant had long leaves and was covered in blue flowers.

"Rani, do you know what we have?" Rani shook her head. *To her it is just a plant. She may be a more experienced alchemist than me, but she knows less about non-magical plants.* "This is Gasparin, one of the best of hot spices, and we have hillsides of it. From the flowers and leaves, we have at least five different types. Do you realise how many merchants will want this? We will almost own the market outside the Caliphate. I was not able to find many seedpods, for some reason it is best picked in the early spring, but I have some samples in my bag." *See, her nose is reacting. Even the flowers and leaves waving in the air give off a sharp and spicy scent.*

"Also, we have the mountain pepper bushes." She removed a small bag and emptied some small round berries on the table. "As well Aine will be glad to know, and Ayesha not glad at all, that we have Allah's Curse." *Rani is still just looking blank.*

Lakshmi sighed. "It distils to one of the best spirits known, but one that it is easy to get addicted to, not like the way that Father Christopher was, but addicted nonetheless. Still, we would not have to worry about that seeing that we are the ones who will hold the supply. We will have so much more to offer merchants. You do not realise how good it is to go out and not just seek the red tansy to make potions to cause the women to miscarry.

"You will want to know that we also have some tea. I have brought some small plants back for Giles to plant closer to us here and Ayesha will be glad to see that we even have kaf. We will need to work out a way to cultivate that as the bushes are very scattered." She waved her arms around excitedly as she said this as if she were taking in the hills and mountains, the whole area where the plants were located.

"Those stupid bandits could have made more money from the plants here than they ever did with their raids. No-one has touched any of this for many, many years and, unlike places that have had people around them all of the time, the plants are lush and not picked out."

"I even think that I have found some of the lichen that is called crotal dubh, although no one knows what that name means, it just comes to us from the past…but it is the only thing that yields a good black dye that does not fade, so we will even have our own supply of that if it tests true. Mind you, it grows very slowly, and we will never have a lot of it. The main thing is, once we can make cloth ourselves, we can die it black and not have it fade."

Astrid
12th Secundus

I t is the night before Christmas and I am the first of the women to give birth. I suppose that is fair. I was the first to start freely fucking. I have made all of Lakshmi's preparations and concerns unnecessary. According to Lakshmi, it was a quick and easy birth. I am not sure if I felt it like that, but she has seen more than me. I now have twin children, a boy and a girl.

They were cleaned up and handed to her to give them suck while Ayesha brought Basil in. *He looks relieved. He has been outside waiting nervously with the priests and Aziz listening to me yelling and swearing. I wonder what he thought. At least he now has a smile on his face and I am so elegant lying with a rug over my legs and naked except for my wedding necklace.*

She indicated each in turn as they lay cradled in her arms and sucking on a breast each. "Husband, meet Freya Astridsdottir, who shall be known, at least until she has established her own name, as 'the Kitten' and Georgiou Akritas. He is the one with the dark hair and scaly skin down his spine and she is the blonde." She smiled broadly.

"But that is my father's name," said Basil with an inane expression on his face.

"Silly, did you think that I didn't listen to you, of course it is. You are leaving your family behind for him and for me. Here is a reminder of them." He leant down to tentatively touch the children and they kissed.

"What is more," Astrid smiled, "if she starts to get teeth like me as she grows older, then you will have to learn to nurse her."

Ayesha

We have been worried, and now Hagar and Rani have returned to Mousehole on the carpet. They had been out on a sweep around the area. Excitedly they reported that Thord was on the way back home.

"He is on his own and sends his greetings and says that he has many tales to tell about the return of the Dwarves. He wouldn't share any of them with us, but he seems to be in very good spirits. He should be back here tomorrow night," said Ayesha.

Chapter XXXV

Thord

After he had been introduced to the new babies, Thord was greeted with a welcome dinner. "T'is is only fittin' for Ambassador. It's good to be back here with plenty to drink 'n' smiling faces instead of t'camp food 'n'dour faces to be found in Dwarvenholme. I ha'missed Lãdi's cookin' so much." He wouldn't be drawn any further and said to wait until after they had all eaten and people could come out of the kitchen.

After all had eaten, Thord was patting his stomach happily and asked everyone to gather around. "I'm used to lots of attention now," There was a twinkle in his voice and a broad wink.

When all had gathered, he started his tale. "T'Dwarves're back in Dwarvenholme," he said. Turning to the mages he said: "I've cautioned'em to stay clear of t'magic rooms, 'n't'ey are now off limits. I told'em t'at we would be up to deal with'em soon. I t'ink it had better be very soon. Someone or another is bound to t'ink t'at t'ey can deal with'em."

He turned back to face everyone. "I ha'gathered'em up from all over T'Land 'n'made sure t'ere were as many delays as I could manage in gettin' t'ere. I saw your tracks on t'way in, but I t'ink t'at we missed you by at least a month. T'others were too busy with rebuildin' t'road as t'ey went," he chuckled, "T'at was my idea, so t'at if'n any noticed your tracks t'ey forgot to mention it to t'others."

"When t'ey got t'ere t'ey quick went t'rough all of t' rooms t'at you had seen and t'en began to explore t' rest. T'ere was a whole nest of t'ose Moonshadow t'ings at t' bottom of t'stairs 'n'several Dwarves were lost before t'ey were wiped out."

"T'ere were also all t'usual hazards 'n'creatures. I was right t'ough. T'ere're also some good food animals. Most of 'em ha'now been rounded up 'n're now t'base of herds. We found another treasure room as well lower down. It was far smaller t'an t' one above, 'n'most of t'treasure had corroded or fallen to pieces, but with what you left 'n'it, t'Dwarves're more t'an happy. All of t'ose who went first're now wealthy. I guess t'at you brought more here." He looked around at some of the jewellery being worn. "Yes, I see t'at you did."

"More Dwarves arrive every day. T' other towns'll soon only have half of t'eir people in t'em, but t'at is right. T'is is t' most important of all of our places 'n'it should ha' t'most people. T'Duke of t'North, Smasher Kharlsbane, wants to proclaim himself King, but his forces are currently outnumbered by t'rest, 'n'even a lot of his own people do not want him to rule us all."

"He cannot just make himself King, however, as I still ha't'Crown 'n'without me giving it, t'ere can be no King. No Dwarf would accept him. T'ey ha'decided t'at t'ere shall be a Mayor of t'city, as t'ere would be under King anyway 'n'T'orgrim Baldursson was elected. He is an old Dwarf of ancient lineage 'n', even if t'ey do not always agree with him, all of t'Dwarves from every area respect him. I gave him my approval,"

"Dwarvenholme is full of light now. T'bats 'n' t'creatures of evil're gone. Dwarves claim shops 'n'start homes. T'forests outside of Dwarvenholme're being slow cleared for timber. Having said t'at, Dwarvenholme a struggles to produce enough food for itself 'n'it is being shipped in 'n't'is will happen for many years to come."

"T'ere is a part-Kharl at Mouthguard, Mellitus, you would have seen him Princess, who hops from foot to foot all of t'time as Dwarves pass t'rough his little garrison with goods 'n' t'ey ha' no interest in trade. I warned him t'ough, t'at if he charges t'Dwarves to pass from Dwarven lands to Dwarven lands, t'en we will build bridge below his fort 'n' no-one'll stay in his tavern. At least this way he gets t' revenue from our stays 'n' his people're sellin' as much food as t'ey can bring in."

"T'at is almost all of general interest. As your Ambassador," he stood and bowed to everyone, "I'm enjoying myself. T'ey do not know how to treat me. I can say what I want 'n'I do. As those who found Dwarvenholme, I've made sure t'at t'voice of Mousehole is heard on equal footin' with any Dwarven village."

After having said this, Thord began to answer questions and to talk more to individuals as the music and dancing started. It was a good night. Rani took him away to inspect the jewellery and gave him some arm bands that had been reserved from the treasure for him. They were of gold and undoubtedly ancient in make and each was a serpent that coiled around the arm. The eyes were small rubies and some mithril had been inlaid in very fine lines to better mark some of the features.

"T'ese'll impress when I get back," he said, "but is t'ere a something t'at

I can keep as wedding gift? My mother is finding me a bride. I should have something to give her to impress her family." Rani let him dig among the jewellery until he found a piece that was too masculine for most of the women, but none of the men wanted.

Chapter XXXVI

Over the next few weeks Mousehole was introduced to Peggy Farmer and Bishal and Valentine Black. Both boys were born on the same day to their different mothers, resulting in a very proud father. They were followed by Aneurin ap Stefan and Bianca Fletcher and then the girls Khātun and Būrān of the Dire Wolves.

Anahita was in labour for over a day giving birth to Būrān and Kāhina was running backwards and forwards, trying to care for Khātun, Hulagu and Anahita all at once. Bianca finally banned her from the birthing room and took over the shuttle, and then finally made her go to bed. She was awake again for the birth.

Goditha
27th Secundus

After this was a small pause of a week before Melissa Mason was born. *Why am I kept out of the birthing room?* "Thou wanted to be the father," said Robin to his sister. "They all wouldn't let me in when Bianca was born, so it is only fair that the same doeth happen to thou. Thou canst a sit out here nervously as the rest of us do. Besides, I think that thy Parminder hates both thee and me at present." *In a way he is right, but it is so hard.*

My little one has been the only birth so far that needed the attendance of our priests, but they tell me that it is just because she is so young and small. Our lovely Melissa is, however, a healthy baby and Parminder is quick to recover. Can I love her more?

Theodora

After she had been to see Goditha, Parminder and their baby, Theodora casually asked Rani: "You have brothers, don't you?"

"Yes, I have two, why do you ask?"

"Nothing, I will talk to you later. It is just an idea."

Lakshmi

"I will be happier when some of our poppies are producing. We need something to make it easier for the mothers…and I am likely to be next to deliver."

We still don't have the opium, but I am so relieved that young George Pitt was not only a trouble-free birth but also the fastest born of all the children so far.

Theodule
2nd Tertius

It worries me that Ruth is having difficulty with the birth. She is a small woman anyway and getting old to have her first child. It was her choice to marry and to have children. Am I to be left a widower again as a result of this?

Joshua and Jeremiah Cephalas are both a surprise and cause of rejoicing. Neither of us priests picked up two life forces, but the identical twins have made my little teacher very happy.

Christopher
18th Tertius

After Theodule's experience, I think that we are also having twins, but this is not something I have practice at, so I am not mentioning it to Bianca.

I *was right. We have twins as well. Bianca has insisted on naming them Rosa and Francesco.* "Rosa was like me in many ways," she said, "but for luck our positions could have been reversed, and you married to her, or I could have died with her. She needs to be remembered and, like me she had no family to do it for her. Our baby will be forever a memorial to her. As for Francesco, he gave me a chance to be more than I was born to be. He is the one who brought me out of Freehold. If it had not been for him, we would never have met."

I suppose that it is just but, if we have more children, I would like the names of my parents to be passed on as well.

9th Tertius

The very next day the last mother to give birth was Verily. She was in so much pain during the labour that Basil had to call on several of the other fathers, for they were now all gathering for each new birth, just as the mothers were starting to do in the birthing room, to help him restrain the Hob from rushing in.

It was made worse when Christopher was called in and Verily was rushed into the prepared room. It took some time, and they were all concerned as Verily's cries grew louder and then stopped, almost in mid-call, but eventually however a beaming, but exhausted Christopher came back out.

"She had some problems, but now, although she will be very tired and sore for a few days, they are all well. There must be something in the water here," he continued. "Verily said that you had chosen Saglamruh for a name if it was a boy. Now go in and see her and think of a name for your second son."

Strong Spirit soon had Sunmak, or Gift, as a name for his brother. Of the mothers, only Astrid and Verily thought that the two boys were beautiful, but the others wisely refrained from saying anything. Bianca thought that they looked a bit like Christopher's gargoyle Azrael, but without the wings. They were certainly not as beautiful as her two, not that any of the other babies were as beautiful as her two.

"If any of them turn out to be mages once they grow up," Rani said to Theodora, "we know they will all be battle mages at least—all of them have been born in the summer. Perhaps that is to the best for the valley."

Christopher
5th Quattro

*S*ummer is, for us all, a time for new beginnings. The children are here to delight the village, Theodule and I have properly blessed the fields, and they are bountiful, and the people are working hard to be good stewards of their gifts by trying to improve their skills.

It is a time of renewal and peace, except of course for those who have to wake at night to feed and care for infants. It seems that Fortunata and Sajāh are well pleased with their foresight and tell me so. They, at least, have alternate nights where they can sleep through the night, at the cost of a little discomfort from swollen breasts.

I have asked Bilqīs who, as a child, did some work on making carpets, if she can do some work for me. I want a prayer rug that has all the right symbols woven into it to take with me when we are away. She is starting by making simple prayer rugs for the Muslims. By the time she gets to the more complex task I hope that she has improved a lot.

Our Princesses are even experimenting with new spells. Rani was very pleased to present Lādi with a small portable stove that heated of its own accord. She is not used to making spells that are not meant to kill people and is so proud of this one. It is almost the first casting that she has done that is not meant to either cast light or kill something. It seems that she was discouraged from such wasteful pursuits in Haven.

Christopher
9th Quattro

*O*ne day, Christopher came running into Rani's study, brushing past Valeria. "I have done it. I cannot do anything for two more days, but it is worth it."

Rani looked up startled. "What can you do? What is worth overdrawing your prayer account that has you so excited?"

Oh yes, an explanation. I did not tell her what I was doing in the way of new thoughts. "I can tell if there is one of the Master's diagrams within a thousand paces of where I am. Do you realise what that means?"

"But we know where several are already, why do we need that spell?"

He began ticking things off on his fingers as he spoke. "We don't know if there are others in the same areas. We don't know where the one is in Darkreach. We don't know where they are in Freehold. Now, I can find out.

We can get rid of the one here, and the ones in Dwarvenholme. We don't need them anymore."

Fatima
10th Quattro

*A*ll summer long Azrael, the gargoyle, has sat on the eave of the hall. *Occasionally, Christopher has fed her something, but mainly she just sits. She was slowly getting a little larger, but like all gargoyles she is very good at just sitting there with her wings furled and her head held in her hands looking out at the world. She has launched herself off, and there is something happening below.*

From her night watch point on the roof she nervously peered over the edge. *There is a fight happening below me. Time to wake people with the Talker. This is an emergency.* She hurried down the stairs. Rani, Theodora, Basil and Fātima converged on the spot. *Azrael is eating something.* Rani pulled her light out of the choli that she had thrown on. *Azrael has killed a bird demon...I think.*

"Better get Father Christopher," Rani said.

I am glad that I did not have to burst in on them, but they are not very awake. I have Christopher in a robe and an equally sleepy Bianca. She just has a kilt and is strapping knives on as she walks. Christopher is almost jumping up and down with excitement.

"I told you all that it was a good idea to bring her back." He turned, "My dear, you can go back to bed. I need to make sure she knows that she did a good thing." Turning again to the others he said: "You realise that this had to have been sent somehow. Possibly it came through our diagram, possibly the long way down the valley. I would bet on the diagram. We really do need to get rid of it. You can all go back to bed now."

He turns to the gargoyle and starts talking to her, telling her what a good girl she is and making a fuss over what she has done. The gargoyle seems to pay very little attention to him. One eye may swivel to him, but she is intent on, before it goes off, eating as much of a creature several times her size as she can. It seems to be going in. It seems that for the rest of my watch I will hear slurping and crunching sounds.

I heard a heavy thump as she came back up and now there is no sign of the bird demon. She seems more than a little bigger, and her stomach is massively distended. Instead of her normal wrinkled self, she sits there on the wall looking like a ball with a head and wings that could not properly fold up at her sides but that stand out like ears protruding on a round bald head.

When they went to check in the mine, the door to the pattern had been opened from the inside. I hear that this confirms that this was the way that the demon entered our valley.

Christopher
12th Quattro

Two days later, and I am ready...I hope...to dispel the Master's symbol in the locked room in the mine before something else is sent. I think my adaptation of a standard miracle will work. I have Rani and Theodora, with the apprentices watching and ready to help if needed, standing by in case there is a backlash from the now free mana. He went to work.

I am blessed. It is dissipating quietly into a reddish mist that is evaporating slowly through the solid roof. We now have a spell that will eliminate the potentially dangerous mind traps that the Masters use, and with my new miracle, we can find out where others are placed if we are near them.

It seems that it is likely that the time of relaxation is coming towards an end and we will have to start back to work soon. We may need to call on the aid of the Saints Melchior, Caspar and Balthasar again.

Chapter XXXVII

Basil
18th Quattro

*I*t is the end of summer and Carausius is back. He says that he has with him the cloth that we ordered and he also brought fine candles, especially ones for the Church that the priests are slowly starting to plan.

He even has two more pack horses with him. Both of them are laden with iron and bronze, we need both of those, and he has a new Insakharl handler, Candidas, to help him with the animals and to leave him free to help with guarding...and I know him well. The man is even using his own real name.

The Princesses have decided that any traders coming to the valley will not be charged for their stay at the inn and so Carausius and his men are to be feted and fed at our expense. After all, it is not as if we need the money. We need what they bring. Now to have a chat with Candidas.

"Greetings, Tribune," said Candidas.

Basil looked around quickly. *Is there someone else here I have not noticed?*

"That was for you," said Candidas, with a grin. "Whatever you are up to here, you must have written a good report about it. I am to tell you that you have been promoted and not just a little way. You have gone straight to being a senior officer. I have a despatch for you, and, when I am here or in your area, I am under your orders. If you want, I am even instructed to stay."

"Greetings, Candidas. Wait until I tell my wife. Of course, I will have to explain what a Tribune is, but she might, just might, be impressed eventually. I will read the despatch and get back to you before you go. Now, go and enjoy the food and drink. We do both very well here. Oh, and that is an order."

They both smiled. Candidas looked around for spectators and, seeing none, removed a large sealed note from his pouch and handed it over.

On getting back to their house, Basil sat down to read. *The note is from*

Strategos Panterius...it commends me on keeping my charge...she is not named...safe and on finding Dwarvenholme. It repeats the news of my promotion and confirms that I am to stay in place...just as well.

My speculation was correct. This is going to be a lifetime job. Is it possible to communicate any other way? Not that I know of...and this bit the Princesses need to know: following instructions from higher up (Hrothnog is not named), if we choose to visit, we will all be free to leave again without hindrance.

Basil sat and thought before writing a reply. He went back out, told Candidas that all was well and handed him the return note. "Mind you, I could be in Ardlark before you if you travel slowly."

"As for orders, I think that it would be good if you can stay on this run and keep your ears open. I especially want to know if anyone...anywhere... is interested in finding out more about Mousehole, or about any of the people here. If they are, keep yourself safe, but try and find out what you can about them. Promise them information, but ask me what to tell them. If anyone tries to get work with Carausius, get the Strategos to look into them. I am still not sure exactly why, but what happens here seems to be very important, and not just locally."

Again, Carausius and his men leave us. This time he has more potions, more gems, the first of our antimony and even some of the gasparin spice, several small bags of it in different strengths. He says he will get a very good price for that as well.

Shilpa and Ruth have warned him that he will need to bring more general things, things that we cannot produce such as more metal, good cloth, different spices, lots of salt and all of the general things that a village needs to function. Even paper is in short supply. Carausius will not make as much on his trips now as he did on his first, but he will still have a good profit with a guaranteed customer and advance orders to fill.

Chapter XXXVIII

29th Sixtus,
the Feast Day of Saint John the Baptist

Eventually, summer ended in autumn, and many of the trees began to turn gold. Even though many of the trees in the surrounding forests were gums, on the upper slopes the beech led the way in changing colour in a spectacular fashion. The people of the valley made their harvests, and began to prepare for the winter, with fodder and hay brought in and with large supplies of timber for the fires stacked ready behind the village wall.

There was still one major event on the calendar of the village that all of them were eagerly looking forward to. Only after it is over will Thord return to the Dwarves. Rani was thinking that it is time for them to start making some of the visits that they have been putting off.

The twenty-ninth of Sixtus, the feast of John the Baptist, was the anniversary of their attack on the village. As it grew closer, Ruth reminded the children of what had happened. The children's daily play even turned more to combat, rather than the simpler and more childish games. One would stalk another as she walked from one part of the village to another, hiding in the shadows and pretending to be Ayesha attacking the guards. Another would be asleep in bed and a sister would jump on them.

The children still had nightmares sometimes, but it seemed that, through their play and acting out the events of the night of their freedom, they were starting to put some of what had happened behind them.

The feast itself was spectacular. They had been preparing for some time for it. All of the new things that they were making were on display, new foods were shown off, new drinks were drunk, and the apprentice mages showed off some of their spells to everyone. Everyone put on their best displays of entertainment, dances were danced, and they all enjoyed themselves.

Astrid, to her chagrin, got completely drunk that evening. She had not had a single drink for six months, and what she had at the feast left her very unsteady indeed. She suffered badly for her enjoyment the next day, when she had to get up early to farewell Thord. She was glad to be able to go back to bed, being woken only to feed her children.

She was not the only one. Thord had also gotten drunk, and had the thought that leaving his departure until the next day might be a better idea as well, but he put the thought aside as he knew that he had to move on. The whole village realised that the time of rest was starting to end. When he left to ride up into the mountains, he had a letter from the Princesses telling the Mayor that the Mice would be making a call on him soon.

Chapter XXXIX

Theodora
33rd Quinque

"I suppose that we should be off to Dwarvenholme," Rani said one night as they were preparing for bed.

"No, we have another visit to make first. Almost a year ago, we went to see the Metropolitan and he gave us Father Theodule, and he also promised to try and succeed at our task if we failed. We have not been back to see him to thank him, and he must be starting to think that we did indeed fail."

"If we go there first, we can talk to him and use the visit as an excuse to see if one of the Master's diagrams is nearby. Not only should we go there, but we should let Father Christopher and Bianca visit all of the outlying hamlets. They can see if there are any men around who might wish to come here."

"While they do this, they can also seek information about any bandit activity and perhaps deal with the killers of Maria's family. These things will act as cover for the Father to set up his search at each stop. Once we have done this, then we will know that there is at least one area, apart from here, that is safe."

My husband was easy to convince, now to work out who should go. The carpet will hold six normal adults in comfort, Bianca is small and her children light, and can travel wrapped up in the warm cloak. This trip will only have Orthodox in it. We can take Danelis and Tabitha to start looking for husbands for them and the other women, so with five on board it will give us some leeway if it is needed.

Next day, when they announced this, Hulagu disrupted all of the plans. "Good," he said, "I need to visit the tribes, but I do not want to be too long away. I could not go until the babies were born, but my family must know that

I am alive, before they declare me dead and mourn. I also must start the hunt for husbands for my köle."

He stops. It is obvious that he wants to say something…looking from me to my love. "How would you feel if I announced the location of Mousehole to the tents? If I do that and say that there are women who seek a partner here, and say why, we can see if anyone comes this way for them."

The mages looked at each other. *Why do that?* "Why can't we just take Anahita and Kāhina out to the tribes and leave them there?" asked Rani.

"Because my köle are wealthy," replied Hulagu emphatically. "Part of the herds of the valley and among the animals that we are gaining should be theirs as dowry instead of just jewellery. If a man is not willing to travel here to their home to try for their hand, then they are not worth much as a husband, and I will not accept them."

That actually makes sense, for all the women actually. He isn't finished, is he? "How would you feel if, when my köle marry, and if their husbands agree, that we will take over running the herds in the upper valley? Mousehole lacks the people to do this properly now, and all that grass is really wasted. This way, they can stay with their children, and the back path is guarded as well. We can grow the herds and make it a rich area instead of just empty grass."

I guess that we need to add Hulagu to the trip, and include a visit to the tribes before we go to Greensin. We will take that other matter under advisement. At least Hulagu is content with that. He has to find husbands first. Getting them to stay in Mousehole afterwards will have to wait until it is seen if they are suitable anyway.

Father Christopher raised the next issue: "If we are visiting the tribes, we will be travelling over Evilhalt. It is a key centre for travel. After all, where was the place where we all just seemed to end up? I think we need to look there first, before we go on. It will take two weeks to look at all of its hamlets, assuming that we find nothing…then we go to the tribes."

"Bianca tells me that Hulagu just wants to find his own tuman and will spread the word through them. That will only be a couple of days, then on to Greensin. We will still be at Dwarvenholme before winter. After all, there is no hurry. We have received nothing yet in the way of a sign to tell us that it is time to come out and be more active. All we do now is tidy up our own area—and the places that we have been active in."

I guess that I have to agree, but each time someone speaks, I can see my time away from my beauty and Fear getting longer and longer. I am not pleased. The problem is that each person who has come to me has come up with a good idea for the trip, and I cannot deny them.

Theodora
34th Quinque

W e set out armed as if for war. Even Danelis and Tabitha are armed, although seeing that Astrid has been teaching Tabitha, we have to be careful with her spear lying along the length of the carpet and the point poking out the front. Only Bianca seemed almost unarmed, she is dressed for the plains, but she has her knives, and two shortswords.

We have gold with us, some for Father Christopher to give to the Church, and another bag to change into other coins of silver, bronze and tin so that we can start collecting some smaller coins. We have so much gold and gems, but so little in the way of smaller coins to use with passing trade. It is a reversal of normal life that we seem to have more mithril coins in the coffers of Mousehole than we have copper. Being unable to give change is one of the things that made us decide not to charge Carausius and his men for their stay.

Christopher

S tefan looks nervous. "I didn't know how to do t'is, seein' t'at my parents wanted me to leave, but I've decided. Can you please speak to my parents for me? Let 'em know t'at I am happy an' well an'll be staying here." He smiled slightly: "An' t'at I'm working with leather more t'an fighting."

"Can you also let 'em know t'at t'ey be grandparents now an't'at Aneurin is doing well an'll grow up wealthy. I wrote note for t'em, but you, bein' a priest an a adding some words to t'at will make it more real for t'em." I was hoping he would do that.

O ur Princess flies us high over the forests. It is odd seeing from above the hamlets along the roads to Erave Town and Kharlsbane and come down out of the east to Evilhalt in the early afternoon. Stefan told us to bring the carpet to the gatehouse and seek permission to enter, rather than just land in the town.

It is a wise precaution, as we were seen approaching some time before, and the town is already getting into a state of defence. Seeing that we are all armed, we might not have been given a chance to explain ourselves if we had just disembarked into the centre of town.

"Just like home," said Bianca. We move, at horseback height, into the town.

"You have to talk to the gate before going in and then fly low. We might as well have walked across, but at least this way we do not get wet feet."

I really do want to see Father Anastasias, but Theodora has insisted that our first call should be on the Baron, Siglevi the Short. "We are not just wanderers now. I am a Princess, well I was a Princess before, but you know what I mean and, and, even when we came here first most of us saw the Baron almost as soon as we arrived."

It is just as well we came straight here through the gawkers in the streets. By the time the gates are closed behind us and the next set opened, and we get to his office, the Father is already with the Baron, waiting with Gregory of Brickshield. Stefan mentioned him, he is the militia commander.

I guess that it is up to me to do the introductions...but where do I start? There is so much to explain. Eventually, it was sorted out and the rulers of two villages were introduced. *From the expression on Theodora's face, I think that she was expecting a little more formality in this. I suppose that, if I am going to keep doing this sort of thing, I should find out how it works. How do I do that?*

"So, you t'ink t'at t'ese bandits were not just band of rogues, but had someone a behind them?" asked Siglevi.

"Oh, we don't just think that, we know it," replied Theodora. "What we don't know is how large a network is behind them, and what they intended to do in the long term. Father Christopher would like to see if they have one of their communication figures here. Mind you, even if he doesn't find one, it doesn't mean that they have no-one here. I believe that you will need to be vigilant on seeing if your priests, any of your priests of any religion at all, get a feel of evil off anyone, even from off people that you know well."

"And just who put you in charge of all this?" asked Siglevi. "What gives you the right to give orders to me? We are not in Darkreach."

"Nor is Mousehole," replied Theodora. "I don't speak for Darkreach and no longer regard myself as a part of it. We have not even talked with them about it. I speak only for my village and am not trying to give you orders. I am sorry if I sounded that way. We tend to get wrapped up in this problem and focus on it; it is often all we think about.

"If you want to know more about the bandits, feel free to ask Tabitha or Danelis. They lived as slaves under the bandits for many years. They can tell you how the village was visited by people from all over the Land, and what was done to the women there. I am just giving a suggestion."

I can see now when she thinks of something. Her eyes get a glint. "After all, I am sure that you would hate to find your trade disrupted by them again. They have done it once. Maybe they can find a way to do it again." *That comment obviously struck home from the looks that are being exchanged among those from Evilhalt.*

Father Anastasias agrees we need to search. I thought he would. It is partly his responsibility that we went out as we did. We will not be with the others tonight. He is taking Bianca and I home, while the rest go to The Slain Enemy. Bianca wants to join them there while I talk with Father Anastasias. We don't have a bathhouse built at Mousehole yet and, for a girl who had not really washed all over until she had come here; she has told me that she misses the experience. I will look after the children...once we have seen Stefan's parents.

At least they are relieved to find out that he is alive and well and more than a little surprised to discover that he now has a child. It is a pity that I have to tactfully skirt around the question of marriage. I need to work on that when we get back home.

Bianca

That night those at the inn had to field requests to perform at the tavern, but this time it was largely left to Danelis and Tabitha to play music. *Neither of them can do more, and although they do play with flute, recorder and shawm, it is not up to what we used to do. Theodora won't do anything, so I should sing a few songs before going back to my husband. I guess that we are, to all intents and purposes, just re-visiting the area and we certainly do not need the money.*

At least the notion of a valley full of beautiful women is starting to get around. It wasn't hard to point out the women to Stefan's friends, who still remember me and, apparently, my husband and their priest had a very public discussion, or so I was told. No-one needs to get up and announce it, but after all, aren't two of the women just here playing? One is even like the Cat that was here a year before, but with different hair and without the teeth that alarmed so many of the local men.

Bianca
35th Quinque

In the morning Christopher, with permission of the Baron, used the Church to test his detection miracle. *At least we can find no evidence of the Masters within Evilhalt. Now we get to go around all the hamlets. Of course, my husband does services as we go, but their own priests come around fairly regularly this close to town, so it is left to me to give an excuse to visit by asking about eligible males that are free in the area while the two unmarried women stay coyly in the background.*

Bianca
10th September

*A*fter two weeks, the area has been searched. There are still more small hamlets springing up on the roads north, but thankfully Theodora has decided they are too far from the town for anyone there to be useful in spying out what goes on now, and too new to have been useful beforehand.

It was also realised that a diagram could even be hidden in the forests somewhere, but, from what they had been told, all of them were in towns or villages, so they were hoping it would stay that way.

Hulagu

*A*t least, since I started being a mage, I understand now why you often have to wait for people to recover. I used to just get impatient. Now our Christian priest is ready, we can leave the khanatai gazar, walled places, of Tulaan golyn nevtrekh, Evilhalt. It is a nice early start.

Now to find where my family should be after the Festival of the Dragon. As they travelled west, well above bowshot, they saw many scattered groups of Khitan,

None are mine. That is where my sister was ambushed, even if she cannot recognise it, and there is where we met. At least she says she recognises this one from the way the trees go up the valley and the ovoo on the hill above. We should think about an ovoo in our valley when we get back.

Towards the middle of the afternoon, a group came into view that was a little larger than most of the others they had seen. Moving towards a rise with another ovoo, which had the start of a small creek springing from beneath it, a clump of over fifty wagons were at the centre of spreading herds of cattle, sheep and goats. Two of the wagons had ger, or circular tents, set up on them, their bases much larger than the wagons beneath and each drawn by many oxen.

This is the group we seek. Even my sister's husband is able to see the Üstei

akh düü, the fur siblings, that bound about, even if he cannot tell them from the ones that attacked him and Astrid. He does need to get out into the wild more.

Our descent is causing some sensation among the tribe as we come down some distance ahead of the first rider on a knoll on the route. It is important that we make no attempt to conceal our landing. Already an ergüül of scouts is moving in our direction.

As they approached Hulagu waited before shouting with joy when they came close enough. *I certainly know their ras-khan at least.* He leapt forward. "Kūrsūl, my cousin."

He has put his bow back into its quiver and leapt out of his saddle with the horse still moving...show off. "We thought that you were dead. We would have held your rites within a month. Now you are back here. Have you traded your horse for a carpet? Why do you travel with those of the khanatai gazar? Have you left the tents behind?"

"Stop, please, you have too many questions. What is more, they are ones that I should answer before my parents and my hetman, Ordu, before I can tell the one who runs their errands. I will tell all tonight. I have news, important news, is all I will say."

"Can you find out if Ordu wishes us to meet him now, or if we should fly on to the campsite? I speak for all here to behave." Kūrsūl nodded and remounted. *His horse had been caught by Bianca. As he mounts, he is looking curiously at my sister, dressed like a maikhand emegai with two babies in slings, as we carry our children, but who openly wears an ornate crucifix around her neck.*

He gives me a glance, and rides off quickly, while the other scouts moved past us and ahead into the plains. Hulagu kept his grin inside himself. *I know what you are thinking. and you are wrong.*

It was not long before Kūrsūl was back. "Follow me. Ordu will see you in his tent now with our grandfather. The city ones can follow on their carpet while you talk." Hulagu nodded and explained what was about to happen. "Bianca, you will come with me to see the hetman." *Christopher looks alarmed.* "Do not worry. She will be safe. We have accepted her as a part of our little tribe at Mousehole, but I need to have her, and her children, accepted here as well."

They were led back through the tuman. *So many curious looks as we pass between them.* Hulagu had Theodora keep the carpet to the same height as the people on horses. "My sister, when we go in, please remember not to touch or tread on the doorsill of the tent. Do not even touch the frame of the door. I have told you this before, but never forget it."

We are at the su-khan's ger and the Üstei akh düü surround us and I see so many people that I know. I have missed my family.

Hulagu directed Theodora to come alongside a ladder leading up to the doorway. He stepped across to the ladder and climbed up to a small platform before stepping into the tent. He then signalled Bianca to do the same, before pointing Theodora to where she should keep the carpet. *Now she has to control herself and stay just there.*

Bianca

I go into a dark and jolting tent. Apart from the feeling of movement, looking inside it is hard to believe that this is on a wagon, but my feet and balance tell me that this is the case. I nearly lost my balance onto the frame but managed to recover. It is an insult to touch it, one so severe that I would be killed.

Entering the gloom, she looked around. *I see several people. One man is seated on a saddle and another sits on a cushion beside him. He looks like a far older Hulagu. The walls are hidden behind carpets and tapestries and light comes only from a dimly glowing image of the sun hanging from the top of the structure. It gives a light like a grey day, comfortable on the eyes, but bright enough to let you see everything, now my eyes are adjusting after the brightness outside.*

The seated people, male and female, are all older. They are the seniors of the group. They all wear weapons but, if I remember my lessons, their embroidered jackets and headpieces show that they are not in a martial frame.

Hulagu is approaching the seated people. "I greet you Ordu, and say that I have finished my wanderjahr, and am now a full member of the tribes. I greet you grandfather, and bring you news of my quest." *He is waving at me.* "This is Bianca of the Horse. She was born a Latin. I speak for her deeds and she may be spoken to. Those of the tents where I now live have accepted her among us, and she has walked the fires. Her husband is outside on the carpet, but he is not one of us. Their children will be raised in the way of the plains."

The two men are looking at me with curiosity. "You speak of her husband," asked Ordu, *the one on the saddle*, "are the children yours or his?"

"They are his. I do now have children, but they are with my köle. That is one of the matters I need to speak to you about. Now, however, I need to know if you will accept Bianca on my word."

"Is this woman fit to be one of the tribes?" asked the other. *He must be Nokaj, Hulagu's grandfather and shamen of the tuman.* "Why do you name her to be of the Horse? There is no clan of the Horse now. There once was such a clan, but it died in the great battle at the start of this age. Do you claim her to be from that time? What is more, she is a Latin, not of the tents at all."

"Grandfather, it is a long story and you had a major part in it. With your permission, we will tell it to you."

Ordu indicated for them to sit and Hulagu began the tale.

"So," Nokaj addressed Bianca, "my grandson has adopted you as his sister."

"Yes, grandfather."

"It is your desire to be accepted into the tents?" he continued.

"Yes, grandfather."

"Do your köle accept her as your sister then?" he asked Hulagu.

"They do, they teach her the ways of the women, and they teach her the dances of the tribes," he replied. "We all teach her the customs and the histories and the stories. She was also accepted as such by the Pack-hunters on our journey east," he added.

"It is too late then to do the tests of adulthood here. They must be done when she returns to your valley with its secret grazing," said Nokaj. "For us, there will be one judgement. We will see how the Üstei akh düü react to her and her children." Ordu nodded,

Bianca had a twinge of doubt then. *What if the great beasts did not accept us? Would my children be safe? Nokaj and Ordu and all of the others are looking closely at me. I must show nothing.* "So, let it be." She rose and turned on her heel and headed out of the door. *This time I time my transit of the door better so that I cannot be thrown against the frame.*

Theodora

It seems to be forever that Hulagu and Bianca are inside the tent-on-wheels as it lurches over the plains. I am getting nervous as the tribe mills around us. Danelis can speak Khitan and is trying to quietly let us know what she hears. At least it is mainly just speculation about why we are here and not much use. Several males are speculating what we women would be like as köle, either assuming that none of us can speak Khitan, or not caring and trying to gauge our reaction, which I am proud to say is just a blank stare in return, but that is the only thing of interest. Eventually Bianca appeared at the door, followed by Hulagu and then two older Khitan men.

Bianca climbed down the ladder and Theodora went to move to get her. *Why is Hulagu waving me away urgently? Bianca has reached the ground and is putting her hands out to the wolves, many of which stand as tall or taller than her, as the ger on wheels lurches onward. The wolves gather around her, and she allows them to smell her and the babies.*

Father Christopher is unsure what he should do, but he is holding still at present. She gives him a look and he subsides a bit.

She has taken Rosa out of her sling and held her onto the back of one of the smaller wolves, which is trying to turn around and see what is happening. Another huge wolf has come up as this was being done and licked the baby, who gurgles happily in response. Bianca replaced her in her sling and did the same with Francesco, only this time on the larger wolf. It is some sort of test. It has to be.

The whole time she had to keep walking to stay up with the cart. When she had replaced him in his sling, she moved ahead and stood looking up at the cart. *She has put out a hand and started scratching the nearest wolf behind the ears. The wolf reacts with pleasure. She said something to one of the men.* "It was 'Do I pass then, grandfather?' I think," said Danelis.

"Keep translating"

One of the men nodded and Danelis continued, "Go then, granddaughter and greet your parents." He turned to Hulagu. "Take her and introduce your sister to the rest of her family." Hulagu grinned, and, without using the ladder, leapt from the cart to the ground and rushed to start doing this. *That is all right. We will just sit here, ignored, on the carpet.*

T *hat night there was a feast. We are fed, but no-one speaks to us. Both Bianca and Hulagu have come to us several times to see if we are all right, but apart from that we may as well not have been there.*

Hulagu said: "The tuman is accepting Bianca as my sister. It is important that this happen without interruption. They now know of what we are doing. and word will be sent to the Pack-hunters and the Axe-beaks, as well as spread to those clans that can marry my köle. Tonight though, is for Bianca's gaining of a family…not to replace you Father, but to replace those that she lost seventeen years ago."

Hulagu

D *uring the night Nokaj sat them both down where the others could hear what was said. He does not acknowledge the presence of the rest of the Mice, but he makes it easy for them. Danelis is repeating everything he says.*

"The fog is still in place over the future," he said. "There are small areas we cannot see into that move around the Land. Only one is fixed and it is a new one in some respects. It is a much larger place than ever it was before, and nothing at all can be seen of it either in this world, or from the Spirit World. Apart from in Darkreach, it is the largest area that has ever been seen that cannot be looked into."

"Is it in the mountains half way between the Gap and the Swamp?" asked Bianca, as Hulagu grinned. When Nokaj nodded with a worried expression, she grinned as well. "That is Mousehole where we all live. It is obvious that Theodora's spell is working well. Do not be concerned with what happens there, it is the moving spots that you cannot see into that will be of concern."

As part of her acceptance, and for the entertainment that all of us try to do, Bianca shows her ability with her knives, just as others show off their skills. She sings the songs of the tents that she has learnt from Anahita and Kāhina, and dances with the other women, stopping only to tend to the babies.

She need not have bothered with the last. They are currently lying happy in a large basket that otherwise contained a litter of wolf pups too young to keep up with the moving tribe on their own and the whole squirming pile is being overseen by their mother as well as by Bianca.

Hulagu
11th September

They left in the morning. *Bianca is hugged by Togotak and Sparetha, her new father and mother, and her many sisters and cousins. She now has a small bag hanging around her neck, as well as her crucifix and several strings of beads. Our mother has a new necklace as well, one of green jade that matches her eyes.*

Still no-one among the Khitan has talked to the other Mice. We are waved away and head north again on the carpet. My sister has tears in her eyes as we go.

"That may be the oddest experience that I have ever had," said Theodora. "I suppose that one of you can explain it all?" she asked.

Bianca and Hulagu looked at each other. Hulagu began: "The tribes rarely have much to do with the city dwellers. Anyone having much to do with outsiders has to undergo purification afterwards. The people of your husband's land do much the same, I believe. If there are Khitan in a group, then they will talk only with the Khitan."

Theodora went to speak, but he held up his hand. "Bianca is now Khitan, so she is treated as would any other person of the tents of another totem who was visiting our clan. The children are as well." He continued: "by doing this, they are not made unclean. Ask Rani about this when you get home. As I said, her people are much the same." *Her husband can explain if she wants more. I have said enough on that.*

Christopher

W *e are flying high. In the distance, I can see the hills of the Dwarves.* As they approached the monastery, Father Christopher pointed below. *There, also headed towards Greensin and seemingly unaware of us above them is a patrol of the Basilica Anthropoi.* "That may even be Praetor Michael again. Are we ourselves this time?"

"Indeed," she replied. "I am a Princess, and you are the head priest of my village. I am sure that you will have no problem getting us an audience this time either." *She is bringing us down.*

Christopher made sure that his helmet was off and his face could be seen. Then, from above and behind he called out: "Praetor Michael, turn around. We bring greetings."

The men below turned, and one member of the patrol started grabbing for his bow, but Michael waved him down. "Who are you and what do you want?" he asked.

"Praetor Michael, you know me. I once was Brother Christopher, but I am now Father Christopher. I was sent on a mission to the east over a year ago. I am now returned, and I need to see the Metropolitan. Is he at his house or is he at the monastery?"

The officer looked hard at Christopher as the carpet came closer. "It is you. For a moment I thought that you were someone else in that armour. I believe he is at his house, Father. Who are these people and what do they do here?"

"That is for the Metropolitan to say in his own good time." *That should be cryptic enough.* "Just allow me to say that they are important." With a wave at the Praetor, he nudged Theodora and she headed the carpet in the direction that Christopher pointed. Behind them, the patrol sped up after them. "Was that too much like Astrid?" The rest of those on the carpet laughed and smiled.

Theodora

T hey landed over a bowshot from the Metropolitan's house. *It is a very large house. For the barbarians it is almost a palace.* She then noted the number of people moving around it. *Of course, she thought, it is just like the palace in Ardlark. It is not just a house for one man and his servants it is also offices and no doubt there are many people who live and work there. Father Christopher walks up and talks to the guards. Now he is waving for us to join him.*

The Metropolitan greeted them warmly and, after they received his blessing, he ushered them inside a large room, calling for refreshments as he did so. "I presume the Khitan woman with blue eyes is the famous Presbytera Bianca that succeeded in turning my monk into a priest," he said. Bianca blushed and nodded.

"A year ago, I sent two priests off on a mission. I was about to send others in search of you. I believe that you may have just beaten Praetor Michael here. Tell me what has happened. I presume these other women will be explained." He waved towards Tabitha and Danelis who sat quietly and in awe of such a high priest.

This time it was Father Christopher who gave the explanations. Hulagu, Danelis and Tabitha were introduced and the women's purpose with them made clear.

At the conclusion, the Metropolitan spoke: "I am sure that you ladies will have no difficulty in finding suitable spouses. I take it they will be your ostensible reason to travel around the hamlets?" Christopher nodded.

"Are all of your ladies as beautiful as these two?" Everyone nodded. "Then you have my blessing. I will let you go and you can search here first and start on the settlements tomorrow." To Christopher he added: "You seem to have grown greatly since I sent you away. You are doing better than I hoped."

"There is another matter. I am not sure if you want to deal with it or leave it to us. We didn't mention, but some slavers appeared at Mousehole while we were at Dwarvenholme. They had two young women with them and a child... about a year ago...can you remember an isolated farmstead to the south of here being attacked and the people being killed? They were a farmer named Beman and his family."

The Metropolitan thought for a moment before picking up a small bell from the table beside him and ringing it. In a little while a small earnest-looking middle-aged man came in. "Andronicus," said the Metropolitan, "did we have a disappearance of a family noted about a year ago? There were..." *he turns to me.*

"A husband and wife, three sons and a daughter, a family called Beman." The Metropolitan turned back to his secretary.

"Yes, Your Eminence. They had a new farm just north of the edge of the woods. The Khitan..." he looks at Hulagu and Bianca. *Hulagu waved to show no offence is taken. Bianca just looks blankly at him.* "...were blamed for taking them as slaves. Their farmstead was sacked, and all the valuables taken, as well as all the livestock."

"It was not the Khitan," said Father Christopher. "The girl was taken as a slave and sold to a couple of men from the Brotherhood and has ended up with us at Mousehole. She will be staying with us now that we have found out that her family are dead. Her parents and the brothers were killed by two of your people to enable the girl to be abducted quietly.

"I don't know what has happened to the bodies or to their flocks. The question is, do you wish us to deal with this, or do you wish to do so yourselves. We have their names and where they were found by the slavers."

That has set the Metropolitan thinking. "I think that this is our business to arrest and try them, you may send someone who knows the details if you wish, and we will get you to testify against them in open court. Do you have means of getting confessions from them?"

"We have two, Your Eminence. Presbytera Bianca can use physical means if it becomes necessary, but I also have a spell that is very effective and does not stress her conscience as much. I am willing to place it at your disposal. I think that it will be best if we might all accompany your men if you do not mind. I am not sure that I want us to be separated for too long when we do not know yet who can be trusted."

"That is fine," said the Metropolitan, "and I appreciate your help with an appropriate conjuration. We have many priests here, but few mages of any power in the area. More correctly, in many respects, we have very few mages of power." He smiled. "Now that this is all sorted out, once you have it all cleared up, where do you go after here?"

"When we finish here we will go to Dwarvenholme and dispel the pentagrams there. After that we go to Darkreach, for family reasons as much as any other, and then we will begin the more dangerous legs of our task. We may have to go to Wolfneck. There, we have to arrest one of its ship owners and question him, regardless of what the rest of the village want. After that, we are undecided as to whether to try Haven, or Freehold or the Caliphate. The Brotherhood will possibly be our last and greatest challenge."

"I will give you a letter for Father Simon at Wolfneck when you need it. That should help you. The Brotherhood will be a great challenge indeed," replied the Metropolitan. "Traders tell me that they prepare for war and have grown mighty. The villages of the north coast seek our aid and talk to the Khitan.

"Freehold will be bad enough, and Christopher, you will either have to not go, or will have to travel in disguise. For some reason, they kidnapped Father Theophilus from Glengate, which is far from them, when he was touring the assarts around the main village. Before any knew of this they took him back to their land, and then burnt him as a heretic.

"They also prepare for war, whether with the Brotherhood, or the Khitan, or the villages of the south coast, none know, nor can we find out. They have gained much wealth lately to increase their armies, none know from where, but there are rumours of many sorts."

"We may know the answer to their wealth," said Father Christopher. When we took Dwarvenholme, we brought to our valley a whole library. Much of it is concerned with travel and several books talk of other lands. We already knew of one of these, that which lies to the north of the Land.

"Some distance to the west of Freehold is another land that is possibly as big as this. It is likely that they have found this and have built it up as a part of their Kingdom. Depending on how long they have been there, they may have twice as many people in their Kingdom as those that we know about here…or perhaps even more. This will mean that, at need, they may be able to double the size of their armies.

"I do not think that these Masters would have control of any nation, except perhaps the Brotherhood, but they may have people that they have corrupted giving advice to the rulers. Beware of anything you hear from there."

"I thank you for that," said the Metropolitan, "and before you go, I think that I will give you letters for the Metropolitans of Darkreach. While all of this matter of the world is significant, in the long run the state of souls is of more importance. We need to see if they are still in Communion with us." *He holds up a hand to stop me.*

"I know my daughter that you feel that you are; but there are many subtle flaws that can enter theology that make a great difference. Even something such as to whether they are still iconodule or even faintly iconoclast is important and has led to strife in the past. I am heartened that Father Christopher tells me that you seem to use all of the same prayers, creeds and rituals, but that still leaves some room for error. I need to be sure."

With that they took their leave and headed off with Father Christopher to the Basilica to make his first search of this area. *I am relieved that he has found nothing in town and now we can go to the house we have been given to stay in. It has been a long day.*

Danelis and Tabitha have many eyes following them, even those of the patrol, which is now waiting outside the Metropolitan's house. I admit that they are both pretty and would tempt me if I were not a happily married woman. It is funny that, instead of moving like the hunter that Astrid is training her to be, Tabitha's walk has developed a distinct sway as she moves, and men follow her as she passes with their eyes.

As for Bianca, even with her babies in their slings, she is moving through the town more like Ayesha does than like a simple animal tender. Most amusingly our simple priest stands in full armour with his hand resting on his mace-head looking more like one of the Basilica Anthropoi than the many other priests around us.

Theodora
12th September

Praetor Michael's patrol had moved out the next day, headed south and the next morning after that the Mice caught up with them. "How do you want to do this?"

"We will ride up and arrest this one, and then we will go down the road and do the same for his friend," said Michael.

"What happens if he sees you coming and is reluctant to come?" asked Theodora. Michael shrugged. "Let the Presbytera Bianca go first," she suggested. "She is trained for this."

Bianca looks surprised, but she is. Ayesha and Basil have both been taking time with her, Ayesha showing her how to stalk and kill, and Basil how to stalk and subdue. This is not a village, but she would at least be moving among buildings soon.

Bianca handed Christopher the children and hopped off the carpet. *See, she unconsciously mimics Basil with moving her shortswords in and out of their sheaths once she was on the ground. Michael still looks dubious.*

"I will do nothing until you arrive, or they notice you," Bianca said to Michael. *She gives Christopher a kiss and heads off before either can object.*

Tabitha hopped off the carpet as well. "I guess then that it is time to see if I have learnt from my training," she said. She looked at Michael: "My teacher has been showing me how to stalk with a spear through the woods. It will be I who will go through the woods near you and try and cut off any attempt to escape."

"I guess that means that I am the archer," Danelis said as she strung her bow and moved away from the patrol.

I am so proud of my girls. They have learnt to be themselves. Christopher gave a chuckle and addressed Michael, *who is still looking surprised.* "Do not worry. We men often feel that way in our village. Now off you go. I am here if I am needed for any cures. Does anyone have allergies to any potions?" *The patrol all shake their heads and Michael signals them forward.*

I will keep station behind them. "Hulagu, prepare a single person spell of sleeping and be ready to throw it." Hulagu started scrabbling to get his small book of incantations from his pouch. *Good, he is already thinking over what he should do and say.*

Our precautions are unnecessary. We have taken the man unawares and he is easily arrested. That is where it stops being simple. He has a wife and children and Bianca is left trying to deal with them until Father Christopher could take over.

This is certainly new to him. How does he tell the woman and children that he knows what their husband and father has done? How does he explain to the woman that he is going to be executed? All he can really do is tell her to come to the Metropolitan's Court at the end of the week and it will all be explained. It isn't very good as an explanation, but none of us have any idea what else to say. We take him away bound and gagged and on a led horse.

The next man is not so easily taken. He lives alone and must have heard something or sensed something. He is only captured when he tries to escape out the back of his hut and meets Bianca waiting there. She has put a blade to his throat, and another further down, as he came around a corner and held him until Michael's men came and secured him. He is also tied, gagged and put on a horse. The two men sit and glare at each other. At least he is a single man. At the next assart that we encounter, Michael tells the neighbours to look after the animals that are left behind and to spread the word as to what is happening.

"Do you realise that any of these buildings, anywhere through this area, could have one of the Master's pentagrams in it?" Christopher asked Theodora as they flew back to Greensin itself.

He is right...but "However, look below. Most of these settlements are very small, little more than assarts, and it would be hard to hide something. I think that it is only in a place where there are more buildings, and many that have more rooms, that you will find anything...of course, that is just a guess, but that is all we can do."

Theodora
17th September

In the next five days, they had told no-one away from the men's home area what was happening with them and they had also tried to fend off any rumours that came to their ears. In the meantime, they had looked at two more hamlets and it was time for the trial.

As we have been travelling around the area, I tell the tale of Mousehole while Christopher searches for any sign of the Masters' work. Danelis and Tabitha provided a distraction for most of the males and Bianca's babies and her story serve for the rest.

Now that it is the trial day, we have finally started talking to people about what is about to happen, but by now we have created an almost festive atmosphere. I gave some money to Andronicus and there is food and refreshment provided, but not enough refreshment for the onlookers to get drunk or unruly on, but enough to make them favourably disposed.

The Basilica Anthropoi are here to keep order, and my Mice that are not a part of what is happening stand armed and ready as well. Despite our caution, until we have finished searching the area, we cannot tell if the Masters have agents in the crowd with instructions to cause trouble and we have to be prepared in case they do.

The prisoners were brought out. They had been kept apart and both were now gagged. *I agree with the Metropolitan. If we need to enchant one it will be the married man. He is already looking at his family and his children, who are sitting guarded near the front, and he is crying.*

The Metropolitan came out onto the porch of his house with Father Christopher and Abbot Theophilus. *Andronicus is already there at a table, ready to take notes and the rest of us are waiting.* The Metropolitan blessed the crowd and began. "I am Basil Tornikes, Metropolitan of the North and senior Metropolitan of the Church Universal west of the Great Range. I am also the temporal ruler here in Greensin in the name of God."

"Behind me are Abbot Theophilus of the Monastery of Saints Cyril and Methodius, over there is Princess Theodora of the village of Mousehole, which lies in the Great Range, Father Christopher, her senior priest is here, and this is Hulagu of the Dire Wolves. He is one of the Khitan and a messenger from them and this matter concerns them as well as us."

"Some of you may be aware that there has been a major problem with bandits and raiders lately. Many of you have suffered to some extent or another. Some traders have not returned from their trips and people, particularly attractive women and girls, have just disappeared. Many have blamed the Khitan for these losses."

"We here have just found out that, until it was freed a year ago, these raiders were based in the village of Mousehole and ventured out from their home in the mountains to go all over the Plains and beyond to spread their evil. They also have confederates and helpers in many areas."

"The women, and I am sorry to say, sometimes even children, who they took have been taken to cater to the baser instincts of the raiders." He looked down at the accused. "Two of the freed slaves are with us here today." He waved towards Tabitha and Danelis. "Some of you have met them."

"One of the last attacks that affected us in this area was around a year ago. The family of Johann Beman, who lived south of here, disappeared along with his flocks and his bees. We now know that two of our own killed him and sold his daughter, Maria, to slavers from the Brotherhood."

"She now lives free in Mousehole, and I have read a letter from her attesting to what happened to her. The slavers who took her are now dead, but before they died, they named these two. The men that are bound in front of you are guilty of the murder of the man, his wife and his sons and the sale of his daughter for rape and forced prostitution."

"I have also read the testimony of the slavers. We will now hear from the men themselves and see what they have to say. If they refuse to talk, and it is needed, the Princess Theodora, who is a powerful mage, will make them talk by magical compulsion or the Presbytera Bianca, Father Christopher's wife, will use methods physical to the same effect."

The Metropolitan speaks in a level and very measured tone. He is not trying to inflame anyone. In a way his words have been even more chilling in their import because of the way they are delivered and the whole audience is quiet and still. Even the children present have sensed something portentous in the atmosphere and gone silent.

As the Metropolitan has spoken, the two accused are looking more and more desperate and there is a look of profound horror on the face of the married man's wife. When they are mentioned, the men really start to look thoroughly wretched.

After a pause, where he looked around the crowd in front of him, the Metropolitan continued: "All of the documents that I have mentioned may be inspected by any who ask after we are finished here, but I am fully satisfied with their truth."

"We will hear from this one first." *He points at the married man and takes a seat.* The guards brought the bound man in front of the Metropolitan, and removed his gag and freed his hands. *Once he is kneeling there, a Bible is produced, and the Metropolitan looks down at him.* "Will you swear before

221

God to tell us the truth, or must we use other means?"

The man looked around at his wife and children, and at the other man and swallowed. His face was streaming with tears. "Forgive me, Your Eminence, I am a sinner. I will swear." He placed his hand on the Bible. "May God strike me dead now if I utter a word of falsehood."

"I am Barton Felders, and this is my older brother Loudon. About a year ago Loudon came to me and said that we could get four gold talents each if we did some work for some men." He swallowed. "I was quick to agree, I had not seen that much money before and I wanted to do better by my family."

"Once I had agreed, he told me that we had to kill Johann Beman and his family and deliver his daughter to the men. We got to keep anything we wanted of Johann's and we had to make it look like it was done by raiders and we had to burn his house. I had just had an argument with Johann because he had claimed an area that I had wanted for my bees, and so I was not hard to convince."

He stops and looks at his wife. If anything, her look of horror has grown worse. "That is how I got all that new stock," he said to her. "We found Johann alone in the woods with his hives and we killed him. His boys came out to look for him, but they were thinking of an accident, so they separated to search and we killed them one by one. We tied Maria up when she went for water and then we went on to the house." He paused for a while.

It is obvious that he doesn't want to say any more, but he looks at us and continues. The words come out in a rush. "While I searched for any valuables in the house, Loudon raped his wife. He had always wanted her, but she had chosen Johann. I swear that I didn't touch her. When he was done, Loudon killed her."

"We dragged her body into the woods with the other bodies and hid them well. When we had taken everything that we wanted, that night we set fire to the house. We delivered the girl to the men, I don't know their names, but they were from the Brotherhood and they had another young woman and a little girl with them on horses."

"A week later, I started saying that I had not seen Johann for a while and eventually others went to check on him and found what we had done. That is the entire truth. So help me God." He threw himself at the Metropolitan's feet. "Please forgive me, Your Eminence, I was weak. I am sorry for my sins."

"My son," said the Metropolitan seriously. "It is not up to me to forgive you here. I will take your confession later, and God will forgive you if your repentance is sincere. However, here I am also a temporal ruler and for these crimes," he looked out over the crowd. *It has grown angry and is starting to mutter,* "of murder, sack, arson and kidnapping…well, they are capital and I can only sentence you to die."

He turned to the guards. "Take him away and hold him until he is confessed before God. He may see his family if they want to see him. Prepare a scaffold for him."

He turned to the older brother. "Bring Loudon here." *This is done, and the gag removed.* "Do you have anything to add? I have a feeling that this is not the first time you have worked for these men? Is that correct? Are you going to die unrepentant?"

Loudon glared at his brother's departing back and then looked at the Metropolitan. *He has passed quickly from anger to having a look of absolute defeat on his face. There is no room for him to move and his guilt is already known. His face shows resignation.* "Your Eminence, it is as my brother said. Yes, I have done things for the men before. I had one more girl to deliver and then I would get to join the bandits myself."

"Barton didn't know this, and he is a bit simple really. I was always able to get him to do what I wanted. My first that I delivered was actually that girl there with the bow." He nodded towards Danelis.

Her eyes go wide, and she takes a step forward. Tabitha restrains her. "We got her from near Warkworth about six years ago. She wouldn't remember me, because she had a bag on her head. A pretty thing she was then, her hair was already silver although she was only fourteen. We weren't allowed to have her though."

"Lucinda, that was Johann's wife, was the first that I was allowed to touch. She was still beautiful, but she was too old to be taken for the slavers." *He stops and thinks a bit.*

"You are going to hang me as well, aren't you?" *the Metropolitan nods.* "All I have left is my soul?" *Again, there is a nod.*

"Then there is another local man who is bound up in all of this, and it is his fault that we are here now. He lives north of here at the hamlet of Northrode. I don't know his name. He sometimes comes to see me when he has orders for me, and it was him who got the Brotherhood men to see me. It may be best if I tell more to someone in private."

He stops and, looking sad, addresses the people in front of him. They are muttering and looking angry. "I am sorry. I know that I was weak, but it only started off with doing little things that seemed to make little difference… and…well…I needed the money, and eventually it was too late." *As he has told the tale, his face has seemed to age. I would say that once he was not a bad man, no worse than the rest of us.*

"Anything to add?" asked the Metropolitan. Loudon shook his head. The Metropolitan addressed the guards. "Take him away, get descriptions from him and prepare him for confession and execution. He may talk to his brother, if either wants to do so."

He bleakly looked out ahead of him and again addressed the crowd. "This is both a sad and a joyous day for us all. It is sad, because evil has been shown to exist in our midst, preying on us. I will be urging all of my priests to be more vigilant and to be firmer with looking at your souls to see if they can feel such sins weighing on you."

"It is joyous because, not only is this blight now removed, but we now know of another, possibly worse villain, and this greater blight will no longer trouble us. Your lives will be safer and your daughters less likely to be prey to the evil that lurks in the shadows. I urge you all to give thanks for this."

"Now, have some food and drink. The executions will be before sunset tonight for those who wish to wait. Please spread word of these events to your friends—and make sure you tell them the full story, and in particular, that deep evil can begin with what seem like only little things." He again blessed the crowd and went into his house, followed by his secretary and the Mice.

"Once you have heard from Loudon and you have told us where this Northrode is, we will be off there. We want to catch this other man before he hears of today's events. Do you want us to bring him back here?"

The Metropolitan nods. "I do. He is ours, and so it is up to us to try him here. Andronicus will give you directions. I must have badly failed my people if something like this could happen here. I need to go aside and pray, unless I am needed for Confessions." *He looks very tired as he blesses us and withdraws upstairs.*

They left behind most of their gear and landed just after dusk near the small hamlet of six houses and a few other buildings, and dispersed. *The moons are both waxing, but they still do not provide a lot of light. Christopher will perform his miracle to find the Masters' pentagram and then will be left holding the babies again, while Bianca heads into the woods with Tabitha.*

Hulagu has already moved off to set himself up to control the path back to Greensin, although all we are expecting is a patrol coming to take our prisoner. Danelis will face the other way. I am pleased with the way we have settled into a useful routine already.

"There is a diagram," said Christopher. He pointed at the building it is in. *It is one of those nearest to us, around a hundred paces away and an outbuilding to a stone house of several rooms that is being added to. It seems to belong to the most prosperous person here and accords with what Loudon told us. It has a third building attached to it, a stable.*

Bianca and Tabitha moved out while the others tried to quietly move a little closer. *Bianca is not as good in the bush at staying quiet and hidden as she is among buildings, but she is learning. Tabitha is being trained by Astrid, who is a hard teacher, and is already better in the wild than Bianca, despite having spent so much of her time in the village.*

Bianca

T *here is a light in the house, and seemingly none in the outbuilding, but I am still checking it first. It seems to be of a much older construction than the other buildings. It has more dark lichens growing on its walls than the house apparently does. Indeed, it is covered by them and the stone underneath them cannot be seen at all, even from as close as I am. The door is closed and locked.*

Bianca listened to the door. *I can hear nothing.* She waved to the main group and beckoned them closer and headed across to the house. *Now that I am among buildings, I am more confident. We will move around to the front of the house, and leave the archers and the Princess to cover the rear. The windows are shuttered, and someone is moving around inside.*

She looked around. *The hamlet seems quiet, but if someone looks out and sees us then we could be taken as raiders ourselves. We need to be quick and take him by surprise.* She quickly mimed to Tabitha what she wanted done and Tabitha grinned. *At least she doesn't have Astrid's teeth, but that grin is more or less the same otherwise.*

Tabitha rested her spear quietly against the wall beside the door while Bianca reversed her grip on her short sword. Tabitha unlaced her top and pulled it wide open. *She unlaces the neck of her chemise completely and pulls it down to her waist to display her breasts.* Tabitha then knocked on the door and stepped back a pace and a bit more to be well out of easy reach of a person inside the building. Bianca flattened herself against the wall.

There must be no suspicion on his part. I can hear movement inside, of footsteps coming to the door and...it opens wide. Even from where I am, he is outlined by the light streaming out from behind him. Come on...there is a semi-naked woman standing before you smiling. Move forward.

The girl is wiggling her breasts seductively at him as she cups them in her hands. That is too much. He does not even look to the side...he involuntarily reaches out and takes a step forward. Bianca clubbed him at the base of the skull with the butt of her shortsword.

He fell forward into Tabitha's arms, and Bianca returned the shortsword to a normal grip and quickly moved into the room. *There seems to be no-one else here.* Tabitha is dragging the body inside and, puts him down. Bianca pointed to the wall where some rope was hanging. Tabitha began tying him up.

Bianca moved quietly from room to room and returned. "There is a door in the kitchen. Open it from the side and wave first so they don't shoot you, then get the others inside. I will check your knots."

"He has been to Mousehole a few times, bringing herbs and other supplies," said Tabitha and kicked the unconscious man in the groin. "He almost bit one of my nipples off once, and I had to be healed. They were debating whether it was worth it to do so, or whether to just kill me. He wanted them to torture me to death."

She pulled aside her top again to show Bianca the faint scar that still remained. She then kicked him again and then went for the others as Bianca had told her to. The Mice gathered in the room. Tabitha pointed at the man for Danelis and started to re-lace her jerkin as the man on the floor came around.

Danelis looked at the figure on the floor and went to get her hammer out. Theodora stopped her. "We need him alive," she said. *He is stirring.* Bianca nodded to the others. She then knelt down and put her hand over the man's mouth as he came alert, groaned and suddenly attempted to curl around the growing pain in his abused groin.

He moaned around Bianca's hand. "Hello, sweetie. We bring you greetings from the Masters." She removed her hand.

"What?" The man looked around. "They didn't say..." *Suddenly he sees Tabitha smiling at him like a cat at a trapped mouse, and his eyes widen and his face goes pale and he changes what he is about to say.* "What Masters? Who are you?"

"Too late...you are ours now. There will be a patrol here soon to take you back to Greensin for trial and execution. Do you want to tell us more about yourself, and what you have done for them while we wait? You can if you wish to entertain us. It doesn't matter all that much. We will find out everything from you at your trial." *The man may stay silent, but his eyes speak volumes.*

Tabitha kicked him again and he yelped loudly. "Do you remember me and what you did to me?" she asked. "I am going to ask the Metropolitan if I can be the one to haul you up to the scaffold. If I cannot do that, then I want the last sight you have before you die to be of my breasts. I want you to go to hell knowing exactly why you are going." She kicked him in the groin again and he gave out an anguished cry.

Christopher looked at the man on the floor. "I can readily sense the evil in him," he said. "He must have avoided every priest in the area to have not been found before now." Just then one of the babies woke and started to demand feeding. Bianca went over to look after them.

Theodora

"We had better talk to the people here. I hope that they are not all like him. It is likely that someone will eventually hear one of the babies and get curious about what is happening in here. Everyone stand ready in case of trouble. Father, come with me."

They began to go from door to door. The patrol had ridden hard and, by the time they arrived an hour later, the whole hamlet had gathered outside. *I need to explain about the trial earlier in the day and what part the man on the ground, his name is Hildric Marchant, played in it all.*

Hildric is denying his part, and alleges that he is innocent, but by that time, with the babies fed, Bianca has started to search the house and come up with a box, which Hulagu has brought to where we all are, and checking with Praetor Michael, opens cautiously by throwing his mace at the lock until it smashes. It is as well he has done it that way. There is a flash as the lock opens. It was trapped. Now they can stare in amazement at the wealth inside, and we have a key.

"So, he has a trapped box," asked one local. "There is nothing wrong with that. He is a trader and has money to protect. What proof have you got that he has done something wrong. Who are you anyway?"

"We are doing the work of the Metropolitan." She pushed Danelis and Tabitha forward. *They can tell their story and explain why they are here, and what Hildric has done to them in the bandit village.*

The patrol shows their letter of authorisation from the Metropolitan to back up all of this. It comes with a warrant of arrest, naming the charges for the crimes that Loudon was able to tell them about. Hildric is still denying the charges, but the rising tones in his voice tend to give him away, and his neighbours are starting to regard his pleas less seriously as time goes by.

Once Hildric had been taken away by the patrol, the Mice then went out to the building that Christopher had indicated. The key fit the door and, as the locals watched, the door was opened. A light was held into the room and a pentagram could be seen on the floor. "It is time to get rid of this," said Theodora. "Everyone, stand well back. Father, can you do your work please." Father Christopher came forward and got out his chalk and went to work.

He has to use stored mana for the whole of the spell this time, but again we have no magical backlash as the restrained mana becomes free, but there is a spectacular flash as something streaks into the sky from it. There was a gasp from the onlookers. *Their fear of the unknown makes them fully realise that this is not an innocent room.*

The Mice searched the building, getting some items of magical virtue to be examined later and then decided to overnight at the house and sent the locals home, having invited them to travel to Greensin on the next day to see their neighbour tried and executed. *We need to set a quiet watch in case the locals resent our interference.* It was not needed.

Theodora
18th September

In the morning, they fed Hildric's animals and invited the neighbours to help themselves to anything they wanted, "It will be forfeit anyway due to his crimes." *Now we return to Greensin with the magic and the money, to hand it to Andronicus.*

The trial of Hildric was held that very afternoon. Two of his neighbours did in fact come along to witness it. "We wanted to see if what you said was true," said one stubbornly to Theodora. "We didn't want to touch his things if he was coming back, and I am still not sure that we believe what you have told us."

"To us, he has not been an evil man. He has done nothing of harm to us and he has been good at hiring people to re-build his house and to work for him so, even if people think it strange that he lives alone, we are used to him and… well…you are strangers, and we do not believe you as much as we believe a neighbour."

Hildric starts by denying everything under oath, despite the testimony of Tabitha and Danelis. I will need to enchant him with all watching.

Now his tune changes. He gives us details of who he has met in the Brotherhood, when he has gone to trade there, and what he has been up to with the bandits. In the course of his confession, several local thefts are cleared up as well. As he speaks several people, ones who have lost relations or stock or even neighbours, cry out in anger.

The crowd are growing very restless and are starting to look forward to his death. It seems that, just as some of his money, and that of Loudon, will go back to Maria in compensation, much of what he owns will need to be sold to cover the rest of his crimes. The two men from Northrode are left shaking their heads. It seems that they are genuine and really had not believed Hildric to be guilty.

It turns out that the brothers Felders are his only agents locally, although there are some people along the coast whom he pays for information. Their names are noted for a later visit.

Hildric died unrepentant, and his last sight before the hood was put over his head was, as promised, of Tabitha's naked breasts, and the last thing that he heard were her taunts that rose into the otherwise shocked, but angry, silence that surrounded this third execution.

I am sure that Father Christopher will have a word with her about forgiveness as a Christian virtue during her next confession. As for me, I wonder if the shocking of local sensibilities with the sight of her bare breasts will, in the long run, increase the appeal of Mousehole from single men, or whether the strength and obvious independence of our women will, in fact, scare men away despite their beauty and their wealth.

Bianca
19th September

The rest of the visit to Greensin was uneventful, although the girls hoped that at least some of the men who had expressed interest in them and their plight would make the long journey to Mousehole.

Those among the men who saw Tabitha's breasts on display might be more interested in coming along to the village for them than those who have sympathy with her plight. At least the women have all decided to follow Hulagu's plan. If someone will not come to Mousehole to court them, then they are not interested in the man.

Few girls in the world are lucky enough to be either pretty or wealthy. The girls of Mousehole are both. They have paid a heavy price for the wealth that they now have. They have paid with the whole of their lives so far. They are not interested in leaving their valley to come somewhere that could be raided easily and, in doing so, to also have to leave all of their friends behind.

They left early in the morning for the flight back. The cool of the day, and especially the wind of their passage, reminded them that winter is again not far off. The babies were wrapped in the magical cloak. The rest wished that they had more of them.

Theodora agreed and promised to make them, or rather to get Rani to. "It is a spell of heat, after all. I am sure that I can easily make one that chills you though," she added cheerfully. *Everyone has declined that offer.*

Chapter XL

Theodora
20th September

*A*ll has been quiet in Mousehole. The herds were brought down from what we are now calling the High Meadow, and provisions were laid in for the winter. We even have gifts from the Metropolitan, half a dozen rose plants.

Lakshmi is very happy with those. "At last, we can think about making our own rose water. It will take a long time before we have enough, but this is, at least, a start for us."

Tabitha and Danelis had an audience of unpaired women as they told of the interest that had been shown in them, and speculated on whether men might actually come to the valley next spring. Hulagu and Bianca went straight into a session away from the rest of the village with Kāhina and Anahita.

It seems that Fear has missed her mummy and she will not leave my side, even at night. I want to make love, but it is not going to happen. "We both go to Dwarvenholme and she comes with us," said Rani after Fear was asleep between them. "I am not being left here alone with her next time. She did not stop asking when you would be back. I didn't even have the bed to myself most nights…and she snores worse than you do."

"I do not…"

"Yes, you do…and it is not new. I checked with Basil long ago. Although he was reluctant to admit it, he noted it before you even left Darkreach."

Christopher
21st September

Early in the morning, Bianca came to see Christopher and gave him a kiss. *She has a very serious expression on her face.* "I love you, my husband," she said, "but there is something that I have to do. It is important to me, to Hulagu and to Anahita and Kāhina, and possibly also to our children, if they wish it to be." She paused.

"I will be away for today and tonight at least. Bryony and Verily will be feeding the children for me. Other women are taking care of Khātun and Būrãn. It is possible that I may not return, but I believe that I will. If I do not, the other three are not to blame. I am doing this by my own choice. I was given that choice while we were away and I could have said no.

"It is very important for me to have a family, and it seems that this is what I must do to have one." *There is a look of pleading on her face. What do I say? She is holding up her hand to forestall me, so it had best be nothing.* "Please, my love, do not make this harder for me. Just tell me that you love me and wish me well."

"I love you and wish you well. This is about you becoming Hulagu's sister, isn't it?" *She nods.* "In that case, I give you my blessing as well. Whatever they do, I am sure that you will pass. I am certain of it, and will pray on the matter as well." He hugged her. "I love you and look forward to celebrating with you."

The four rode out, heading up to the chilly High Meadow with several bundles on their horses and leading a sheep on a rope, and with extra horses along with them. All of them were dressed as if they were riding off for war.

Christopher
22nd September

After Mass the next day, Christopher went to wait anxiously on the village wall. Theodule and Ruth joined him. "I am sure that your Presbytera will be fine," said Theodule.

"I don't know what they are doing," said Ruth. *There is a touch of frustration in her voice as she speaks. She really does want to find out as much about the world as she can.* "I tried to find out from Anahita, so that I could teach the custom to the children, but she said that I would have to do it to find out, and then I would not be able to tell anyone about it afterwards anyway.

However, I have confidence in Bianca. She is stronger for her size than the other two girls and she has proven herself to be able to survive when others would not do so."

They waited until lunch time, with the other two talking and Christopher silent most of the time and generally praying. Occasionally, others would join them in looking up at the path.

The others left to eat and returned, bringing food for Christopher. *I should eat something.* He nibbled a bit in an absent-minded way. *Will I become a widower today? I am not sure that I realised fully how much I love my wife until now when the possibility of her loss arises.*

I fully realise how Basil felt while Astrid was away on the first probe of Mousehole. I am at least sure that I can give an adequate answer if someone asks the same sort of questions as Basil asked before we attacked the bandit village.

It was well after lunch before there was any movement to be seen on the trail. With his eyesight, Christopher could not make out how many horses were coming down the trail. *Luckily Ayesha, who has also spent a lot of time on the wall, is there.* "There are six horses," she said. "Bianca's three and three for the others. Allah is merciful, four of them have riders. They are all there." *There is relief in her voice.*

Christopher turned and hugged her. "Thank you. I pray that one day you feel as happy as I do now." *She looks surprised. I know that she was not sitting here worried about my wife. She is worried about Hulagu.*

After greeting Christopher, the four Khitan went to see the mages as soon as they had returned and cared for their horses. Christopher took his wife's hand and went along.

"The dragon is coming," said Hulagu, with a concerned look on his face. The other Khitan nodded at his words. "Not now, not next week, but we now know that the dragon is coming here to attack, and try and kill us. It will probably be here at some time after mid-winter, but before summer is fully come."

"Have you become a seer?" asked Rani.

"I cannot tell you how I know," he replied, "but I do know. I also know that we cannot fight it with just bows and maces. It is too mighty. It is the strongest of its kind that exists anywhere in the world. It is stronger than the Dragon of the Rock. It is so large and so strong that we cannot even allow it to come into the valley of Mousehole. Our children and our herds will die if it does."

"We have told you of this threat, now it is up to you to find a way for us to kill it. The carpet is too large and too slow, and it will burn too easily, but there must be something that you can do to stop it. That is why you are our Princesses. We will fight it for you, and die for you if we must, but it is up to you to find a way for us to do this without us all dying needlessly."

The two Princesses looked at each other. *They both look worried. They do not have an immediate answer.* "Thank you for letting us know about this. We always considered that it was likely, but it is good to be sure. If we have that much time, I am sure that we will think of something," said Rani. *She may sound confident, but she does not look it. I can tell when a person is dissembling.* "Please leave it with us, and we will think about it while we are away on our next trips."

Chapter XLI

Rani
28th September

W*aiting a little meant that I was able to enchant a new warm cloak for each traveller, and still leave one for the person who has the guard duty at the valley entrance.*

True to what she said, Rani insisted that she and Fear would be on the trip. "After all, this is a friendly visit. There should be no danger to us, and having a child with us emphasises our friendship. What is more, she has to start learning these diplomatic things at some time. You grew up in a palace, as did Ayesha. I am still making mistakes learning to be a Princess, and she has even more to learn. What better way can there be than to visit the neighbours in a friendly way?"

Ayesha was taken with them. *As Princesses we do not get a lot of obedience sometimes. Ayesha and Basil gave Theo-dear a choice of which one would go, and Ayesha is coming in a servant role. They were not happy that they were left out of the last trip and insisted that one of them has to be with her at all times. I don't matter apparently.*

We leave Basil in charge of the kitchen and bring Lādi with us. She has spent over sixteen years, most of her life, in the valley. I meant it as a holiday for her, but she is insisting on bringing supplies of her own. "You don't know what cooks they have and remember what Thord said about their supplies. I am not seeing you starve, just because the Dwarves are more interested in rebuilding their city than in feeding visitors."

We have Christopher to cast the needed miracles to rid us of these patterns, and then we have Harald. Having been brought up among Dwarves, he is eager to see the lost city and, seeing we need a visible guard, we may as well have one who thinks like a Dwarf anyway.

Rani stood looking at the very fully loaded carpet before they left. *We are close to the limit of lift, and there is no space left on it.* "We need you to make us a second and larger one."

Theodora thought for a bit. "I would have to be seriously overdrawn to do it. Over winter I will see if there is a way I can, but it is not as easy as the spell that I used to hide the valley." *Obviously, my wife has already thought about such a spell.* "That is why the Caliphate does not use them all of the time," continued Theodora, by way of explanation.

"Flying carpets are rare. I don't know where the bandits got this one from, but I am sure that the Caliphate is missing it. Besides which, I don't think that Bilqīs is able to weave one well enough yet. Did you see her last attempt? It will work on a floor for a few years as long as it does not get much traffic on it, but I wouldn't want to trust my life to it. It may be many years before she is ready, but at least she is starting to show the little girls how to do it. She says that, at seventeen, her fingers are far too old to do a really good job."

Ayesha leant over their shoulders. "What is more," she said, "I have not seen many, but this is the fastest carpet I have ever seen. Usually a carpet can either carry a load and move slowly, or carry very little and move fast. This does both. I may not be any good with magic, but I am willing to say that no-one in the Caliphate could make it today. If you know carpets you can see, just by looking at it, that it is woven in a very old pattern."

Theodora nodded and added: "What you need to hope is that Bilqīs can repair it when it gets a hole. I hope that it survives the dragon, and that we can think of something to do about it."

"It seems to me that, the more powerful I get as a mage, the more that is demanded of me. It makes me wonder how, if that is the case for me, if the Granther ever gets time to even rule, let alone relax."

I am glad of these new cloaks. The air is rapidly getting colder as we travel. Winter is just around the corner and we still have one trip to make after this one, and it is a long one. After having left the valley by the gate, they flew around its southern outskirts and then directly up into the mountains.

I can see the trees around the valley, often deciduous, being replaced by the towering mountain gums and hardier upland conifers. Looking north they stared into the bowl of the Upper Meadow. *It shows little sign of being grazed all summer. Only in a few small patches, mainly near the stream, does the grass look any shorter at all. There is, however, a small hut.* "No-one mentioned that," said Theodora. "What else have they been doing over summer that no-one talked about?"

"Do you realise that we didn't do anything about Aziz's old tribe all summer?"

"Next year," said Theodora. "Somehow I think that visit would not have counted as resting."

As we move closer to Dwarvenholme and look further up into the mountains, I can see that the permanent snow on the peaks is already edging further down the slopes, and some of the valleys are starting to fill with their winter blanket. Above us the gums are shrinking and becoming more twisted and the plants of heath and the upper slopes are starting to dominate. As they went, Rani was holding Fear tightly on her lap and pointing all of these things out to her.

They came up their river to the Dwarvenholme road and turned right. *The road that had been almost non-existent, the track that we struggled over with the cart breaking a wheel, is almost a proper road again, at least as far south as Dwarvenholme.*

All of the trees have been cleared off it, all of the centuries of dirt have been cleaned away, and even some of the stone paving has been replaced. All it needs is traffic. I can see a Dwarven gang hard at work on it where a landslide has taken a section away. We almost lost a wheel getting around that slip; soon it is going to be as if the rock fall never existed, and now I can hear the faint noise of a large horn being blown in a call from ahead.

They arrived near lunchtime. *I nearly didn't recognise the entrance. The skeletons of past Dwarves that attacked us and all of the trees that were outside have disappeared. The pathways up from the road have been restored completely. The rocks are gone off the paths. Some have been used and others now lie in piles waiting to be.*

A sentry stands on a watch platform high above the gate. We didn't even notice that it existed when we were here. There are no stairs up to it that I can see, so unless Dwarves have learnt to fly, this means that it is accessed from inside. The sentry is heralding our approach with another short tune on his horn, and Dwarves working below on the platform stop and stare up at us as we approach. It seems that we are expected as there is no apparent fuss about our approach.

Gradually, Theodora brought the carpet down to the main platform, stopping in the middle of it in front of the door. They took their time getting off the carpet and ready. Theodora and Rani moved towards the door each holding one of Fear's hands. Striding behind them as guard was Harald, looking around as he went.

Ayesha and Lãdi were left with the carpet. Ayesha had her bow strung and was making moves to unpack the carpet, ready to take things inside, but she stayed alert in case there was trouble. She needn't have bothered. Thord was already hurrying out of the gates with his hands outstretched in welcome. Behind him they could see some more Dwarves approaching.

*W*e are greeted by one who is tall for a Dwarf and broad with it. He has a grey beard and hair. "Welcome, again I believe, to Dwarvenholme 'n' t'Race will t'ank you forever for what you've done here. I am T'orgrim Baldursson, t'Mayor of Dwarvenholme, at least until t'findin' of t'King."

"T'smilin' fool who greeted you first is livin' happy on our t'anks. One day he may come to his senses 'n' rejoin us, but in t'meantime you'll be pleased to hear t'at he serves your interests well." *Thord's face takes on a look of exaggerated hurt and wounded innocence, which fools no-one.*

He continues: "You come to clear t'relics of t'Masters, I believe, 'n' we'll be glad. Our Druids tell me t'at safely performin' such task is beyond t'eir ken at present, but t'ey be keen to learn. In t'meantime come 'n' see what we've done to restore Dwarvenholme. We still ha'years of work ahead of us, but it be work t'at any Dwarf'll be glad to do."

"T'roads're priority 'n' Thord would not tell us how you arrived here 'n' spirited away some of the treasure without our permission." *He smiles at that.* "When you let us know which path you ha'used, we'll clear it so t'at we may trade with you for food, 'n' I believe, gems 'n' metal."

"We thank you for your welcome," said Theodora, "I am Princess Theodora, and this is my husband Rani, and our daughter Fear." *This statement elicits no response at all from the Dwarf...something to store away for later thought.* Theodora waved a hand: "Our guard here is Harald Pitt." *Harald interrupts waving at Dwarves he knows to give a short bow.* "He was brought up among Dwarves in the Hills in the Northern Plains. Behind us you see Ayesha and Lãdi, who were brought up in the Caliphate."

"Please show us the wonders you have here. We saw only a pale fraction of the glory that will again be Dwarvenholme on our last visit, and we look forward to seeing it more properly now that the Dwarves have returned and have begun restoring its glory to the way that it once was and should be again."

They were taken inside and shown what was to be seen. *I note that many of the nails we left have been moved, although they are still being used. Now they are placed in the roof. Thorgrim notes my look.*

"Aye, we still use t'nails, 'n' we t'ank you for'em. T'ey ha'made our task far easier. Eventual t'ey'll be replaced with somethin' grander, but just now t'ey let us concentrate on lightin' areas t'at you did not visit."

In the entrance hall, it was easy to hear, and indeed to smell, that the rooms of stables along it were now in use, as were the guard rooms. *Dwarvenholme is coming back to life.*

In place of bats and dung, the grand concourse is now full of light and scurrying Dwarves. The smell is even gone, although from the strength of the incense being burnt in several places, it may be merely banished for a while. It may be some time before it leaves the rocks completely.

Looking around and up they could see that the balconies were being repaired and some of the alcoves, mainly those at ground level, already had shops in place in them. *It seems that there are eight levels here in this immense space.*

Around us rises a clamour. In this huge empty void, it is a little thin compared to Pavitra Phāṭaka. I have quickly grown accustomed to the quiet of the village, broken only by Norbert's hammer and the cries of children. Next to that, this is almost a continuous din.

They stopped and stared around them. Eventually Ayesha and Lãdi, together with other Dwarves carrying their belongings, joined them and they also just stared.

"It is already as big as Yarmūk," declared Lãdi, naming the village she grew up in.

"And Yāqūsa," added Ayesha. "It seems so much larger now that we can see all of it."

Thorgrim and Thord are both beaming with pride. "T'rest of t'Land must be wonderin' what is happenin' to t'Dwarves," said Thorgrim. "Near half of us're either here or bringing t'ings here. It is a great time.

"All we need is t'King to make it complete, 'n' if we lack him, t'en we will ha' more time to ready it for him. Who knows, perhaps he'll be born here. T'at would be good 'n' would save many arguments. T'Finder insists he does not yet know him, 'n' on t'is we must trust him."

Lãdi and Ayesha went off with their attendants and, after some more looking around Thorgrim said: "I will allow T'ord to show you to where you'll stay. It is on the T'rone Level, where t'Masters were, 'n' I presume, where you will be workin'.

"I notice t'at you ha' brought food. It is as well; our supplies here tend more to t'portable 'n' t'storable t'an to t'palatable. T'ord probable told you t'at. He never stops complainin' 'n' missing your cook 'n' her work. T'is is one of t't'ings t'at will change 'n' at least t'fungi fields ha'plenty to grow on." He sighed and then politely took his leave and they began the long walk up the stairs.

This time it is easier. The stairs are now well lit and we can lean out and look far up and down the shaft. We can even hear others using it. Coming towards us are living Dwarves, rather than the animated remains of their ancestors. It is still, however, a long climb.

Fear, as children do when the exercise they are doing is not of their choosing, is complaining well before we reach the top. As they went, Theodora explained to Harald and to Fear what had happened and where. *Her explanations attract attention and, while our arrival may have been expected by some, it is obvious that not everyone has heard about it.*

That night, on Harald and Thord's advice, they held a small feast for the Mayor and a few others among the leaders of the Dwarves. *It is lucky that Lãdi expected that, and brought the portable stove and more food than we would have otherwise needed.*

Theodora
29th September

The next day, they got to work on dismissing the pentagrams working into the floors of the nearby rooms. *It is slow work, but getting safer and safer as we grow accustomed to the spell. The first casting had been the riskiest, but now it is getting to be an almost routine enchantment.*

"The surviving Masters, wherever they are, must be feeling this," said Theodora. "There is always a feeling of pain and anguish when something you have made is dis-spelled. Losing them at this rate must hurt—even for them."

When they were not working, they were taken on tours of Dwarvenholme by Thord. *Now we can use the carpet to travel up and down the stairs. Seeing that we are just going up and down and there is no wind, if we leave most of our stuff behind, and are all careful and take it slowly, it is safe to fit an eighth person on board.*

They still did not return until what might be night. Thord took them to the base of the stairs and the workings there and back. *As we go, I can see envious looks coming from those who are trudging up and down the hard way. Dwarvenholme turns out to have twelve main levels and many smaller ones.*

When they reached the bottom, it was revealed to be a mine. *The level above it was still being built when Dwarvenholme was lost. It was to have housed smelting and other smelly trades that would have been brought down from above. It is obvious that once this city held many more people than any city now in the world and it was intended to have room for many more.*

Vast ventilation shafts interlace the levels and the spells there are being restored, slowly, to keep the air fresh so far beneath the ground. You know when you are near those shafts as the roaring wind in them seems able to be heard even through the rock. Eventually spells will be used to calm the noise, but for the moment, those enchantments are less important than making it possible to work everywhere in Dwarvenholme without Dwarves passing out from stale or foul air. It is a lot of work.

Theodora
6th October

Eventually, the work was done. *It has taken a very long time; the largest Pattern is left until last. Christopher was unsure if his standard miracle would be able to handle it. He has to modify the one he has been using, but he is so familiar with them now that it is possible. With the diagrams gone, it seems that there is almost a perceptible lift in the spirit of the city. There is no reason for this, but looking round, that is the way it seems to be.*

That night the Dwarves hosted them for a dinner, although it turned out, from the fact that a Dwarf in an apron kept coming and talking quietly to Lãdi, that she might have had a hand in it as well. *There are a lot of mushrooms, of different sorts, among the dinner dishes, even as sauces on the pork-like meat.*

"When you get that road down to us built, we will work out how to trade. I think that we may have some greens and herbs that your cooks will appreciate, and even some hot spices and drinks. As well, I think that we had a good year for onions and root vegetables. You do seem to have plenty of dried pulses though." *I tried as hard as I could to make that sound like a compliment, but I fear it was not a success.*

Rani
7th October

In the morning, they were bidden farewell and they headed back to Mousehole. *The last of the nearby visits have been made. The next visit that we make has to be the trip to Darkreach. We will wait at least a month for that one, and leave Mousehole much closer to the onset of the real winter. It is unlikely that there will be any threat to the village when the snows lie deep and it will be hard to get the dragon to stir in such weather.*

On the trip back to Mousehole, and before they headed down the northern flank of their valley, with the mountain of the dragon very visible on their right, the carpet rocked suddenly and violently, and an excited Theodora said: "I have an idea. If you can make some sort of weapon, I think that I can give our people a chance to get close enough to use it, and still have a chance to stay clear of its breath. It will be dangerous, but it should work."

She will not be drawn any more on details, and we have to land and let Lādi take a turn controlling the carpet as Theo-dear is soon too distracted to steer properly and keeps veering off course and rocking the carpet.

Chapter XLII

Hulagu
7th October

W ell, the carpet is back, but Theodora's mind is not. She has just jumped off and called for Stefan. They are in a heads-together conference as they are walking to his workshop and Stefan is already jumping about. From up here on watch I can see covered objects going into his workshop and everyone else being kept out.

N ow Dulcie has been called in, and the sound of hammering and sawing comes from her locked workshop as well, and she and Tabitha then start carrying things draped with cloth to Stefan's workshop, where there is more hammering. No-one will say anything, just grinning when asked and we are all just told to wait.

Hulagu
13th October

I t is a week later that Theodora has brought out the old jars from wherever they were kept, and started going around collecting hair and nails, and other things, from everyone. The carpet has even been sent to collect from Thord, taking food with it.

I guess Theodora is brewing a major spell again. She will not say what it is, even to us apprentices, but is humming happily as she goes around the *village. Sometimes she can be very annoying, just like a small child with a hidden treasure. She has even collected from all of the children.*

The next day, word came out that everyone was banned from casting or even using spells in the village for the next few days.

Hulagu
16th October

Theodora *has called everyone together outside the hall. Stefan, Dulcie and Tabitha are standing there proudly in a row. Behind them is a large covered lump.* Theodora smiled and eventually spoke as she looked around them. "Hulagu has told us that the dragon will be coming to Mousehole after winter is over."

So that is what it is about. She looks around her. They all know that by now. Was she expecting to keep that secret in a community this small? She sighed.

"Several of you have asked about how we might deal with major threats and others have complained that we need another carpet. We cannot make one of those yet, but we may have something even better for what we need." *Her voice is sounding almost smug.* "Behold," she waved a hand, and Stefan and the others moved away and whipped the cloth off what they had concealed so far.

What in the name of the spirits bastard children is that? It looks a bit like a saddle and has obviously started out as one left over from the bandits. It can never be used on a horse again. It stands on three carved wooden legs a short pace off the ground. It has a bow case and two covered quivers attached to it and a small projection out of the front of it to which short reins are attached.

Is it meant to train people how to ride? I have heard the people of the khanatai gazar have toy horses for children, but it has no head at the front nor the rockers that I hear such horses usually have.

Astrid is almost bursting out laughing, but the four up front look proud. No-one else is saying anything, and the makers are looking fit to burst. People are looking at each other in puzzlement. I don't want to be the first to ask. It seems that everyone is the same, even Rani. "All right," Astrid, *predictably,* asked, "what is that?"

"I am very glad you asked," said Theodora. "Hulagu, please come here… please put this on. Make sure it is tight and secure around your waist." *All right what is this? She has given me a leather thing. It is a belt with a large metal ring on each side of it. Once it is on, she continues.*

"Now please sit on this as you would sit on a horse." He did this. "Now think of it as if it were a horse, a horse of the air. Be gentle with it, and think of slowly walking a horse, but as if it were in the air." Hulagu concentrated.

The saddle is rising. By the Sky Spirit, it is flying. "Turn it with the reins," said Theodora. "You should be able to use your knees as you do on a horse, but the reins will be easier to use for now."

"I want everyone to move up on to the roof of the Mouse Hall, quickly. Hulagu, just stop there until we are all upstairs." *They are all rushing upstairs, now they are all excited, but not as excited as I am.*

When they have reached the top, Theodora looks at me and calls down. "Now, Hulagu, you will see that on each side of you there is a strap and a buckle. I don't want you to feel insulted, but please make sure you fasten yourself on tightly with the belt—as tight as you can."

Curious, and looking around and finding straps and buckles, Hulagu obeyed. "Now, do what you want with it. You can go as fast as you want and, if we have done it right, you should even be able to fly on your side. I will urge you to be cautious when you try something new. I think that this will be a skill that is different to anything that anyone has ever done before. It may look a little like riding, in some ways, but I am sure that it will take near as much learning to master."

Hulagu, in reflex, dug his heels into where a horse would be. *It is as if it is alive. It has taken off.* Faster and faster he flew, faster than the fastest horse, and then far faster still. *I am flying faster than the fastest birds.*

He started moving it around and, at one stage ended up flying upside down over the watchers making 'whooping' noises with the quivers hanging down past him. *It is lucky that they are lidded. I must bring it back. Theodora is beckoning at me.*

"We will be making as many of these as we can," said Theodora. "I am thinking we will eventually need at least twenty. Everyone that can learn to use one will get one. We think that we can now out-fly the dragon. Now we just have to work out how to use these to get us in a position to kill it."

"Best of all, no-one who is not of Mousehole can use them. Even those children we now have can eventually be taught. I thought that I was not going to be able to do this, but I thought only about carpets and brooms, which for some reason are traditional for flying."

"Eventually," she said looking from one to another of the trainee mages, "I thought, why not use something that is meant to be ridden on, and that wants to be ridden instead of something that was meant for another purpose. That will reduce the cost of the spell...and it worked. Adding that, to making it so that only the people of this valley can use them, well, I was just able to perform the conjuration."

Rani ran up and kissed her. "This will give us an advantage in any battle, let alone against a dragon. We need molotails when we go to Darkreach. We can drop those on armies from above them and only magic will be able to touch us, and we can cope with that as well."

Hulagu
30th October

I may not be much use yet, but so much magic is being made that Harald has begun digging out one of the largest empty spaces of the mine, to be used for the storage of items that will take several days to complete otherwise only one item can be made at once.

Soon the increasing number of saddles became popular, so popular that people rode their saddle to the fields or out to the watch point. *Even Astrid has had a try. I never thought that I would see that. She can use the saddle, but she cannot use her long bow from it nor her spear.* "It is useless to me except as transport."

Rani is determined and seems to be using her army mind hard. Eleanor, who is the best of us with using a lance, is soon hard at work training flyers. Norbert is also soon hard at work, modifying mail and helmets while Fortunata, Astrid and Parminder are sewing uniforms for everyone.

Rani wants to make a show of our visit, so that we do not appear to be below the notice of a mighty Empire.

Eventually, Astrid has to admit that the saddles are fun, "Just like sailing, or a good run downhill on skis." *She is having less fun now Rani is insisting on us learning to fly in perfect formations, and be able to change direction as if we are one. We are not perfect, but lots of hard work will make us better. We are improving almost every day.* Rani insisted on them moving just right, even above them learning to shoot their bows or use their lances from the saddles.

"We hopefully will not have to be in combat on this trip, but presenting a good appearance is important," she said. "From what Theodora tells me, the Darkreach heavy cavalry make ours in the west look like amateurs. We have to be able to impress them."

Hulagu dealt with the grumblers shortly. "She is treating us just as Haven treats their cavalry. They move as one and hit hard and can move quickly away and regroup. On our saddles, we can do it even better, and the cavalry of Haven do not know how to use bows or magic.

"Some of you saw how good her escort looked arriving at Evilhalt. In a short time, we will look better." His voice bore certainty.

Soon, most of them were practicing in mail similar to that worn by

Theodora. After a while, the seamstresses brought out a pile of folded blue cloth. The riders put them on over their armour as tabards bearing an image on gold of a mouse sitting up on its haunches over their hearts. Flowing from attachments on their helmets were streamers of blue cloth and their lances had, near their tips, pennons with the same mouse on them.

Theodora

T *hey listen to Astrid in the air and it is all looking good.*
Rani had been working inside and came out for some fresh air in time to see the riders in their new panoply sweeping past in a row. "Where did the mouse come from?" she asked.

"Fortunata insisted on it. She grew up in Freehold after all. That is one of the things she can remember from growing up as a beggar. The rich people, and the people who worked for them, apparently have badges on their clothes there. She thought that being rich meant you should have a badge. She is now rich, so she wants us to have a badge. She is working on banners for our walls now.

Rani nodded thoughtfully for a moment. "Good idea," she said.

Chapter XLIII

Theodora
31st October

*W*e *will leave for Ardlark straight after Astrid's mid-winter fire. It doesn't matter how cold the weather is when we travel, and that is the usual limit placed on any extensive travel in the mountains. My dark beauty has her warmed cloaks for all of the people who will be going. Now that we have my saddles as well as the carpet, we can take many more people if we choose to.*

Although the spell remains the same, the way the saddles are made is being changed as we learn more about how to use them, and now they all even have saddlebags, and some of the Mice have gotten Stefan to modify their saddles in special ways. Bianca has had a set of buckles put on each side of her usual saddle, so that she can carry her babies in what look suspiciously like baby quivers lined with wool and blankets. Astrid, Anahita and Kāhina have quickly copied her in this.

Astrid
2nd November

*I*n *the early light of the morning we set off.* Others accompanied them to the gate and Lakshmi went on to the lookout. As they left the lookout they climbed for altitude, Astrid looked back to Verily, who was controlling the carpet. "Try for more speed."

Except for our scouts, who can scoot around as they will, our experience so far shows that most saddle-riders feel very sluggish being tied to the carpet. In the van are Hulagu, Kãhina and Anahita, as scouts, flying a long way ahead of the rest and spread well out and having fun. The others ride with me.

Why did Rani make me command while we are in the air? Damn her. I want to be with the others out front. I am at the point and Valeria, Fãtima, Ayesha and Bianca are formed up behind me. Oh, I know what she said about my experience with ships and ski…and I have to admit that skiing, rather than riding, is the skill that is closest to using the saddles.

It is a pity that few in The Land, and no others among us, have the skill. The others use their reins. Mine are looped onto my saddle and I control my mount just by shifting my weight in the seat and the stirrups.

Astrid looked around. *I have two fliers on the same level as the carpet, and one rides above and one below. Behind the carpet are Basil and Bilqîs, flying side by side. The scouts have their bows out and their lances tucked away in holders. The others fly with their lances at an angle.*

With no threat to be seen, and flying well above any bow's range, even well enhanced, we all have the mail veils on the helmets raised. We will only fly like this when there are people who can see us, and Basil tells me that the Darkreach forts in the hills and Forest Watch, on its hill to the east will all, most likely be watching.

Every now and then, to keep people alert and stop them getting bored, Astrid blew a whistle and waved her arms and changed from that formation from the square arrow, to a flat arrow with a point and two or three trailing from it or a line formation. She spread them out and then closed them up, moved them up and moved them down, and made their relatively slow pace through the air at least an occasion for practice, rather than a slow procession.

Astrid led them east of Forest Watch, the most isolated of Darkreach's watch towers. *I once wondered why it was placed on its lonely hill. Now that I know where all the roads run through the area, its location finally makes sense. If the people there know where the roads run around them, and have the right equipment, they can watch for movement on the roads from Evilhalt to Mousehole and Kharlsbane, as well as the Mousehole road itself. They might even see the junction of the Mousehole road and the path up into Dwarvenholme.*

If all of these roads were clear and busy, it is a location that cries out for a watch garrison. It may be near useless now with how few people move through the area, but no major movement of people, or in particular armies, can take place near the Gap without the watchers knowing, if they are alert and know where they should look.

As she looked at it, she could see a beacon fire had been lit on it. *It glows briefly with just its flame and then throws up a column of black smoke. Our arrival at Mouthguard will now be expected.*

They stopped soon after that for lunch, to feed and change babies and to stretch their legs. *Even with the carpet slowing us down it does not take much longer to sight Mouthguard and some traffic on the roads around it.*

Despite it being the middle of winter, so many Dwarves are still on the road trudging through the snow that their road can be seen from the sky as a dark strip laid across the white of the rest of the landscape. They have even taken to working on the tracks between Kharlsbane and Mouthguard, and making them into something more of a road. That will take many years to complete, but the long-lived Dwarves are never deterred by how long a project will take.

Astrid called for a flat arrow formation, summoning the scouts back, with Hulagu to take her position and the girls to take the ends of the formation. *I note, from the agitation I can see…an ant's nest with water poured on it would be about right…that the keep has worked out what the beacon fire was about and has seen our approach.*

She halted the flight well out of the range of shot, even for a ballista. Soaring down closer to the ground, she flew on alone. She looked back. *All the lances are held correctly. Ahead is a keep with a nervous collection of soldiers. Now, what is the name Thord told me…ah yes.*

She flew up to the keep at the level of a horse's rider. "Greetings, I am here to see Mellitus to get some travel documents to go on to Ardlark. We are an Embassy from the village of Mousehole, the Dwarves may have mentioned us, and we are on the way to Ardlark for our Princesses to see His Imperial Majesty," she smiled her toothiest grin at them and waited.

A Kharl, a Kichic-Kharl archer, scurried inside and returned quickly with an Insakharl. *He must have been waiting somewhere nearby, he is that prompt.* "I am Mellitus," he said, "and who are you? What do you want?"

"I am Astrid the Cat, and we are going to Ardlark as an Embassy from Mousehole. I am in charge of the guard. We thought that, wanting to do the right thing; we would get travel documents here, rather than just fly in."

"You could be a threat," *Mellitus looks and sounds very unsure, he is stalling. I am sure that the only other entrants into Darkreach from the outside world have been a few merchants. Most of the traffic that he has seen so far will have been from Darkreach traders going out and passing Dwarves. According to what Basil has told me, few outsiders will be going in and none so strongly armed.* "I am not sure if we should let you in."

"Oh, you cannot stop us if we do want to go in. We can just fly over you if we want to. As for being a threat…" She turned and made the arranged hand signal that would bring Basil forward, "I think that I would like you to meet my husband." She waited, refusing to say more. When Basil came up to join them, she introduced him.

"Mellitus, this is my husband, Tribune Basil Akritas of the Antikataskopeía. He reports directly to Strategos Panterius, I believe," she smiled sweetly. "You do know who he is, don't you? Husband dear, please say hello to the nice man who is about to give us travel documents."

"Hello," said Basil. "What is the delay?" he asked in his best military voice. "Do you wish to see my sigil?" He reached into his pouch and started pulling it out. Mellitus swallowed. *He is caught like a fish on a hook and he knows it.* Basil showed it to him. *Except for sealing letters, I don't think that he has used it since he was given it.*

"I will just be a moment," said Mellitus very quickly. *He is glancing nervously at the sigil in Basil's hand as he goes.* He turned to go back inside and then remembered something, turned again and obviously started counting.

"In case you are having trouble, there are two and a half hands of adults and a hand and one of children." *I am enjoying this.* "Do you want our names? No, we are diplomats, it should not be necessary."

Theodora told me, and I happen to agree with her, to avoid any mention of the presence of the Princess. I cannot lie while I do it though. Offering names and then arguing against the idea is a good way to achieve both objects.

The Insakharl headed inside and came back in a few minutes with a piece of paper. Astrid drew nearer and took it and, without looking at it...*after all, I still cannot really read more than a few words of Darkspeech the silly way that they write it...*she handed it to Basil.

He looks at it, "That seems to be in order, but you have who is in charge of the Embassy wrong, still that is no moment. Let us go."

Astrid took the paper back and tucked it in her pouch. She then waved her hand in the air in one of her hand signals and pointed up the pass. Verily turned the carpet and the others wheeled with her. Basil sped back to his position and Astrid flew ahead of the rest at her best speed.

With that piece of paper to be shown, I will take the lead until Nameless Keep, at least. She indicated more height and they rose to half way to the level of the forts, riding a thousand paces in the air above the Methul River. *It is flowing underneath us in the centre of the broad valley that cleaves the mountains in two, like an axe-mark though a fallen log.*

Directly below, I can see the light winter traffic on the river and the activity of the hamlets springing up along its cold length. Even I am glad of the warmth of the cloaks. I note that, if the bright winter sunshine high up in the pass momentarily fools a rider into throwing a cloak off, the speed of our passage makes the wind cut through our clothes in an instant and soon prompts us to put them back on.

Chapter XLIV

Astrid
2nd November

T heodora has decided that we should spend the night at some little hamlet that was springing up at the head of navigation of the Methul when she first came through. That must be it. I hope that Theodora remembers the disguise for her eyes. Basil tells me that this took three days and we have done it in a few short hours.

My husband didn't mention crops, but there are some stone-walled fields now on the north slope of the valley, where the hard-pressed crops can catch some sun, and I can see a small flock of sheep let out into one of them with a bale of hay. A few small houses, some of them still being added to, a couple of large barns, as well as what looks like a warehouse by the water's edge, make up the rest of the settlement. Theodora thought there would be an inn now, and there is. It has a sign with a head painted on it and water flowing out of the open mouth. I cannot read the writing. From behind Basil said, "The River's Head."

While the others stayed mounted, Astrid went in calling loudly for the innkeeper. He was obviously not used to such large and loud Insakharl women and seemed terrified. "It is winter, we don't have enough rooms ready," he said wringing his hands.

"That is all right," *Take a conciliatory tone. I shouldn't tease someone who is about to prepare my food.* "We will wait here and feed babies and have something to eat and drink before your fire. That will give you time to prepare, we are early for the meal anyway and would appreciate a chance to just rest." He tugged his forelock and scurried away.

Astrid called the others in to where she waited. The saddles had been made to fit through most doorways and so, when the landlord returned into his main room with a girl servant, some tables had been moved aside and the saddles were lined up along a wall. The carpet was rolled up on top of them and under Ayesha's watchful eye. *If he is taken aback by soldiers, having doffed their mail, then breastfeeding, he didn't show it beyond a widening of his eyes. Good boy.*

Tactfully, and nervously, he cleared his throat, "I have to ask to see your papers please."

"Of course." Astrid dug the piece of paper out of her pouch.

"You are not from here then?" he asked inanely as she was doing this.

"Most of us aren't, but the two with black eyes are. I am an Insakharl from outside the Empire. We don't all have the eyes where I am from."

He inspected the paper. "That is in order, thank you. Just let this girl know what you want and I will see about rooms. We may not have enough for all of you to sleep in. I am afraid that you will have to make do with barracks."

"A barracks will do for us, but if you have five rooms for us, well then that will do as well. If you have six, then four will share one. Most of us are small." *I talked with Basil about costs and can now just pay.* She pressed some money into his hand. *He is obviously pleased with what he sees. He smiles, touches his forehead again and hurried off. It is nice to have people defer to me.* Soon there was a bustle and the clatter of noise from above them that signalled efforts to make more rooms ready as they gave their orders for drinks.

"I am going to have a look at the kitchen," said Basil in Hindi. "Some of these places are acceptable and some aren't. We didn't stay the night here on the way out, so I don't know." He wandered out the back following the waitress.

The food is acceptable, given the short notice, but not what we are used to. "It is fairly normal Darkreach tavern food," said Basil. "The kitchen is clean though, and that is the most important thing."

They spent a quiet and fairly comfortable night and headed off after Astrid had paid the innkeeper the rest of his bill. His eyes went wide at the sight of the ancient and unfamiliar golden coins he was handed, and he could not resist biting one before obviously deciding that gold is gold, regardless of what it looks like.

They came up to the huge bulk of Nameless Keep well before lunch on the next day. *As it grows in front of us, I can see that it might be impregnable to any normal army, but unless its defences are augmented, it is as open to slaughter from the air as a baby seal lying on the ice. The castle behind its*

walls is as vulnerable to us as the spread-out surrounding village would be to an army on the ground.

Still, she obeyed Theodora's injunction and flew down to the entrance to be polite. *Christopher has indicated that he wants to check here for one of the Master's pentagrams. We can do little now if he finds one, but due to its key spot for trade, it would be a good place for the Masters to have placed an agent, at least.*

Astrid flew up to the gate of the keep and produced her papers. *They are handed back with barely a glance. The looks are reserved for the saddles. This garrison seems much more casual than the one on the border. It is marvellous, once you are inside. If you have the right papers, everyone is much more relaxed and they don't ask questions at all, even though I can see that several want to.*

As they had lunch and fed babies in a village inn, Christopher performed his miracle. He finished and shook his head. "There is one here in the village," he said. "Do you want us to do anything about it?"

Theodora and Basil looked at each other. "I am on detached duty," said Basil. "I could do something if I wanted to, but it might get the local officers upset with me. I haven't even checked in with them, and I won't. I think it is best to report this to my Strategos first, and allow him to take it from there. Such news is a good gift for him." Theodora and Rani concurred and they flew off after eating. Christopher discretely pointed out the building he had found to Basil as they rose and Basil made a note of its location.

*D*espite it being winter, the air from Nameless Keep to Sasar gets warmer and warmer as the day progresses, and we fly rapidly over the way posts that had seemed so far apart when Theodora told of leaving Darkreach. Soon the air we fly through is warmer than Mousehole gets in summer and the cloaks are being put away.

Even from a distance it is possible to see where Sasar is. The great gouge that is being taken from the hill behind it can be seen for many miles. Over many centuries, terrace after terrace had been driven back into the slope and then eliminated gradually from below. Although there is a long way for them to go, gradually the hill is being eaten away.

*W*e may have been glad to drop in at Sasar to eat, but we are also very glad to leave. The red dust from the great iron mine coats everything.

It is like the dust from peat moss and flavours the food if the wind blows the wrong way...and it is blowing.

Only the Alat-Kharl and Greydkharl people seem happy to be there. From what I can see, it is a place of hard work and hard drinking, and with little else to commend it.

N ow, Sasar *looks good. The air grows even hotter and far drier as we move further into the Great Plain. I have never been this hot, even in a sauna. That must be the Great Bitter Lake to the left of the road. Aziz, with his eyes being more sensitive to light than those of the humans, has to travel with his eyes closed and Verily has bound a cloth around them to help him.*

To the right, the massif of the dead, which was crowned by the ancient barrows, and watched over by Deathguard Tower, came into view spread beneath them. Theodora had said it was large, but she did not tell half of it. *The view from above shows you what you cannot see from the ground. There are over a hand of huge conical tumuli, each a large hill in its own right and countless smaller ones. Who built these? What happened to their people? Why do we know nothing of them? Why are there not even legends?*

T hey came to a stop before the gates of the keep and, again, Astrid flew on forward with their pass to have it inspected by the guards. *This is easy. I am soon waving them all in. I note that the Princess and my husband are getting some second looks from the garrison. It seems that they are remembered by some.*

Bianca

A s *we set up in the accommodation, and being more relaxed now than he had been at Nameless Keep, my husband wants to find the local priest for a 'professional chat.' I had better go with him, I suppose.*

The local priest, Father Theodorus Daphopates, is very surprised to see him. Christopher is the first priest from outside the Empire that he has heard of in Darkreach. Now that my husband has gone back and fetched my Bible, it will be the last I see of him tonight. They are already head down checking if they both use the same text. I suppose that it has to be done. I am going to get some rest.

Theodora

T his is the first place where there is genuine curiosity about us and our mission and the fact that we have a Hobgoblin with us. What is more, he is dressed as the rest of us are and he has a Human wife. Probably due to being on continual combat alert because of where they are, the garrison (and almost everyone is a part of the garrison, even the innkeeper and the waitresses), are interested in anything that happens that might affect them.

I have to be careful about letting on who Basil and I really are, and ask them to keep the tale quiet among themselves until they were told otherwise, but I need to tell them what is happening. I am sure that, if anyone in Darkreach will readily believe in the Masters and their actions, it will be the people that live here.

After the tale was complete, Basil had to go with two officers to introduce them to Father Christopher. Apparently, they want an immediate check for any pentagrams in the area. Basil tells me that the fact that it was negative produced immediate relief on their faces. I suppose that they have enough to worry about.

I noticed the looks that passed when I mentioned that the attack on us had probably been engineered by the Masters. Basil also told me that he saw the looks passing between the officers and is willing to bet that the intensity of patrols is about to be stepped up and that the seals will be more closely inspected for a long while, especially the ones that are far away from the Keep.

Apart from the tale of what brings us here, I think that the garrison are disappointed not to see any entertainment, particularly seeing that we have only three males and we women are all so beautiful.

However, as Fātima, in her heavily accented Darkspeech, told one admirer, a huge dark-green Isci-Kharl sergeant, as big as Aziz and with his rank clearly tattooed on his bare arms: "if you wish to court us, you now know where we live, and it is not just us, there are other women there as well."

Basil
3rd November

T*he next morning, we have headed out while it is still cool. It won't last,
but this is so much more comfortable than on the ride out. The way
stations laid out along the road across the Great Plain slipped below us,
and Nu-I lake and the village of Dochra are in view in time for an early
lunch. Again, just as at their last stop, it is impossible to avoid their past. The
Princess is addressed as Salimah al Sabah by several people and the local
garrison are deferring to me.*

*Seeing several here knew at least a little about me, I might as well take
advantage of it.* He went up to the garrison sergeant: "Greetings, sergeant,"
and saluted with his fist to his heart. The sergeant looked surprised.

"You did not want to be recognised last time you were here," he said.

"That is true, but circumstances are very much changed now. I am Tribune
Basil Akritas and I work directly under my Strategos on a special assignment."
*The sergeant's eyes have grown wide. I am probably the most senior officer of
my Corps that he has met, or at least the most senior that has openly admitted
his rank.*

"Salimah al Sabah is actually a Special Personage," *I hope that he heard
the illuminated capital letters on front of the last two words. Ah yes, his eyes
open wider.* "one that I am tasked to look after. We have been out of the Empire
since you last saw us and I know nothing about what has gone on here during
that time. I need to know if anything unusual has occurred while we have been
away."

"Unusual?" asked the sergeant.

"Rebellions, strange rumours, peculiar crimes, unexplained mysteries…
anything really. I will know what I want to hear of when I hear it."

The sergeant sat back. *The question, particularly being asked in this quiet
town, seems to puzzle him.* "Sir, it has all been quiet, very quiet." *I can almost
see him straining to find something to mention. He wants to find something…
and there is a touch of relief in his voice to not totally disappoint a senior
officer.*

"The only thing that I can think of at all was that one of the Navy's great
dromonds disappeared late in the spring, one of the fireships from Antdrudge
going on the way to Ardlark. It had been refurbished and re-armed, and was on
a training cruise in fine weather and it just disappeared. It didn't even arrive in
port in Pain. Apparently, a search was mounted and nothing at all was found,
even by the mages.

"It caused quite a commotion and there was a review of everything that had to do with flame weapons. All of the troops even had to go through all their training again with them in case it was due to an accident. Is that what you were after, Sir?"

"It may well be," *Late spring would be soon after we took Dwarvenholme. Why a dromond?* "In spring…yes it could be. Thank you, sergeant, it may well be exactly what I was looking for." *Yes, the more I think about it, the more that it seems quite likely.*

He returned to the inn and told the Princesses. "It could well be something fleeing our attack or with no place to go home to, but how they got the dromond or where they went, I have no idea."

The Princesses may thank me, but they do not see the relevance, do they? Basil sighed. *They are really not used to looking for any conspiracies that might be around them. It is just as well that I am here to look for them.*

That night, for the first time since leaving home, Theodora urged them to entertain. "This is where Basil and I met, and it is important to me," she said. "Besides, there is local Muslim presence here and we have to start thinking about the promises we have made to Bilqīs and Fātima and the others. We might even find someone for Ayesha." She turned to Ayesha: "Wouldn't you like a man, or a partner at any rate?" *For some reason Ayesha blushed and is lost for words.*

To the sound of nay, oud, buzuq, and drum there was dancing and singing and storytelling. *I can sit back, cuddle my wife, and just watch…although it seems that I may have to play some chess as well.*

The tale of the Mice is told and the position of the women explained. The women have had to refuse several offers on the spot, again taking the line that suitors had to come to the valley to be taken seriously. Several men looked at the women themselves and then at the jewellery that they are wearing, made more obvious by their attire, and have expressions of thought on their faces.

Verily has complained that she is out of practice for dancing, her muscles are all sore and that Aziz will be caring for the children at least one night a week while she gets fit again.

The Alat-Kharl who had played the hammered dulcimer at their last visit had made himself a new—and better—one. Verily immediately bought it off him, at what had to be a very handsome price, judging from the bemused expression on his face.

She also got him to show her a bit of how to play it. "It is the one happy memory of my childhood," she explained to the others as she sat there with it on a table in front of her, "sitting in chapel and listening to one of these. I want to learn to play it and this nice Kharl is making that possible for me."

Nice Kharl? From the expression on his face as he has noticed a few of his soldiers listening in. The sergeant is obviously not sure if he likes being called 'nice', but he is more than happy with the money he is receiving.

Chapter XLV

Astrid
4th November

W*e are on the final leg to Ardlark. We are high above a road with people going each way on it. The plains grow more fertile, and more and more settlements and farms appear, spreading out from the road. The temperature is staying mild for us as we fly into a cool breeze.* Bilqîs flew close to Astrid. "The air smells funny," she said.

"That is the smell of the sea. I hate to say it, but I have missed it. Look ahead. That must be Ardlark. God, Basil, you were right. It is huge. What are those big buildings?"

"The really big one that looks like a hill is the Palace." *He is pointing as he talks; trying to call loudly enough that all can hear what he says.* "That is where we are headed, and where the Princess grew up. That big round one is the Circus. That is where combats take place. It will hold most of the people of Ardlark."

"The very long one is the Hippodrome. That is for racing horses and chariots and other things in. Father, that building with the big dome is the main basilica, it is named after Sancta Thomaïs, she is our patron saint. I will take you there.

"Ayesha, the one beside it with the towers is for you, that is the main mosque. All of those big buildings leading up to the Palace are where the business of Empire is done. They are Courts of Law and for people who collect the taxes, and the people who look after food, and pay the army, and train officers and all sorts of things.

"There is a University, and the different Churches teach their priests in some of the buildings. That big mass of low buildings over there is the main market; there are lots of small ones. The huge round building with water in the centre near the sea is the Arsenal. It is where the Fleet docks. The big squares

…there…there…there…and there, they are Army bases. Each house at least a tagma in a permanent base."

"Now, we had better tidy up and look sharp. They will be looking at us already. Bring us down near that gate there." *He is pointing at a huge gate, one of several set in the three lines of walls that made up the outer boundary of Ardlark proper. Outside the walls the fields begin, even though there are still some houses and small settlements along the many roads. So many people, so many farms.*

Astrid put them all into a flat arrow, with the carpet at the head behind her, while she sped ahead to the gate. She sped along the wall, stopped in front of the gate and hopped off with a flourish. *I need to make sure all of the people gathered here can see that I have no weapons in my hands. Looking at me is a large collection of Insakharl guards. Several have bows, not just nocked, but drawn and the rest have shortswords out.*

"Hello, I am Astrid the Cat, and here are our papers," she moved towards the only one there who had no weapon out. *Like the rest of those with swords, he wears bronze lamellar armour with greaves, but his helm has a crest on it. He must be an officer. I wonder if he outranks Basil. Let's not get us shot now, but this could be fun.*

She smiled and continued. "We are an Embassy from the independent village of Mousehole and we are here to speak to Hrothnog. He is expecting us, not necessarily now, but he did send us an invitation."

"I will send word to the Palace," he waved his hand and the archers lowered their bows. They kept them drawn. *Different hand signals to the ones we use.* "You can wait here. Move your people off the road and near the wall where we can watch them."

"I don't think so. It is hot here in the sun and we have babies that will need feeding soon. What is your name and rank?"

"I am Ducenarius Monoastres Gabras," replied the officer stuffily.

"Thank you" She waved for Basil to draw nearer. "I don't know exactly, but I think a Tribune is a higher rank isn't it?" The guard commander nodded. "Then may I introduce my husband Tribune Basil Akritas."

Yes, from the expression on the officer's face when Basil saluted him and produced his sigil, I am going to enjoy this visit a lot. Basil said he had been given a high rank. It must be a really high rank. I have difficulty with any rank above ship's captain. "Husband, this is Ducenarius Monoastres Gabras and he wants us to wait here. Freya and Georgiou need feeding and changing. I think that we should go on to the Palace and do that. Don't you?"

I can see Basil sighing inside over my tweaking noses. He can live with it. "Ducenarius, Strategos Panterius wants to hear from me now. His Imperial Majesty will probably want to see us within the hour. You wouldn't want us to have to explain why our children are present and crying during that audience, would you now? I think that it would be wise all around to let us in. Our papers are in order and it is up to us to behave ourselves and see our way to where we have to be. Isn't it?"

The officer is nervous. Basil may not be in a Darkreach uniform, but it is some sort of uniform and he has the right sigil. Basil said that those things are personal and changed to black in the wrong hands and he is dropping the right names to gain immediate attention. He is waving behind him again. "Let them in," he commanded, as if it were his own idea.

"Thank you for your co-operation," said Basil and turned to his wife switching to Hindi. "Stop teasing everyone you meet, Puss. If you keep doing it, then one day you will accidentally do it to Hrothnog, and I love you very much and would miss you." *It is not as much fun when he pats my butt with mail on before he goes back to his saddle.*

"Form pairs, half in front, half behind. Basil, quick, come to the front and show me which way to go." She looked through the series of gates at the packed streets and added: "Keep a tight formation just over their heads." *We pass into Ardlark, looking about us in wonder at the number and variety of people and at the buildings around us while below, as we fly, people are looking back up at us with the same expression on their faces.*

B asil led them through one huge archway after another, straight up the main boulevard. *Even with my lack of experience in cities I would have been able to find the Palace unaided. It lies straight ahead, and everything leads to it.*

Three times we have to pass under other arches. There are no walls attached to them, and it looks like there never have been. They just seem to be there just for the joy of having them. On one of them people, not guards, just people, are moving around watching us from the walled top and it looked like all of them have stairs inside.

From our height as we fly, I can see over some of the walls along the way. In courtyards, fountains played. It looks like what Ayesha has described of her home.

Below us are the people of Darkreach. There are several kinds of Kharl: Humans dressed either in Muslim dress and in long robes, or in trews and short tunics, and even some of the huge Insak-div. There are pack animals of nearly every sort as well as carts, sedan chairs, chariots, wagons and porters. The smell and the noise drift up to us.

As we go up what Basil calls a boulevard, major streets join from both sides. In the centre of every of these intersections there stands a tall post with stairs winding around it to the top. At the top of each of them, in a fenced platform, there is a person in uniform with a whistle and a paddle in each hand wearing a big flat hat. We are flying at a level just above them. The people on the platforms are blowing their whistles and waving their paddles and trying to keep the throng of people in order. It doesn't seem to work very well.

As they went Basil leant across to Astrid. "Let me take the lead in talking to people from now on, Puss." *He can do that. I am not sure that I can say anything sensible anyway.*

Basil has brought us to a halt before a set of open doors that dwarf even those of the city gates, and even of Dwarvenholme. The wall they are mounted in seems more of a cliff rather than just a wall. It is well over four times as high as the Hall of Mice. The gate has more guards, and I can see more of them walking the walls above. The Palace then rises in layers behind this outer wall.

Basil dismounts from his saddle and approaches the gate and salutes: "Greetings," he said. "I am Tribune Basil Akritas to see Strategos Panterius. Take these people to one of the suites set aside for a visiting Dukas, one of the ones with a balcony, so that they can land. I will walk to see the Strategos, so their guide can ride on the carpet to show them the way."

He turned, expecting to be obeyed, "Aziz, take over my saddle." *Aziz moves forward and mounts. The guards are staring at him. They have never seen anyone like him before; so large, with grey skin and even bigger teeth than any Kharl has. Basil turns to me.*

"When the guide arrives, form them up behind the carpet and follow it. I will be with you soon." He turned again to the guard commander. *There has been no movement. I don't think that the officer is used to visitors giving him orders.*

"Hurry up, man!" *The officer shakes his head and finally springs into action. It is a Tribune giving the orders after all. One person is despatched at a run. He will be trying to get to the apartment first. Basil has been walking to the gate. He turns again.* "Oh, and take your time flying where he tells you to go. Give them time to get the rooms ready."

A Human woman, dressed in the manner of the Caliphate has nervously come out of the gate and anxiously mounted the carpet when bidden. "Excellencies, I will show you where to go," she said, *she is looking around at our odd assemblage, all in armour, except for a young child, and she is visibly armed with several knives.*

The servant is leading us around the wall until we are over the sea near what Basil has called the Arsenal. Now we are closer to it, I can see that it is a huge round shed with ships under it, on sloping ramps formed up in a circle out of the water. In the middle is a large round pool of water, several virgates in size, with a ship, its masts still up, being backed up to a long ramp. A wide gap in the circle leads along a short and walled canal to a small lake with docks, and then along another canal to the actual harbour.

Astrid brought the saddle to beside the carpet. *The girl is getting Theodora to climb. I will bet she will be petrified when she realises that she has been patting a Princess on the shoulder, and she points above the wall, to the building which has layers of balconies. She pointed to near the top and swallows.*

"I am sorry, but I am not sure which one you will be in, and I have never seen the Palace from this side. Can we please wait?" she asked. *She is nervous, and unsure of the rank of the people she is with or who to even talk to. She probably thought that the Insakharl woman is the most familiar.*

Without comment, Theodora held the carpet in place until some shutters were thrown open on a door, and a servant appeared on a balcony and waved at them. *The girl supposedly directing them pointed with some relief, and now we are headed towards that balcony and, following the carpet, pair after pair, we get to land.*

Dismounting and leaving the saddles outside for the moment, we enter a room that is as big as the main hall at Mousehole. It has seats and tables and many doors and corridors led off from it. Servants are scurrying about with bedding and other less identifiable things.

An older woman, with grey hair and a severe expression on her face, is approaching us. She could be Sajāh's sister. She has a small flock of servants behind her, and as she walks, she is looking from one to another trying to establish who to address. She has given up and, standing a little way away, addresses us all.

"Honorii, I am Thamar Lydina, the Magister Cubicularius, the chief servant, for these sets of rooms. We are still preparing them for you, but please allow my staff to take your things and get you in place."

Theodora is in the lead and she turns to us and uses Hindi. "Once the children are fed, then please change into your good clothes. We don't know when we will be received, I am sure that Basil will arrange that, but we can leave the young children with the servants. Valeria, you have time off from your duties here, just watch the way that they do things."

Behind her, this Magister Cubicularius has noted which one is giving the instructions…and she cannot speak Hindi.

265

Chapter XLVI

Basil
4th November

Basil headed through familiar corridors, dodging the servants, clerks and soldiers going about their many tasks. *If I report first, we might be better placed when the Princesses actually get to see His Imperial Majesty. At least we might know which way the wind blows.*

Eventually, he arrived at the Strategos' office, passing through a room of clerks and entered his antechamber. The door was open to the office, but he went up to the secretary, a short Insakharl woman with black hair and a faint cast of green to her skin.

"Tribune Basil Akritas to see the Strategos." The woman made to rise.

"Basil?" A curious voice came from within the room. "Come in."

Basil entered and saluted. The Strategos was rising from behind a desk covered in paper. "Reporting, sir."

"Is it just you, or is your charge here as well?"

Basil closed the door behind him. The Strategos waved him to a chair and took one himself. "She is here as well, sir, but only temporarily. She and her partner have brought an Embassy here. I am not sure of their exact purpose, but we are still on the trail of those Masters I wrote to you about. We have discovered one of their devices in Nameless Keep already on our way in. As well, I have heard of the missing dromond."

My boss looks much older in such a short space of time, and his normally tidy room is a mess with papers and books everywhere.

The Strategos grunted and pointed at his desk. "That is what all those papers are about. Despite what we have made everyone do with re-training with fire weapons, that is a distraction. We know that its disappearance is not an accident and we know that it still exists...somewhere, but that is about all that we do know."

"Sir, it seems to have disappeared very soon after we defeated the Masters. It is my belief, although the Princesses seem to dismiss this, but I think that they are wrong, that the Masters are involved in its loss. After we defeated them, we think that there is still at least a hand, and possibly up to two, of them around. I don't know why they wanted the ship, or how they got it, or what they are doing with it now, but I think they did it.

"We know that they are still active, dispatching their servants around, we know they have at least one pentagram here and they probably have more." He stopped. *I would not have dared speak like this in giving the Strategos advice before I left Darkreach. Maybe my wife's attitudes are rubbing off on me, or maybe it is just my new rank. I will continue.*

"I would advise not dis-spelling the one we found. Keep a watch on it, and see who visits. Investigate them and anyone who has dealings with them. That way you might find out what happened to the ship, or at least prevent another one from going missing."

The Strategos looks at me and thinks for a moment before nodding. A small smile appears on his face briefly. "Any other advice from a new senior officer?" he asked.

Basil looked a trifle abashed. "Sorry, sir. I have grown unused to discipline and...well you have not met my wife yet. She has scant regard for authority, any authority. She teases the Princesses all of the time, and I am sure, is the only person not one of them who regularly causes a member of the Imperial family to blush. "Where we live is very isolated and there are very few of us. We are all forced to have to think in order for us to survive.

"I have to say that Her Highness is doing much better with her role than I thought she would. Moreover, her husband is a Havenite Battle Mage, and she copes well in getting us to act together in combat. Neither is experienced in ruling a village however, and life is a little...unorganised, occasionally.

"By the way, I still have the Princess incognito at present, until we can learn how the Emperor wishes to treat our visit. I have had us installed in one of the suites set aside for a visiting Dukas. I thought it best as we are well out of the way of family members and are more inconspicuous staying there. Mind you, we flew here and so most of the city saw us arrive. Hopefully, they just do not know who we are."

"You flew?"

"Yes, sir. Sorry, sir. I should start at the beginning..."

Sometime later it was: "As well, our village priest, Father Christopher is also charged by his Metropolitan to talk with our Metropolitan, and to see if we are still communicate with the Orthodox in the west. I have seen no differences, but I am no theologian.

"Finally, sir, on a personal note, if it is permitted, I would like to let my brother and sister in law meet with their niece and nephew, and let their children meet their cousins. My wife would also like to meet my relations."

The Strategos thought. "First, I think that we should go straight away to the Emperor and have a brief word with him, before he hears of it all from another source. Come on." He arose and looking in a mirror to see if he was presentable, headed out of the door, followed by Basil.

"We are off to see the Emperor, and may be some time," he told the secretary. "Get my next appointments, and anyone else who wants me to come back tomorrow...unless it is of earth-shaking importance."

With that they retraced the trip they had made when Basil was first sent on his assignment. *At least until I get there, I have a little less fear. I still have awe of my Emperor, due to my familiarity with Theodora and her work as a major mage...and her snoring.*

They arrived at the Emperor's office. *I am sure that there are the same people on duty that were here when I was sent out. My perspectives have changed indeed. The young woman now looks fairly ordinary in my eyes.*

The Strategos goes across and says something quietly to the man seated at the desk. Again, the man beckons to the messengers. This time it is the young man who rises and goes into the office. The man behind the desk now looks at me, not as if I am a prospective horse purchase as he had before, but as if I have run my first race and come second. Now, I start to feel nervous. Damn.

He schooled his face to look impassive and tried to calm his beating heart. *It was easier facing that damn bandit chief one-on-one than doing this.*

"Come," said the young man and ushered them into the Imperial presence. *This time the Emperor, the God-King, is dressed mainly in gold silk, although it has designs that are worked in gold on the gold. He still looks the same though, and I can feel my heart beating even faster. At least now I am used to the eyes. Seeing the same eyes in the morning bleary with sleep or after a hard night of celebration gives a person a totally different perspective on them. The Emperor has that sort of smile on his face again.*

Blank mind...blank mind. If I have to think, think only about what I am asked. Don't think about Astrid or what she would say now. Damn, that is a thought.

"I have been waiting for you," said Hrothnog. *The voice has the same terrify-*

ing tones. "I presume that it was my granddaughter that rode on the carpet that flew past here an hour ago."

He points to a corner of the room. There are three chairs there and a table with kaf and food on it. I didn't notice that last time. "Sit and tell me everything that was not in the report and why you are here now." *I am being told to sit in the Imperial Presence. I am terrified. No-one sits; no-one eats before Hrothnog...no-one...ever.*

"Sit and eat. I will tell no-one you ate, if you do not." With a terrified glance at his superior, Basil once again launched into his story. *This time I leave out the personal asides.* Occasionally, Hrothnog interrupted him and made him expand on what he meant or thought.

"My granddaughter has grown since she left here," Hrothnog eventually said, when Basil had finished. "When she left, she was like a spoilt child, playing at being Royal and with no thought beyond tomorrow. There are many here among her cousins who are like that. You say that she has taken the responsibility of a child, one that is not her own?"

"Yes, Your Majesty."

"Does she treat her like a pet, like a small dog or as a parent does?"

That is an odd question to give me pause. How can I judge a member of the Imperial family for another? I can only be honest.

"She treats her as my mother treated me. She makes her see right and wrong. She hugs her and she scolds her if she is wrong. She comforts her when she cries in the night. She regards her as her daughter, and in return Fear thinks of her as her mother. She goes to the Princess Rani as I would have gone to my father, but to the Princess Theodora as her mother."

"And she loves this Rani person?"

"I believe so, Your Majesty. It started as a casual indulgence; or perhaps just curiosity but, from watching them, they engage in all of the casual intimacies that a married couple engage in. *Ayesha, she is the Caliphate ghazi sent on the same task as I by her cousin, she says that they complete sentences for each other like an old married couple, and she is right.*

"They are of one body and, usually, of one mind. I cannot speak about what they do in private, but the one disagreement they have had in public was on a moral principle over Azizsevgili, the Hobgoblin captive who has since married one of our women. Rani would not accept him as a proper person and the Princess Theodora upbraided her and made her treat him as you would have everyone treated in the Empire, regardless of their race. He and his wife and children are with us now."

Hrothnog nodded. "Why do you think they wish to see me?"

I have thought about that question all the way here. "If I may be so bold, Your Majesty, I think that the Princess craves your approval of her actions, and to know that she might continue in Mousehole. I have heard her say several times that we are too small to survive on our own without support.

"One day, someone will decide that they want our riches, and we are rich; very, very rich, and we will only get richer. Every day even our youngest women wear gems to work in the fields that the ladies of the Court will envy when they see them.

"We currently have the support of the Dwarves, but they are Dwarves and busy on their own business, and will not be distracted by anything short of the Final Battle, and maybe not even then. We need more people, even more women, but mainly men who will be suitable. Verily chose Aziz to wed, and I would venture to suggest that we might even find places with some of our women for some good Alat-Kharl among the men you send."

"She may underestimate the strength of your village," said Hrothnog. "I have tried to look into it since I found out about it, and the shield that is in place stops even me. If she can do that, and make those things that flew past my window, she has grown much since she left here and is getting to be a mage of power. How strong is her partner?"

"Your Majesty, they refer to each other as husband and wife, as do the other two women in Mousehole who are married." Out of the side of his eye, Basil saw the look on his Strategos' face. *I just casually corrected Hrothnog… oh shit*. "I am sorry Your Majesty. I did not think…I apologise." Hrothnog waved away his apology.

"Her husband, how strong is she?"

"Your Majesty, the Princess Rani is a powerful mage in battle. Much more formidable in combat than your granddaughter, but the Princess Theodora attempts, and succeeds at non-battle spells that make her husband nervous. She is continually pleased that she thinks of ways to do things that others have not thought of. The flying saddles are an example. Only we of the village can fly them, no-one else. I do not understand these things, but apparently this makes it easier to make them."

"They are to help us deal with our next threat. Hulagu, he is our male Khitan, says that we will be attacked by the dragon that lives south of the gap by summer. He will not say how he knows, but the other Khitan back him up on this. Theodora has made the saddles so that we can outfly the dragon and hopefully kill it. It is now up to Rani to think of the weapons and tactics to defeat it. Your granddaughter leans on her husband in those matters."

"Your Khitan, why have they not gone back to their tribes?"

"No-one exactly knows, except for the Presbytera Bianca, and she is now adopted as a Khitan, and so she will not say what she knows. The two women who are his slaves, but do not behave like slaves do elsewhere, are hoping that husbands will come for them, and will agree to stay in the valley with them."

"How can a priest's wife become a Khitan?"

I have been in here for over an hour now, and I am feeling exhausted. "Your Majesty, she behaved as a Khitan would, and knew the tribes before she met her priest. She was raised as a schismatic from the far west and had to adapt more to become Orthodox than she had to change her ways to become Khitan. Again, not being Khitan, we do not know the details. They do not discuss these things with others. Sometimes the Presbytera is just a priest's wife, the same as any other priest's wife, and sometimes she is a Khitan. It is like night and day as she switches from one personality to the other. Her husband, and the other Khitan seem happy to accept this."

Hrothnog paused in his questions and pointed briefly at the pot of kaf. Steam began to come from its spout. "You have not eaten or drunk anything. Do so now. That is an order. Next, I want to hear about this assassin from the Caliphate."

Basil obediently poured himself a cup and took a pastry. "She calls herself a ghazi…" *Damn I have done it again, oh well.* "It means Holy Warrior. She is sort of like a female warrior-priest. She leads the other Islamic women in prayer, and I am not sure if she actually wants one of their real priests to come to the valley.

"Astrid, my wife, thinks that she is in love with Hulagu, but will not admit it, even to herself. She is, like me, on a lifetime mission. She has more difficulty in her mission than I do, as I am not sure that she can enter the Caliphate again as easily as I have entered here. I do not think that she has even made an attempt to report, and the Caliph was possibly very glad to see her go away and out of his land. She is good at her job, very good, and she trains some of the women, and even me, in some of the things that she has learnt. She has made us swear not to pass these things on without her permission, but I can say that it was worth that oath to learn."

"Now tell me about your wife. I do not believe that I told you to marry."

You didn't tell me not to either. "It started off in the same way as your granddaughter's romance, Your Majesty. We were both more than a little drunk and seeking something. I woke in the morning and realised that I was in love."

"You had not forbidden me this, and, if I was going to be away for my lifetime, the Princess would still live longer than me. I wanted children to take over my task. My wife and I are still in some discussion over this, but she sort of accepts the possibility that they will inherit my task. We now have two fine children.

"In fact, our village is blessed with children. We have two priests, and they are diligent in their duties. None of the children has died, and although one came close, no mother has died in giving birth.

"My wife is an Insakharl from Wolfneck, and we must go there soon to cleanse it of her intended husband at least. He is an agent of the Masters. She is beautiful and strong and brave. She stood alone against the entire Hobgoblin force, admittedly she had magic to help her, but she would have done so without it."

"So, your little village wishes to cleanse the whole world of these Masters, does it?"

"Your Majesty, we have only just realised that there is far more to the world than the Land. You would have to ask the Princesses, but I believe that this is what they somehow intend. When we go out of the village, with the possibility of dying or of killing some of the Masters or their creatures; more always want to go along than we can take. We have a village of plenty, and yet everyone is willing to risk their lives.

"The women hate the Masters for what was done to them. They also hate their servants and they want to wipe them all out." He paused and continued with some embarrassment in his voice, "And the rest of us are getting the same way.

"While I was away last, Astrid took two of the women to her bed to keep them company, and she told me of having to hold one of them every night as she moaned and cried out in her dreams about what had been done to her as a small child on the night she first arrived, pleading with a man to stop continually raping her.

"Verily (she is the one who is married to the Hob) was also brought in as a child and she cannot readily accept a normal Human, either man or woman, as a lover. Until she had Aziz, she was scarcely Human herself in the way that she acted. Some of the others are similar, especially the children.

"I thought that this attitude might change when we had new children in the village, but it now looks as if the new-born children have made everyone feel that this task is more important now."

By now, I may as well continue and risk asking a question. "Your Majesty, if you found these creatures here and caught them, what would you do?"

"From what you have reported," said Hrothnog, his voice now even more menacing, "they would die slowly and horribly, several times each at least. I have had it done before to such. Now, I think it is time to see my granddaughter."

He put something that was sewn on his sleeve to his lips and spoke into it. "Get my granddaughter and her husband, and bring them to the private audience chamber. They are in one of the guest suites. Tell her to come as herself, not in disguise. Let them bring their priest, and the Insakharl woman as well. Let me know when they are here."

He turned back to the two in front of him. "While we wait, we will discuss your future, young man…"

Chapter XLVII

Theodora
4th November

"You were the one who wanted to come here," Rani said to Theodora as they nervously waited out on the veranda, and with the city spread out below them, scarce noticed. "What do you want out of it? He will want to know that."

"I am not sure. I was hoping that he would accept us, and help us find anything of the Masters that might be in Darkreach. Apart from that, I don't know. I do know that we have been waiting for a very long time and Basil has not returned yet. I thought that he would see us straight away once Basil told him that we were here."

"Basil said to stay with my disguise on in case it had to be a secret visit, and then he tells the people at Dochra who he is, and Astrid has been telling everyone almost everything,"

I feel unhappy and even a trifle sulky. Getting back in the Palace is making me more like my old self before I left here. I don't like that. She was just about to say something when a servant knocked at the door and entered without pausing. He was dressed in green silk trousers and a vest.

"His Imperial Majesty, the God-King Hrothnog, commands his granddaughter to come before him, as herself, and with her husband, and her priest and the Insakharl woman," he said. "One of you is his granddaughter?" Theodora raised a hand briefly as she started to take her eye disguise off. "Where are your husband and the others?"

"My husband is here. He said my husband, did he?" *There is a shocked look on the young man's face. He is obviously not used to being questioned about his tasks when he gives the Emperor's commands. He nods.*

Theodora turned to Rani: "That means that Basil has talked to him." She turned back to the messenger. "The others are probably in their rooms." They went out to the central room. "Father Christopher, Astrid, where are you?" Father Christopher appeared, followed, from another room, by Astrid. Others came from their rooms. *Astrid has a baby at each breast and her good dress is unlaced.* "We are summoned."

"And I have just started feeding these two. He will have to wait." *I thought that he was surprised before. The idea that an order from Hrothnog might not be obeyed promptly has made his mouth fall open in shock.* Bianca noticed this and nudged the two Khitan girls. They moved forward.

"We will look after them now, and you can do the same for us later," said Anahita, starting to unlace her top.

"Tuck yourself in, put some pads there and let me help you lace up." *I just shocked the messenger again.*

Bianca turned to check her husband's presentation. She gave him a kiss and said quietly...*not quiet enough...*"it is your turn to keep an eye on Astrid. You are to somehow make sure that she does or says nothing foolish." *Christopher glances at Astrid. He realises exactly what his wife means.*

We are ready to leave in only a few minutes. The messenger is obviously agitated by even this delay, and more so when only I increased my pace to match his. "I am not trying to talk to the ruler of half of our world when I am all out of breath," said Rani. "It is going to be hard enough for us all without that on top."

As we emerge from our rooms there are servants moving around, and they will be able to see that my Insakharl eyes have now transformed into those of a member of the Imperial family. Gossip about that will soon be speeding through the Palace. We go through several corridors and down some stairs and a set of large doors. The messenger opened them and ushered them inside.

It is a bare room, palatial, but not large. There is another, smaller, door on the other side of the room and in front of that is a large, and ornate, chair. It is covered with gems on its sides and front and the rest, apart from the cushion, is gilt. The messenger closed the doors behind them and then bowed.

"Wait here, please," he said, and left through the other door.

Rani and Theodora stood close to the chair, with Christopher and Astrid behind them. Astrid turned to Christopher. "Basil says that he can read your mind in some way," she said, "so try and think of something else if you are not answering a question."

"Something else?" asked Christopher.

"Yes, Father. Run through a liturgy, or something like that prayer you said over and over in Dwarvenholme in your head instead of letting your thoughts run. I am going to think about finding husbands for our single women. That should keep my mind occupied, or at least keep him amused. It will probably be easier for you." *She gives a slightly nervous smile.*

Soon the door at the other end of the room opened, and the Granther emerges dressed in golden silk. He is followed by an older man dressed in a dark uniform, then Basil, still dusty in the armour he arrived in, and finally a few servants or secretaries. The Granther takes the chair and the older man stands behind him. Basil gives a salute to the Granther, and then moves to stand beside Astrid and takes her hand.

Astrid

"Chairs," said the figure in a voice that sounded full of doom. *My God... I laughed at Basil when he described the voice. He even looks the same, sort of, you can at least see though that Theodora is related. It is not just the eyes. The bones are the same in the cheeks. Oops...think marriage, how to get husbands, good husbands for the women.*

"Fetch chairs for them all, and tables, kaf and food," said Hrothnog. Servants scurried away. "Granddaughter," he said, "you are looking well. I have been hearing about your marvellous valley, and what you have done out among the barbarians. I am pleased that I let you run away from here. After all this time you are finally growing up. Now, introduce me."

Theodora

I am thunderstruck. Of course, Basil would report everything. He wouldn't even think not to. He wants introductions, even though he must already know who everyone is. "Yes, Granther. This is my husband, the Princess Rani." *I cannot gesture..I am holding Rani's hand very tightly already.*

"...And behind me you see Father Christopher, he is here to help us find anything left by the Masters and then," she turned, "holding your Tribune's hand is his wife, Astrid." *Basil has looked down. He did the same as me. He has quickly released her hand, but Astrid has reached out and grabbed it back and squeezed. I am sure that her hand is trembling. Astrid is actually nervous.*

Astrid

Chairs began to appear. *Two for the Princesses are at the front, and three behind them, one to the right for Father Christopher and two to the left for us.* Three tables also appeared in front of them and another in front of Hrothnog. *A chair has also come for the older man. It was placed beside and behind the Emperor, and he has gratefully sunk into it. Is that Basil's Strategos?* Trays appeared with kaf fragrant with cardamom.

Do they have a room somewhere where there is always food, and kaf is continually brewed, just in case it is needed? Hrothnog gave a slight start and looked at her. *Marriages; think about marriages.*

Theodora

When everything was organised, and the servants had either left or moved to stand ready for the next request, Hrothnog spoke again. "Theodora, what is it you want of me?" The two women exchanged glances. *Rani's face has 'I told you so' written all over it.*

"Granther," *Calm down…take a very deep breath.* She raised her hands and started pointing to a finger each time she made a point. *I need to make sure that I don't leave something out.*

"I want your permission to stay in Mousehole with Rani, and yet to still raise our daughter as a Princess of Darkreach."

"Second, I want a treaty between you and us, as between any two States, respecting each other, and recognising each other and promising support as it is needed. Basil will have already told you that we have found out one thing you did not already know about—at Nameless Keep—and there may well be more."

"Thirdly, if we are attacked by Haven, or the Swamp, or even the Caliphate, we want you to promise to either send help or to avenge us."

"Fourth, we want open trade with you without tolls at the border. You have a trader coming to us already. He has already increased his load to us, and we are happy with him and we trust him. Allow us to trade through him with you, not necessarily exclusively, but to a large part."

"Fifth, if we send you anyone, because we fear being overrun, I want them accepted as a citizen of the Empire with all of the rights that they should have."

"Sixthly, if any of your people wish to come and try for the hand of any of ours, then you will allow them to freely come." She changed her count to her other hand.

"Lastly, we might send you an Ambassador. We have one with the Dwarves. If we do, I would like you to accept them." *Breathe again. I forgot to.* Hrothnog sat silent for a while.

"Are you sure that is all, granddaughter? You do not wish something to destroy the dragon with? You do not want a tagma of troops to come back with you?"

"No Granther. I have thought about this, and what I have asked of you anyone in our position would ask. If I asked for what you suggest, then we are always going to be beholden to you and all will think...no...all will know... that we are just an extension of Darkreach into the mountains and they will harden their hearts against us."

Hrothnog thought momentarily and then inclined his head. "Very wise. Then it is agreed." He turned to where a scribe stood behind him near the wall. *He has been writing the whole time!* "Write that up properly in formal language, and make two copies for our signatures."

He turned back to the front. "Now for the rest of you. Father, you may talk to our priests. I think that you should find that your Metropolitan has nothing to worry about, and we will ask you to check all of Ardlark, as you checked when you entered the Empire. As you do this, please show our priests what you do, so that it may be done throughout the realm." *Father Christopher has signified assent.*

Astrid

"**N**ow, let us see this marvellous woman who has stolen one of my officers from me." *Is that me? I can feel myself blushing.* "I see that we did wrong to allow your people to stay abandoned for so long. Still, what is done; is done." *He is looking hard at me. There is calculation in his eyes.*

"You have had a task held in your mind. Send the girl you think most of to me. I will know her, and she will be happy with me. With my gift of minds, she can always be safe with me from taking her to places she does not want to go. I have been thinking of taking another wife for a while. I think that we will suit each other very well. You have my granddaughter now, and I will have one of yours, and a young mage to boot, as a wife to seal our agreement. Do you agree?"

He is asking me for agreement. It must be Fātima he has found me thinking of in my mind. There is an almost imperceptible nod as I thought her name.

"Emperor, I will talk to her for you as her go-between. If it is her wish, then I will be glad for her." *Be damned with serious.* "And I hope that she will be as happy with you as I am with Basil."

I am rewarded with shocked looks from the servants. In their minds Imperial wives do not have to be happy. They are an Imperial wife.

Your eyes are twinkling. I have amused you.

Theodora

"What is more…" *He is back to us now. Who does he mean? Damn Astrid.* "You should appoint her your Ambassador. She will know the mind of your village, and if she keeps her marvellous saddle or you bring her another when your immediate need is passed, she can get a message to you quickly."

He paused in thought for a moment. "In addition, Theodora, I think that I have a request for you, and note that I do say request. You have grown up more since you left here than you did in the last one hundred and twenty years that you spent in the Palace. Do you want more children than the one you now have?" *Of course I do.*

"You do realise that you have deliberately put yourself in a position where that is nearly impossible, do you not?" *Rub it in why don't you?* "When my wife has children, and she almost certainly will, then if she agrees, when they are weaned and old enough, they will be sent to you to foster and school until they are of age. Do you agree with that, and do you agree, woman husband of my granddaughter?"

Who does he mean? There is obviously something that Astrid knows about at least one of the women that I do not. Is it wrong that my ancestor wants to have sex? Does any of that actually matter? No, not really, I suppose. "Of course, Granther." *My husband is already agreeing, even if she is not sure about what she is agreeing to.*

"Good, then this audience is done. Cat girl, get me an answer soon, then you may visit my Tribune's family. You may talk about any of this as you wish. I am not going to keep it secret." *We all stand, and Hrothnog sweeps out of the room followed by his servants and the older man.*

Astrid

hen he has gone, the other four turn towards me. Basil spoke first: "Who does he mean, and what did his comments imply?"

I feel very smug. "He meant Fātima, and the rest is not my secret to tell." *I note that Father Christopher suddenly has a look of understanding on his face. I think that I will share the attention.* "Breaking a secret is wrong, isn't it, Father?" *They can now all look at the priest.*

"We can go back to our rooms and I can see how our children are, and ask Fātima if she wants to go from being just a slave girl, one with not even any knowledge of her parents, to being the Empress of Darkreach."

"Please tell no-one about this until I have asked her." She then led the way out of the room. *I am the one on an Imperial mission. The Princesses can trail after me.*

Chapter XLVIII

Astrid
4th November

Astrid went straight away to see Fātima. She was out on the balcony with Bilqīs, looking at the view. "Fātima, I need to speak to you alone. Bilqīs, can you please leave us. You will find out why soon enough."

When she ushered the little mage back into their main room Astrid closed the door behind her, leaving the two of them alone on the balcony. She looked at the young woman beside her who was looking curiously back at her. *Now how do I do this...delicately?* "Do you like that view?"

"It is marvellous," replied Fātima. *She is wondering where this is leading.* "It is so alive, so different. All I can remember really are vague memories of a poor life before I was taken, and then, of course, the village and until recently those were not good memories to have. All of this, what you see..." she waved a hand to what was spread out below "...it is, well, indescribable. It is beyond anything I imagined."

Good start. "You remember what you asked me for when we talked about husbands." *Fātima bows her head slightly. There is a hint of blush in her skin.*

"Yes," she said in a low voice.

"Do you still want that?"

"I do. I could accept anyone who will keep me safe, and yet give me what I want. I don't know how that will happen, but I know that this is what I want. I dreamt of being free once and did not know how that would happen, and yet it did. You and your people have made me expect to have my dreams to come true."

"Anyone?"

"Anyone. I want children of course," she waved dismissively, "but, and I know it is wrong, but I need more. I want to be satisfied, to have release and

283

in my own way to be fully happy."

Astrid came over and hugged her before standing back, and now waved her hand at the view that she had been admiring earlier. "Then how would you like to be Empress of all of this?"

She then had to explain what she meant and what the potential groom looked and sounded like, and assured the girl that the offer was genuine and reassured her that she would still be from Mousehole and would not be abandoned, and that she would be their Ambassador in Ardlark. *I am not mentioning the fostering. Her new husband will have to talk to his wife about that himself.*

Fātima thought for a few moments. "Do you think that he will give me everything that I want and still be kind?"

I have been thinking about that exact question, and its many ramifications, spoken and unspoken, as I returned here. "All of the time that you are with him he sees right inside you somehow and you will never, ever, have a single secret that you can keep from him. Having said that, I do think that, because he can do that, he, whatever he is, may be the only creature who will ever be wholly able to be what you want in a man."

Fātima nodded. "Then I say yes wholeheartedly."

"Excellent. Now please allow me to tell everyone. If you look back through the windows, you will see that they are all gathered and watching us and have no idea what this is all about." They turned around and Astrid waved through the glass as she smiled at them.

The room behind us, through the impossibly large glass doors, is full of people and all of them are watching us on the balcony. Even the servants passing through have somehow realised that something important is happening, and are trying to find out what it is by lingering at the edges of the gathering, or pretending to carry cushions or sheets from one place to another. Astrid threw the doors open and, taking Fātima by the hand, stepped inside.

"Mousehole will need a new spinner and weaver. Please allow me to introduce to you Fātima bint al-Fa'r, daughter of the Mouse, Empress-in-waiting of Darkreach, and betrothed bride to be of Hrothnog. She will also be the Ambassador of Mousehole to the Empire."

There is a servant who, despite all of her training, is simply standing there with her mouth open with an armful of sheets that are about to fall out of her arms. She will do.

"Be a good girl and run and let the Emperor know that he has a wedding to arrange and a bride to meet." Astrid gave her a push. She turned to the Princesses: "I hope that we have a necklace with us, or else one of us will have to go back and get one. Princess, come and greet your new step-grandmother."

Astrid
5th November

The wedding was set for three weeks' time. Apparently, there were certain guests who had to come, and even though, according to Basil, a courier could get to all the places of the Empire very quickly, even if he would not say how, the guests still had to get back to Ardlark. In the meantime, the Mice enjoyed themselves in Ardlark.

Basil's family is delighted to see him, and even more happy to discover that he is now a senior officer, married, and a father. While they were happy with that news, they are even more delighted to discover that the family has an invitation to attend the Emperor's wedding.

Astrid even pressed money on Loukia, her sister in law, so that they would not be embarrassed in terms of clothing, and then had fun with her going to spend the money. *Basil is right. I fit in with his family and his one sister who is currently in Ardlark, Olympias, who is in the Navy, does have a sense of humour just like mine. Some of the better dressmakers in Ardlark will take a while to recover from some aspects of this wedding.*

Ayesha

My first visit has to be to the Mosque. First, she went just as a worshipper. *I admit that I am shocked. Sometimes the women here wear veils and sometimes they do not. At least they all cover their heads when going to mosque.* It was only after that first exploration that she nervously introduced herself to the Imam at the main mosque.

He knows about the Imperial wedding, but has not yet received the notification that he will be performing it. Astrid has not gotten around to that bit. After that news, anything else I tell him is strictly secondary. I thought that me being a ghazi, and also leading prayer would shock him as much as it would shock the Mullahs at home. I am wrong. He dismissed that with a wave of the hand as being totally unimportant.

"In Darkreach, anyone can be in the military and for many poor women it is seen as a good way to get away from small villages, and to find a good husband," the Imam, Iyãd ibn Walïd, said. "If they are stationed somewhere away from a mosque, it is far better that a woman leads the prayer than that they not pray. Is that not the case in the Caliphate?" *I have shocked him with my answer, but he has his mind firmly on more important matters and will not be distracted.* "Now, back to the wedding…"

At least I have got out of him a commitment to find some good potential husbands who are men of good character, devout and hard working. I just remembered that Astrid said that shearers, spinners and weavers are especially needed. The Imam thought a bit about that and said that he would send a letter to the Imam at Brinkhold.

"They make a lot of cloth there, but the town is…well, many want to leave there. For many the army is an option, but surely those who wish to stay in the trade that Allah, the Wise, has given them to do, would be best served staying in that trade if they can. I am sure we will find you some men." *A thought has struck him.* "What if we find women or girls, orphans perhaps? This trader Carausius, he is reliable and will get them there safely?"

Ayesha sighed in resignation. *I know where he is going with that thought.* "Only send women or girls if they are useful. We do not want women who are useless, but if the girl is bright and has skills and is, preferably, pretty so that she does not feel left out, it is far better to send her to us than to let her find… another way to survive or to stay in that way."

The Imam took my meaning immediately and smiles. I can see that he is looking forward to culling the ranks of women of fallen virtue and giving those who deserve and want it a worthy life again. Allah is indeed Merciful.

Theodora
6th November

I *have to negotiate my way around my family. Unlike Astrid, who comes back, most nights, full of tales of laughter and chaos, I am finding that introducing Rani, explaining her status, why I left, and why I now will be living outside Darkreach is hard work and no fun at all.*

More than ever, I know that living with my large supply of relations, all of whom have more concern for bloody protocol and status than anything else, is like trying to live under a pile of heavy blankets with no light and very little air to breathe.

I wish that I was already back at home with only a dragon to worry about. Even Fear has some problems, although she may be too young to understand some of them. I hope. Theodora soon discovered that some of the family objected to Fear's adoption into the Imperial family.

Fear

E xcept for some excursions, I have to spend my time at the school for the Palace. I miss Ruth and I miss all of my cousins. This is much more boring, even though mummy Theodora tells me it is important, and that I have to be a good girl, or I will not be going to the wedding. I am not sure if the wedding is worth it.

Even worse than being just boring, all of these children with golden eyes, eyes that are just like my mother's eyes, are not nice. They don't believe my stories when they ask me about myself and where I came from. They treat me as if I am somehow less than them. Some of the teachers are just as bad.

That changed when Theodora found her crying one afternoon in her room, and after comforting her, went storming out. One of the teachers is not there today, and two of the worst of the children now look at me as if they are scared of me.

That is even more the case now that Ayesha has returned to giving me some of the training that she had been giving to all of the young girls back in Mousehole. I was not wearing my blades, now Ayesha says that I have to wear them everywhere—even in class—regardless of what the teachers might think.

It got even better after Ayesha and Basil took me to the markets and bought me some beautiful matched blades of my own, enhanced ones with swirling patterns in the blades just like Basil's, not just ones that are left over from the bandits.

My cousins at home will be envious. Although everyone here has a belt knife, none of the other children in the school carry any real weapons, or even know what to do with them yet. I think that is silly. What would you do if someone attacked you by surprise and you were not armed?

Rani
8th November

I t is interesting here. In some ways it is as stultifying as living under, what I now realise, are the restrictions of caste. In others, it is freer. Ardlark is so much bigger and provides more scope than Pavitra Phāṭaka in so many ways.

She made a visit to the University, to discover that here Magic was just one of the faculties in a much larger institution. What is more, anyone can attend

University if they can afford it, and if you pass the exams to get there and are too poor to afford to go, the Empire even grants a stipend to the students so that they can attend. The students on the stipend have to live in barracks and live there under rules, but in Darkreach people are used to that. In return for being taught, they have to serve the Empire for at least ten years upon graduating.

This means that a goodly supply of physicians, teachers, mages and other professionals end up in even the smallest villages of the Empire. I wish Haven would do that. I know now that too many of the people, particularly the poor ones, in the outlying villages die when they need not, and live lives that are poorer than they should be.

She even went along to see a school where students from several races were taught. *And taught by a tiny teacher who, and I have to smile at this, despite being obviously more than half Kharl, reminds me so very much of Ruth.*

Aziz

W e are having a very enjoyable time. There are whole areas of the city where the soldiers exercise and practice and drink. Verily and I have found them all. I am a Hob, and yet no-one cares about our race, and we take the babies along and they usually end up being cared for by some of the locals, who are fascinated by us very strange strangers with Imperial cachet.

Theodora

E ventually, I get to visit the Grey Doe. I have decided not to be Salimah al Sabah, but myself. Astrid has scouted the location for her husband. I have to take her and Ayesha with me inside. We arrive and leave Basil with the saddles, in the street in front of the inn.

Everyone now knows, or at least thinks they know, who rides the saddles and who lead the party. According to Astrid the city is awash with rumour and information, so that even my entry into the main room causes a sensation. Astrid, with her spear does not help. Maryam bint Suliman has come out into the common room, wiping her hands and full of consternation.

She is dragged out by the hand by an excited Saidah. "I told you, I told you," *she is crying out.* "You didn't believe me. See, it is Salimah, who is really the Princess."

Theodora held out her hands towards the innkeeper. *She is now bowing down, as are the rest of the room.* "Stop that and stand up. I came here to thank you for looking after me and sheltering me when I needed it. You were the people who started me on my journey and I would not have been able to leave the Empire without your help. I owe you and the people here a huge debt of gratitude that I can never repay." *I think that she is very nervous being thanked by an Imperial Princess.*

Only a few of the people staying in the inn had been there when Salimah had stayed there, but Theodora made sure that she talked to all of them, and even to all of the servants, giving all of the latter little presents that Ayesha had already bought for the purpose.

Astrid has left Ayesha to look suspiciously around the room. She put aside her spear, and took Saidah in hand to hear her side of the story, so as to give me time and space for my conversations. Eventually, I can get to her to thank her as well. "I now have an adopted daughter who is nearly your age. Would you like to come to the Palace and meet her?"

Fear
9th November

S o, it was agreed, and I have gained a companion in Ardlark who accepts me as just another girl, although one who has had a very different life. Fear even disappeared once with Saidah, disappeared that is to all except their silent and unseen companions of the Antikataskopeía who shadowed them.

We simply went to the docks and looked at the ships tied up there and ate some sweets as we sat on a seat by the wharf. It was all very exciting and well worth being scolded for by my mummies when I got home. I was safe. I had my knives, and Ayesha said that she was proud of how well I snuck out.

Christopher

A fter introducing himself and Bianca to the Metropolitan of Ardlark, Tarasios Garidos, Father Christopher handed over the missive from Metropolitan Basil, and they settled down to a long talk. *I really should have noticed when Bianca went back to the palace to change and to find the other*

Khitan. She left a message for me with a servant.

Christopher ended up dividing his time between searching for artefacts of the Masters and giving some guest lectures at the University in Theology.

Here it seems that a priest is taught in a school as well as in a church. I have to admit surprise, although it does make sense, to discover that, although they have their own separate instruction in their own faiths, my students include not only Orthodox students, but also Muslims and Druids from among the Kharl, as many classes, such as rhetoric and law, are shared between them.

Bianca

W e Khitan are spending a lot of time at the Hippodrome. We can watch races, we can take part in races, and we talk horses with the breeders. Apart from the local heavy horses for the kataphractoi, ours are generally better, but it is hard to resist buying a few for breeding. We may be the first to contact Carausius to bring goods back to the valley for us, but I guarantee that we are not the last.

The saddles cause a sensation, and there is great disappointment when we show that we are the only ones who can ride them. My stupid brother ends up having to be healed after one incident of showing off his skill. He failed to take the bend sharply enough at one end of the hippodrome. We were very hard on him when he regained consciousness, although admittedly mainly because he could have irreparably damaged the saddle.

Astrid

I am going to shake this city up, being in charge of the bride's side for the wedding. Our trader and his wife are coming to the event as well. "He was named in the Treaty. That makes him important enough to be there."

I thought that Carausius was more than happy with the new profits he was making. Apparently, being both a simple merchant's wife and yet also going to the Imperial marriage is something beyond his wife's ken, and all of her friends are agog at the news.

Valeria

Valeria ended up at school. *Once this Thamar woman, the head domestic for this part of the palace, discovered that in Mousehole I am the servant for the Princesses, it seems that I am marked for some intensive training, and not for a holiday after all. Luckily, this learning about makeup and hair and clothes is actually my idea of fun, and the fact that some of the servants liked to party and dance after work does not hurt either.*

I hardly ever get to my room, except sometimes to sleep. It is also lucky that there are thousands of Palace servants to care for Fear and the Princesses. I'm not needed to actually do any real work. I just get to play with hair and makeup and clothes every day and dance all night. This is the best trip ever.

Bilqis

I *will end up alternating between the mages at the University, and two crafts workers that I have located; a glassblower and a carpet maker. My lack of full literacy is actually a big problem for me and I resolve to pay even more attention to Ruth when I get home. The University are having difficulty placing me as a mage. I am going to stop going there.*

The Princesses are generally far better teachers than the ones here. These are so conservative in their views on what magic can do and how to apply it. Do not over extend yourself, do not take risks. Life is about risks.

At least I have more time to practice with my trade masters. I want to mix magic and glass and carpets, and create things that glow, one way or another. I am hardly in my rooms, and often smell a little singed when I get there, but I am glad of the servants who can fix holes and get me new clothes. I am exhausted.

Chapter XLIX

Astrid
15th November

G radually, the Palace is filling up with guests, some even trying to make themselves known to the Princesses, or the Empress in waiting, and Ardlark itself is on taking a festive air. I will make sure that this wedding is unlike anything that Darkreach has ever seen in living memory.

To the horror of the staider of Hrothnog's descendants, I have more say in the way it is set up than they do. Even with the staff, my ideas on how a wedding feast should run cause consternation. To them, it is bad enough that a Tribune of the Antikataskopeía is in the kitchen giving them instructions on particular dishes, but to be told that the wedding dancers will include a Princess of the Empire and that the bride will not have a father present, but instead will have another woman standing in his stead is almost too much.

The Khitan and Verily have to get new dancing clothes and sabres as they insisted on doing what, for their village, is a normal practice in front of the Court. I wonder how they will feel doing this once they actually meet the groom.

At least Fãtima seems pleased with what I am doing, even if she is tied up in her duties already. She has even met her husband to be, and while awed and more than a little timid about the magnitude of what she had agreed to, she seems to concur with my assessment of her future mate.

Just as importantly, I was present for the whole meeting and think that Hrothnog similarly approves of his new wife. With only me and a servant present he went out of his way to, somewhat awkwardly, charm her. I had to try hard to suppress my thoughts about how quaint it was and I ended up thinking a lot about fishing for whales in the northern seas.

Christopher
21st November

I have a map of Ardlark and its environs from this Panterius of Basil's, and now even have my own staff from his office, as well as a pair of priests to teach. Each afternoon, after I leave the University, I work out where I will go the next day, and when I arrive there on a saddle with Basil to direct me, my detail will be there with an area for me to use that was set aside away from prying eyes.

It could be in a church, a mosque, even taverns, and once I am sure it was a brothel. They must all be doing a lot of riding. Apart from the local priests, all of them, whatever race they are, even the two who are Insak-div, have the same sort of look that Basil does when he is working.

My officer in charge tells me that he has often used mages before, but he hadn't realised the value of using a priest until we had indicated to his men a few people, ones that they had just noticed while they were walking around, who gave off an aura of evil. Every single one turns out to be wanted for one crime or another. It seems that the priests in Darkreach stay confined only to the religious duties unless they are asked.

It is only two days until the wedding. There was only one other area to check, and we get success with the search, at last. We are in a fishing hamlet to the north of Ardlark, close to the city, but so small that it only has a visiting priest some of the time. I know which house it is straight away.

"I have found one. We shall take a casual stroll, and you can all try to look less like my guard when we do it, please. You realise that I talk to the people in the villages each time. This time I will make sure that I go past the place and show you which it is."

As with the place found in Nameless Keep, this house would now have a constant watch placed on it, and anyone associated with it would be followed and everything about them found out. Some might later find themselves in a cell with a mage, and a keen and urgent desire to be somewhere else. The last settlement that they checked, to the south of Ardlark, but otherwise similar to the previous one, had nothing of importance to be seen or found.

Astrid
23rd November

H rothnog used the wedding to announce His Treaty with the independent village of Mousehole, and to inform His subjects of the status of His wife as an Ambassador. Her necklace is of diamonds. At least we brought one in case of need. I hope that I have done the right thing by arranging it, but Fãtima seems happy.

Even the groom seems less rigid. I hesitate to use the word happy in connection to him. I am sick of trying to find things to think about and totally give up trying to hide my thoughts from the Emperor. It doesn't seem to have any effect anyway apart from provoking small smiles in my direction when I am particularly indelicate on any subject.

C arausius and his wife are sitting alone in a corner, ignored by the nobles, they need a chat.

Astrid was soon headed for the Princesses, dragging the trader's poor wife behind her. *Now to stop her bowing herself to death. I need to keep her upright.* "Theodora…I want you to meet Theodora." *The Princess, so addressed, looked puzzled. At least this Theodora has stopped trying to bow.*

"One of the reasons that Carausius was so affected on seeing you was that you and his wife share a name. It turns out that her great whatever grandmother was born on the same day as you and was given the same name out of respect, and the senior women of each generation of her family since have all been named after you. He didn't think to mention this." *At least the Princess looks astonished.*

"There is even a daughter of near my age around, who I am going to call the Little Theodora…which the Father tells me is said as Theodora Lígo, and I want you to make Carausius promise that he will bring her with him on his next trip to us. They have no sons and she is the oldest daughter, so she will inherit the business and our trade, and so she should learn to deal with you rather than have someone do the trade for her and possibly cheat her."

After obtaining this promise, Astrid took the trader and his wife to meet Basil's family, who were just as glad as the trader to meet someone who would talk to them.

*I*f I thought that the servants were shocked at some of the things I insisted on, I did not have the imagination to encompass the reaction to us from the nobility of Darkreach once they saw the Mice in action at the wedding.

The whole party from Mousehole, and our guests, went through the assemblage like a gale of wind through a dense fog. From our dress to our behaviour, everything we do always seems to be a shock to someone. The fact that we all go armed in the Palace, even Fear, and even at the wedding is a sensation.

Apart from some guards, and some attending officers, we are the only people at the wedding who are armed. My spear, even though it is left leaning against a light stand for most of the night, causes continual shock.

The clothes that I had made for myself and Basil's female relations are entirely new in design. The men insisted on uniform, even if they are the lowest ranked persons present, but for the women, loose silk trousers, gathered into boots and a short tight silk bodice show off our figures and jewellery very well.

The Khitan dance, from which I copied the dancer's tops, is at least well received, although I heard a few shocked comments that included the word 'Presbytera' and Theodora's name is mentioned in shocked tones many times. That the guests should have their own wedding dance, and one of them a Princess, is almost the last word.

Valeria has many of the men, even men with golden eyes seeking the exotic, chasing her but, while she is happy to dance with them and drink with them, she also seems to be firm with insisting on anyone who wants more to come to the valley. Ayesha is the only one of the Mice who will be going to bed fully sober and even she seemed to enjoy herself. At least she has danced some dances, even if the bride herself had to join the musicians to help play tunes that the Mice all know, but which are unfamiliar here.

Astrid looked around her when Fatima took the stage. *This may be the last straw for some of them. I just wish that I could capture the array of emotions displayed on the faces of the attending nobles. The musicians look like they will die. Given how much Fātima loves music—they had better get used to her joining them. At least every time I check the groom he looks, and I really do have to use the word now…almost happy.*

That is odd. There is a little group over there in the corner around one of the musicians that seems happy to do those Freehold dances. I wonder who they are. Now what does Basil want from me?

Olympias

I t was a fun night until a dance brought me face to face with the Drungarius of my flotilla, Zampea. It turns out that she is only here as an official partner to our Strategos, and she does not know how to react at seeing her junior officer dressed in such a fashion and at the Imperial wedding.

I had to catch my brother and introduce him before my explanation was accepted. The fact that my brother outranks the Drungarius, and is in the Antikataskopeía, made quite an impression. So did Astrid, when she came over to see what we were doing and was then introduced.

Basil is at least familiar. Astrid is not, in any way. She offered, if Zampea wanted more confirmation on my, her sister's, right to be there, to introduce Zampea to the Princesses or to take her to see Hrothnog or his bride but Zampea grew discomfited and declined in a flustered way.

It is not helped by the fact that Astrid totally refuses to call the Emperor by any of his titles. He isn't her ruler after all. "Stuffy fool," Astrid muttered as the woman fled. I am left trying to smother a smile, I hope with some success.

Astrid

B y the end of the night, Astrid thought she realised what Hrothnog was doing. Darkreach is, despite its apparent vitality, almost completely rigid in the way people act and think. People are so set in their traditions, and their certain ways of doing things, that Hrothnog is using we Mice to be...what did Father Christopher call it? That is right...iconoclasts who might stir the Empire out of its complacency, and wake up some of its inhabitants from the sleep of centuries.

Olympias' officer is a good example. She is dead from the neck up. They may be outwardly calm and orderly and safe, but it is at a cost. Lack of change means that they, well, they don't know how to change. From what I have heard and seen, although life is far better for most of the people who live here, Darkreach is just as closed off to change in any important way as Haven is.

Chapter L

Astrid
24th November

It is early morning, but the bride and groom are here to see us off in a family farewell. Fātima thanked Astrid very much. *Her face is flushed and, she moves a little tenderly, but she is very happy, happier than I have seen her. I note that Hrothnog even seems a touch younger looking and more alive, if that is even the right word.*

When they left together with hugs, tears and kisses, only Astrid had been game enough to hug and kiss the groom, and even he looked surprised at that. *The servants look like they will die of shock, as does Basil. You were not reading me at the time. Now, listen to this. 'I know one reason that you have done all of this'.* She then outlined her idea in her head. She received an inclination of the head in return, which she grinned at and then returned.

"Puss, that was the Emperor, of whom over half of the world is in terror, that you just grabbed and kissed in public," Basil said when they had left.

"He didn't object to it," *and that honest answer has left my husband open-mouthed and completely speechless.*

That night, when they were alone, she told him about her conclusions that, it seems, were otherwise only known to the Emperor. They both agreed that this was something that, if the Emperor wanted known more widely, he could let it be known himself. They decided that they wouldn't tell anyone—even the Princesses.

Basil
26th November

O nce again, I leave Darkreach with my wife showing her gift for the comic tale by acting out the Imperial wedding, especially the reaction of various nobles and Strategoi that they possibly knew of, in the inns.

Twice, I have had to stop her from being arrested. I am sure that the officers who had been about to perform the arrests were glad of my intervention, from the expressions on their faces, when she got to the part about her kissing the Emperor.

This time, Theodora has made no attempt to disguise her features or to hide who she is, and, between the two women, we are managing to cause quite a disturbance as we leave.

Chapter LI

Astrid
27th November

Although we enjoyed the visit, I am sure that we will all be glad to return home to Mousehole, even if we do have to fly these last legs while feeling our way through the bleakness of a blizzard. Although the magical cloaks keep us all warm as we fly, we are still getting soaked with melted snow. It is not even clean dry snow. These southern mountains have snow that is all damp and clinging.

Despite that, I want home. I do not want to stay longer at Mouthguard, even though it was fun describing the wedding to Mellitus and watching his reaction, particularly when I told of kissing Hrothnog. It was nearly matched by his face when I went to Theodora and got hold of the Treaty to show it to him. "No duties on goods, mind you, and free passage. We will see you the next time we come through to visit."

Rani

It seems that Thord prefers our food at Mousehole to that at Dwarvenholme. He is here to spend the winter with us. "T'reconstruction, it continues," he said, "but Dwarvenholme is very cold in winter, 'n' 'll stay t'at way until t'ere are many more people t'ere 'n' t'ey ha'much more of t'city repaired. T'ere is just so much t'at t'ey ha'to make or repair 'n' it is so hard to keep it all warm."

"Every day people find t'ings t'at're rusted 'n' not workin' 'n' water leaks everywhere. T'Mayor asked where t'water came from for t'city 'n' everyone just looked at each other. I went to find out to give Hillstrider a run. It turns out t'at t'ere is a dam hidden in t'mountains above Dwarvenholme, with its own abandoned village, 'n' a whole series of tunnels 'n' aqueducts that lead back to the city. Dwarves from village used to care for it all once. T'entrance to t'repair tunnels was a hidden in a landfall. T'ere're so many breaks, cracks 'n' holes t'at it is a wonder any water at all a gets into t'city. Most of t'repairs to t'at'll have to wait'til summer. Half of it is under snow 'n' t'rest you just cannot get to."

We need to give him a copy of the Treaty with Darkreach to take back to Dwarvenholme when he returns. "We will need to work out a proper agreement with the Dwarves. You are the Ambassador. Use this to negotiate with and see what you can arrange. Unless it is pretty much the same as this you should check with us before signing anything."

"You want me to run up 'n' down?" asked Thord.

"When we have dealt with the dragon, we can probably send a messenger up weekly on a saddle..." she smiled, "and even bring some supplies up to you. People will enjoy going up for a ride and it will let us keep an eye on the area as well."

*W*hy we had come back without Fātima is taking some explaining to the rest of the Mice. I admit that it sounds unbelievable, and my wife has brought out our copy of the Treaty and is working everyone through it to convince them.

I was there, and I still find it hard to believe that one of our own, a former slave, is now an Empress and, not only that, but an Empress to an Emperor that most of us grew up to fear. I am still not sure what Astrid did or why.

Rani

*N*ow that we are back to our winter routine, my wife and I can settle down to working out how to defeat a dragon with only nine mages, seven of them very weak, and around twenty useful troops, when the dragon can easily destroy a whole army, and has probably done so more than once before and has most likely eaten whole towns of people.

Thankfully, like all of its kind, it spends most of its life asleep, usually waking only every year or two to gorge itself on large and easy to catch animals, possibly even from the giant beasts of the Swamp. It will normally eat until it can barely fly and then return to its lair to sleep on its golden bed. Few know much about dragons. No-one even knows why they seem to like to collect gold and gems as they just seem to sleep on them.

We have the advantage of knowing that it is coming and, being a dragon and lazy, it will probably come straight to us, but only when it is warm enough. According to legend, which is all we have, the gigantic red dragons do not like cold weather. It makes them sluggish. So, again according to legend, that is why they prefer to show themselves only in the warmth of summer. Those few scraps are all we have to work out a way to deal with the beast.

Chapter LII

Rani
27th November

Harald has been hard at work while we were away. We now have, deep in the mine, a storage room to put magic items in while they are being worked on. We can put them there while we wait to add to the enchantments.

This way, with care, no spells will be cast too near the incomplete items being made, and they are unlikely to pick up any influences that are not meant to be in them. It means that our trainee mages can safely go back to work in the village itself, practicing as they need to. Their spells should not have the strength to reach that far and through rock.

Now that I have the time to complete the tests on Maria, it seems that she has the potential to be a strong mage. I can add her to the apprentice roster. She will have to work hard to try and catch up with the others. At least she is like Naeve in that respect. She comes from a long line of farmers and the chance to be something else is exciting to her.

Theodora
32nd November

I started making lightning wands before we even left for Darkreach. I don't like it, but it is my best idea so far, and although it will take very many hits with them to kill or even hurt a dragon, at least with the saddle's speed and manoeuvrability we might have that chance and their range should be enough to keep their users away from the breath of the dragon, I hope.

I wish that we knew more about them. I could find little even in the libraries of Ardlark, except enough to give me hope that a dragon's breath will not be able to reach the end of its tail or the tips of its wings.

We have arrows as well, many of them enchanted, but they are just flea bites to the creature. We need to think of something better than just arrows and wands. My dusky love, my hardened battle mage, cried herself to sleep last night in despair at how many of our people could die if this is all we have. She thinks that she is failing our little village.

Rani
34th November

Like my wife, all I can do is make wands. They are as powerful as I can manage, and, if I do not make them rechargeable, that is powerful indeed. One wand on its own will kill several elephants. Many people think that the red dragons are proof against fire, but I know better.*

At least we were able to confirm that much in Ardlark. They are flesh just like any other beast. There is just a lot more of that flesh on a dragon than there is on any other known creature. I cannot see how we can get enough people in the air with enough wands to kill it. We can hurt it, but that will not be enough. There has to be something else that we can do that will kill it. I just do not know what it is…yet.

I keep coming back to a control spell, but even though I was born under the sign of the dragon, and so will have an advantage in that, what with the automatic resistance that dragons have to magic, the same sort of resistance that mages develop with time only far more so, I am just not powerful enough to do it in a battle unless the fight takes place directly over the village itself, and I can stand in the pentagram on the roof. I cannot even do it for a short time if I am away from there. I don't think that anyone except my grandfather-in-law could. Unless I overdraw my account, I will have only half the needed mana even standing there. Even if I have Theodora's supply of mana as well, I cannot do it.

I keep trying to think of new things, but I know that Theo-dear is better at new spells than I am and she has had no ideas to help me. She is sticking to what she knows while she thinks and, seeing that she is not being distracted by making new flying saddles, she is at least making a new fully charged wand every two weeks.

Each of them is a very powerful weapon, but even so I know, that unless we are amazingly lucky, or I come up with a better idea, more than a few of my people will die if this is all they have. She expressed this gloomy thought to Father Christopher one day when she needed someone to talk to.

He beamed. "Before you go out to fight the beast," he said, "everyone who is to fight must come and see me at the same time. I have been wondering what I could do for the battle, and you have just told me," he paused and smiled broadly. "A good blessing can often work miracles. I will pray for the luck of those who will fight the beast to improve. I hope that God will find that this is in His favour." *Has he no sense of the irony of his words?*

Christopher
2nd December

O *n every clear day, the villagers practice wheeling around the sky with the saddles. Aziz has tried to adapt a game he had learnt from the Kharl, called by its unimaginative fans simply 'ball', into an aerial game to give them something to force them to become quicker at turns, but it wouldn't work without a special flying ball, and no-one has time to make one of those. They end up playing child's games of tag with each other. I wish that they wouldn't.*

They may be child's games, but we are being kept busy fixing injuries. Playing tag while mounted on fast moving objects travelling through the sky can often lead to more than bruises as people spin out of control from impacts. We have had several broken bones as well as lesser scrapes and cuts. Luckily none of the injuries anyone has received have been permanent, but it is just a matter of time.

Rani

I *watch these games in the sky and try to work out who will be best to go into battle for us. We have ten saddles, and Theo-dear is not going to make any more for the time being. At present, we have five major fire wands and two of lightning, but that will soon increase.*

What will be our best tactics? The number of saddles sets our maximum limits. Do we keep working until each rider has one of each wand, or do we send our best out with two each? Did we use arrows as well? I can make far more arrows than I can wands, but the wands are likely to hit. How about martobulli or lances? Would they even be useful at the speeds they will be flying at?

She looked at the riders playing in the sky. *These people trust me. I am making life and death decisions for us—for the riders, and even for the village itself. We have to tackle the dragon well away from the village. That much is plain.*

The sheer size of the beast means that, in death, its fall will crush anything beneath it. Fighting over the village will mean that, even if it is killed, we could have victory and yet still be defeated as we lose all that we love beneath its fall. At all costs, we have to keep it away from our homes, and yet I still have to keep an option as a final defence.

My wife and I have to be ready, if all else fails, to stand in the pentagram and use one last spell each, the strongest that we can muster, using every carat of overdrawn and stored mana so that the casting will probably lead to our own deaths. I can see no other option.

That means that we cannot go out. Like a real general, I will be sending others out to die for me. However, unlike many real generals, I know and love these people, and I despair over having to make such a hard set of decisions.

Which of those beautiful children down below just starting to take their first steps will end up with only one parent or with none at all? All four of the Khitan, including Bianca, want to go. I have no chance at all of stopping Astrid, even with a direct order, and both Basil and Ayesha will regard it as their duty.

With the help of Astrid, Tabitha is getting as bad as her teacher is, but she has no child, while on the other hand Goditha will want to defend her Parminder and their Melissa. At least I can argue that an earth mage is not the best to be fighting in the air.

The priests have to stay behind from the fight, but they will want to be nearby, and they have to have someone who can use the carpet to take them to try and save anyone who falls in the battle. My Princess and I will be too distracted to do that.

Why is it my dharma to be born a Battle Mage? Everyone knows that I am, and they automatically trust me to make the decisions in battle and they will do what I ask. Couldn't someone else have this task? I know what Father Christopher will say about that if I ask him. He has said it often enough in his sermons.

Damn the man, I can now think in his theology better than I can in my own. Parminder did it before marrying. Maybe I should convert as well. No, I cannot bring myself to do that. I have to try and keep some tiny part of myself true to my upbringing, and pray that Kartikeya, God of Battles, takes this into account.

Parminder
5th December

All winter I have been practicing with my listening to animals. I prayed to Saint Francis for aid, and I am finally starting to be able to use some range in my communicating with them. Most importantly, I am starting to get the horses and the cats to answer when I talk to them. Their talk is simple, they are, after all, only animals, and it is usually directed to their wants and needs.

I am often followed by the cats whenever they are hungry, which is much of the time. They now realise that I am a human they can actually tell what they want, and they are not backward in saying what it is. It is ideal, from their point of view.

I can usually bribe them to do things that I want them to do as well, not that there is much that I want from the cats. Although, by getting them to change where they sleep, we now have fewer mice annoying us Mice.

My skill does make it easier for me to handle the horses, and I am learning to see using their eyes and other senses at greater and greater ranges. I can keep track of anything that happens in the village if there is a cat or a horse nearby. Sometimes that is embarrassing if I do not shut it off.

Sometimes I enjoy being away from the cats. Riding through the sky over the hills on a patrol, and learning the area is ideal. Wait, what is that? She stopped her saddle and flew back and followed the thoughts.

There is another animal that I can contact. I need to concentrate, not call after the others. Astrid and Anahita will notice soon enough and come back for me. I need to land, here in the snow. It is deep and up to my waist. Perhaps I should have stayed on the saddle. There is a cave buried here, almost hidden under an ice overhang. The thoughts come from there.

"What are you up to?" asked Astrid. *She hovers alongside me.* Parminder held her finger to her lips and moved away from the saddles so that she could peer into the cave.

She smiled and turned. *It is marvellous.* "I cannot see anything in there, but she just gave birth." The other two have a puzzled look on their faces. "There is no danger. I would sense that, but now I know that I can hear bears as well. The mother bear is asleep, but she has only just had cubs. I can hear them."

She hopped back on her saddle and re-joined her patrol. *I will come back here as soon as I can to try and get through the sleepy thoughts and talk with the cubs.*

Parminder
8th December

I am having more and more success each time I visit the bears. A parrot? I wonder…on a saddle I can fly as fast as the birds. I wonder if I can… Bird after bird. I will keep trying.

Goditha
12th December

My little one has found success at last with a bird, and a good one as well. I suppose that I should get the Princesses to look up. She waved at the mages walking towards the mine and pointed up. *Eventually they notice. Now they see my Parminder riding on her saddle with an eagle perched on the front of it.*

Norbert
15th December

It has taken me a while, and two tries, to get this right. Never have I cast anything so large before. I have used almost all the bronze that Carausius brought in, but we now have this huge bronze gong to signal to all in the valley if we need to be alert.

He stood back to admire his handiwork hanging on top of the Hall of Mice for whoever is on watch to use.

Harald, Goditha and I have done a good job. The frame is fastened strongly into the rock of the wall itself. It is tied firmly to the four corners of the iron frame that it is hanging from, but, with the strong breeze that is blowing, I can hear the gong humming softly to itself. Beside it we have this huge padded hammer of timber and leather that will have to be used with both hands to beat it with. Now to test it.

*I*t works better than I thought it would. A good strike can be heard in all of the houses and even, faintly, in the mine. It was marvellous to hear it echoing its way up the valley until its noise was finally drowned by the falls. It can be heard clearly at the watch point and in almost all of the areas that people will most likely be hunting in.

We can now tell the whole village when something is happening. One stroke meant 'gather,' two meant 'danger' and three meant…well, for now anything more than two means that the dragon is upon us. Just time for you to kiss your lover and say goodbye was how Astrid put it.

Ayesha
16th December

I think that Astrid has the right idea. We may be friendly with Darkreach, but they do not need to know every time that we fly out and Forest Watch can, I am sure, see our valley. We should keep wearing our rings and amulets when we are out on patrol on the saddles. Invisible we can soar high over the whole area and do so unseen by others.

It is a pity that we still have to fly through the gate. The mage Princesses have established, by carefully climbing higher on the carpet and waiting to feel a sense of magic, that there is a field of some sort over the valley. They may not have established just what it does, but it is there.

All of the birds can pass through it easily. What it will do to people we still don't know, and it is not a good time to find out. We actually have the two shields now. The smaller holds just the valley, except for the path over the falls and the entrance gap, but outside it is the one that Theodora put in place to hide what we do. At least we don't need to worry about it, as it extends much further up into the meadows and along the Mousehole road in both directions.

Chapter LIII

Verily
18th December

It is a lovely morning to be on watch. She blew and watched her breath stream away in the light breeze. *The gate buzzer...who is on outside watch?* "Theodule...is everything fine?"

"Yes, it is Astrid," said the priest. "She is back early and has not stopped to say why." *Curious, where is she then?*

"Try and show no reaction," said Astrid's voice from behind her. *Damn. I gave a small jump.* "I need to have Rani up here fast. We are being watched."

Verily raised the talker and summoned Rani. "On the hillside above the mine, but outside the inner shield, there is a man. He must have come in at night and has hidden himself well. I only saw him when I was directly above him. What do you want to do?"

"You have not seen him before?" asked Rani.

"No," said Astrid. "I flew close and he grew nervous. He must have felt my presence. He is a Christian of some sort. He has a black crucifix embroidered into his leather jacket, but he also has some sort of bent stick there as well. He..."

Oh, double damn. "A bent stick, could it be a flail?"

I cannot see her, but that pause means that she is thinking. "Yes, that would make sense," she finally replied. "What does that mean?"

"He is from the Brotherhood, and not just one of their slavers who is lost either. He is one of the cursed Flails of God, one of their Holy Enquirers. They are the hard men who enforce their rules. They have no pity and no humour. I can remember very little of my past outside really, but I can remember being made to be very afraid of them as a child. I think that most of the people are afraid of them. Why would he be here?"

"I was about to ask the same," said Rani. "The only way that we can find out is to capture him and bring him here. Astrid, go below and dismount where he cannot see the saddle. Get Ayesha and Basil as backup, and meet me where you leave your saddle. I will get the carpet and meet you there. Astrid... Astrid? Damn, I wish that she would remember just for once that we cannot see her when she simply nods."

Rani

I *have the carpet, and there is Astrid's saddle visible on the other side of the courtyard and out of sight from a watcher, but there is no sign of Astrid. I can try and look casual, but I feel as if I am walking naked through the University.*

Rani carried the carpet across to where the saddle was out of sight and unrolled it. Parminder came past with Melissa riding on her hip and giving a quizzical glance. "Keep going and don't look at me. We are being watched and they may see you and get curious." *Why is it taking so long for Basil to appear?*

Basil is dressed and armed, and has several small ropes and one of the small sets of shackles that he purchased in Darkreach on his belt. If I look carefully, he is holding someone's hand. He sat on the carpet. "We are all here," he said. "I have hold of Astrid and she has hold of Ayesha...I think."

"I do," said Astrid's voice.

"Right then. We are using the carpet because we will need to bring him back. Astrid, is there anywhere near him where we can land without him seeing us?"

There was a long pause. "Sorry, I nodded...I think so," said Astrid's voice.

"Then this is what we will do. Ayesha will take the saddle here and follow us. Astrid will direct me, and we will land where she says. Once we are there we will work out if Ayesha needs to go alone on the saddle, or if we can put down close enough and she and Basil can go. Ayesha, we need to arrest him, not kill him."

What might be a hand just squeezed my shoulder. It is disconcerting. Mages have a chance of seeing many invisible things, but Ayesha's charm seems to be far better than the usual run of these things, and even Astrid's far weaker one is hard to see through most of the time.

"Basil, that is why you are here, you are to secure him and make sure that he cannot kill himself. I know a little of them. He must be one of their scouts, as well as an Inquisitor, and he will kill himself rather than give us any information if that is what he has been instructed. Can you do that?"

"I thought that might be why you wanted me," said Basil. "I have a gag here. That one from the woman bandit, it was meant for something else, but it will also stop him biting his tongue. I can secure the rest of him easily, but I think that I had better get a priest, just in case."

As if on cue, Father Christopher came out of his house. Basil called him over and he was added to the carpet. When the purpose of the trip was explained, he insisted on going to get some supplies and went into the birthing area.

It is now becoming more than a birthing area. It is now more fully a proper chapel and also the place where the priests and others do most of their healing and medical work, and where we have the supplies. He needs supplies. He came back in a few minutes with a bag and a pouch. "Ready," he said.

Rani looked around. *Everyone is still in place; at least I presume Astrid is. Basil seems to be having some problems with an invisible hand and that is usually a sign that Astrid is nearby.* She took off, waved to Verily on the roof and they headed for the gate.

When they reached it, Basil hopped off the carpet and did gate service. He waited until the carpet was through and then left the gate open for a while longer. *Hopefully Ayesha was through as well before he closed it.* He then regained the carpet.

"Where to?"

"Go down the road under the cover of the hills and then keep going until the second valley," said the invisible Astrid. "Keep low, and then we should be able to sneak up into the mountains." Rani headed the carpet south, keeping it at the height of a horse.

"Keep a good look out," said Astrid. "I didn't see any others, but I could have missed them." *She does not sound as if that is likely.* As they went up the second valley she spoke again. "Well, he is probably alone."

"Why do you say that?" asked Rani.

"Slow down and edge to the left towards that bunch of trees against the cliff." Rani did as she was told. "Now please stop here and let me off." Again, Rani complied. *I can feel the carpet shift as Astrid climbs off...and we wait until we are told...it shifts again.* "He is on his own, well supplied and with good equipment."

"Stop being mysterious. How do you know that?"

"Because his horse is behind the trees with his campsite," said Astrid. "From the amount of gear there, I would guess that anything magical has been left behind here. He may come back here tonight, but I doubt it. There is fodder laid aside for his horse and the leather bucket of water he has hanging up for it has in it enough for another day at least."

"Now let us go and catch him and then someone can look after the horse and bring it back for the herd."

Rani headed off again, following Astrid's soft directions. Soon she was flying up the slope, barely clearing the rocks and shrubs there. They approached the crest. "Wait here," said Astrid. *Again, the carpet shifts. Again, there is a pause and then it moves again.*

"Go up the ridge to there…oh, I have to stop pointing. Look ahead and you will see a big rock about a hand by ten away on the ridge. Cross the ridge behind that and then drop down into the valley."

She started directing quietly and then softly, just above a whisper, said: "Ayesha, catch my hand…it is over Basil's head…she has…now land straight ahead and let me off. Ayesha, keep hold of my hand. I will squeeze your hand if I think that we can get Basil up to him unseen. You do the same. If you squeeze, land so I know where you are and then drop my hand and wait for me to come back with him, we will be gone for a little while. Everyone try to keep quiet, and that means no praying, Father."

Again, the carpet rocks and we are left to stare at an empty valley and to listen suspiciously to the small sounds around us. A few birds are hunting among the rocks, and in the distance I can hear a few black cockatoos making the day rowdy from the pine trees where they are feeding.

The winter sun passed overhead, and a few clouds drifted along in the pale sky. *It doesn't look like there will be more snow tonight at least. Eventually there is a whisper from Astrid.*

"Darling, take my hand. We can get you to within two hands of paces of him unseen. Try and be quiet. Stop when I let go of your hand and I will call you when you should come forward. Rani, come forward when you hear me call Basil." *I am just here to steer the carpet.*

Basil

O*ff and hold out my hand. I can feel my wife take it and we try and move forward quietly. At least on this slope there are few twigs to break. We are behind a rock, and she has dropped my hand.* He stopped. *Now wait…* "Basil" *and run.*

There is a man lying in a gap between rocks. He dived down and put the man's hands behind him and shackled them and then put the gag in his mouth. He then turned to his legs and completed pinioning them.

A groan, our spy is recovering… He looked up. *The carpet is already in place and Astrid and Ayesha are in full view. Astrid has a grin on her face.*

Basil turned back to the man and started stripping him of anything that could be a weapon. By the time he had finished the man was struggling and glaring at him and trying to speak.

"He is ready to go. My dear, give me a hand." Together they loaded him on the carpet, then Basil picked up all the things that the man had brought with him, and they returned to Mousehole, letting Ayesha pick up his horse on the way back, while Astrid took over the saddle. Several times the man tried hard to throw himself off the carpet, so Rani travelled low and slowly, just in case he succeeded. *I will keep a fast hold on him for the same reason.*

Chapter LIV

Rani
18th December

*D*espite the Brotherhood man's struggles, Basil has him trussed up in the whipping frame. My wife has sent Valeria around to make sure everyone knows and slowly they are beginning to congregate. Another prisoner is interesting to all and this one is known to none of them. I can hear several wondering what he is here for. He must know it is useless, but he is still struggling and glares at the people gathering around. Ruth is ready to write down what he says.

Astrid has appeared, pulling Make behind her by the arm. The girl still refuses to believe what she is told. At least she now admits that the men were not necessarily trying to do her a favour when they brought her to Mousehole. She has also stopped protesting when people tell her their stories.

In a way that is a big improvement, but she still will not let go of her Brotherhood dress and she holds fast to the habits that she learnt there. She is now the only person in the whole village that does not at least occasionally come of their own will to hear the priests preach. She only comes to a service if she is forced to attend. On seeing the man, she is showing fear. She has tried to get out of Astrid's grip without being seen by him. Astrid has not allowed this, and the girl is where she will see and hear it all.

Princess is still preparing her truth spell. "You were spying on our village, so I am about to question you. It is unlikely that you are here with honest intent, for if that was the case you would have come to our front door and we would have let you in. You will be given no choice but to answer our questions honestly and, once we know all about you, we will determine your fate. If we find that you have committed crimes, then you will be judged and punished."

She is ready. Rani stood back as her wife began to chant. After she had finished admonishing him not to kill himself and to answer fully and truthfully the man's gag was removed. Rani moved forward.

"Who are you and what are you doing here?"

"I am named The Vengeance of the Lord is Mine Quester," replied the man. *There is no reluctance in his voice, but almost a sound of pride.* "I am an orphan of God-fearing parents who was raised by the Church, illumed in the Light of God's Word and trained by the Church as a Seeker of the Flail of God."

"I have been sent here to investigate this den of devil worshippers and idolaters and to take word on it back to the Church that it might be exposed for what it is to the world and destroyed."

"Who sent you, and who told you the lie that we worship devils?"

"I was sent by Brother Job Sword-of-God, the head of the Flails of God acting under the Word of the Disciples. He told me that you worship the devil, so it must be true. Brother Job cannot tell a lie when he speaks for the Church, and I can even see one of the devils sitting on a roof up there reporting what it sees to its master in the underworld."

Rani checked where the man was looking. *Sure enough, Azrael is sitting in his view.* "That is a gargoyle, and they kill and eat demons. As all should know, they are creatures of good and fight the Enemy." As she turned back she caught sight of the expression on the face of Father Christopher and turned to him. *His face bears a very puzzled expression.* "What is the matter?"

"The man is not evil. Like Make, he actually believes that what he has been told is right." *He shakes his head in amazement.* "I suppose that he will do evil if he has been told that it is right and good to do so, but he is not evil himself. He is a bit like Matthias, the slaver. He truly does believe that he is doing the will of God." He turned to the scout. "Isn't that right?"

"Of course it is right. If you do not acknowledge the Words of the Prophet as supreme in your life, then you must be a devil worshipper." *Make is nodding at these words.* "It does not matter what is said or done by or to you, as you were destined to be condemned to an afterlife of damnation and torment from the moment of creation by the Merciful God.

"You cannot judge me to be a criminal, because I act to obey the Word of God as spoken by His Prophet on Earth. Anything I do in furtherance of his orders cannot be a crime. It must be a Holy Act simply because The Prophet speaks for God on this world and in the present. He has been given this instruction from God who speaks to him regularly. It is only if I act on my own will and without an order from the Prophet that I can commit a sin. I have always done exactly as I was ordered, and so I am completely without sin."

"What exactly were you told to do?"

"I was to find out what happened to two missionaries who were sent here,

Brothers Amos and Matthias. If it was possible I was to kill, or better yet return with, any apostates that I find here, any that were born to the Faith but who are now living without it."

Make gave vent to a squeak on hearing this, and Rani glared at her "But the information I was to find out on you is far more important. I am to evaluate your defences and report back on them, as well as what I can find of your numbers and your power. If I had a chance I was to capture and question any I could and then kill them. If they were female then, if I could, I was to know them carnally, and was to do this in such a fashion that it would put blame on the Khitan."

"So, you acknowledge that you are a rapist?"

"It is not rape. You can only commit a rape on a free woman. By capturing a known criminal, I have made that criminal a slave. You cannot rape a slave."

"What if a woman you capture is not a criminal?"

"She would be a criminal. You are all criminal. Brother Job has said so."

That gives me pause. The man's logic is making my head spin in its circularity. How can he live like that, accepting another's will completely and ignoring his own inner voices and not permitting himself to have any doubts as to his acts? Perhaps he has no inner voice, no conscience. Perhaps I can come from another direction.

Astrid has given Bryony and Goditha charge of Make. Rani gestured to them to bring her forward. *Make has to be made to come.* "This girl here is Make Me to Know My Transgressions. She was brought here by the slavers Amos and Matthias to be sold and used for sex by bandits. If you could, you would use her the same way, and either force her to go back to your perverted land or else kill her?" *Make has slumped and almost fainted. Luckily, Goditha has caught her.*

The man nodded. "I was told of her. She was not brought here to be sold for sex, although it would not matter if she was. She was brought to cook and be their servant by the missionaries who were charged with bringing the word of God to the heathen. You must have killed them and made them martyrs for their work. I praise the Lord that they are now sitting at the right hand of God, basking in His Glory."

"They were questioned and made no attempt to be missionaries. They admitted their connivance at murder and they admitted that they were sent by a man called Micah to sell the woman Make and a child for sex. I can show you the records of their questioning if you wish to know the exact words."

"I know that you are all devil worshippers, so I know that you are lying to me. You have no proof. Anything that you show me will have been made up by you to support your lies. I was directly told that the men were missionaries by Brother Job, so that is what they were. It appears that I am also destined by

God to be a martyr, so I give thanks to the Lord that my dying will likewise bear witness to my faith."

Rani looked at Christopher and Theodule. *They are talking quietly to each other and shaking their heads.* "Are you absolutely sure that he is not evil?"

"Unfortunately, we are," said Christopher. "He believes that what he has said is right. In their hearts an evil person, as the slavers were, knows the difference between good and evil and, however they justify it, they know that what they do is evil. This poor man does not know what real good and evil are. He has been taught that the words of his priests are always right and always good and that any who oppose them are automatically evil." He turned to the scout again. "Isn't that right?"

The scout nodded "Of course. The truth is fully written in the Bible and is explained so that we might understand it in the Revelations of the Prophets and in the pronouncements that their successors make. How can the written or revealed words of God be evil or wrong in any way?" *There is genuine puzzlement in his voice.*

"How can His representatives on this world be in error in any way? That would deny the Perfection of the All-wise Lord and Creator. Once all is revealed there can be no possibility of error. God's Will is made manifest to us and will not be denied. His Dominion over the whole world will be achieved in time. That is inevitable before the completion of the End Times."

This questioning is not going the way that I expected. "Have you killed any man or woman?"

"Only those who deserved it, and that I was told to kill," was the reply.

"How do you know that they deserved to die?"

"Some tried to prevent me doing my work, some refused to honestly answer when they were confronted as demon worshippers, and some tried to run away from me when I went to question them. Only the guilty run from the Flails of God. The innocent have nothing to fear from us."

"So, you admit that you find some people innocent? Do you then release them?"

"Of course, none of those that I have killed were innocent. If they were innocent, I would not have been sent after them. Brother Job, or Brother Micah, has declared them as sinners, otherwise we would not have arrested them. They start by denying their wrongdoing and maintaining their innocence but, eventually, when they are confronted with the instruments of truth, they will confess their evil and go to the Holy Fire repentant, to be ushered into an eternity in purgatory."

"So, you will always torture people and not ask them the truth as I ask you now?"

"It is written in the Revelations that 'only through pain is the devil burnt out of the soul of a sinner,' so it is wrong to use any other method to find the truth in a Holy matter. For the sake of their soul, torture must be made as painful and as protracted as is possible to ensure that no truth is left hidden behind the lies that they start with.

"Sometimes you have to continue to question them over a matter of weeks so that they will finally abandon their lies and admit to what you know is true. It is well known that, in the end, torture will always give you the real answers, the ones that you seek."

"So then, we should torture you? We can do that if you wish." *Bianca is absolutely horrified at my suggestion.*

"There is no need. I have given you the truth. If I had not been ordered to kill myself rather than tell you this, there would have been no need for you to use any compulsion. You are not seeking Holy Truth, just a truth of this world."

"But you just said that only through pain can we reach the truth."

"You are not interested in the real truth," said Vengeance. "For instance, you keep referring to the Brothers as slavers, when you must know they were missionaries. You would know this because firstly, they would have told you this themselves, and secondly, I have already told you that Brother Job told me that this was the case, so you have no excuse for your ignorance."

"What if this Job is wrong?"

"He is not wrong, and he cannot be mistaken. He was speaking as a Prophet when he gave his orders, so his words are thus shown directly to be the spoken Words of God."

Rani looked around the Mice. "Does anyone have questions for this man?"

Unexpectedly Make speaks up. "What would you have me do?" she asked timidly.

"You should have me released," said Vengeance, "and return with me to the Brotherhood of Believers along with any others who were born there. There you will be fully questioned as to the depth of your sins, and when you have admitted your part in killing the missionaries, worshipping Satan, fornication, and your other undoubted sins you will be burnt as a consort of devils."

"But I have done nothing wrong," bleated Make. "I have kept all of the commandments, I have prayed every day as I was taught. I have lived my life sinless."

"You have not. I know this because I was told that I might find you here fornicating with devils, and plotting the overthrow of the Chosen of God, and so I find you. If you are walking free, you must be consorting with these evil doers. You were judged as condemned before you were born, and now we see the proof open before God and His Angels, and all with eyes on this world."

Make fell to the ground. *Make has really fainted now and Goditha was too slow.*

"Mummy," said Fear to Theodora, tugging on her sleeve with worry in her voice, "does that man want to kill me as well?"

"He does," said Theodora. "But do not worry little one. Your mummies will not let him succeed. We know that the men he serves do not worship God, instead they serve the Masters. He thinks that his leaders serve God, but we know they do not. They really serve the Devil and we will defeat them. Isn't that right?" she asked Christopher. *He is looking at the Brotherhood agent as if he is a serpent in our midst.*

"Yes, little one," said Christopher to Fear, shaking himself. "Your mummies will protect you from the evil rulers of that place, and what is more, your grandfather will do the same. These men have perverted the Word of God away from words of love and acceptance, and have twisted the minds of men. Although he is condemned from his own mouth as a sinner according to the world, this man is not fully to blame for his actions, as he believes that the sins he has committed are not sins. He does not worship the devil himself, even though the man who gave him his orders does so."

"Blasphemy," interjected Vengeance. "You speak blasphemy. You should be beheaded."

Christopher ignored him and turned to Rani. "What will you do with him? He has committed no crimes against us, apart from his spying, so we cannot kill him, according to our law in the village so far, without committing a sin ourselves. But if you release him, you will aid the work of the devil through this Brother Job and the Masters.

"Although it would be heresy to suggest that, because he does not know that he sins he is fully guiltless, he has as yet done nothing to break the law that you have laid out so far, which admittedly is not very much, and far less than exists in other areas." *I will ignore Christopher's broad hints on the subject of making a new law on the spot.*

"Is there anything you have to add about your activities? Have you actually done anything to anyone here?" *Vengeance shakes his head.* "Then, with the concurrence of my consort," she patted Theodora's hand. *His face shows horror... I hope that I can make you suffer...* "for the moment, until we have a better solution, we temporarily condemn this man to be kept incarcerated until he sees the error of his ways and repents of his beliefs, even if that is for the rest of his life.

"We charge you both," she looked at Christopher and Theodule, "to try to show him how badly he is in error and to turn him from his path." She sighed and turned to Basil. "Take him down and lock him up and ensure that Make is never allowed to be alone with him." Basil moved to comply. "While the spell lasts, see what magic his gear holds and all those other things that policemen do."

She turned again to the Vengeance. "When the spell lifts, will you try and kill yourself? Will you try and escape?"

"I was only to kill myself to stop you gaining information. You have the information. To kill myself now would be a mortal sin and I would end up beside you in hell if I killed myself. However, it was so ordered. It is my duty to escape and, as an agent of the Lord, if I cannot get home with what I know, to destroy as many of you as I can to prevent you interfering with the work of the Lord in this place."

"Good, then may you rot in shackles in our cells until you see the error of your path."

Rani turned to address the Mice. "You can see what evil exists outside of here. It is not just the bandits who were evil, and their evil was at least open. They served the same creatures as this man's leaders do. The evil of his rulers is concealed beneath a mask of holiness that they display to the world. It is clear that both the bandits and the Brotherhood act only for the interests of the Masters, and the evil that they represent. They are the two faces of this evil.

"It seems that the point of us waiting, that I saw in my reading, is now clear. We must stamp out all of the agents of the Masters, regardless of where they are or how powerful they are. We have cleared their agents from some of the north and, at least some from Darkreach. I think that we can trust the Emperor to remove the rest from there.

"We still must act against those in Wolfneck, the south, and in Freehold. It is likely that none of these others are rulers where they live, but somehow our little village will have to take on the Brotherhood, or at least its leaders, and remove the influence of the Masters there.

"Perhaps once we have done that our task will be done. It will be hard, but will only come after we have killed the dragon. If anyone has ideas on how we should do this, please come and talk with me." She paused briefly and looked at the sky. "The day is now late. Let us have a small celebration tonight that we have taken another step against our enemies."

Christopher

B asil has taken him away. I need to think and pray before I confront him again. Ayesha's face has a look of deep concern on it. He went over to her. "What is the matter?"

"He used words about his so-called prophets that are very similar to those that I heard from some of my teachers about our duty of obedience to the Caliph," she said.

"I know well that this man's priests are evil. So, if they are evil and use the same words as those imams that taught me, does it follow that my teachers and the Caliph are also both evil? Could it be that, despite the way I feel, I am the same sort of person that he is? I pray to the most merciful Allah that this is not the case."

"I do not have the wisdom to answer that question of obedience for you." *Be diplomatic.* "I do know that you have talked for a very long time with the imams in Darkreach on matters of faith. When you did that, did they say to you the same sort of things to you as those who taught you did?"

After a pause Ayesha said: "No, they didn't." *She sounds surprised with herself and her face shows signs of relief.* "They talked about our individual responsibility before Allah for our own deeds, and the good or evil that we do, and ensuring the safety of the innocent, of any creed, before all else. They said the state and the ruler could only make laws that had to fit everyone, not just those of one faith. Laws could not make moral judgements on religious matters that affected only the individual and they talked a lot about mercy and compassion and understanding."

She sounds surprised. "They sounded more like you, as a matter of fact. I should have made sure you met some of them. I am certain that you would like each other." *I did meet them. That is why I asked you that question.*

I will ignore the compliment. "Then, if you truly believe that the Darkreach imams are good and holy men, I suggest that you try and listen to their words more than to the words of your teachers. It is even possible that some of your teachers may have been influenced by the Masters and their ideas. We do not know."

"They may innocently think that what they teach is the Word of God and be like Vengeance; fooled by the devil instead. It may even be that this influence is what led to the changes that took place in my Church in Freehold."

"I do not know these answers, and I am afraid that you will have to pray on this matter yourself. I will help you if I can, but my beliefs are different to yours. I can only try to give you honest advice, although I can tell you this much, you do not believe what I believe, but I cannot find the slightest taint of evil in your soul, and you know that I can feel that in a person, particularly one I am near for much of the time. In yourself, you are a good person and seek to fight evil. Does that help?"

"Thank you, Father, it does. I will read my Qur'an and pray on this to Allah, the Compassionate."

Chapter LV

Christopher
20th December

T he village is turning back to its winter tasks. With Fātima gone, the fleece is piling up and the production of cloth has slowed, but we still have some from what Carausius brought in, but Astrid complains of thinking twice before making something.

The advent of Vengeance on our doorstep, and the menace that he represents, have made the play with the saddles and weapons both more urgent and far grimmer.

In the meantime, Rani works the trainee mages hard on their spells, while the Princesses make more wands. Theodora confesses despair in not being able to think of any spell that will save our people from having to actually fight the dragon.

Theodule and I spend most of our time with Vengeance. He can quote verbatim large amounts of the writing of his Prophets, but he has little exposure to the actual Bible. Apparently, it is read from very little in the Churches of the Brotherhood. When I checked with Make, she admitted that she had heard only little bits of it, usually a prohibition of some sort that is repeated after a while. The sermons are always drawn from the words of their Prophets. These are used to explain what the Bible actually means to say.

"How can they call themselves Christian, when they ignore most of the Words of Christ?" Theodule asked.

I have been thinking exactly the same thing. What they do to slaves they do to the least and so they do to Christ. "What they speak they even twist around to justify sin. and they ignore what is inconvenient."

Theodora

*I**t is nice to sit in a warm study, even if my nose is tickled by smoke from the* charcoal in the brazier behind me. If we survive the dragon, we must look at* *some other form of heating.* Behind her she could hear sounds of domesticity from the house and she could see similar scenes being enacted outside, through the small panes of glass that were bound by lead into a window in front of her.

I have forgotten to look at that sword. I carried it all the way in my saddle bag, and it took up so much room there, ever since we killed the Wight who had it near Deathguard. What with everything else that has happened, I had completely forgotten I even had it.

If Astrid can read the writing on the tablet at the start of the road then, perhaps, she can read what is written on the sword as well and, at any rate, Christopher should look at the magic on it. It may not help, but it is obviously a fell blade.

She went rummaging around her house and found, eventually, that the blade had been put in the bottom of a box. Taking it in hand, she went out looking for Astrid and found her just about to set out on a hunt and to do some scouting.

"I really do not know how your people call Darkspeech your own, when you have forgotten how to read it," Astrid said as she traced out the words with her finger. "Look, it says clearly 'My name is Wrath. Wayland made me. Mighty am I.'"

"You can see it is one of our swords. It has the five lobes on top of the pommel that only our swords in Wolfneck seem to have, but we have no-one now in Wolfneck who could make something as fine as this. What is more, I have never heard of a smith called Wayland. I have seen a sword that the owner called Wrath, but it isn't nearly as good as this one. Is that all? Can we go hunt now?"

Theodora thanked her and went in search of Father Christopher. *He and Theodule are measuring and pacing off an area outside the village wall with string and sticking sticks in to the near frozen ground. Goditha is with them and she has a large piece of vellum in her hands. The breath of everyone is steaming in the winter air. I take comfort that the weather is still far too cold to lure the dragon out of its lair. It is nearly too cold to lure me out of mine.* "Fathers; are you free?"

"Yes", said Christopher. "We are just planning out some ideas for a basilica and a school. It will take the last of our poorer grazing land, but it is time we started to think of something more permanent than just using the hall, and it will take a long time to build it all, so we may as well start. None of us have any experience in this sort of work, and we need to think carefully about what we are going to do, and to work out what we can from our memories of other places."

"Then I will leave you with this sword to look at, that I brought forth from Darkreach. I keep forgetting it and Astrid has now told me what it says on it."

Well, that has set him off. He has left the other two and is immediately hurrying off to the chapel to see what he might found out about the old blade.

C hristopher is in a very excited state indeed. "It is strong…very strong," he said. "It is enhanced to both add to its ability to strike a blow, and to enhance the damage when it does so. Even more important is that this Wayland made it to kill dragons and other Wyrms. Not only will it hit them easier, but, if the blow is good enough it has an enhancement on it that may…not 'will,' mind you…but only 'may'…kill the beast almost instantly."

"I think, but only think mind you, that it may have been made for smaller beasts than ours, or perhaps ours was smaller when this was made, but if someone is brave and lucky enough to get close to such a dread beast alive and can use it against the Wyrm stoutly, then this blade has a chance of solving our problem at a single stroke."

He is waving the bare blade around in his fist as he speaks. "I think it is like the enchantments that you put on the maces we used against the Masters, but Wrath holds a far stronger set of charms".

"I thank you. Now, I need to work out if we have someone who can use it against the dragon. Do not mention this to anyone yet."

I will lay this one on my husband. I am the only one in the valley who can both ride a saddle well, and yet still use a sword competently, but I do not think that my love will allow me to take it into the battle on a mere chance of success.

Rani

T his sword is both a blessing and a curse. It is a blessing in that it possibly gives a means of destroying the dragon, but it is also a massive gamble, particularly for the one who will have to wield it.

If we rely on it and it does not work for any reason, then we will lose our fight. Try as I might I can think of no smart solution to the problem. The dragon has probably destroyed armies in its past. What makes me think that a mere tiny village can come up with a way to defeat it without loss?

In my mind, I have made up a list of who can do what in the fight to come. I dare not write it down. This sword changes everything. This is a huge risk. Princess and Stefan are the only ones who can actually use a normal sword competently. My love is not going because I need her here to go with me in a final casting.

As for Stefan, he is not a confident flyer at all. He can travel safely and move around, but he lacks the agility that the Khitan or, in particular, Astrid have. He can really only do straight flight.

Ruth

A strid can easily read what is written on that sword, can she? In among the books I am cataloguing there is an odd scrap of vellum. I thought that it was just a place marker when I put it aside, and still think that, but it has that writing on it that was meaningless to me and the Princess when I showed her. She went and found it again and took it to Astrid.

"See…there is a large circle with nothing beside it and there are twelve small circles. Each has something written beside it in dwarf runes, but they make no sense."

"Of course, they make sense," said Astrid. "Well sort of anyway. It is a list of names. I guess they are all of towns because that one," *she points to the third on the list,* "says something that sounds like 'Pavitra Phāṭaka' if you say it, and the way I speak Hindi may be bad, but I know that is what they call Sacred Gate, and that," *she points two down,* "is Ardlark, and that," *she points at the next one,* "says Amtrage, and I am sure that Theodora once told us when we were in Evilhalt that that is what the town of Antdrudge in Darkreach used to be called."

"That one says 'Muzel' and that will be us in Mousehole. That one says 'Cwyfodi Mwd'—which makes no sense at all—unless 'Mwd' is supposed to be 'Mud', in which case that could be Bryony's village, because that is the only town I have ever heard of with 'mud' in its name, and even if these are old names, it has probably always been muddy. Who knows what a 'Cwyfodi' is? But mud would still be mud."

"The others" *she points at them as she reads them out,* "are 'Nahmess', 'Khmel', 'Topudle', 'Ovendle', 'Graecin', 'Gil-Gand-Rask' and 'Graemsle'. You have been teaching me the geography of the Land, and there is a town called 'Toppuddle' in Freehold—that would be 'Topudle.' There is also a village there called 'Camelback'. I am sure that would be 'Khmel' because that is the cloth you get from camels. I am also betting that 'Ovendle' is 'Owendale' in the Brotherhood and 'Graecin' is 'Greensin'. Would 'Graemsle' be 'Greatkin'?" she asked. Ruth nodded in thought.

"We also know that there is a circle at Nameless Keep. I wonder if that is what 'Nahmess' has become today?" I always thought that calling a castle 'nameless' was very silly. What if it came from another name, and it didn't actually mean what we thought it did?

Ruth shrugged. "It could be, and if it is then what we have here is a list that someone, or something, wrote out of all the circles used by the Masters. You also forgot to mention Gil-Gand-Rask. It is a real place, and it still has that name. It is both the town and the island to the south of Haven."

What a thrill this is. "If this is what we think it is, then we don't have to look for where the circles are anymore. We now know where we need to go to destroy them. I think that it is time to go and see the Princesses with this."

Christopher
23rd December

We were expecting a new round of pregnancies to be coming up soon. It seems that whatever we do here will always be limited by this factor for some time at least until the women decide that they have had enough.

What I did not expect was who the first of the next round would be. It seems that young Valeria did more than just dance while she was in Darkreach. She came to me about a cold and I only picked up the pregnancy by accident. It is at a very early stage, and she has not mentioned it in Confession, nor has she asked me anything, so it is polite to say nothing myself. She has said nothing to Theodule either, and we agree that it is up to her to raise the matter, or at least to ask about the changes in herself. So far, she has been silent.

Hulagu
29th December

There are still patches of snow lingering in shadowed places, but it seems that this is spring in the mountains. At least, like the plains, the hillsides are full of colour and now we have our trader back. I had better tell the Princesses.

"He has a lot with him this time. Two carts as well as his packhorses, and the string of beasts that he is delivering for us, horses, cattle and sheep. There are four women and another man with him as well as the other three."

"He says that it his turn to be mysterious and he won't say anything until he arrives tomorrow except that he has letters and lots of metal. He just looked smug and those idiot guards of his had big grins plastered all over their ugly faces."

Chapter LVI

Norbert
30th December

S o once again we wait on our trader. He had better bring more metal. With all of the repairs that are being made to the buildings, I am almost out and having to scavenge rusty bits to make nails and hinges. We need a new plough, and fittings for the second cart, and I cannot do those.

It always seems to be iron that is in the shortest supply and places the most limits on doing anything, but that is the case anywhere. Why is iron so scarce? I am sure that people use magic so much simply because we lack sufficient quantities of the right metals to work with and to make enough tools. Magic may be hard to work with, but finding enough iron is even harder and more seem able to work with magic than with metals.

Astrid

C arausius' arrival is starting to look a bit like a procession. Some of our villagers are going out to look over the people he has with him. Out in front walks Karas, behind him Candidas is driving one cart, with the packhorses and a string of unladen horses strung behind on a series of leads, one behind the other, then comes Carausius tending the horses and walking with three women dressed in Caliphate fashion and huddled together as if they are uncertain of their reception and a little afraid. With them is a man who is dressed more for a city than the mountains.

Next in the procession is a young woman driving a second cart, and then some cattle and several sheep, then finally Festus walks in the rear looking *more like a shepherd than a guard. The woman on the cart is armed much as Candidas, with shortswords and light leather armour, and she has a shield propped beside her.*

Of the three Caliphate women, only one, a tiny girl as small as Bilqīs and as pretty, has a bow and the others, one not much taller and another who is above average in height, have only daggers.

The man, likewise, has only daggers, but he walks like a man who is sure of himself. His eyes keep looking from woman to woman, not resting on any, but passing on as he sees new ones, and he is rejecting each one...he is seeking someone. I'll keep an eye on him and who he seeks.

"Greetings, Carausius, and welcome back to the valley of Mice. I suppose that you are going to keep close as to who these people are, even from me, despite me getting you a much sought-after wedding invitation, one that probably still has you dining out on the strength of your stories from it and your new connections."

"Alas, I must" he replied in a tone of fake regret. "I am sorely grieved, but I am sure that you understand that your Princesses will not want to be kept waiting forlornly while we chat idly outside and keep them waiting."

"Your incredibly false sadness is betrayed by that grin. Come on up to the hall. Can you say what you have with you at least?"

"Only that you should leave the second cart strictly alone and allow us to unpack it. Most of what it has on it is just iron, but there are some wooden boxes on board that should not be touched and should be handled with care. Let Candidas and the girl driving it unload that one and let no-one touch the boxes afterwards."

Now they are before the stables and Candidas, Festus and Karas are *starting to unload the carts and packs and put the horses inside. The Khitan are ignoring the rest and fussing over the horses that they bought in Ardlark. Bianca told me that they will now have enough beasts to start building a proper herd and also have remounts available at the same time. Naeve is behaving even worse over the sheep and cattle. They didn't tell her about them.*

The rest trooped into the hall. *Carausius is followed by his charges and the rest of the village in a gaggle, all trying to find out what they can and commenting on the new arrivals. At least they are using Hindi.*

The new man is interesting, but he seems to pay no attention to anyone... wait...he and Valeria, standing behind the Princesses, have locked gazes. He has smiled, and she has blushed in return, and nearly dropped the bag that she is holding. Well, our first suitor arrives. I will teach him to try and keep secrets, and I might steal some of Carausius' thunder.

"Your Excellencies. I present our trader Carausius who brings with him iron, something that needs careful handling, some more girls and a suitor for your attendant Valeria." *I have another blush from Valeria, a surprised look from both Carausius and the Princesses, a sharp look from the man and various noises of approval from the Mice. The idea that, at last, a suitor had arrived for at least one of them seems to have general approval.*

"How did you...I didn't say anything...have you started to read minds?" stuttered Carausius. Astrid just looked smug. *Christopher and Theodule are nodding to each other...almost as if they expected this.*

"Stop being a clown, Astrid, and let Carausius get on with explaining. Greetings, Carausius," said Rani with a touch of annoyance. "What do you have for us this time?"

"I have brought all of the ordered goods, including a quantity of good metal, iron, copper, tin, pewter and lead. I have two packhorses with enough good slate on them for one large roof or two small ones or else many repairs.

"It is marvellous what my new connections can do. Because of them I have even managed to obtain a supply of molotails of the most powerful sort. I figured that they could come in useful against your dragon...that is the stuff that needs to be handled carefully.

"I have some candles and incense, more cloth, spices, seeds and even some tree seedlings of apples, apricots and quinces. They should grow well here, and I have not noticed any so far. I have..." And here he stopped and began to dig in a large flat pouch hanging at his side. "I nearly forgot. I have letters, just like I was one of the Oxys Dromos, the Imperial messengers."

He started looking through them and handing them out. "That is one for the Princesses from their Ambassador, the Empress, beloved be her name. One for Basil from his brother...and for Astrid from Basil's sister...and for Ayesha from the Imam of the main mosque, and finally one for Father Christopher from Metropolitan Tarasios. I have been told by all of them that I have to wait for replies. Now, where was I...oh yes.

"I have introductions, even if Astrid spoilt one surprise. The man here is Nikephorus Cheilas, and he is the first man to come along with me to seek a bride. He tells me that he already knows your waiting woman and that he wants to marry her. I don't know how she feels, but he has brought a reference to the Princesses from Thamar Lydas, the Magister Cubicularius of where you stayed, that I have seen, or I would not have brought him.

"These three women have been sent by the Imam Iyād ibn Walīd, and he probably has said more in his letter to Ayesha, but he told me that they are some of the girls he discussed with her from Ardlark, and that he awaits a reply from Brinkhold and that he hopes to have some men to send along soon."

"They do not come empty handed, but he sends them—and this takes up a lot of space on one of the carts—with tools of their trade to set them up. They have looms and wheels." *From the expressions on the girl's faces, this is news to them.*

"I will let them tell their own stories, and they certainly have stories, but the shortest one with the bow is called Yumn." *An elaborate obeisance towards the Princesses...never done that before and has no clue.* "She tells me that she is a skilled carpet maker. The other short one is Rabi'ah and the taller is Zafirah." *The girls each make a deep obeisance when their names are mentioned, but not as bad as the first.* "I have been told that they are both spinners and weavers. I am not able to judge these things, but the Imam assures me that this is true."

He looked around and grabbed the other girl and dragged her forward "And this is my daughter Theodora, whom Astrid called Theodora Lígo, and demanded that I bring her along. She has come with me, on this trip at least. As you are aware, I have no son and so, and Astrid is right in this, she should learn the business. Hopefully one day she will get herself a husband who will do the hard work for her. But for the present..."

"Well," said Rani, looking at her wife, "let us get on with negotiations. Astrid, Ayesha, Bianca, can you take these young ladies aside and find out all about them. I am interested in why we have more women instead of potential husbands, but that can wait."

"Princess," said Ayesha, "that is, in fact my fault and I fully take the blame; may Allah, the Merciful, forgive me. I told the Imam that, although we needed men most, we would even be interested in the right girls with the right skills and...background, if you take my meaning. We will talk with them and see if that is the case."

She turned to the three girls and gestured commandingly. "Come with us and we will talk." *The three new girls are looking at us as if we will bite them and are clustering close together as we leave.*

Ayesha

W e will put them at ease. Hall of Mice, seats and kaf with locum and baklava. Ayesha smiled. *I remember how the Princess had tried to put me at ease as I was sent out on this mission, what seems to be a lifetime ago. Now I sit in a similar fashion as I work out how to deal with the life of another.*

Astrid and Bianca are just looking at me to take the lead and I am unsure where to begin. For a start, what language will we use? Astrid and Bianca have no Arabic, but then Bianca has very little Darkspeech, but her sense probably doesn't need language. Darkspeech it is then.

"I am Ayesha bint Hāritha. I am a ghazi from the Caliphate, and it seems, the spiritual leader of the Faithful in this village, which is called Mousehole. This is Astrid the Cat. She is a hunter from the north and is married to a Tribune of the Antikataskopeía." *The three girls look scared at that, particularly with Astrid smiling that quite carnivorous smile of hers at them.*

"The other woman is the Presbytera Bianca, the wife of one of our Christian priests." Bianca heard her name and smiled. "She does not speak Darkspeech, but she has her own ways of finding out if you tell lies that do not need her to understand a word of what you say. She only needs to be near you when you speak." *Now they looked terrified...no I needed to say that.*

"Now, you are going to tell us all about yourselves and why the Imam sent you to us." *They look at each other. None want to be first.* "Come on, speak up." *Again, they exchange looks.*

The smallest spoke first, looking from one to another of the three sitting in front of her. "If your Excellencies would be pleased…"

Astrid interrupted her. "We are not Excellencies. I am just a hunter, and Ayesha is…well, she is a warrior, and Bianca is…what Bianca is. None of us is really noble. It is only our Princesses who are Excellencies. You can just call us by our names. Now, continue."

"Yes, Ex…umm Astrid. I am Yumn. I am an orphan. My parents were carpet makers, but they were very poor and could not seem to ever get out of debt. When they died, there was no money for me to have, and I had no connections and could expect little as mahr, a dowry, from a husband, nor had I anything to give him. Their loom was even taken from me by a moneylender to settle some of their debt, so I could not earn anything."

"I had no other skills, and was too small for the army, and so I entered into a contract that would earn me better money than I could get otherwise, in the hope that I could get enough to set up my own business. After some time, I was approached by the Imam, after prayers and he asked my story and a week later he asked if I wanted to come to a place where I could make a fresh start. My work was not what I had hoped it would be, and I was glad to say yes."

Now I understand … 'enter a contract' indeed. "You were a prostitute. You were all prostitutes." *They don't look happy at that.* "I thought so. The Imam took my meaning." She turned to the other Mice and changed to Latin. "I offered him a place to send girls like this, good girls who had no choices, and who wanted to make a new start. Let us see what the other two have to say." She turned back to the Darkreach girls. "Continue."

"You do not mind that we sold our bodies?" asked Yumn, with a tone of wonder in her voice.

"Most of the women in our village have done that, one way or another," said Astrid dismissively and with a wave of her hand. "It is of no importance. Women often do what women must do in order to survive. Who is next?"

"If it pleases you, I am Zafirah," said the tall one of the three, and the plainest, but still a more than attractive girl. "My family also had no money, and a moneylender was threatening us. I have two brothers and three sisters, all younger than me. I sold myself to pay off the debt and give my parents some extra money, so that the rest of my family would stay free."

"The Imam also talked with me. In fact, he talked to all of the women of the Faith in our line of work. We are the only ones who he talked to a second time who then decided to come. Many did not want to leave the city for an uncertain future away from home in the wilds."

"I did not want to leave my parents and siblings, but I was lost to them anyway. Carausius told us that the imam bought us as slaves to free us, and we now owe him a huge debt that we cannot repay, but because of him I can now start a new life." She looked at the third girl.

"I am Rabi'ah." *Her voice is bitter even in saying her own name.* "My father is a drunk and a fool, and he sold me to a slaver as none would give mahr to a daughter of such a man, and with what he got for me, he could drink more and not be burdened with the expense of keeping me. I did what I was told. Even doing what I did was better than my life had been."

"I had fourteen more years left of my time, and I was counting the days. I am glad to be free and will make no trouble. We are spinners and weavers and we will work hard just to be free."

The others are nodding, and so we now make a decision in the name of Allah, the Compassionate. Ayesha switched to Hindi. "I think that we should let them stay."

Astrid

W*ho cares what they did?* Astrid turned to Bianca "Did your sense, whatever it is, do anything?"

"No. Was I supposed to find something?" was the reply.

"Only if they were lying, I suppose. I agree with Ayesha. So what if they sold their bodies. That is between them and their God, and their priest sent them to us. I will report back to the Princesses."

"Bianca should go back and have a talk with this Nikephorus fellow with her husband, and Ayesha, you can keep these three occupied by showing them the village." Ayesha went to object. "You can speak Arabic. We only have a few words of it. They may still have other things to say, and you can best put them at ease. We cannot."

She switched back to Darkspeech. "Girls, finish your kaf and sweets, and then Ayesha will show you around the village, and we will see where you can set up your looms if you decide to stay." She stood and took Bianca away, leaving Ayesha with the three.

Astrid and Bianca arrived just as the trade negotiations were finished. *They must have gone well, as Carausius, Ruth, and Shilpa all look happy. Theodora has just called Nikephorus up and is getting Valeria to where she can see her. We are just in time.* Bianca and Astrid edged forward. *Bianca has grabbed Christopher.*

"Young man," Theodora said in Darkspeech. "I think that you can now explain yourself."

"Excellency," he said, "I was a praetor koubikoularios, an upper servant," *I am not the only blank face he saw...* "in the Imperial household, and I met your serving woman when you visited, and she was learning in our schools. We danced, and we enjoyed ourselves and then, when she had left, I realised that she meant more to me than just a brief relationship. So, I decided to follow her and seek your approval to ask for her hand in matrimony."

"If she chooses to come back to Ardlark, I will have my job back. If she prefers to remain here, which I suspect she will, I will then seek to find a position with you. I have brought with me a reference from both my superior, and from the Magister Cubicularius Thamar, whom you know."

"Assuming that we let you stay, and that is not pre-empting anything that Valeria may say, what would you bring to us?" asked Rani.

"Excellency, I am an experienced personal attendant. I speak most of the languages of Darkreach, although I admit that this is not likely to be of much use here. I have skills in cooking, in makeup and beauty care, and in running a household, and I brought with me a good quantity of useful supplies along these lines," he replied.

Valeria is obviously thinking she is just speaking to herself. She quietly added: "And he dances divinely." *Now she realises that she spoke aloud and blushes. He is as well. How sweet.*

"You do realise the past that lies behind most of the women here?" Theodora asked. *She is looking at Valeria as much as at the man.*

"Yes Excellency," he replied. "Your story is much told in the Empire and our new, and much beloved, Empress has made no secret of it. She stands as an example of strength of character to women throughout the Empire. The Emperor has chosen a bride from Mousehole. I hope that he does not mind if I follow his example."

Theodora continued. "You do realise that, if you come here, you are leaving Darkreach behind. You will owe allegiance to us in our valley, not the Emperor."

"As you have yourself done. That was made clear to me before I left," Nikephorus replied. "I have been told that the Emperor himself happily gives us permission to do this if we wish and, from what I hear, this is even included in your Treaty with him." Theodora nodded.

Theodora and Rani then looked at each other and then at Christopher and Bianca. "I believe him to be a good man," said Christopher.

"And I feel nothing untoward from him," said Bianca.

"In that case," said Theodora. "You have our permission to proceed. We will discuss other issues later."

Everyone in the room is now looking at one or another of the pair.

"Here? Now?" asked Nikephorus, looking around him.

"Yes," said Theodora. "You really do not realise how much what you are about to do means to many of the women here. They have a right to see you ask." *Nikephorus is looking at the circle of expectant faces before him and swallowing. He looks very nervous now. This is something that is far beyond his experience.* He moved forward, and bowed, elegantly, to the Princesses and, moving past them so they had to turn to see, he knelt before Valeria.

"My beloved lady, from the moment that you left Ardlark, my life has been barren and desolate and as if it were ashes. My heart was empty, food has had no flavour and nothing I have seen or done has given me any joy. I ask you, in your benevolence, to grant me the boon of life again and bring spring into the winter of my existence by agreeing to be my wife."

He has been working on that and has it memorised. He is looking up at Valeria and she is just blushing. She is lost…there is silence. Oh hell, someone has to… She moved up and nudged Valeria. "Say something, anything, but say something."

"I will," *Well, that came out more as a squeak than anything else. It seems popular though; we have general cheering and ululation and a hug from him.*

"Christopher," said Theodora, "take them aside and make arrangements."

Christopher

I *had better be honest with them about what Theodule and I have found out.* He turned to Valeria. "Before you go any further, did you know that you are with child?"

Well, at least Nikephorus looks delighted and Valeria is blushing again. "I didn't know. It must be yours. You are the only man I have had since we were freed."

Basil

Basil went to see Candidas where he was working unloading the carts. "Greetings, Tribune," he said. "Have you come to give me a hand with some honest work?"

"I try and avoid such, but I will if I must." Basil grinned. "Do you have anything to report to me?"

"Nothing serious from the Strategos, except that he was pleased with the visit, and that his superior seems to be very pleased." Basil nodded. "However, I had an interesting conversation in Nameless Keep. A man came up to me and asked if it was true that I was coming here."

"I confirmed I was and he said that he was thinking of trading in this direction, and that he was willing to pay for information about the village. I pretended to be interested and took him for far too much money for such information. He paid so much that he cannot be an honest trader. Let me know what to say, and I will go back and sell it to him for even more before getting someone to keep a very close eye on him and his friends."

"I will talk with the Princesses, and we will let you know what we want them to think. It will probably be something that points in totally the wrong direction to where we intend to strike next. Is there anything else?"

"On a personal note, do you mind if I lay court to my boss' daughter?" *Well, that was a surprise.* "I get on well with her, she is wealthy, and is going to be even more so, she is good looking, in fact she is really quite a catch, and I am probably going to be on this run for the rest of my life and she could be as well.

"If that is the case, then I would prefer to have someone to keep warm with than to be lonely the whole time like Karas and have to pay for companionship, or with a wife at one end of a long trip like Festus and Carausius. You are combining your job and your pleasure. Why cannot I do the same? Maybe my children can report to yours in the future."

"I hadn't thought of it that way but go ahead. How do you think she feels?"

"I drive one cart, she drives the other. At night, we talk about all sorts of things…at present, that is all. Her father is there the whole time, what more can we do? Having some time off together here will be my first chance to be alone with her on the trip, and probably my last. I guess that I had better soon find out her opinion."

Astrid

A strid took Theodora Lígo in hand, and started showing her the village, and what was being done there, and what they hoped to produce and what they needed. *Most of all she wants to know what I know of her father's man, Candidas.* "I think that it would be better if we asked my husband about him," *See, I can be diplomatic.*

W ell, it seems that Ayesha already has Rabi'ah, Yumn and Zafirah installed in the spare workshop-residences that are still left vacant. They will have to sleep in the barracks for the present, but the workshop will need to be made liveable. More sheep's intestines stretched over timber frames to fill empty gaps as windows, and more outside doors to be hastily made. At least the only suitable building has a good roof already.

Chapter LVII

Goditha
30th December

T heodora may be announcing the wedding, and Nikephorus may be keeping a straight face, but Valeria has a big grin on her face and is making a gesture indicating what she wants to do tonight.

Now Fortunata has grabbed Valeria and that is the dress being organised, and Nikephorus is left standing with nothing to do and looking around. Goditha nudged her brother. *He agrees.* They started forward.

"Cometh, thou. Alloweth me to go and change. I am not going to be gettin' any more work done today, and Robin isn't busy anyway. I think it is time that we got thee to relax a bit. We are going to give thee thy bachelor send-off. I thinkest that I know where Aine has a crock or two of ale that she won't be mindin' us broachin' before thy wedding. We can gather the other men and thee can get to know them."

Nikephorus is spluttering. I can see from his eyes that he knows me a woman despite my close-cropped hair, me being just wearing kilt and apron, and is wondering what to say.

"No protests. Thou hast been dismissed for the day. See, Ayesha is already in thy place. She may not be as good as thee are, but she and Basil were a lookin' after them afore they came here and Ayesha knows what to do as she is a Princess herself...sort of, anyway." She headed off to put some clothes on instead of her work kilt and apron, and was soon back to them in shoes, a pair of hose and a jerkin.

Robin and Nikephorus are chatting out on the veranda and the other men are starting to gather as well. They all have the same idea that I do. Nikephorus looks from one to the other of us. I dress the same, and we look alike, except for my tits. He will learn that from afar, I am the one with the sword, and Robin has a bow or just a dagger otherwise.

"Sister," said Robin, "thou didst promise us beer. Where is it?" Goditha led them off.

Nikephorus

S*he is a very good-looking woman, despite the lack of hair on her head. She is married to a girl, and she acts like a man, but she is a good host. The other men accept her as one of them and I am really going to have to work hard to stay sober tonight.*

I*may have heard of the Imperial wedding, but I didn't work at it and I may not be prepared for what is happening to me. I expected the priests, but that is about where it ends. My bride being given away by a woman from Haven, and that woman, her employer is a bit of a shock.*

The bridal gift has left me floored. Obviously, the Empress got one and my bride told me that she was wealthy, but I was thinking on a lower level than what is becoming apparent. Now Khitan dances and then a Caliphate dance, with a Princess of the Blood taking part in it. I had heard the shocked reports about that.

At least I am able to show my skill with the dances that my wife enjoys, and now it seems that if my wife wants a rest, someone else will have me up. I am not sure how the other men will like it, but it seems that I have promised the women to teach the other men how to dance better. At least I am not the only one with skills. I didn't know that young Yumn could play the oud.

Basil
32nd December

A*fter a day's rest, and now finally having seen a village wedding at home, we can send Carausius back to Darkreach with new orders for goods and a whole new satchel of letters. It seems that we have four new residents.*

Candidas has a whole batch of rumours to be sent out into the world that will hopefully send the Masters setting the wrong defences, and Theodora Lígo has some encouragement about her prospective suitor from my wife.

They even spent most of last night talking and dancing together, even if they did sleep apart.

I think it best that all we passed on was that we believed that he was a good prospect with honourable intentions and an intention of staying with her or her father for the long haul. The rest Candidas will have to tell her himself if anything comes of it. As I said: 'Despite what you may think, Puss, we are supposed to be a largely secret police force after all.' I don't think that my wife believes me on that.

Rani

W ith the trader gone, it is time to sit down with a wax tablet and return to thinking about the combat that is coming, the dragon. If we do not succeed at this, then everything else is futile. The key to it lies in how well we use the saddles.

We have more than enough riders for them. Not all are great with them, but we have my wife and I, as well as Astrid, Hulagu, Kāhina, Anahita, Valeria, Ayesha, Bianca, Basil, Bilqīs, Bryony, Stefan, Verily, Lādi, Naeve, Sajāh, Lakshmi, Robin, Elizabeth, Umm, Aine, and Hagar who are all good enough at riding them. Many of them cannot handle weapons well enough, though.

I need to keep the mages here as a reserve, and that includes the apprentices, so that we can draw on their mana if need be. That still leaves three hands of riders and an upset Hulagu. Can he accept staying back as a mage? He will have to.

Stefan is the worst of those at riding, but the best with a sword, so if he is going to use the sword 'Wrath', then he has to be in a saddle and Astrid will just have to make him better at riding.

Hagar can ride well enough, but she can scarce use a weapon at all, although anyone can use a wand. What if it comes down to more physical combat? It is likely. Aine can at least use a bow and sword, but Umm, one of the most skilled riders, is no better than Hagar with weapons. The same applies to Sajāh. Elizabeth is skilled at throwing things; perhaps she can use the molotails. Robin can use a foot bow very well, but the best that can be said was that he is getting better with using a Khitan bow from the saddle, with the arrow on the other side. Ruth is only just able to be considered on the riding list, like Stefan, but she is used to throwing a javelin, so she has to be considered for using molotails.

Lakshmi is a superb rider, but I am not about to allow someone who really can only use daggers as weapons to take on the dragon. After her wands are *exhausted, she is likely to try and prove herself by jumping on to the beast's back and attacking it. Verily is just the same, so she is also out.*

Bianca can at least use a sling, and we have a good supply of magic bullets for that weapon, and Christopher and Theodule can easily make more. Valeria cannot use a horse bow well, but she can use one. Lãdi can use a sling, she is another who can go. If I count Bryony, who has mastered horse bow quicker than Robin, even if he is by far the better archer on foot.

That still leaves me too many choices. Perhaps I should just keep the ten in mind and see what happens on the day. She sighed.

Chapter LVIII

Hulagu
1st Undecim

T *he morning has begun in as normal a fashion as any other begins in
Mousehole. That is good.* Hulagu left for the lookout before dawn on a
saddle with his breakfast in his saddlebags and Bianca and Bilqīs, who had
handled the second of the night watches on the roof, started to hand over to
Goditha, who had the first day watch.

The Mice had learnt some lessons from when they first took over the
village, and one was, that two people had to take duty there at night to keep
a watch out for each other. However, they had also decided that only one
person was needed on the roof during the day, and they were there mainly to
act as a relay point from the outside lookout, and to keep a watch around the
mountains and the cliffs behind the village.

Hulagu

I *t is important to make all of the checks. Before going to the gate, I need to
check the borders of the lower valley, in the pre-dawn light, using the magic
detection wand as much as my sight.*

*I have a clear sky above me and, although Terror is only the faintest sliver
waxing as it sets on the western horizon, Panic is a trifle higher, much fuller
and lends more light. With the last of the stars glimmering faintly, the lack of
clouds means that there is plenty of light as the east grows white behind the
peaks.*

He moved to the gate, was let out and went, slowly and cautiously, up to the lookout. *Time to report.* "I am here. There is nothing to be seen, and I am about to start using the wands and the telescope."

Goditha

*H*e takes it so seriously. Hurry up, and let Bianca and Bilqīs go to bed after their watch. The custom of waiting until the lookout gives the all clear makes sense, but he is always so slow.*

The cliffs and the fields grow clearer in the growing light. It promises to be a fine day. I can clearly see the yards, and now the gardens, the archery butts.. finally the fields and the mine entrance come into sharp focus. The far mountains are lit up, the gold on their tips slowly spreading down their slopes.

Hulagu

*B*efore landing, I check the immediate area around the lookout, first with my eyes from out of bow shot, and then with the magic detection rod. I report, and land and then start to do the same to the whole area around me. There is nothing to be seen or detected, the same as it is on almost every morning but, when you have enemies, getting sloppy is likely to get you killed and I have no intention of making that mistake.*

He reported again. *Now I check further afield. Eventually, I look right out to the horizon to look for any smoke. As is becoming fairly common, there is a faint smudge of smoke to be seen from the direction of Dwarvenholme. It is visible only with the direct light of the growing sun behind it. Am I happy? Yes. Time to report, and let last night's watch go to bed while I settle in for another watch.*

I keep my eyes on anything close by, use the telescope regularly, particularly in the direction of the dragon's lair, and then use the magic detector over the whole area. I try to make sure that the order that I look at things is different each time, in case someone is watching for patterns, but that is often hard.

The smell of kaf from the warm sealed pot rose into his nostrils as he opened it. *I never had it to drink before coming to Mousehole, but now it means mornings to me.*

Bianca

B efore bed, we each have sunrise services, the first for me and the second in the day for the Muslims. The new girls have quickly gotten used to a female voice calling them to prayer, and my husband always waits until Ayesha has finished with her prayers before calling for the Orthros service.

He has said that he is sure that God would understand that it is better to get on with your neighbours rather than fight them, and besides, this way many come straight from prayers to sermon. How many priests can say that? It shocked all of the new arrivals.

It seems that more attention is paid to religion, any religion, in Mousehole than they were used to in their normal lives. Most non-Muslims outside the valley are content, at most, to attend something weekly. In Mousehole, most of the Christians manage at least two services each day and sometimes more.

Unless they are unable to do so due to their work, the Muslims have their six prayers, and even our pagans, who have no priests of their own, usually manage to come to at least one of Christopher's a day, even when they still do their own private prayers.

Christopher said that he thinks the more uncertain that your life is and the lower your own personal chance of survival, the more likely it is that you are going to pay attention to the one thing that could at least give you an afterlife and maybe even keep you alive longer in this one.

O rthros is over, and the smell of breakfast is floating gently through the village from the communal kitchen and from people's houses. Mothers can be heard dressing and feeding daughters for school, and some of the babies need changing or feeding and they are letting everyone know about it.

Hulagu

T he sun is fully above the mountains to the east. Time for another check. There is a moving dot in the sky to the north-east. It is hard to pick up against the bulk of the Mountain of the Dragon behind it, but it is there.

Bracing the telescope against a rock so that it would not shake and make it harder to see, Hulagu kept watching, checking to see if there was any sideways movement.

No, it is coming straight for us. It is a hand of hands of thousands of paces *away, and only the vast size of what is coming (it has to be the dragon) makes it visible at that distance. It is the same size to my eyes as a raven at, say, eighty paces. If it were in clear sky it would stand out easily, but only my keen sight lets me see it as a red fleck against the mountain backdrop behind.*

What do I do next? I know what Rani wants, with me inside the village, but she is used to battles of mass. I am more used to manoeuvre, and tactics that will work against the Zaan may work against a dragon. Tar-khan Siramon's elephants cannot be stopped in a charge, but if you harass them from the flanks and rear, you can sometimes turn them from their objective, despite someone they respect giving orders to the great beast.

I am outside now, and in a position to harass the dragon as it approaches. I have two wands and my arrows and my lance. It may be that I can distract it away from the village, and give the rest a chance to defeat it far enough away so that its fall need not destroy all we hold dear. That is, if we can defeat it.

First, I will call in what I have seen, and then wait for Rani to call back before I fly off. Then I have to lay down everything that I do not need, the talker, the telescope and the magic detector, along with any food that I do not want immediately.

He called Goditha and then waited for Rani to call back. While waiting he strung his bow and put it in its quiver, making sure that it and his arrows were laced down. *Now the gong sounds loud in its tocsin, calling the village to attention. Next, I eat. I have no idea when next I will get a chance.*

He paid particular attention to his felt guardian in his prayers this morning, as he explained what he would do and asked for help. He had just explained about the children, and was working on his sister and his köle when Rani called.

Goditha

I *wonder what he wants.* "The dragon is coming to attack us now. I will soon go and try and draw it away from the valley, while everyone prepares to fight it. If I fail to return, tell my köle that I love them and the children, and regret that I do not have husbands for them yet. Tell them that they will belong to my sister if I do not return. She will have to do what I did not. Get Rani to call me when she arrives up there."

Oh shit. I need to do something...the gong. She watched herself walk over to the gong and take its beater in her hands from where it hung. *The shaft feels rough beneath my hands. Am I just more sensitive?*

"Booong..." *Once, its voice rings through the valley. The morning bustle below, even that of the children, is already silent as all look up towards me on the roof.*

"Booong…" *The sound of the second stroke starts them moving again. Heads and bodies are popping out of doors and windows; others are diving inside to get armour and weapons. All are still silent.*

"Booong…" *It is the third and final stroke and the confirmation of what is about to descend on us. There are tears on my cheeks. Noise is starting again, a cacophony, as people yell and call to each other and rehearsed plans are put in place. All I can do is wipe my face and stand here. Will I still have a family when this is over?*

I can see Rani running, holding the sari she is wearing up at the front. It is a garb not meant for running in. She is stripping it as she runs to me. All those others who might have to fight head off to prepare for what is about to come. Ruth is calling for the children, even the babies. They are off into the mine where, even if the worst happens, they may still survive and let our village keep going through them.

Hulagu

"**W**hat is happening?" Rani asked.

"I managed to see it soon after it took off. I have watched it carefully. It is coming straight for us, but even such a beast will take at least half an hour to reach us. It is a long way away. There is time for the good Father to make his service. If I fly straight out, I may be able to delay it further."

He explained his logic to Rani. *She is muttering to herself, so she is probably unhappy, but her general silence must mean she agrees with me.* "So, I am about to set off. Give my respect and best wishes to all, and I wish you good hunting in your task. May we all fight with honour and may our deeds today live long in the tales of the bards."

"Fight well, but try and stay alive," *comes the reluctant reply over the Talker.* "There is far greater honour in having the sense to retreat at the right time than in throwing your life away foolishly. Do you hear me?"

"I hear your words, and I will heed them. I know that I wish to hold my children again, but I am leaving now. I am going to leave the talker here for whoever will come out next to relay what is happening. I will leave everything that I do not need to fight with.

"Please pass my regards to everyone and good hunting. I will see you all later, perhaps in this life, or perhaps in the spirit lands where we all shall go one day. Today, it will be as the spirits will it."

Chapter LIX

Canute Jakubsen
1st Undecim

I have given the alarm. I will bet that I am the first, anywhere, to see it on the move. Not only is its mountain closer to us in Dwarvenholme, but its exit from its lair is silhouetted against the sky from here at the watch post.

We were told of its presence by the Mice and by Thord, and the tales of our race have mentioned it with respect and fear, but none of those now alive have seen one of the few red dragons that are known of this close before. It has always been a distant object in the sky to those now alive.

The horns of alarm are blowing but, even as I watch, it flies across my sight. It is ignoring the closer target for one that it seems aimed at like an arrow. I admit to mixed feelings. It must be going to Mousehole.

I wonder if they will survive and, indeed, if they do not, what will happen to the village and its riches. I am on duty, but behind me I can hear an argument. Some are saying that the Mice will indeed triumph, and that we should be getting ready to head towards the dragon's lair to see what is there. I am betting that our Mayor will take caution over avarice.

Togrül dol Glavan

Life in this westernmost Darkreach outpost on its distant and lonely mountain, the one that is called Forest Watch, is generally boring. It is not as cold or dangerous as life can be in the other outposts in the actual mountains. I will take boring. We can see several roads with our strong telescopes, but we have few visitors.

Lately, my movement log has begun to show more entries as Dwarves return to their home, and occasionally we even see one of the people from this new village with the unlikely name flying through the sky.

In the entire history of this outpost it is usually only once a year, and sometimes not even that, that the sergeant in charge gets to record the giant dragon and its movements, as it seeks food before returning back to its lair to sleep.

Once, in a time still recorded from during The Burning, it had destroyed most of this outpost and eaten their mounts. Only a few of the garrison from then had survived by hiding and by good fortune. The volume recording that day, kept below in the record room, has blackened edges.

Now, during my turn on watch, and my hand of months of this tour in charge, I get to see the great beast in the far, far distance, near three hands of hands of thousands of paces away. To the naked eye it is just a dot in the sky, but using the telescope mounted on its post on the eastern wall it can clearly be seen.

From its course, it is no menace to us and our mounts, or even Mouthguard this time. It is heading straight for the new village. Standing orders said that everyone has to be woken up when it is seen, so I have a scout on the iron triangle sounding out its alarm.

After everyone had been roused, they all stood on the walls and watched. *As per orders, I will consult with my second patrol commander and our mage, and we will order the beacon fire to be lit.*

Regardless of what happens, Mouthguard needs to know that something is afoot in the mountains and life is not likely to be the same again. Once the fire is alight, and I have seen an answering light from the distant keep, I will order the dumping of copper dust into the fire to turn the flame green and indicate that the menace is not a present danger to the Empire.

We really need something better than this. It may have served for more than a thousand years, but I am sure that we can do better.

Once they acknowledge, it will be up to them to send out their patrols toward me and, once I know more of what is happening, I will send my second sergeant out with her Kichic-Kharl troops to find out more about the dragon. I had better get them and their wolves ready to set out as soon as there is something for them to go towards either in the south-east or, perhaps, in a more southerly direction. Waiting will see.

Chapter LX

Rani
1st Undecim

Rani hurried down from the roof of the hall to find almost the whole village, except those who had been designated to care for the children, gathered. *They need to hear what will happen next.* Thoughtfully she looked out at them all.

"We have nearly half an hour before the dragon will reach here. Bianca, you have just come off watch and are not rested. You will not be going out." *Bianca looks downcast, and Anahita pats her shoulder, but Christopher looks relieved.*

"Bryony, when we are finished here, take some of the strong arrows and go to the watch point. You have an essential role. You are to communicate what happens outside to us inside the valley, and to direct the priests on the carpet to where they are needed. You are to use your arrows as you need if the dragon comes close." *She and Stefan are not worrying about anyone watching as they say goodbye. Next, then…*

"Thord, you are to go onto the hill over the mine on Hillstrider. Your job is the same as Bryony's, but from the other side of the village." Thord nodded.

"Elizabeth, you are to go with the children. I have decided that your weapons are too short a range for this task. This leaves Eleanor taking the carpet with the priests. I do not want to hear of any of you on the carpet getting in combat, or indeed going anywhere near the dragon. It is your job to find the fallen and the damaged and to heal them as you can."

"Astrid, you will be in charge of the attack. You know how to attack a whale with small boats when it can eat you all. Now is the time to apply this in the air. You will have Kãhina, Anahita, Valeria, Ayesha, Basil, Lãdi and Aine," she said, naming a mix of the best riders blended with those experienced at fighting on horseback and with longer range weapons. "You will each have two wands, two molotails, and as many arrows or sling bullets as you can carry."

"Stefan, as we have discussed, your role is to be the most dangerous. You must get close, and go for the heart or the head as it seems best. You will have Ayesha's ring to help you but, like mages, dragons can resist magic, so it may be able to see through the glamour of the ring. Do not rely on it, but be like Astrid is with her ring. Try to be just as stealthy with it on as when it is not in use. How you can do that in the air, I am not sure, but try."

"As for tactics, do what Astrid says, but remember all of you, that Stefan will be trying to get close to the dragon from underneath. Try not to fire anything there. Remember that your wands have just a little bit more range than its breath probably does, and it will only take one breath from the beast to kill you. We have been able to give you no protection from its breath, or its teeth for that matter. You will have no second chances."

"We think that you are faster. Try and attack from the rear or the sides or, even better, from above its tail. Its breath should not reach you there. If you can, concentrate your fire on one spot and try and weaken something. If you can bring it down, then it should take damage from the fall and…I have said all of this before, haven't I?"

The chorus of nodding heads says yes. "In that case, I believe that the good Fathers want to see you all in the healing chapel regardless of your religion. It is small, but all of those going outside must be there, and as many others as we can fit in."

Christopher

W*e must be quick. Short confessions and absolving for those of our flock who practice the rite, and once these are all dealt with inside the chapel, it is time for a few words.* "As those who were at Orthros would know, today is the Feast day of the Archangel Michael." He indicated the image on his crucifix.

"Michael is sacred both to Christians and Muslims as the Strategos of the Heavenly Host and he has special patronage over victory. He, like St Georgiou, is usually depicted in victory over a dragon as a symbol for the devil. Today, we will be contemplating this image for its more literal meaning.

"We will be praying over you and asking God to increase the luck of all who are involved in our enterprise, if it pleases Him to do so, and I hope those not of our faith will not be offended. I am sure that God, however you worship

Him, will listen to our prayers in the spirit in which they are meant." *It is time now for me to gather mana from Father Theodule and to say the words of the Miracle.*

D*one and I feel content. Now the benediction and...* "We also have had these tokens made for you to wear and we have blessed them beforehand." Theodule began handing our strips of purple cloth, which had two conjoined Greek letters painted on them in gold.

"There is a legend that has been passed down in our church of an ancient ruler who had a vision from God with this symbol in it, together with the words 'touto nika' or 'conquer with this sign'. I hope that this charm will also aid our task. Feel free to take one each."

"I will take two," said Anahita. "I will take one for Hulagu, in case I can give it to him." People took the strips of cloth from Theodule and began to tie them about their persons, or have others tie them on them. *Partners and friends are using them as a way of perhaps saying goodbye, exchanging a kiss or a hug as the task is completed.*

As they dispersed Rani moved up. "You used all of your mana then, didn't you?" *Well, yes.* "How then will you cure us if needed?"

Christopher sighed. "We have storage devices with us with more mana of course, and we had Lakshmi make us more potion of Sleepwell." He held up his hand to forestall what Rani was about to say. "Yes, we are well aware of the risks. Remember that I know too well the pain that the addiction brings... and I may not be as lucky next time around. We will take as many doses as we need to administer the cures we need to make.

"It is better that we should have people alive to tend us in our pain than that we go without the pain and have none survive. For it is written in the Gospels that: 'greater love hath no man than this; that a man lay down his life for his friends.' Others are going forth to physically combat the beast and put their lives in danger. Can we in conscience do any less?

"We have discussed this between ourselves, and with our spouses. The Presbyteras are not happy with the decision, but they accept the necessity of what we do. I ask you not to mention this to anyone, lest they be reluctant to take healing from us. Now, let us go out and do what we have to do, and may God have mercy upon all of our souls."

Bianca

E veryone is running to their saddles as last goodbyes are said. Basil and Astrid are the only couple who are flying out, and neither wants to be the first to drop their hand. I may lose my husband, my new brother, and his köle and thus be responsible for six children.

Thord is already headed out from the stables and heading past those going to the mines. Astrid has promised him that they will get drunk tonight. For once, I hope that they can. Bryony will be dropped off by the carpet at the lookout, and so she climbs on that.

One by one they ascend into the sky. Astrid has called for the riders to form line behind her and, waving sombrely to those staying, they are headed to the gate. The mages are headed towards the roof. I hope that they will not be needed, for if they are, then the rest will be lost. Now I need to gather the rest of the adults, get breakfasts and other essential essentials and follow the last of the children into the mine.

Chapter LXI

Hulagu
1st Undecim

Hulagu sped through the sky, climbing as he did so and veering to the right. *If I am lucky, the dragon will ignore me until I attack. No, that isn't going to happen. It is a long way off still, but it looks like it is rising in response to my move. That means that it has seen me, reckoned me to be a threat and so left its straight course.*

He kept going, travelling as fast as he ever had and moving to the side. *Looking at the forest below the dragon though, it seems to me that the dragon may be travelling nearly as fast as I am. Maybe our advantage in speed will be less than we had hoped. I pray to my guardian spirit, to the Khünd Chono, that I have the ability to dodge better than my opponent; otherwise this will be a short fight.*

At least ten minutes have passed. Glancing to my left, I can see glimpses of the river, the one that we now know to be the Tulky Wash, as it flows from its origin on the Mountain of the Dragon down into the Swamp. Looking to my right, I can see snatches of the road to Dwarvenholme from the Gap.

I am veering right and am now higher than the Mountain of the Dragon itself. The dragon seems unsure whether to keep following me, or to turn more directly back towards the valley. It doesn't have much time to decide but, being such a massive beast, it seems to be far happier when it travels in a long glide, only flapping its wings when it needs to. Maybe that will force its decision.

However high it goes, I have to go higher. He checked and tightened the straps that held him to the saddle, checked once again that everything was secure and not going to fall off when he made sudden moves and then readied a wand.

It has decided. It has given me a look, and now drops into a glide for Mousehole, ignoring me as a small object flying above it. Hulagu kept climbing but stopped moving further towards the main mountain ranges.

The time came when they passed each other. *The dragon briefly turned its head up and back to check on me again. It seems to have some difficulty with taking a prolonged look in any direction other than down. Anything else makes it steer erratically. I suppose that a dragon must spend most of its flying life looking down for prey. There is little to interest it that will be higher in the sky than it. I am about to change that.*

He put the saddle into a dive. *It is a risky move, but I am going to get close to it for my first pass. I want its attention. I have the rising sun to my left, and am coming out of the clear sky in a near vertical dive. It is something that the dragon probably cannot do. It may not think of this as something that can be done to it.*

I want to pass close by the back of the left wing. I can see one of the ribs near the end of the wing. It is like the wing bones of a bat; those that stiffen the wing, rather than the single outstretched bone of the flying furry lizards. That is my prime target. The dragon is looking behind, trying to spot me. It looks to the other side and away from me.

He went past firing the wand in a blast of lightning. *Hit.* He swooped down past the wing and under the dragon's tail as a gout of flame washed above where he had been. *The dragon is turning around to look for me as I complete my loop around its tail and again fire...and hit, at the same spot...dropping down.*

This time, I continue past the dragon's tail and away. Just as well. It has flamed under its body where I would have been if I had done the same. It seems to have lost sight of me. Good, I guessed right. It learns fast. I have to change my attack each time. One small touch of that flaming breath and I am dead.

Hulagu rode away and looked back. *I have succeeded at one thing at least. The dragon is turning away from Mousehole. I now have its undivided attention. On one level, that is a good thing. Now I have to change tactics. It is time for me to revert to a time-honoured Khitan practice.*

He put the wand away in its pouch, fastening it, and being careful that he remembered that the one on the left had used two charges, and unlaced the bow and arrow quivers. *This is going to be less accurate. I will be firing from a very long range with these arrows and I thank my father for the enchantments woven into this weapon.*

I can risk closing to a range where I will be more likely to hit, but there, even a slight miscalculation will put me within range of the dragon. I am sure that it will not misjudge the distance, even if I do. The key to being successful will be to keep the distance close enough that it thinks that it has a chance to catch me and keep the shots far enough apart that I do not run out of shafts before the dragon loses interest in me.

Once his bow was out, he took careful aim and fired. *My luck is in. The dragon has either not seen the arrow or else ignored it as being below its notice. That is its error.* An explosion announced it hitting the dragon on the nose. *One arrow will do less than half what the wand will do, and is easier to miss with, but it will all add up and that shot had to have hurt it in more than its pride.*

It turns out that it was ignoring the arrow. The next one he fired was flamed out of the sky with a minor puff from the beast. *I can try changing my point of aim.* It ignored one shot at its wing, but it flicked past the tip and missed the beast. *A puff of flame from below on a hillside tells where the arrow landed.*

I will try something else, a plunging shot. Normally, this would not work, but this beast is so big that...A hit on its back and a brief flame in my direction and gaping jaws as it roars. He fired again into the sky. *The dragon realises what I am doing and allows itself to move left...not enough, anything with a wing span of five hundred paces makes a huge target and now I hit its right wing.*

Damn, it has decided that I cannot be caught and is turning away, back towards Mousehole. It has to be driven by something. I cannot imagine a normal beast not wanting to follow me and eliminate me for my temerity. Now I have to use a wand again. The bow went back in its case and was locked down, the arrow quiver was closed and quickly laced, and the wand came out again.

He came up to the tail. *If I fly directly behind the beast, then it might not see me.* He drew level with the tail. *Ahead, the beast is glancing back. I am right. It has difficulty seeing me here, but then I cannot fire where I want. I have no choice. I will have to get closer.*

He flew past the tip of the tail, a huge diamond of leathery red skin moving side to side through the air. I have an idea. The dragon looks a bit like a Tailed Leather-wing. It is far larger, has more bat-like wings and four legs and no fur, but that is what it looks like. A Tailed Leather-wing without the tip of its tail cannot fly properly as it cannot steer.

Now, how do I do this? He took aim at the base of the diamond shape. *It is a harder shot than aiming at the vast wings and body, but...* He concentrated his aim and fired and pulled the saddle to a stop straight away. He stopped dead. *The belt around me is almost cutting me in two, but just as well, my blast has galvanised the tail into thrashing through the sky where I would have been. If I had kept going, I would have been swatted aside like a gnat. It has not liked that at all. I will keep doing this.*

The second time is not as easy. Although it makes its flying more erratic, the dragon has realised what I am doing, and its tail lashes out at random. I have to be quick to dodge or else risk firing from a range where I am more likely to miss. And I just did that, wasting a bolt.

Again, he closed and fired and stopped. *This time I have gotten too close and the very tip of the tail, only the last hand, casually flicked me as it passed. The dragon probably didn't even notice the touch, but it is enough of an impact to send me spinning through the sky in agony.*

He fought for control of the saddle through the pain and a growing blackness. He regained control just paces from the trees towards which he had been despatched. In pain, and through a growing fog he looked down. *My left leg is crushed. I can see my trousers are wet with blood, and the pain is intense. Damn not having a healing potion with me. Even if I somehow survive, I may have lost the leg.*

He focussed on the beast now ahead as well as above him. *I might just have one more try at the beast left in me.* He was just heading back to the dragon for a last attack when he heard a cry from above and towards the valley. Hulagu looked up.

I have delayed the dragon perhaps even enough. The rest of the fliers have engaged the beast while I fought to stave off blacking out and regain control of my saddle. I am being hailed by the priests on the carpet as it is dropping towards me. I just might survive this fight after all. He felt a wave of relief pass through him even as he fought for consciousness against the growing blackness.

Chapter LXII

Astrid
1st Undecim

As Eleanor headed up to the lookout to drop Bryony, Astrid was already moving the saddle riders into the formation that she had decided upon. *I have them in a crescent with me at the centre and Kāhina and Anahita at the ends. To the left, between Astrid and Anahita, are Valeria and Basil. On the other side are Lādi and Aine. Ayesha, the most skilled rider bar me, is below holding onto a rope, the other end of which is being held by an invisible Stefan.*

Far ahead, I can see that Hulagu still survives from the flashes of the discharges of his wands. He must be using one of Theodora's wands, as I can see a glint of lightning in the sky and, if I listen hard, a faint 'crack.' The dragon fights back with gouts of flame.

"He is still there." *That was a sigh of relief from below me.* "Now we climb and go as fast as we can. Keep your formation with the wings advancing and getting a hundred ahead. We need to pass a hand of hundreds of paces above it before we swoop back down. Do not be distracted. Stefan, detach when I say so. Forward." *If any could see my face, I know that I have the predatory look on it of a great cat about to pounce.*

Astrid had been climbing as she watched Hulagu's tactics. *I will work with what he is doing. It is good. I will keep two held forward and two on each side. That way, whichever direction the dragon turns in there would be two on its tail. We will open with a thrown molotail each from above as we go for our positions.* She yelled instructions. *I wish that my voice was louder.*

The carpet is falling back and dropping away to the side and down. Kāhina is moving to join me while Anahita and Valeria, Ayesha and Basil and Lādi and Aine formed pairs. Ayesha is waving the hand that had been holding the rope. Stefan must have chosen his own time and is now on his way.

They flew on and, just as she was about to give the signal to drop in attack, she saw Hulagu's luck run out as he was sent spinning through the air. "Down." Each with a molotail held ready, they dropped onto the dragon. *It is turning around to where Hulagu spins helpless through the air.*

It must have been absorbed completely in its combat with Hulagu. It didn't see us coming. We are a complete surprise to it. "Throw" *Eight arms hurl their deadly cargo before wheeling to take up our positions. We are at the front, Lādi and Aine to the rear and the others on the flanks.*

Kāhina, Anahita, Ayesha and Aine get their bows, and the rest of us reach for a wand, as six of the molotails hit and explode in flame. The others are on a long fall to the ground where only the wetness of early spring prevents the hillsides from going up in smoke. The devices fall among the eucalypt forests of the middle slopes. Unnoticed by anyone else, oily smoke erupts skyward from their impact sites.

The dragon gives vent to a mighty roar. I felt that. It is enveloped in a series of fireballs that join together across its back in a rolling explosion, and I feel the wash of heat from that as well. The contents of the molotails cling to its skin and the dragon roars in pain and twists around while still flying on, the flame is dripping from its flanks and wings.

It has a tactic for this. It is drawing its wings in and shaking itself, dropping like a stone, but freeing itself of much of its flaming burden, now cascading as a rain of fire through the sky. Stefan, is he still alive?

The move nearly halved the amount of burning liquid on it. I wonder if this is a tactic that it remembers from fights in its far-distant youth, when dragons must have been smaller and perhaps more plentiful, and dragon may have fought dragon as a regular occurrence.

We were caught out by its sudden fall, but now our archers take advantage of its inattention to fire from above the beast into its vast back. It is hard to miss. They just aim for the centre of its body. They have explosive shafts; each hit adds a spurt of flame to the conflagration below. The four with ready wands take position as the dragon again begins to rise towards us. We have the upper hand over the beast.

Each arrow, although powerful enough to perhaps kill a person on its own, is individually only doing a tiny amount of damage to the great beast, as little as an ant bite would do to a person, but it is all adding up. If we can keep this up, it can do nothing to us and our greater height and its slower rise means that we can easily stay outside the range of its breath while continuing to harm it.

She signalled for the others to continue the attack like this, while she looked around and took stock.

Yes, Hulagu has moved the fight away from the direct line to the village. Now the dragon, in trying to climb towards us and rid itself of its tormentors, has become even more careless of its direction and we are headed out over the forested slopes, more towards the Darkreach outpost than anywhere else. It is lucky for us and we will take advantage of this while we can.

Bryony

I am supposed to say what is happening, but I can only pass on what I see and that is hard. I see no people. Even with the telescope, it is mainly the dragon rising and falling in the sky...its changes of direction and sudden turns, some lightning bolts, but none of them since the ball of flame surrounded the dragon. That must have been the molotails and then it dropped and flew out and started to rise again.

At least it is not coming towards us now. It is particularly important when I have just a bow, and am placed so as to be under the dragon when it flies into the village.

Still, my greatest fear is for Stefan. The father of my child is somewhere out there with the most dangerous role of them all, and because of what he carries, if he is injured and knocked unconscious at some time in the fight, none will ever find him. He is undetectable and that works each way, for both enemy and for friend. Even now he could be unconscious and bleeding to death as he flies past the priests and no one will ever know.

He just accepts what scraps I give him. Have I even told him that I love him for what he is? What he has done for me? I had thought that I would never want another commitment, but I already have one baby with him, and I may have another on the way, so why do I feel the way that I do?

I need to think about where I want to go with my life. My old one is well and truly behind me. I have cut it off. Am I ready to start a new one? In the meantime, I will pray and hope, but who do I pray to?

Chapter LXIII

Stefan
1st Undecim

*A*strid has not said to go yet, but I heard her orders and the time to go is now. Stefan separated from the rest of the flight and dropped. *I want to be well below the dragon as I approach, so that any flame it lets out will not accidentally toast me.* He looked up.

I have to be as aware of my friend's fire, as much as I am of that from the dragon. Damn, Hulagu is spinning away and the dragon is turning to finish him off. The carpet is dropping. Eleanor is heading it towards where she thinks Hulagu is headed.

S'blood, what is that...the molotails? Even here I felt the wash of heat, as they drop on the beast and the impact of its roar of pain and rage. To the right, most of them hit on the dragon. That one sailed past only a few paces away as it heads to the ground. It was hard to pick out as it dropped, but I was lucky to see and avoid it in time.

S'truth, down, down. The beast is dropping, and shedding fire and I am under it all. Dodge around plummeting dragon to crush and sheets of flame to burn... It is shaking like a wet dog, and flying like one as well.

Now I am out from under the damn beast and that was an arrow that just went past. Thanks folks. Drop again in a dive to attempt to regain the shadow...we are low...its wing tip just hit the top of a giant Swamp Gum and demolished it, and I am still avoiding flaming drops.

Stefan heard a rain of smaller explosions. *More arrow fire. For some reason Astrid is using the less powerful weapons rather than the wands.* He looked up and around. *Of course. The riders are in pairs above the dragon, and one of each pair can keep up a constant rain of arrows, while they last, and still stay clear of its blasts.*

Such pinpricks will not kill it but while it is distracted it will let me get close, even if the dragon sees through my magic or even looks in my direction. He rose, now fully under the dragon and safe from arrow fire and being seen.

Safe I might be, but I am here to do a job, not to be safe. I have a broadsword. It is a weapon that is meant to be used by one person attacking another person while both are standing firmly on the ground and hacking and slashing at each other. Even if you are on a horse attacking someone you hope to have a more suitable blade.

Here I am, flying through the air, about to attack another flying target that isn't even vaguely humanoid. What idiot made a weapon to kill a dragon, and made it the worst possible weapon for the job? Why not use a lance or a spear at least? The only things that would be worse are a dagger or a rapier, and I am sure that Ayesha could somehow make a dagger a much better proposition.

He looked above him, and flew backwards and forwards underneath the great beast. *There is not a single point of vulnerability I can see. I am supposed to deliver a mighty blow that will despatch the beast, but that will only be possible if there is something for me to attack that might be vital to it. Dear Saint Jude and Saint Michael, I will keep flying around and maybe one of you will show me this mythical place for me to strike a killing blow.*

Chapter LXIV

Astrid
lst Undecim

D*amn. The beast has realised that we are distracting it and it is turning back towards Mousehole. We are running out of arrows; not that they are having a lot of effect anyway. Sure, I can see bleeding wounds on the beast. There are even a couple of places where there are holes in the wings that I could fly through, but none of this seems to slow it down, and its breath is still a mighty blast that will cook any of us instantly.*

What do I try next? Valeria has her own horse bow and supply of arrows and Lãdi has a sling and a supply of magically enhanced bullets. They can keep up their own fire after the four firing now run out. She waved her arms and shouted, rotating and changing positions. *Now I have Anahita and Valeria ahead of the dragon, on its right. Lãdi and Aine are ahead and to the left, Kãhina and I behind and to the left, and Ayesha and Basil are behind to the right. We are still well above the dragon, but this will change.*

I wonder where Stefan is. Those are the last few arrows, now for new instructions. Keep the front flyers high. Drop the rear ones and we prepare to use wands. She called instructions out to the others. *The first run is mine. It must have been Hulagu who did that damage to the beast's tail and that is a good place to start.*

She fired the wand, pulled out and indicated the target. *One by one, we do our runs in. Fire, and out in a different way. Lightning, flame and air fists are pounding away at it. At least the dragon cannot readily flame us here, it is too far from its vast jaws unless it contorts itself or turns itself around. We only have to fear its lashing tail—only—and what happened to Hulagu shows that to be a real fear. We cannot afford a touch from such a massive object.*

Christopher

H ulagu is hit. "Get to him." *I see Theodule is sipping on the Sleepwell. It is that time when we must. I can feel my mana return.* As they came closer, and ignoring the closing dragon, Christopher grabbed hold of the rope that he had attached between Theodule and himself, while Theodule stood up precariously on the plunging carpet and attempted to catch the saddle.

Hulagu has not even noticed us, is he conscious? Eleanor has called out several times. Eventually he has seen us, his eyes full of pain; he is slumped, almost dead. Theodule has him...fighting the saddle...a hand on it steadies it. Theodule has the first miracle this time.

They looked at each other. "Do a simple bone-set on the leg first, then a major cure. He is just still conscious, and that should restore him enough that a lot of fluid and some rest will see him get back into the fight, if he is needed, and so that he can hold that saddle steady. I won't be needed on this one." *Theodule nods in agreement and he prays while I keep an eye for where we will be needed next.*

Astrid

M *y tactics are slowly working. Between the arrows still coming from in front of it, and that it is flying into, and the blasts from the wands onto its tail, the dragon is clearly unhappy. From what I can see, we are losing about half of the arrows to its breath, but what they do is less important than the damage that we are doing with the wands.*

I can see bone. The good thing is that the end of the tail has to be near to being severed and that will, at least, make it harder for the beast to manoeuvre. As well it is obvious, from the number of close encounters that we have had with the lashing tail just missing us, that Father Christopher's prayers have been answered.

The number of times that we have turned aside at the last moment, ducked or dodged and been missed is, well, miraculous. I owe real attention at services for at least a month out of gratitude.

Maybe it is about time for me to pick a saint as my special patron. Bianca has a serious devotion to Saint Ursula, and swears that her saint had been instrumental in her revenge on the bandits. When this is over, I will think about it, but I don't think that the virgin Saint is for me.

The bad thing is that the dragon has nearly halved the distance to Mouse-hole. Will what we are doing work in time?

Chapter LXV

Stefan
lst Undecim

I *have looked at the whole underbelly of the beast. There is no place that is vulnerable. Anything that may once have been a soft spot now has enough gems and gold embedded in it from the dragon sleeping on them that it is now armoured with treasure.* He looked out from under and saw the archers firing.

I should be able to safely fly out a little way, I hope. I have to look out for the dragon's neck as it dodges around firing blasts of fire at arrows and archers, but that is fairly easy. There is my target. There...at the junction of wing and body on the right of the dragon, only visible if you are as close as I am and with time to look for it.

There is a patch of skin that slowly moves in and out. It is just like one of the blood vessels on a person's neck near their shoulder, only it is as big across as my whole body and pumps more slowly. It won't be easy and I will get just one shot at this.

Where is everyone? He looked around and then flew as fast as he could ahead of the dragon before turning around and heading back.

I have Wrath over behind my back to give me the maximum swing. I need to time this right. As I fly at the beast, I will get just one slash with the sword and then I will hit the dragon with my saddle...hard. There is nowhere for me to dodge, and no other way to do it. I hope that I will survive the impact, but it should work, and my woman and my son may live. That is more important.

Chapter LXVI

Astrid
1st Undecim

"**B**asil!" *Our luck has run out at the same time as we finally succeed in our attacks on the tail. My husband is the worst of our riders, and his fireball has hit the dragon and finally caused the tail to break, the same break has caused it to flop in a direction that was totally unexpected. There didn't seem any force in the blow that hit him, but there does not need to be. He is dropping. I have him, so does Anahita. Can we wrestle him to the carpet? Thank God, it is rising. Hulagu is alive and alongside it.*

"He has taken a blow to the chest." *As if he needed to hear that.*

"He is far better than he was last time I had to cure him," Christopher said to Theodule. "Hulagu, you have had enough rest. You can take over from him, but be more careful this time. Basil, I just need to do a plain cure on you this time. I want you to stay awake now," and he started chanting.

Chapter LXVII

Stefan
1st Undecim

By Saint Michael, what was that roar? Can I still hear? That blast just
missed me. No distractions. Add the momentum of my charge to my swing
and damn the consequences. "For Bryony and Aneurin!"

The sword struck the tough hide. *It is like hitting a practice target of hay-
stuffed linen clad in a suit of mail worn over really thick padding, rather than
hitting a normal beast. It cuts through the throbbing place on the skin. I am
able to twist and hit with the base of my saddle and now I am bathed in the hot
and steaming gore of the dragon.*

*I have it in my mouth. I was screaming something as I flew in, God alone
knows what. That tastes foul.* Coughing and spluttering, he struggled to see
and to find his way clear.

*I am flying sideways over the body of the dragon, while spinning around
like a God-damned top. I need to get clear before I become the unwitting
target of one of my friends and so that I can see what I did. Did it work?*

Astrid

They were flying back up from the priests on the carpet when the dragon
gave a start. *Something is pouring from the dragon. Could that be blood?
It looks like a waterfall, a vast red waterfall. Has Stefan succeeded? Where is
he?* "Stop shooting. We could hit Stefan."

The dragon has stopped flying. It seems to have entered a glide and is just getting as much distance as it can. Perhaps it knows that it is doomed, but it still wants to savage the valley.

She looked ahead of where she was now flying over the back of the beast. *It might just still make the valley if it keeps going. Damn. We will still have to do something. But what else can we do? The dragon seems to be dying, but something is keeping it going single-mindedly. Surely, it is under some form of geas of control.*

Stefan

D*amn this blood in my eyes! That was Astrid I just went past. I should reappear. They might be holding fire because of me.* He turned to join the others above the beast and pulled the ring off, keeping it tightly held in his left hand as he fumbled to open a pouch.

Astrid

W*e are all flying above the dragon now. Stefan is here. He is covered in blood. He looks like someone who has been inside a whale while it is being flensed. Now I know what to do, he is now safe, but the beast is still flying, just.* She looked around.

"The left wing, get above it! If it turns to take us, then it will fail in its glide. With its tail gone it is finding it hard to steer. We only need a bit more. Fire everything you have left."

The others acknowledged her words by wheeling and taking places only two hands of paces away from the wing, and pouring everything they still had onto it. *They are starting with the rest of the molotails. The stench of burning flesh and whatever is in molotails fills the nostrils. Now for the crackle of lightning or the 'whoosh' of fireballs, depending on what wands people have left.*

Damn it. It is dying and still it draws nearer and nearer to the valley. Whoever or whatever is controlling it is going to make its death count. The dragon now is completely ignoring us.

Astrid looked ahead. *I can make out Bryony on the watch point preparing to add her almost useless fire to what we are already pouring into the flying behemoth.* She looked around. *The archers have switched back to bows but I am out of everything.* "Find a joint and concentrate on it. Stefan can you do something with that sword again?"

Stefan

"**I** can." *If there was a blood vessel on one side, it should be there on the other as well. Out with Wrath again; it is bloody in my scabbard and in my hand.*

He flew hard and, confident that it would be there as he flew over the wing, swung low down from his saddle. Again, he had swung well, and the blood cascaded out. *It is a shallower wound, but this time there is more effect. Add it to what the other fliers have already done to the wing it is enough. There is a sound like a banshee's wail, only it is a deep bass banshee, and at a volume that makes my head ring in pain. Its left wing is giving way and folding in on itself.*

I can see Bryony standing there shooting. Now the beast is plummeting to the left, hitting the ground with a sound like the end of the world. First the tip of a wing hits the ground, then the body of the beast, and then the second wing drapes over the body. The tip of it comes down nearly reaching the road below. Cliffs are falling. Bryony has dropped her bow and is on her knees. We will live. We will all live.

Now it is silent, for a moment. A chorus of bush birds are letting their concern be heard. There is the sound of falling trees echoing around.

My last blow, or maybe the previous one, was fatal. Maybe the beast was already dead, and its joints were locked, and the last blow just unlocked the wing. Who knows? Who cares? The dragon, our greatest fear, and the thing that has been preventing us from thinking further ahead, now lies dead in a heap on the cliffs outside the village.

Bryony

I think that is Stefan who did that…the bloody figure on a saddle with a sword waving in the air and yelling something. I fired one shot and that is all. I nearly fell off the cliff when it struck.

Now, ahead of me I can see its open eyes, yellow rather than a metallic gold and slitted like those of a cat. They are open and staring, gradually glazing over as the last remnants of life leave them. In death, it forms a vast mound on top of the cliff above the road. Its skeleton will stay in place there to serve as an entrance marker to the valley for generations to come.

Astrid

W *e did it! By Saint Michael, by Saint George, we did it.* Astrid looped her saddle around as she flew. *Each of the others is doing something similar. We are all alive, us, our children, even the chickens. My head is ringing from that last cry and I cannot hear properly, but I can still see.*

A vast weight has been lifted from my shoulders, and what is more, I have just led a war party on my own and triumphed. It may have been due to luck and good preparation over months, but the skald's tales will talk about me. I will make sure of it. She looked to the side at the bloody figure beside her... *And of Stefan of course.* She grinned and turned to look for her husband back near the carpet. *I wonder if we can get someone to look after the babies tonight.*

A *triumphant return, and why does Rani look like that? What haven't we done?* "We already have lots of wealth," said Rani to the riders, "but Lakshmi and Harald have pointed out to me that the dragon will have even more in its cave. While we may not need what is there, if we do not stake our claim on it, and at least take the choicest pieces, then we will lose prestige in the area. That fight may even have been seen by the Bear Folk in the swamp. We now need to take the rewards. Are you able to fly, or do you want someone who was not in the fight to do so?"

Astrid paused. *Rani is actually asking my opinion. The miracles continue.* "Let Stefan, Basil and Hulagu wash and put on clean clothes. We will have something to eat and drink and others can fetch us a new supply of arrows while we do that. The ones who killed the beast should have the first reward, but one of you mages should take Theodule or Christopher's place on the carpet. We have no magic left and who knows what will be there. We will leave behind everything but the bare minimum to carry back as much as we can."

"So let it be;" said Rani. She looked at Theodora. "You may have more mana, but I am better in a fight without preparation. I will go." Theodora nodded.

Rani

W e could not have left it much longer. Already, I can see a large group of Dwarves have set out from Dwarvenholme, and those who were on the road have turned aside and are already at the base of the Mountain of the Dragon. It is still a long climb for them.

T hey were to be disappointed, at least in part. By the time the first Dwarves reached the huge cave that the dragon had taken and then modified for its own purposes, the saddles had made three trips to the cave, changing riders after the first. The carpet had made two trips.

Even without counting what was buried in the hide of the dragon, they had brought back to the valley far more treasure than they had obtained from Dwarvenholme. They still left behind as much or more than they had left in the Dwarven city. In the end, they had needed to use picks to do it; mining huge lumps of gold and gems as they did, but the bed of the vast beast had lost its top layers of compressed and almost unrecognisable plunder into the ever-growing treasury of the Mice.

Cast

Aelfgifu: 8 year old adopted daughter of Eleanor and Robin.

Aine: A woman from The Swamp, she is now the brewer and distiller for Mousehole. Marries Aaron.

Amos: A slaver from the Brotherhood, brother of Matthias, executed at Mousehole.

Anahita of the Axe-beaks: Khitan girl from Mousehole and Hulagu's köle, she is the mother of Būrãn.

Anastasius, Father: Chief Orthodox priest for Evilhalt.

Aneurin ap Stefan: Son of Bryony and Stefan.

Astrid Tostisdottir (the Cat): A part-Kharl girl from Wolfneck, in the far north of The Land. She is married to Basil. Her children are Freya Astridsdottir, 'the Kitten' and Georgiou Akritas. She is attractive, but for a strong jaw & lengthened incisors. Astrid is tall and statuesque, with pale blonde hair and dark green eyes. She can lap up drinks & purrs when having sex.

Ayesha: A ghazi or assassin of the Caliphate assigned by a Princess to guard Theodora. She is one of the rare women of that culture who is allowed independence and has received an education at Misr-al-Mãr as a ghazi (holy warrior). She is a minor daughter of Hãritha, the Sheik of Yãqũsa.

Aziz (Azizsevgili or Brave Lover): Hobgoblin captured during the attack on Mousehole. He falls in love with Verily and converts to the Orthodox faith and marries Verily. Their sons are Saglamruh (Strong Spirit) and Sunmak (Gift). His former name is Saygaanzaamrat (Plundered Emerald).

Barton Felders: Younger brother of Loudon. They sold Maria to the Brotherhood slavers.

Basil Akritas or Kutsulbalik (nickname from great-grandfather): Is a mostly human (one sixteenth Kharl) who appears as a youth just out of his apprenticeship (although he is ten years older). He is an experienced secret police officer of Darkreach. He comes from Southpoint from a military family and is now married to Astrid and living in Mousehole assigned to guard Theodora by Hrothnog.

Basil Tornikes: Metropolitan of the North at Greensin.

Bianca: A foundling from Trekvarna now living in Mousehole and married to Father Christopher. Their children are Rosa and Francesco. She can smell treachery.

Bianca Fletcher: Daughter of Robin and Eleanor.

Bilqĩs: A tiny girl, from a trade background in the Caliphate, she now lives in Mousehole as an apprentice mage. She has some ability as a glassblower.

Bjarni the Talker: Guard commander and Greeter for Kharlsbane.

Bjorn Strikefast: Dwarven Baron of Ironcone in the South-West Mountains.

Bryony verch Daffyd: A freckled red-head from Rising Mud in the Swamp. Her husband (Conan) and father were killed at her wedding and she was brought to Mousehole. She now lives with Stefan and her son is Aneurin ap Stefan.

Būrãn of the Dire Wolves: The daughter of Anahita of the Axe-beaks and Hulagu.

Candidas: An animal handler for Carausius from his second trip on. He is also a Darkreach agent and will be marrying Theodora Lígo.

Canute Jakubsen: A Dwarven sentry.

Carausius Holobolus: Darkreach trader in fabric, spices or anything else. His guards are Karas & Festus, animal handler is Candidas, his wife is Theodora and his daughter is Theodora Lígo.

Christopher Palamas, Father: The chief Orthodox priest for Mousehole and husband of Bianca. Their children are Rosa and Francesco. He is a very holy, but diplomatic, man and a dedicated healer.

Cnut Stonecleaver: Dwarven Baron of North Hole in the Northern Mountains.

Danelis: From Warkworth, she now lives in Mousehole where she usually helps Harald in the mine. She also helps on the farm. She has a minor ability with telekinesis and is short with silver-coloured hair.

Dar Lagrange: An ancient philosopher.

Dharmal: Dwarf and leader of the brigands who attack Bianca's caravan. He ruled Mousehole and acted as the main servant of the Masters in The Land. He was executed after the Mice overturned him.

Dulcie: From Bathmor in The Swamp. She is now the Mousehole carpenter and marries Jordan.

Eleanor: A caravan guard from Topwin in Freehold she now lives in Mousehole and works as a jeweller. She is married to Robin Fletcher and is one of the first in the village to fall pregnant. They have adopted Aelfgifu, Gemma and Repent and have a daughter Bianca.

Elizabeth: An orphan from Trekvarna in Freehold who now lives in Mousehole. She is a skilled musician and assistant brewer.

Fãtima: She comes from an unknown background in the Caliphate. As Fatima bint al-Fa'r (Fatima, daughter of the Mouse) she marries Hrothnog as the

Empress of Darkreach and Ambassador of the Mice.

Fear the Lord Your God Thatcher: At 7 years old, she is the adopted daughter of Rani and Theodora.

Festus: A part-Kharl & guard for Carausius, a Darkreach trader in spices etc.

Fortunata: Dressmaker and embroiderer for Mousehole. She is the first wife of Norbert and her son is Valentine.

Francesco Palamas: The son of Bianca and Christopher, twin brother to Rosa.

Freya Astridsdottir: Twin sister of Georgios Akritas, daughter of Astrid and Basil. They were the first children born in Mousehole to live. Loves cats.

Gemma: A 9 year old child, adopted daughter of Eleanor and Robin.

George Pitt: Son of Lakshmi and Harald.

Georgios Akritas: Twin brother of Freya Astridsdottir, daughter of Astrid and Basil. He is named after Basil's father. They were the first children born in Mousehole to live. Good at fixing things.

Giles Ploughman: A farmer at Mousehole. He is married to Naeve.

Goditha: Sister to Robin Fletcher and married to Parminder. She is the mason of Mousehole and an apprentice mage. She is regarded as the father of Melissa Mason.

Gregory of Brickshield: Militia commander for Evilhalt.

Gurinder: An 11 year old child and sister of Parminder.

Hagar: From a farming family outside Dimashq in the Caliphate, she lives in Mousehole as the village butcher.

Harald Pitt: Miner at Mousehole. He marries Lakshmi and their son is George.

Hildric Marchant: An agent of the Masters in the independent villages of the north, he is based in Northrode near Greensin and acting as a trader.

Hrolfr Strongarm: Dwarven Baron of Oldike in the South-West Mountains.

Hrothnog: The immortal God-King of Darkreach and great-great grandfather of Theodora. He is now married to Fātima.

Hulagu: A young Khitan tribesman with ten toes. His tribe and totem is the Dire Wolf. He becomes a part of Mousehole. His daughters are Khātun (with Kāhina) and Būrān (with Anahita).

Ironfist: Dwarven Baron of Defcor in the Northern Mountains.

Iyād ibn Walīd: Imam of the main mosque in Ardlark.

Jeremiah Cephalas: The son of Ruth and Theodule and identical twin of Joshua.

Job Sword-of-God, Brother: Second Disciple and head of the Flails of God.

Johann Beman: Murdered father of Maria.

Joshua Cephalas: Son of Ruth and Theodule and identical twin of Jeremiah.

Kāhina of the Pack Hunters: Hulagu's köle and mother of Khātun of the Dire Wolves.

Khãtun of the Dire Wolves: Daughter of Kãhina of the Pack Hunters and Hulagu.

Karas: Part-Kharl guard for Carausius, a Darkreach trader in spices etc.

Kũrsũl: Cousin of Hulagu.

Lãdi: From the Caliphate, she is the chief cook at Mousehole and very skilled.

Lakshmi: Former Havenite, she has converted and is now Orthodox and married to Harald Pitt. Their son is George. She is the apothecary and midwife for Mousehole.

Leonas of Goldentide: He is Captain of the militia of Erave Town.

Loudon Felders: Older brother of Barton. They sold Maria to the Brotherhood slavers.

Loukia Akritina: Wife of Basil's brother.

Loukia Tzetzina: Cooper and cabinet maker from Mistledross. She lost her family in an earthquake and has moved to Mousehole.

Lucinda Beman: Murdered mother of Maria.

Make me to know my transgressions: A young woman from the Brotherhood brought as a slave to restock Mousehole.

Maria Beman: A kidnapped woman from near Greensin, daughter of Johann Beman, brought to Mousehole by slavers after it was freed.

Maryam bint Sulieman: Owner of the 'The Grey Doe', an inn in Ardlark that caters only to well-to-do women of any race.

Masters, the: Animated skeletons of the old Dwarven Druids with the ability to use magic as air-mages. They may now longer exist, or there may be more somewhere.

Matthias: A slaver from the Brotherhood, brother of Amos, executed at Mousehole.

Melissa Mason: Daughter of Goditha and Parminder.

Mellitus: Insakharl customs officer at Mouthgard.

Micah: A man in the Brotherhood in charge of taxation. He finds people who owe taxes who may sell the women in their household as slaves.

Michael: Praetor or leader in the Basilica Anthropoi.

Naeve Milker: Former Freegate dairymaid who now runs the herds of Mousehole. She can become catatonic under stress. She becomes an apprentice mage and marries Giles. Her daughter is Peggy Farmer.

Nikephorus Cheilas: He was an upper servant (Praetor koubikoularios) in the Palace at Darkreach, he is now married to Valeria and father to her child.

Nokaj: Grandfather of Hulagu, senior shaman to his tuman.

Norbert Black: He is skilled as a blacksmith, weapons smith and armourer. In Mousehole he marries both Fortunata and Sajãh. His sons are Valentine (with Fortunata) and Bishal (with Sajãh).

Olympias Akritina: Basil's sister, a junior officer in the navy in charge of a small fast scout and messenger boat.

Ordu: Hetman or leader of Hulagu's tuman.

Panterius, Strategos (General): In charge of the Darkreach Antikataskopeía.

Parminder: Assistant cook and sometimes dressmaker at Mousehole, she marries Goditha and is sister to Gurinder. She becomes an apprentice mage and is a xeno-telepath. Her daughter is Melissa Mason.

Peggy Farmer: Daughter of Giles and Naeve.

Ploughman, Giles: Chief farmer at Mousehole, he is married to Naeve and his daughter is Peggy.

Rabi'ah: A poor spinner and weaver from Ardlark. Her drunken father sold her into slavery. She is sent by her Imam to Mousehole.

Rani Rai: A former Havenite Battle Mage and now co-Princess of Mousehole. She has broken caste and is married to Theodora and has adopted Fear.

Repent of this thy wickedness: A 6 year old slave brought from the Brotherhood to help restock Mousehole. She is adopted by Eleanor and Robin.

Robin Fletcher: Fletcher and bowyer for Mousehole. He is married to Eleanor and they have adopted Aelfgifu, Gemma and Repent and have a daughter Bianca.

Rosa Palamas: Daughter of Bianca and Christopher, twin sister to Francesco.

Roxanna: A 9 year old adopted daughter of Sajãh, Norbert and Fortunata.

Ruhayma: A 10 year old adopted daughter of Sajãh, Norbert and Fortunata.

Ruth: Former Freehold merchant and now teacher of the village children in Mousehole. She is married to Father Theodule and their identical twin sons are Joshua and Jeremiah.

Saidah: A young girl who works at 'The Grey Doe', an inn in Ardlark, now nine years old.

Sajãh: From the Caliphate, she is the Seneschal of Mousehole under the Princesses. She is second wife of Norbert Black. Adopted mother of Roxanna and Ruhayma and mother of Bishal.

Salimah al Sabah: Theodora's alias when she is not being herself.

Shilpa: Former Havenite trader and now assistant smith in Mousehole. She takes Vishal as her partner.

Siglevi the Short: Baron of Evilhalt.

Simon of Richfield: A traveller and chronicler from before The Burning and even from before the Schism of the Church. He wrote a book called 'My Travels Over the Land and Beyond'.

Smasher Kharlsbane, Duke: ruler of Kharlsbane and the Northern Dwarves.

Snorri Trueheart: Dwarven Count and the ruler of Copperlevy in the Hills in the Northern Plains.

Sparetha: Mother of Hulagu, master horsewoman and trainer, fletcher, very skilled archer. Her mother is 'from the east' (actually the west) and was a thrall.

Stefan: A young soldier from Evilhalt. He is now in charge of the militia of Mousehole and lives with Bryony. Their son is Aneurin ap Stefan. He is also a leatherworker and has an inherited magical sword called Smiter.

Stefano of Erave Town: Son of Leonas, student at the school.

Stronghand: A Dwarf and Mayor of Diamondroot.

Svein: A man of Wolfneck and 'suitor' to Astrid. He is an ugly (very Kharlish appearance), violent drunkard and around 40 years old. Owns a ship and is a rival of Astrid's father. He is the Northern agent for the Masters.

Tabitha: Born in a farming hamlet near Erave Town, she now lives in Mousehole as an assistant carpenter and cook. She has one green eye and one blue one. Cats like her.

Thamar Lydina: The Magister Cubicularius, or chief servant, of the rooms reserved for special guests in the Palace at Ardlark.

The Vengeance of the Lord is Mine Quester: Brotherhood scout and Inquisitor from the Flails of God who comes to Mousehole to spy on it.

Theodora do Hrothnog: Great-great-granddaughter of Hrothnog. She is not entirely human, a mage and, at 120 years, is far older than the late teens that she appears to have. She is now Princess of Mousehole with her husband, Rani and their adopted daughter Fear.

Theodora Cephalou: Wife of Carausius.

Theodora Lígo: Daughter of Carausius.

Theodorus Daphopates, Father: The Orthodox priest stationed at Deathguard Tower.

Theodule, Brother: A former monk and now assistant to Father Christopher at Mousehole. He marries Ruth and their identical twin sons are Joshua and Jeremiah.

Thord: A shorter and broad humanoid of the species locally known as a Dwarf. He comes from Kharlsbane in the Northern Mountains, but is now Mousehole's Ambassador to the Dwarves. He rides a sheep called Hillstrider.

Thorfinn Deepdelver: Dwarven Duke and ruler of the Hills in the Northern Plains.

Thorgrim Baldursson: New Mayor of Dwarvenholme. He is tall and broad with grey hair and beard.

Thorkil: An outlaw from Wolfneck in Dharmal's brigands. He was killed in the attack on the bandit village. He was a paedophile.

Togotak: Father of Hulagu, master horseman, married to Sparetha. He is a better rider than her.

Toğrül dol Glavan: Senior Sergeant of the Border Regiment of Darkreach, in charge at Forest Watch.

Tosti: Father of Astrid and Father Thorstein.

Umm: Slave of the bandits from a poor farming family in the Caliphate, she is now a spinner and weaver in Mousehole and helps in the kitchen. She is now the senior wife of Atã ibn Rãfi.

Valeria: A 17 year old from Deeryas on the south coast, she is now the servant of Rani and Theodora and has married Nikephorus.

Verily I Rejoice in the Lord Tiller: A former Brotherhood slave and, now an assistant cook and apprentice mage in Mousehole. She can 'smell' magic and has married Aziz. Their sons are Saglamruh (Strong Spirit) and Sunmak (Gift).

Yumn: Orphan carpet maker from Ardlark who became a prostitute to raise a dowry or get enough for a loom. She is sent by her Imam to Mousehole. She becomes junior wife to Tãriq.

Zafirah: A poor spinner and weaver from Ardlark who sells herself into slavery to pay the family debts. She is sent by her Imam to Mousehole. She becomes junior wife to Atã.

Zampea: Drungarius (or Commodore) of Olympias Akritas' original flotilla.

Glossary

Anne, Saint: Christian Patron Saint of those who right the undead and protect against evil, also of those who return from the dead.

Andrew, Saint: Christian Saint, Feast Day 30th November, patron of fishermen.

Antdrudge: A town in the north of Darkreach.

Antikataskopeía: A part of the Darkreach Army who are also police. Sometimes they are in uniform and sometimes they are not. The term may be translated as 'secret police', but they are responsible for looking for subversion, spies and treason as much as normal criminals.

Ardlark: capital of Darkreach.

Asvayujau: Hindu Goddess of good luck, joy and fortune.

Betterberries: One of many magical herbs, if picked at the right time each Betterberry will have a tiny amount of healing power. You can eat a lot of them.

Brinkhold: A town in the south of Darkreach.

Brotherhood: A semi-Christian nation in the north-west of The Land.

Calendar: There are twelve months to the year. In order: Primus, Secundus, Tertius, Quattro, Quinque, Sixtus, September, October, November, December, Undecim, and Duodecimus.

Choli: The blouse top worn by Havenite women under a sari; it usually has short sleeves and buttons at the front leaving a bare midriff.

Cokhane: A flying bloodsucking beast found underground.

Cosmas, Saint: Always associated with Saint Damien as the Orthodox Christian patrons of healing. Their images are always dressed like men of the Caliphate and they have medical tools around them. Their Feast Day is 7th Duodecimus.

Darkreach: The Empire to the east of the mountains that is ruled by Hrothnog.

Deafcor: A Dwarven town.

Deathguard Tower: A Darkreach fortification guarding an ancient burial field.

Deathshrew: A small, but very dangerous underground predator.

Dharma: A Hindu concept, the shape or destiny laid out for us.

Dhatr: Hindu God of health and magic.

Diamondroot: A Dwarven town.

Ergüül: Khitan for a patrol or smallest unit.

Flashfever: A disease that occurs within an hour of infection. The victim develops a severe fever and, without intervention, dies in a few hours.

Francis, Saint: Christian Saint, Feast Day 4th October, patron of animals.

Freehold: A Kingdom in the west of The Land.

Ganesh: Hindu God, known as the Remover of Obstacles, he is the son of Shiva & Parvati, elephant headed and rides a mouse, God of knowledge & divination.

Ger: Khitan for a tent or yurt.

Gotar: Any fibre that is made from the fleece of goats.

Granther, the: A term used by the Darkreach Imperial family to refer to Hrothnog.

Grey Doe: A tavern in Ardark run by Maryam bint Suliman which was important as a means of allowing Theodora to escape Darkreach.

Haven: A Kingdom in south of the Land.

Healbush: A leafy herb found in the mountains. A potion made from it has minor curative effects and tastes very spicy.

John the Baptist, Saint: Orthodox Saint, his Feast Day in 29th Sixtus and he is the patron of pilgrims and others who travel for the faith.

Jude, Saint: Christian Saint, Feast Day 17th Undecim. He is the patron of those who are desperate and have only a forlorn hope of success.

Kartikeya: Hindu God of Battles.

Khanatai gazar: Khitan phrase for 'walled places', the fixed settlements.

Khitan: A group of tribes inhabiting the plains.

Khmel: Any cloth or fibre made from camels.

Khünd Chono: Khitan phrase for a Dire Wolf and also a clan name.

Köle: A Khitan word meaning something between 'prisoner' and 'slave'.

Kron: The name given to the sun of Vhast.

Lacrima Christi: Greek phrase and expletive for 'Christ's tears'.

Lamia: A form of demon that is a nagin, a snake demon. It takes the appearance of a snake up to fifty metres long with the body and head of a six-armed giantess. It can use a variety of weapons and is a fearsome opponent.

Luke, Saint: Christian Saint, Feast Day 18th October, patron saint of physicians.

Magister Cubicularius: Greek for Head Servant. A department head.

Mahr: Arabic word. It means something like 'dowry', but both sides are expected to bring something.

Maikhand emegai: Khitan phrase for a Khitan woman, literally 'woman of the tents'.

Maskirovka: A Darkspeech word, in the Wolfneck dialect, meaning a tactic of deception.

Masters, the: A group of undead mages who have control over Dwarvenholme.

Melchior, Caspar and Balthasar Saints: Orthodox Saints, Their Feast Day on Twelfth Night (25th Secundus) is also known as the Feast of the Magi. They are patrons of the giving of gifts and of righteous prophesy.

Moonshadows: A carnivore that feeds off the electrical energy of their victims. They are hard to detect and each attack they make will take away a function, thought, hearing, sight until death occurs.

Night Moths: A carrion-eating moth that have a strong contact poison and can also be a vector for flashfever. They will wait for a victim to die and then will settle down and wait for it to rot to the right consistency.

North Hole: A Dwarven town.

Our Lady: Mary, for the Christians the Mother of God and the Patron Saint of Mothers. Feast Day 12th November.

Ovoo: A Khitan shrine, mainly used by travellers, but also in other ceremonies.

Pain: A town in the north of Darkreach.

Pavitra Phāṭaka: Capital of Haven and often called Sacred Gate.

Praetor koubikoularios: Greek for an upper servant, a section head.

Prthivi: Hindu Goddess of the element of Earth and the planet itself.

Pusan: Hindu God of herdsmen, but more importantly of roads, paths and travellers.

Ras-khan: The leader of a Khitan ergüül or patrol.

Ratri: Hindu goddess of love, carnal desire, lust, passion and sexual pleasure. She is the female counterpart and chief consort of Kamadeva.

Sh-hone: A cloth made from a form of kelp.

Slain Enemy, The: A tavern in Evilhalt.

Sleepwell: A rare tree found in the southern forest. Its leaves can be made into a potion that will give the imbiber's body the equivalent effects to a night's sleep without penalty. It can cause addiction.

Spilk: A form of silk made from the webs of certain spiders. It has some magical correspondences.

Su-khan: The leader of a tuman, a Khitan sub-tribe.

Tagma: A Darkreach Army unit of around 14,400 troops.

Talker: A magical device that lets people talk to each other at a distance.

Talent: For the Independent villages, this is a gold coin that weighs 20g and is worth 2,000 follis.

Tulaan golyn nevtrekh: Khitan name for Evilhalt. 'Battle River Crossing'

Üstei akh düü: Khitan phrase. It is the term for the totem animals of a tribe.

Vitalis, Saint: Christian Saint, Feast Day 24th Undecim, he is the patron of merchants and traders.

Walla: Any cloth made form the wool of llamas, alpaca and similar animals.

War Tigers: A strange mammalian carnivore with a metallic exterior and eyes that are a type of gem. They are found underground and in some ruins.

Winifred, Saint: A Christian saint, Feast Day 19th Primus, she is one of the patrons of healing, particularly of those hurt in combat.

Zaan: The Khitan Clan of the Elephant.

More details of many of the towns, plants and animals of Vhast can be found through the author's website or Patreon postings along with many short stories set in the world of Vhast.